PENGUIN BOOKS

THE ADVENTURES

SIR ARTHUR CONAN DOYLE

PENGUIN BOOKS

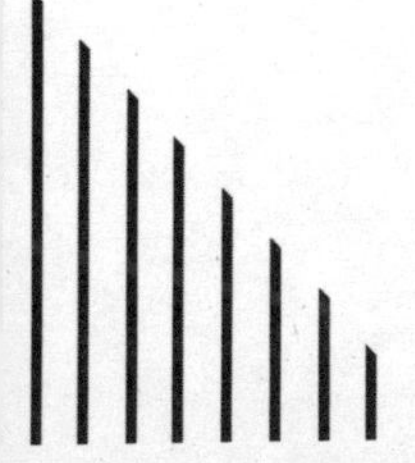

PENGUIN BOOKS

Published by the Penguin Group
Penguin Books Ltd, 80 Strand, London WC2R 0RL, England
Penguin Group (USA) Inc., 375 Hudson Street, New York, New York 10014, USA
Penguin Group (Canada), 90 Eglinton Avenue East, Suite 700, Toronto, Ontario, Canada M4P 2Y3
(a division of Pearson Penguin Canada Inc.)
Penguin Ireland, 25 St Stephen's Green, Dublin 2, Ireland (a division of Penguin Books Ltd)
Penguin Group (Australia), 250 Camberwell Road, Camberwell, Victoria 3124, Australia
(a division of Pearson Australia Group Pty Ltd)
Penguin Books India Pvt Ltd, 11 Community Centre, Panchsheel Park, New Delhi – 110 017, India
Penguin Group (NZ), 67 Apollo Drive, Rosedale, Auckland 0632, New Zealand
(a division of Pearson New Zealand Ltd)
Penguin Books (South Africa) (Pty) Ltd, 24 Sturdee Avenue, Rosebank,
Johannesburg 2196, South Africa

Penguin Books Ltd, Registered Offices: 80 Strand, London WC2R 0RL, England

penguin.com

The Extraordinary Cases of Sherlock Holmes first published in Puffin Books 1988
The Great Adventures of Sherlock Holmes first published in Puffin Books 1990
Both reissued in Puffin Classics 1994
Published in this collection 2011
002 – 10 9 8 7 6 5 4 3 2

The Extraordinary Cases of Sherlock Holmes: 'The Adventures of the Speckled Band'
and 'The Adventure of the Blue Carbuncle' first published in *The Adventures of Sherlock Holmes*, 1892;
'Silver Blaze', 'The Musgrave Ritual' and 'The Reigate Puzzle' first published in *Memoirs of Sherlock
Holmes*, 1894; 'The Adventure of the Dancing Men' and 'The
Adventure of the Six Napoleons' first published in *The Return of Sherlock Holmes*, 1905; 'The Missing
Three-Quarter' first published in *The Case Book of Sherlock Holmes*, 1927

The Great Adventures of Sherlock Holmes: 'The Solitary Cyclist', 'Charles Augustus Milverton', 'Black
Peter', 'The Golden Pince-Nez' and 'The Priory School' first published in *The Return of Sherlock
Holmes*, 1905; 'The Beryl Coronet', 'The Engineer's Thumb' and 'The Red-Headed League' first
published in *The Adventures of Sherlock Holmes*, 1892

All rights reserved

Set in 12/15pt Plantin
Printed in Great Britain by Clays Ltd, St Ives plc

British Library Cataloguing in Publication Data
A CIP catalogue record for this book is available from the British Library

ISBN: 978-0-141-33973-3

www.greenpenguin.co.uk

Penguin Books is committed to a sustainable
future for our business, our readers and our planet.
This book is made from Forest Stewardship
Council™ certified paper.

Contents

THE ADVENTURE OF THE SPECKLED BAND

On glancing over my notes of the seventy-odd cases in which I have during the last eight years studied the methods of my friend Sherlock Holmes, I find many tragic, some comic, a large number merely strange, but none commonplace; for, working as he did rather for the love of his art than for the acquirement of wealth, he refused to associate himself with any investigation which did not tend towards the unusual, and even the fantastic. Of all these varied cases, however, I cannot recall any which presented more singular features than that which was associated with the well-known Surrey family of the Roylotts of Stoke Moran. The events in question occurred in the early days of my association with Holmes, when we were sharing rooms as bachelors in Baker Street. It is possible that I might have placed them upon record before, but a promise of secrecy was made at the time, from which I have only been freed during the last month by the untimely death of the lady to whom the pledge was given. It is perhaps as well that the facts should now come to light, for I have reasons to know that there are widespread rumours as to the death of Dr Grimesby Roylott which tend to make the matter even more terrible than the truth.

It was early in April in the year '83 that I woke one morning to find Sherlock Holmes standing, fully dressed, by the side of my bed. He was a late riser, as a rule, and as the clock on the mantelpiece showed me that it was only a quarter-past seven, I blinked up at him in some surprise, and perhaps just a little resentment, for I was myself regular in my habits.

'Very sorry to knock you up, Watson,' said he, 'but it's the common lot this morning. Mrs Hudson has been knocked up, she retorted upon me, and I on you.'

'What is it, then – a fire?'

'No; a client. It seems that a young lady has arrived in a considerable state of excitement, who insists upon seeing me. She is waiting now in the sitting-room. Now, when young ladies wander about the metropolis at this hour of the morning, and knock sleepy people up out of their beds, I presume that it is something very pressing which they have to communicate. Should it prove to be an interesting case, you would, I am sure, wish to follow it from the outset. I thought, at any rate, that I should call you and give you the chance.'

'My dear fellow, I would not miss it for anything.'

I had no keener pleasure than in following Holmes in his professional investigations, and in admiring the rapid deductions, as swift as intuitions, and yet always founded on a logical basis, with which he unravelled the problems which were submitted to him. I rapidly threw on my clothes and was ready in a few minutes to accompany my friend down to the sitting-room. A lady dressed in black and heavily veiled, who had been sitting in the window, rose as we entered.

'Good-morning, madam,' said Holmes cheerily. 'My name is Sherlock Holmes. This is my intimate friend and associate, Dr Watson, before whom you can speak as freely as before myself. Ha! I am glad to see that Mrs Hudson has had the good sense to light the fire. Pray draw up to it, and I shall order you a cup of hot coffee, for I observe that you are shivering.'

'It is not cold which makes me shiver,' said the woman in a low voice, changing her seat as requested.

'What, then?'

'It is fear, Mr Holmes. It is terror.' She raised her veil as she spoke, and we could see that she was indeed in a pitiable state of agitation, her face all drawn and grey, with restless, frightened eyes, like those of some haunted animal. Her features and figure were those of a woman of thirty, but her hair was shot with premature grey, and her expression was weary and haggard. Sherlock Holmes ran her over with one of his quick, all-comprehensive glances.

'You must not fear,' said he soothingly, bending

forward and patting her forearm. 'We shall soon set matters right, I have no doubt. You have come in by train this morning, I see.'

'You know me, then?'

'No, but I observe the second half of a return ticket in the palm of your left glove. You must have started early, and yet you had a good drive in a dog-cart, along heavy roads, before you reached the station.'

The lady gave a violent start and stared in bewilderment at my companion.

'There is no mystery, my dear madam,' said he, smiling. 'The left arm of your jacket is spattered with mud in no less than seven places. The marks are perfectly fresh. There is no vehicle save a dog-cart which throws up mud in that way, and then only when you sit on the left-hand side of the driver.'

'Whatever your reasons may be, you are perfectly correct,' said she. 'I started from home before six, reached Leatherhead at twenty past, and came in by the first train to Waterloo. Sir, I can stand this strain no longer; I shall go mad if it continues. I have no one to turn to – none, save only one, who cares for me, and he, poor fellow, can be of little aid. I have heard of you, Mr Holmes; I have heard of you from Mrs Farintosh, whom you helped in the hour of her sore need. It was from her that I had your address. Oh, sir, do you not think that you could help me, too, and at least throw a little light through the dense darkness which surrounds me? At present it is out of my power to reward you for your services, but in a month or six weeks I shall be married, with the control of my own income, and then at least you shall not find me ungrateful.'

Holmes turned to his desk and, unlocking it, drew out a small case-book, which he consulted.

'Farintosh,' said he. 'Ah yes, I recall the case; it was concerned with an opal tiara. I think it was before your time, Watson. I can only say, madam, that I shall be happy to devote the same care to your case as I did to that of your friend. As to reward, my profession is its own reward; but you are at liberty to defray whatever expenses I may be put to, at the time which suits you best. And now I beg that you will lay before us everything that may help us in forming an opinion upon the matter.'

'Alas!' replied our visitor, 'the very horror of my situation lies in the fact that my fears are so vague, and my suspicions depend so entirely upon small points, which might seem trivial to another, that even he to whom of all others I have a right to look for help and advice looks upon all that I tell him about it as the fancies of a nervous woman. He does not say so, but I can read it from his soothing answers and averted eyes. But I have heard, Mr Holmes, that you can see deeply into the manifold wickedness of the human heart. You may advise me how to walk amid the dangers which encompass me.'

'I am all attention, madam.'

'My name is Helen Stoner, and I am living with my stepfather, who is the last survivor of one of the oldest Saxon families in England, the Roylotts of Stoke Moran, on the western border of Surrey.'

Holmes nodded his head. 'The name is familiar to me,' said he.

'The family was at one time among the richest in England, and the estates extended over the borders into Berkshire in the north, and Hampshire in the west. In the last century, however, four successive heirs were of a dissolute and wasteful disposition, and the family ruin was eventually completed by a gambler in the days of the Regency. Nothing was left save a few acres of ground, and the two-hundred-year-old house, which is itself crushed under a heavy mortgage. The last squire dragged out his existence there, living the horrible life of an aristocratic pauper; but his only son, my stepfather, seeing that he must adapt himself to the new conditions, obtained an advance from a relative, which enabled him to take a medical degree and went out to Calcutta, where, by his professional skill and his force of character, he established a large practice. In a fit of anger, however, caused by some robberies which had been perpetrated in the house, he beat his native butler to death and narrowly escaped a capital sentence. As it was, he suffered a long term of imprisonment and afterwards returned to England a morose and disappointed man.

'When Dr Roylott was in India he married my mother, Mrs Stoner, the young widow of Major-General Stoner, of the Bengal Artillery. My sister Julia and I were twins, and we were only two years old at the time of my mother's re-marriage. She had a considerable sum of money – not less than £1000 a year – and this she bequeathed to Dr Roylott entirely while we resided with him, with a provision that a certain annual sum should be allowed to each of us in the event of our marriage. Shortly after our return to England my mother died – she was killed eight years ago in a railway accident near Crewe. Dr Roylott then abandoned his attempts to establish himself in practice in London and took us to live with him in the old ancestral house at Stoke Moran. The money which my mother had left was enough for all our wants, and there seemed to be no obstacle to our happiness.

'But a terrible change came over our stepfather about this time. Instead of making friends and exchanging visits with our neighbours, who had at first been overjoyed to see a Roylott of Stoke Moran back in the old family seat, he shut himself up in his house and seldom came out save to indulge in furious quarrels with whoever might cross his path. Violence of temper approaching to mania has been hereditary in the men of the

family, and in my stepfather's case it had, I believe, been intensified by his long residence in the
tropics. A series of disgraceful brawls took place,
two of which ended in the police-court, until at
last he became the terror of the village, and the
folks would fly at his approach, for he is a man of
immense strength, and absolutely uncontrollable
in his anger.

'Last week he hurled the local blacksmith over
a parapet into a stream, and it was only by paying
over all the money which I could gather together
that I was able to avert another public exposure.
He had no friends at all save the wandering gypsies, and he would give these vagabonds leave to
encamp upon the few acres of bramble-covered
land which represent the family estate, and would
accept in return the hospitality of their tents,
wandering away with them sometimes for weeks
on end. He has a passion also for Indian animals,
which are sent over to him by a correspondent,
and he has at this moment a cheetah and a baboon,
which wander freely over his grounds and are
feared by the villagers almost as much as their
master.

'You can imagine from what I say that my poor
sister Julia and I had no great pleasure in our
lives. No servant would stay with us, and for a
long time we did all the work of the house. She
was but thirty at the time of her death, and yet
her hair had already begun to whiten, even as
mine has.'

'Your sister is dead, then?'

'She died just two years ago, and it is of her death that I wish to speak to you. You can understand that, living the life which I have described, we were little likely to see anyone of our own age and position. We had, however, an aunt, my mother's maiden sister, Miss Honoria Westphail, who lives near Harrow, and we were occasionally allowed to pay short visits at this lady's house. Julia went there at Christmas two years ago, and met there a half-pay major of marines, to whom she became engaged. My stepfather learned of the engagement when my sister returned and offered no objection to the marriage; but within a fortnight of the day which had been fixed for the wedding, the terrible event occurred which has deprived me of my only companion.'

Sherlock Holmes had been leaning back in his chair with his eyes closed and his head sunk in a cushion, but he half opened his lids now and glanced across at his visitor.

'Pray be precise as to details,' said he.

'It is easy for me to be so, for every event of that dreadful time is seared into my memory. The manor-house is, as I have already said, very old, and only one wing is now inhabited. The bedrooms in this wing are on the ground floor, the sitting-rooms being in the central block of the buildings. Of these bedrooms the first is Dr Roylott's, the second my sister's, and the third my own. There is no communication between them, but they all open out into the same corridor. Do I make myself plain?'

'Perfectly so.'

'The windows of the three rooms open out upon the lawn. The fatal night Dr Roylott had gone to his room early, though we knew that he had not retired to rest, for my sister was troubled by the smell of the strong Indian cigars which it was his custom to smoke. She left her room, therefore, and came into mine, where she sat for some time, chatting about her approaching wedding. At eleven o'clock she rose to leave me, but she paused at the door and looked back.

'"Tell me, Helen," said she, "have you ever heard anyone whistle in the dead of the night?"

'"Never," said I.

'"I suppose that you could not possibly whistle, yourself, in your sleep?"

'"Certainly not. But why?"

'"Because during the last few nights I have always, about three in the morning, heard a low, clear whistle. I am a light sleeper, and it has awakened me. I cannot tell where it came from – perhaps from the next room, perhaps from the lawn. I thought that I would just ask you whether you had heard it."

'"No, I have not. It must be those wretched gypsies in the plantation."

'"Very likely. And yet if it were on the lawn, I wonder that you did not hear it also."

'"Ah, but I sleep more heavily than you."

'"Well, it is of no great consequence, at any rate." She smiled back at me, closed my door, and a few moments later I heard her key turn in the lock.'

'Indeed,' said Holmes. 'Was it your custom always to lock yourselves in at night?'

'Always.'

'And why?'

'I think that I mentioned to you that the doctor kept a cheetah and a baboon. We had no feeling of security unless our doors were locked.'

'Quite so. Pray proceed with your statement.'

'I could not sleep that night. A vague feeling of impending misfortune impressed me. My sister and I, you will recollect, were twins, and you know how subtle are the links which bind two souls which are so closely allied. It was a wild night. The wind was howling outside, and the rain was beating and splashing against the windows. Suddenly, amid all the hubbub of the gale, there burst forth the wild scream of a terrified woman. I knew that it was my sister's voice. I sprang from my bed, wrapped a shawl round me, and rushed into the corridor. As I opened my door I seemed to hear a low whistle, such as my sister described, and a few moments later a clanging sound, as if a mass of metal had fallen. As I ran down the passage, my sister's door was unlocked, and revolved slowly upon its hinges. I stared at it horror-stricken, not knowing what was about to issue from it. By the light of the corridor-lamp I saw my sister appear at the opening, her face blanched with terror, her hands groping for help, her whole figure swaying to and fro like that of a drunkard. I ran to her and threw my arms round her, but at that moment her knees seemed to give way and she fell to the ground. She writhed as one who is in terrible pain, and her limbs were dreadfully convulsed. At first I thought that she had not recognized me, but as I bent over her she suddenly shrieked out in a voice which I shall never forget, "Oh, my God! Helen! It was the band! The speckled band!" There was something else which she would fain have said, and she stabbed with her finger into the air in the direction of the doctor's room, but a fresh convulsion seized her and choked her words. I rushed out, calling loudly for my stepfather, and I met him hastening from his room in his dressing-gown. When he reached my sister's side she was unconscious, and though he poured brandy down her throat and sent for medical aid from the village, all efforts were in vain, for she slowly sank and died without having recovered her consciousness. Such was the dreadful end of my beloved sister.'

'One moment,' said Holmes; 'are you sure about this whistle and metallic sound? Could you swear to it?'

'That was what the county coroner asked me at the inquiry. It is my strong impression that I heard it, and yet, among the crash of the gale and the creaking of an old house, I may possibly have been deceived.'

'Was your sister dressed?'

'No, she was in her night-dress. In her right hand was found the charred stump of a match, and in her left a match-box.'

'Showing that she had struck a light and looked about her when the alarm took place. That is important. And what conclusions did the coroner come to?'

'He investigated the case with great care, for Dr Roylott's conduct had long been notorious in the county, but he was unable to find any satisfactory cause of death. My evidence showed that the door had been fastened upon the inner side, and the windows were blocked by old-fashioned shutters with broad iron bars, which were secured every night. The walls were carefully sounded, and were shown to be quite solid all round, and the flooring was also thoroughly examined, with the same result. The chimney is wide, but is barred up by four large staples. It is certain, therefore, that my sister was quite alone when she met her end. Besides, there were no marks of any violence upon her.'

'How about poison?'

'The doctors examined her for it, but without success.'

'What do you think that this unfortunate lady died of, then?'

'It is my belief that she died of pure fear and

nervous shock, though what it was that frightened her I cannot imagine.'

'Were there gypsies in the plantation at the time?'

'Yes, there are nearly always some there.'

'Ah, and what did you gather from this allusion to a band – a speckled band?'

'Sometimes I have thought that it was merely the wild talk of delirium, sometimes that it may have referred to some band of people, perhaps to these very gypsies in the plantation. I do not know whether the spotted handkerchiefs which so many of them wear over their heads might have suggested the strange adjective which she used.'

Holmes shook his head like a man who is far from being satisfied.

'These are very deep waters,' said he; 'pray go on with your narrative.'

'Two years have passed since then, and my life has been until lately lonelier than ever. A month ago, however, a dear friend, whom I have known for many years, has done me the honour to ask my hand in marriage. His name is Armitage – Percy Armitage – the second son of Mr Armitage, of Crane Water, near Reading. My stepfather has offered no opposition to the match, and we are to be married in the course of the spring. Two days ago some repairs were started in the west wing of the building, and my bedroom wall has been pierced, so that I have had to move into the chamber in which my sister died, and to sleep in the very bed in which she slept. Imagine, then, my thrill of terror when last night, as I lay awake, thinking over her terrible fate, I suddenly heard in the silence of the night the low whistle which had been the herald of her own death. I sprang up and lit the lamp, but nothing was to be seen in the room. I was too shaken to go to bed again, however, so I dressed, and as soon as it was daylight I slipped down, got a dog-cart at the Crown Inn, which is opposite, and drove to Leatherhead, from whence I have come on this morning with the one object of seeing you and asking your advice.'

'You have done wisely,' said my friend. 'But have you told me all?'

'Yes, all.'

'Miss Raylott, you have not. You are screening your stepfather.'

'Why, what do you mean?'

For answer Holmes pushed back the frill of black lace which fringed the hand that lay upon our visitor's knee. Five little livid spots, the marks of four fingers and a thumb, were printed upon the white wrist.

'You have been cruelly used,' said Holmes.

The lady coloured deeply and covered over her injured wrist. 'He is a hard man,' she said, 'and perhaps he hardly knows his own strength.'

There was a long silence, during which Holmes leaned his chin upon his hands and stared into the crackling fire.

'This is a very deep business,' he said at last.

'There are a thousand details which I should desire to know before I decide upon our course of action. Yet we have not a moment to lose. If we were to come to Stoke Moran today, would it be possible for us to see over these rooms without the knowledge of your stepfather?'

'As it happens, he spoke of coming into town today upon some most important business. It is probable that he will be away all day, and that there would be nothing to disturb you. We have a housekeeper now, but she is old and foolish, and I could easily get her out of the way.'

'Excellent. You are not averse to this trip, Watson?'

'By no means.'

'Then we shall both come. What are you going to do yourself?'

'I have one or two things which I would wish to do now that I am in town. But I shall return by the twelve o'clock train, so as to be there in time for your coming.'

'And you may expect us early in the afternoon. I have myself some small business matters to attend to. Will you not wait and breakfast?'

'No, I must go. My heart is lightened already since I have confided my trouble to you. I shall look forward to seeing you again this afternoon.' She dropped her thick black veil over her face and glided from the room.

'And what do you think of it all, Watson?' asked Sherlock Holmes, leaning back in his chair.

'It seems to me to be a most dark and sinister business.'

'Dark enough and sinister enough.'

'Yet if the lady is correct in saying that the flooring and walls are sound, and that the door, window, and chimney are impassable, then her sister must have been undoubtedly alone when she met her mysterious end.'

'What becomes, then, of these nocturnal whistles, and what of the very peculiar words of the dying woman?'

'I cannot think.'

'When you combine the ideas of whistles at night, the presence of a band of gypsies who are on intimate terms with this old doctor, the fact that we have every reason to believe that the doctor has an interest in preventing his stepdaughter's marriage, the dying allusion to a band, and, finally, the fact that Miss Helen Stoner heard a metallic clang, which might have been caused by one of those metal bars that secured the shutters falling back into its place, I think that there is good ground to think that the mystery may be cleared along those lines.'

'But what, then, did the gypsies do?'

'I cannot imagine.'

'I see many objections to any such theory.'

'And so do I. It is precisely for that reason that we are going to Stoke Moran this day. I want to see whether the objections are fatal, or if they may be explained away. But what in the name of the devil!'

The ejaculation had been drawn from my companion by the fact that our door had been suddenly dashed open, and that a huge man had framed himself in the aperture. His costume was a peculiar mixture of the professional and of the agricultural, having a black top-hat, a long frock-coat and a pair of high gaiters, with a hunting-crop swinging in his hand. So tall was he that his hat actually brushed the cross bar of the doorway, and his breadth seemed to span it across from side to side. A large face, seared with a thousand wrinkles, burned yellow with the sun, and marked with every evil passion, was turned from one to the other of us, while his deep-set, bile-shot eyes, and his high, thin, fleshless nose, gave him somewhat the resemblance to a fierce old bird of prey.

'Which of you is Holmes?' asked this apparition.

'My name, sir; but you have the advantage of me,' said my companion quietly.

'I am Dr Grimesby Roylott, of Stoke Moran.'

'Indeed, Doctor,' said Holmes blandly. 'Pray take a seat.'

'I will do nothing of the kind. My stepdaughter has been here. I have traced her. What has she been saying to you?'

'It is a little cold for the time of the year,' said Holmes.

'What has she been saying to you?' screamed the old man furiously.

'But I have heard that the crocuses promise well,' continued my companion imperturbably.

'Ha! You put me off, do you?' said our new visitor, taking a step forward and shaking his hunting-crop. 'I know you, you scoundrel! I have heard of you before. You are Holmes, the meddler.'

My friend smiled.

'Holmes, the busybody!'

His smile broadened.

'Holmes, the Scotland Yard Jack-in-office!'

Holmes chuckled heartily. 'Your conversation is most entertaining,' said he. 'When you go out close the door, for there is a decided draught.'

'I will go when I have said my say. Don't you dare to meddle with my affairs. I know that Miss Stoner has been here. I traced her! I am a dangerous man to fall foul of! See here.' He stepped swiftly forward, seized the poker, and bent it into a curve with his huge brown hands.

'See that you keep yourself out of my grip,' he snarled, and hurling the twisted poker into the fireplace he strode out of the room.

'He seems a very amiable person,' said Holmes, laughing. 'I am not quite so bulky, but if he had remained I might have shown him that my grip was not much more feeble than his own.' As he spoke he picked up the steel poker and, with a sudden effort, straightened it out again.

'Fancy his having the insolence to confound me with the official detective force! This incident gives zest to our investigation, however, and I only trust that our little friend will not suffer from her imprudence in allowing this brute to trace her. And now, Watson, we shall order breakfast, and afterwards I shall walk down to Doctors' Commons, where I hope to get some data which may help us in this matter.'

It was nearly one o'clock when Sherlock Holmes returned from his excursion. He held in his hand a sheet of blue paper, scrawled over with notes and figures.

'I have seen the will of the deceased wife,' said he. 'To determine its exact meaning I have been obliged to work out the present prices of the investments with which it is concerned. The total income, which at the time of the wife's death was little short of £1100, is now, through the fall in agricultural prices, not more than £750. Each daughter can claim an income of £250, in case of marriage. It is evident, therefore, that if both girls had married, this beauty would have had a mere pittance, while even one of them would cripple him to a very serious extent. My morning's work has not been wasted, since it has proved that he has the very strongest motives for standing in the way of anything of the sort. And now, Watson, this is too serious for dawdling, especially as the old man is aware that we are interesting ourselves in his affairs; so if you are ready, we shall call a cab and drive to Waterloo. I should be very much obliged if you would slip your revolver into your pocket. An Eley's No. 2 is an excellent argument with gentlemen who can twist steel pokers into knots. That and a toothbrush are, I think, all that we need.'

At Waterloo we were fortunate in catching a train for Leatherhead, where we hired a trap at the station inn and drove for four or five miles through the lovely Surrey lanes. It was a perfect day, with a bright sun and a few fleecy clouds in the heavens. The trees and wayside hedges were just throwing out their first green shoots, and the air was full of the pleasant smell of the moist earth. To me at least there was a strange contrast between the sweet promise of the spring and this sinister quest upon which we were engaged. My companion sat in the front of the trap, his arms folded, his hat pulled down over his eyes, and his chin sunk upon his breast, buried in the deepest thought. Suddenly, however, he started, tapped me on the shoulder, and pointed over the meadows.

'Look there!' said he.

A heavily timbered park stretched up in a gentle slope, thickening into a grove at the highest point. From amid the branches there jutted out the grey gables and high roof-tree of a very old mansion.

'Stoke Moran?' said he.

'Yes, sir, that be the house of Dr Grimesby Roylott,' remarked the driver.

'There is some building going on there,' said Holmes; 'that is where we are going.'

'There's the village,' said the driver, pointing to a cluster of roofs some distance to the left; 'but if you want to get to the house, you'll find it shorter to get over this stile, and so by the foot-path over the fields. There it is, where the lady is walking.'

'And the lady, I fancy, is Miss Stoner,' observed Holmes, shading his eyes. 'Yes, I think we had better do as you suggest.'

We got off, paid our fare, and the trap rattled back on its way to Leatherhead.

'I thought it as well,' said Holmes as we climbed the stile, 'that this fellow should think we had come here as architects, or on some definite business. It may stop his gossip. Good-afternoon, Miss Stoner. You see that we have been as good as our word.'

Our client of the morning had hurried forward to meet us with a face which spoke her joy. 'I have been waiting so eagerly for you,' she cried, shaking hands with us warmly. 'All has turned out splendidly. Dr Roylott has gone to town, and it is unlikely that he will be back before evening.'

'We have had the pleasure of making the doctor's acquaintance,' said Holmes, and in a few words he sketched out what had occurred. Miss Stoner turned white to the lips as she listened.

'Good heavens!' she cried, 'he has followed me, then.'

'So it appears.'

'He is so cunning that I never know when I am safe from him. What will he say when he returns?'

'He must guard himself, for he may find that there is someone more cunning than himself upon his track. You must lock yourself up from him tonight. If he is violent, we shall take you away to your aunt's at Harrow. Now, we must make the best use of our time, so kindly take us at once to the rooms which we are to examine.'

The building was of grey, lichen-blotched stone, with a high central portion and two curving wings, like the claws of a crab, thrown out on each side. In one of these wings the windows were broken and blocked with wooden boards, while the roof was partly caved in, a picture of ruin. The central portion was in little better repair, but the right-hand block was comparatively modern, and the blinds in the windows, with the blue smoke curling up from the chimneys, showed that this was where the family resided. Some scaffolding had been erected against the end wall, and the stone-work had been broken into, but there were no signs of any workmen at the moment of our visit. Holmes walked slowly up and down the ill-trimmed lawn and examined with deep attention the outsides of the windows.

'This, I take it, belongs to the room in which you used to sleep, the centre one to your sister's, and the one next to the main building to Dr Roylott's chamber?'

'Exactly so. But I am now sleeping in the middle one.'

'Pending the alterations, as I understand. By the way, there does not seem to be any very pressing need for repairs at that end wall.'

'There were none. I believe that it was an excuse to move me from my room.'

'Ah! that is suggestive. Now, on the other side of this narrow wing runs the corridor from which these three rooms open. There are windows in it, of course?'

'Yes, but very small ones. Too narrow for anyone to pass through.'

'As you both locked your doors at night, your rooms were unapproachable from that side. Now, would you have the kindness to go into your room and bar your shutters?'

Miss Stoner did so, and Holmes, after a careful examination through the open window, endeavoured in every way to force the shutter open, but without success. There was no slit through which a knife could be passed to raise the bar. Then with his lens he tested the hinges, but they were of solid iron, built firmly into the massive masonry. 'Hum!' said he, scratching his chin in some perplexity, 'my theory certainly presents some difficulties. No one could pass these shutters if they were bolted. Well, we shall see if the inside throws any light upon the matter.'

A small side door led into the whitewashed corridor from which the three bedrooms opened.

Holmes refused to examine the third chamber, so we passed at once to the second, that in which Miss Stoner was now sleeping, and in which her sister had met with her fate. It was a homely little room, with a low ceiling and a gaping fireplace, after the fashion of old country-houses. A brown chest of drawers stood in one corner, a narrow white-counterpaned bed in another, and a dressing-table on the left-hand side of the window. These articles, with two small wicker-work chairs, made up all the furniture in the room save for a square of Wilton carpet in the centre. The boards round and the panelling of the walls were of brown, worm-eaten oak, so old and discoloured that it may have dated from the original building of the house. Holmes drew one of the chairs into a corner and sat silent, while his eyes travelled round and round and up and down, taking in every detail of the apartment.

'Where does the bell communicate with?' he asked at last, pointing to a thick bell-rope which hung down beside the bed, the tassel actually lying upon the pillow.

'It goes to the housekeeper's room.'

'It looks newer than the other things?'

'Yes, it was only put there a couple of years ago.'

'Your sister asked for it, I suppose?'

'No, I never heard of her using it. We used always to get what we wanted for ourselves.'

'Indeed, it seemed unnecessary to put so nice a

bell-pull there. You will excuse me for a few minutes while I satisfy myself as to this floor.' He threw himself down upon his face with his lens in his hand and crawled swiftly backward and forward, examining minutely the cracks between the boards. Then he did the same with the woodwork with which the chamber was panelled. Finally he walked over to the bed and spent some time in staring at it and in running his eye up and down the wall. Finally he took the bell-rope in his hand and gave it a brisk tug.

'Why, it's a dummy,' said he.

'Won't it ring?'

'No, it is not even attached to a wire. This is very interesting. You can see now that it is fastened to a hook just above where the little opening for the ventilator is.'

'How very absurd! I never noticed that before.'

'Very strange!' muttered Holmes, pulling at the rope. 'There are one or two very singular points about this room. For example, what a fool a builder must be to open a ventilator into another room, when, with the same trouble, he might have communicated with the outside air!'

'That is also quite modern,' said the lady.

'Done about the same time as the bell-rope?' remarked Holmes.

'Yes, there were several little changes carried out about that time.'

'They seem to have been of a most interesting character – dummy bell-ropes, and ventilators which do not ventilate. With your permission, Miss Stoner, we shall now carry our researches into the inner apartment.'

Dr Grimesby Roylott's chamber was larger than that of his stepdaughter, but was as plainly furnished. A camp-bed, a small wooden shelf full of books, mostly of a technical character, an armchair beside the bed, a plain wooden chair against the wall, a round table, and a large iron safe were the principal things which met the eye. Holmes walked slowly round and examined each and all of them with the keenest interest.

'What's in here?' he asked, tapping the safe.

'My stepfather's business papers.'

'Oh! You have seen inside, then?'

'Only once, some years ago. I remember that it was full of papers.'

'There isn't a cat in it, for example?'

'No. What a strange idea!'

'Well, look at this!' He took up a small saucer of milk which stood on the top of it.

'No; we don't keep a cat. But there is a cheetah and a baboon.'

'Ah, yes, of course! Well, a cheetah is just a big cat, and yet a saucer of milk does not go very far in satisfying its wants, I daresay. There is one point which I should wish to determine.' He squatted down in front of the wooden chair and examined the seat of it with the greatest attention.

'Thank you. That is quite settled,' said he,

rising and putting his lens in his pocket. 'Hello! Here is something interesting!'

The object which had caught his eye was a small dog lash hung on one corner of the bed. The lash, however, was curled upon itself and tied so as to make a loop of whipcord.

'What do you make of that, Watson?'

'It is a common enough lash. But I don't know why it should be tied.'

'That is not quite so common, is it? Ah, me! it's a wicked world, and when a clever man turns his brains to crime it is the worst of all. I think that I have seen enough now, Miss Stoner, and with your permission we shall walk out upon the lawn.'

I had never seen my friend's face so grim or his brow so dark as it was when we turned from the scene of this investigation. We had walked several times up and down the lawn, neither Miss Stoner nor myself liking to break in upon his thoughts before he roused himself from his reverie.

'It is very essential, Miss Stoner,' said he, 'that you should absolutely follow my advice in every respect.'

'I shall most certainly do so.'

'The matter is too serious for any hesitation. Your life may depend upon your compliance.'

'I assure you that I am in your hands.'

'In the first place, both my friend and I must spend the night in your room.'

Both Miss Stoner and I gazed at him in astonishment.

'Yes, it must be so. Let me explain. I believe that that is the village inn over there?'

'Yes, that is the Crown.'

'Very, good. Your windows would be visible from there?'

'Certainly.'

'You must confine yourself to your room, on pretence of a headache, when your stepfather comes back. Then when you hear him retire for the night, you must open the shutters of your window, undo the hasp, put your lamp there as a signal to us, and then withdraw quietly with everything which you are likely to want into the room which you used to occupy. I have no doubt that, in spite of the repairs, you could manage there for one night.'

'Oh, yes, easily.'

'The rest you will leave in our hands.'

'But what will you do?'

'We shall spend the night in your room, and we shall investigate the cause of this noise which has disturbed you.'

'I believe, Mr Holmes, that you have already made up your mind,' said Miss Stoner, laying her hand upon my companion's sleeve.

'Perhaps I have.'

'Then, for pity's sake, tell me what was the cause of my sister's death.'

'I should prefer to have clearer proofs before I speak.'

'You can at least tell me whether my own

thought is correct, and if she died from some sudden fright.'

'No, I do not think so. I think that there was probably some more tangible cause. And now, Miss Stoner, we must leave you, for if Dr Roylott returned and saw us our journey would be in vain. Goodbye, and be brave, for if you will do what I have told you you may rest assured that we shall soon drive away the dangers that threaten you.'

Sherlock Holmes and I had no difficult in engaging a bedroom and sitting-room at the Crown Inn. They were on the upper floor, and from our window we could command a view of the avenue gate, and of the inhabited wing of Stoke Moran Manor House. At dusk we saw Dr Grimesby Roylott drive past, his huge form looming up beside the little figure of the lad who drove him. The boy had some slight difficulty in undoing the heavy iron gates, and we heard the hoarse roar of the doctor's voice and saw the fury with which he shook his clinched fists at him. The trap drove on, and a few minutes later we saw a sudden light spring up among the trees as the lamp was lit in one of the sitting-rooms.

'Do you know, Watson,' said Holmes as we sat together in the gathering darkness, 'I have really some scruples as to taking you tonight. There is a distinct element of danger.'

'Can I be of assistance?'

'Your presence might be invaluable.'

'Then I shall certainly come.'

'It is very kind of you.'

'You speak of danger. You have evidently seen more in these rooms than was visible to me.'

'No, but I fancy that I may have deduced a little more. I imagine that you saw all that I did.'

'I saw nothing remarkable save the bell-rope, and what purpose that could answer I confess is more than I can imagine.'

'You saw the ventilator, too?'

'Yes, but I do not think that it is such a very unusual thing to have a small opening between two rooms. It was so small that a rat could hardly pass through.'

'I knew that we should find a ventilator before ever we came to Stoke Moran.'

'My dear Holmes!'

'Oh, yes, I did. You remember in her statement she said that her sister could smell Dr Roylott's cigar. Now, of course that suggested at once that there must be a communication between the two rooms. It could only be a small one, or it would have been remarked upon at the coroner's inquiry. I deduced a ventilator.'

'But what harm can there be in that?'

'Well, there is at least a curious coincidence of dates. A ventilator is made, a cord is hung, and a lady who sleeps in the bed dies. Does not that strike you?'

'I cannot as yet see any connection.'

'Did you observe anything very peculiar about that bed?'

'No.'

'It was clamped to the floor. Did you ever see a bed fastened like that before?'

'I cannot say that I have.'

'The lady could not move her bed. It must always be in the same relative position to the ventilator and to the rope – or so we may call it, since it was clearly never meant for a bell-pull.'

'Holmes,' I cried, 'I seem to see dimly what you are hinting at. We are only just in time to prevent some subtle and horrible crime.'

'Subtle enough and horrible enough. When a doctor does go wrong he is the first of criminals. He has nerve and he has knowledge. Palmer and Pritchard were among the heads of their profession. This man strikes even deeper, but I think, Watson, that we shall be able to strike deeper still. But we shall have horrors enough before the night is over; for goodness' sake let us have a quiet pipe and turn our minds for a few hours to something more cheerful.'

About nine o'clock the light among the trees was extinguished, and all was dark in the direction of the Manor House. Two hours passed slowly away, and then, suddenly, just at the stroke of eleven, a single bright light shone out right in front of us.

'That is our signal,' said Holmes, springing to his feet; 'it comes from the middle window.'

As we passed out he exchanged a few words with the landlord, explaining that we were going on a late visit to an acquaintance, and that it was possible that we might spend the night there. A moment later we were out on the dark road, a chill wind blowing in our faces, and one yellow light twinkling in front of us through the gloom to guide us on our sombre errand.

There was little difficulty in entering the grounds, for unrepaired breaches gaped in the old park wall. Making our way among the trees, we reached the lawn, crossed it, and were about to enter through the window when out from a clump of laurel bushes there darted what seemed to be a hideous and distorted child, who threw itself upon the grass with writhing limbs and then ran swiftly across the lawn into the darkness.

'My God!' I whispered; 'did you see it?'

Holmes was for the moment as startled as I. His hand closed like a vice upon my wrist in his agitation. Then he broke into a low laugh and put his lips to my ear.

'It is a nice household,' he murmured. 'That is the baboon.'

I had forgotten the strange pets which the doctor affected. There was a cheetah, too; perhaps we might find it upon our shoulders at any moment. I confess that I felt easier in my mind when, after following Holmes's example and slipping off my shoes, I found myself inside the bedroom. My companion noiselessly closed the shutters, moved the lamp on to the table, and cast his eyes round the room. All was as we had seen it in the daytime. Then creeping up to me and making a trumpet of his hand, he whispered into my ear again so gently that it was all that I could do to distinguish the words:

'The least sound would be fatal to our plans.'

I nodded to show that I had heard.

'We must sit without light. He would see it through the ventilator.'

I nodded again.

'Do not go asleep; your very life may depend upon it. Have your pistol ready in case we should need it. I will sit on the side of the bed, and you in that chair.'

I took out my revolver and laid it on the corner of the table.

Holmes had brought up a long thin cane, and this he placed upon the bed beside him. By it he laid the box of matches and the stump of a candle. Then he turned down the lamp, and we were left in darkness.

How shall I ever forget that dreadful vigil? I could not hear a sound, not even the drawing of a breath, and yet I knew that my companion sat open-eyed, within a few feet of me, in the same state of nervous tension in which I was myself. The shutters cut off the least ray of light, and we waited in absolute darkness. From outside came the occasional cry of a night-bird, and once at our very window a long-drawn catlike whine, which told us that the cheetah was indeed at liberty. Far away we could hear the deep tones of the parish clock, which boomed out every quarter of an hour. How long they seemed, those quarters! Twelve struck, and one and two and three, and still we sat waiting silently for whatever might befall.

Suddenly there was the momentary gleam of a light up in the direction of the ventilator, which vanished immediately, but was succeeded by a strong smell of burning oil and heated metal. Someone in the next room had lit a dark-lantern. I heard a gentle sound of movement, and then all was silent once more, though the smell grew stronger. For half an hour I sat with straining ears. Then suddenly another sound became audible – a very gentle, soothing sound, like that of a small jet of steam escaping continually from a kettle. The instant that we heard it, Holmes sprang from the bed, struck a match, and lashed furiously with his cane at the bell-pull.

'You see it, Watson?' he yelled. 'You see it?'

But I saw nothing. At the moment when Holmes struck the light I heard a low, clear whistle, but the sudden glare flashing into my weary eyes made it impossible for me to tell what it was at which my friend lashed so savagely. I could, however, see that his face was deadly pale and filled with horror and loathing.

He had ceased to strike and was gazing up at the ventilator when suddenly there broke from the silence of the night the most horrible cry to which I have ever listened. It swelled up louder and louder, a hoarse yell of pain and fear and anger all mingled in the one dreadful shriek. They say that away down in the village, and even in the distant parsonage, that cry raised the sleepers from their beds. It struck cold to our hearts, and I stood gazing at Holmes, and he at me, until the last echoes of it had died away into the silence from which it rose.

'What can it mean?' I gasped.

'It means that it is all over,' Holmes answered. 'And perhaps, after all, it is for the best. Take your pistol, and we will enter Dr Roylott's room.'

With a grave face he lit the lamp and led the way down the corridor. Twice he struck at the chamber door without any reply from within. Then he turned the handle and entered, I at his heels, with the cocked pistol in my hand.

It was a singular sight which met our eyes. On the table stood a dark-lantern with the shutter half open, throwing a brilliant beam of light upon the iron safe, the door of which was ajar. Beside this table, on the wooden chair, sat Dr Grimesby Roylott, clad in a long grey dressing-gown, his bare ankles protruding beneath, and his feet thrust into red heelless Turkish slippers. Across his lap lay the short stock with the long lash which we had noticed during the day. His chin was cocked upward and his eyes were fixed in a dreadful, rigid stare at the corner of the ceiling. Round his brow he had a peculiar yellow band, with brownish speckles, which seemed to be bound tightly round his head. As we entered he made neither sound nor motion.

'The band! the speckled band!' whispered Holmes.

I took a step forward. In an instant his strange headgear began to move, and there reared itself from among his hair the squat diamond-shaped head and puffed neck of a loathsome serpent.

'It is a swamp adder!' cried Holmes; 'the deadliest snake in India. He has died within ten seconds of being bitten. Violence does, in truth, recoil upon the violent, and the schemer falls into the pit which he digs for another. Let us thrust this creature back into its den, and we can then remove Miss Stoner to some place of shelter and let the county police know what has happened.'

As he spoke he drew the dog-whip swiftly from the dead man's lap, and throwing the noose round the reptile's neck he drew it from its horrid perch and, carrying it at arm's length, threw it into the iron safe, which he closed upon it.

Such are the true facts of the death of Dr Grimesby Roylott, of Stoke Moran. It is not necessary that I should prolong a narrative which has already run to too great a length by telling how we broke the sad news to the terrified girl, how we conveyed her by the morning train to the care of her good aunt at Harrow, of how the slow process of official inquiry came to the conclusion that the doctor met his fate while indiscreetly playing with a dangerous pet. The little which I had yet to learn of the case was told me by Sherlock Holmes as we travelled back next day.

'I had', said he, 'come to an entirely erroneous conclusion which shows, my dear Watson, how dangerous it always is to reason from insufficient data. The presence of the gypsies, and the use of the word "band", which was used by the poor girl, no doubt to explain the appearance which she had caught a hurried glimpse of by the light of her match, were sufficient to put me upon an entirely wrong scent. I can only claim the merit that I instantly reconsidered my position when, however, it became clear to me that whatever danger threatened an occupant of the room could not come either from the window or the door. My attention was speedily drawn, as I have already remarked to you, to this ventilator, and to the bell-rope which hung down to the bed. The discovery that this was a dummy, and that the bed was clamped to the floor, instantly gave rise to the suspicion that the rope was there as a bridge for something passing through the hole and coming to the bed. The idea of a snake instantly occurred to me, and when I coupled it with my knowledge that the doctor was furnished with a supply of creatures from India, I felt that I was probably on the right track. The idea of using a form of poison which could not possibly be discovered by any chemical test was just such a one as would occur to a clever and ruthless man who had had an Eastern training. The rapidity with which such a poison would take effect would also, from his point of view, be an advantage. It would be a sharp-eyed coroner, indeed, who could distinguish the two little dark punctures which would show where the poison fangs had done their work. Then I thought of the whistle. Of course he must recall the snake before the morning light revealed it to the victim. He had trained it, probably by the use of the milk which we saw, to return to him when summoned. He would put it through this ventilator at the hour that he thought best, with the certainty that it would crawl down the rope and land on the bed. It might or might not bite the occupant, perhaps she might escape every night for a week, but sooner or later she must fall a victim.

'I had come to these conclusions before ever I had entered his room. An inspection of his chair showed me that he had been in the habit of standing on it, which of course would be necessary in order that he should reach the ventilator. The sight of the safe, the saucer of milk, and the loop of whipcord were enough to finally dispel any doubts which may have remained. The metallic clang heard by Miss Stoner was obviously caused by her stepfather hastily closing the door of his safe upon its terrible occupant. Having once made up my mind, you know the steps which I took in order to put the matter to the proof. I heard the creature hiss as I have no doubt that you did also, and I instantly lit the light and attacked it.'

'With the result of driving it through the ventilator.'

'And also with the result of causing it to turn upon its master at the other side. Some of the blows of my cane came home and roused its snakish temper, so that it flew upon the first person it saw. In this way I am no doubt indirectly responsible for Dr Grimesby Roylott's death, and I cannot say that it is likely to weigh very heavily upon my conscience.'

The Adventure of the Blue Carbuncle

I had called upon my friend Sherlock Holmes upon the second morning after Christmas, with the intention of wishing him the compliments of the season. He was lounging upon the sofa in a purple dressing-gown, a pipe-rack within his reach upon the right, and a pile of crumpled morning papers, evidently newly studied, near at hand. Beside the couch was a wooden chair, and on the angle of the back hung a very seedy and disreputable hard-felt hat, much the worse for wear, and cracked in several places. A lens and a forceps lying upon the seat of the chair suggested that the hat had been suspended in this manner for the purpose of examination.

'You are engaged,' said I; 'perhaps I interrupt you.'

'Not at all. I am glad to have a friend with whom I can discuss my results. The matter is a perfectly trivial one' – he jerked his thumb in the direction of the old hat – 'but there are points in connection with it which are not entirely devoid of interest and even of instruction.'

I seated myself in his armchair and warmed my

hands before his crackling fire, for a sharp frost had set in, and the windows were thick with the ice crystals. 'I suppose', I remarked, 'that, homely as it looks, this thing has some deadly story linked on to it – that it is the clue which will guide you in the solution of some mystery and the punishment of some crime.'

'No, no. No crime,' said Sherlock Holmes, laughing. 'Only one of those whimsical little incidents which will happen when you have four million human beings all jostling each other within the space of a few square miles. Amid the action and reaction of so dense a swarm of humanity, every possible combination of events may be expected to take place, and many a little problem will be presented which may be striking and bizarre without being criminal. We have already had experience of such.'

'So much so,' I remarked, 'that of the last six cases which I have added to my notes, three have been entirely free of any legal crime.'

'Precisely. You allude to my attempt to recover the Irene Adler papers, to the singular case of Miss Mary Sutherland, and to the adventure of the man with the twisted lip. Well, I have no doubt that this small matter will fall into the same innocent category. You know Peterson, the commissionaire?'

'Yes.'

'It is to him that this trophy belongs.'

'It is his hat.'

'No, no; he found it. Its owner is unknown. I beg that you will look upon it not as a battered billycock but as an intellectual problem. And, first, as to how it came here. It arrived upon Christmas morning, in company with a good fat goose, which is, I have no doubt, roasting at this moment in front of Peterson's fire. The facts are these: about four o'clock on Christmas morning, Peterson, who, as you know, is a very honest fellow, was returning from some small jollification and was making his way homeward down Tottenham Court Road. In front of him he saw, in the gaslight, a tallish man, walking with a slight stagger, and carrying a white goose slung over his shoulder. As he reached the corner of Goodge Street, a row broke out between this stranger and a little knot of roughs. One of the latter knocked off the man's hat, on which he raised his stick to defend himself and, swinging it over his head, smashed the shop window behind him. Peterson had rushed forward to protect the stranger from his assailants; but the man, shocked at having broken the window, and seeing an official-looking person in uniform rushing towards him, dropped his goose, took to his heels, and vanished amid the labyrinth of small streets which lie at the back of Tottenham Court Road. The roughs had also fled at the appearance of Peterson, so that he was left in possession of the field of battle, and also of the spoils of victory in the shape of this battered hat and a most unimpeachable Christmas goose.'

'Which surely he restored to their owner?'

'My dear fellow, there lies the problem. It is true that "For Mrs Henry Baker" was printed upon a small card which was tied to the bird's left leg, and it is also true that the initials "H.B." are legible upon the lining of this hat; but as there are some thousands of Bakers, and some hundreds of Henry Bakers in this city of ours, it is not easy to restore lost property to any one of them.'

'What, then, did Peterson do?'

'He brought round both hat and goose to me on Christmas morning, knowing that even the smallest problems are of interest to me. The goose we retained until this morning, when there were signs that, in spite of the slight frost, it would be well that it should be eaten without unnecessary delay. Its finder has carried it off, therefore, to fulfil the ultimate destiny of a goose, while I continue to retain the hat of the unknown gentleman who lost his Christmas dinner.'

'Did he not advertise?'

'No.'

'Then, what clue could you have as to his identity?'

'Only as much as we can deduce.'

'From his hat?'

'Precisely.'

'But you are joking. What can you gather from this old battered felt?'

'Here is my lens. You know my methods. What

can you gather yourself as to the individuality of the man who has worn this article?'

I took the tattered object in my hands and turned it over rather ruefully. It was a very ordinary black hat of the usual round shape, hard and much the worse for wear. The lining had been of red silk, but was a good deal discoloured. There was no maker's name; but, as Holmes had remarked, the initials 'H.B.' were scrawled upon one side. It was pierced in the brim for a hat-securer, but the elastic was missing. For the rest, it was cracked, exceedingly dusty, and spotted in several places, although there seemed to have been some attempt to hide the discoloured patches by smearing them with ink.

'I can see nothing,' said I, handing it back to my friend.

'On the contrary, Watson, you can see every-thing. You fail, however, to reason from what you see. You are too timid in drawing your inferences.'

'Then, pray tell me what it is that you can infer from this hat?'

He picked it up and gazed at it in the peculiar introspective fashion which was characteristic of him. 'It is perhaps less suggestive than it might have been,' he remarked, 'and yet there are a few inferences which are very distinct, and a few others which represent at least a strong balance of probability. That the man was highly intellectual is of course obvious upon the face of it, and also that he was fairly well-to-do within the last three years, although he has now fallen upon evil days. He had foresight, but has less now than formerly, pointing to a moral retrogression, which, when taken with the decline of his fortunes, seems to indicate some evil influence, probably drink, at work upon him. This may account also for the obvious fact that his wife has ceased to love him.'

'My dear Holmes!'

'He has, however, retained some degree of self-respect,' he continued, disregarding my remonstrance. 'He is a man who leads a sedentary life, goes out little, is out of training entirely, is middle-aged, has grizzled hair which he has had cut within the last few days, and which he anoints with lime-cream. These are the more patent facts which are to be deduced from his hat. Also, by the way, that it is extremely improbable that he has gas laid on in his house.'

'You are certainly joking, Holmes.'

'Not in the least. Is it possible that even now, when I give you these results, you are unable to see how they are attained?'

'I have no doubt that I am very stupid, but I must confess that I am unable to follow you. For example, how did you deduce that this man was intellectual?'

For answer Holmes clapped the hat upon his head. It came right over the forehead and settled upon the bridge of his nose. 'It is a question of cubic capacity,' said he; 'a man with so large a brain must have something in it.'

'The decline of his fortunes, then?'

'This hat is three years old. These flat brims curled at the edge came in then. Its a hat of the very best quality. Look at the band of ribbed silk and the excellent lining. If this man could afford to buy so expensive a hat three years ago, and has had no hat since, then he has assuredly gone down in the world.'

'Well, that is clear enough, certainly. But how about the foresight and the moral retrogression?'

Sherlock Holmes laughed. 'Here is the foresight,' said he, putting his finger upon the little disc and loop of the hat-securer. 'They are never sold upon hats. If this man ordered one, it is a sign of a certain amount of foresight, since he went out of his way to take this precaution against the wind. But since we see that he has broken the elastic and has not troubled to replace it, it is obvious that he has less foresight now than formerly, which is a distinct proof of a weakening nature. On the other hand, he has endeavoured to conceal some of these stains upon the felt by daubing them with ink, which is a sign that he has not entirely lost his self-respect.'

'Your reasoning is certainly plausible.'

'The further points, that he is middle-aged, that his hair is grizzled, that it has been recently cut, and that he uses lime-cream, are all to be gathered from a close examination of the lower part of the lining. The lens discloses a large number of hair-ends, clean cut by the scissors of the barber. They all appear to be adhesive, and there is a distinct odour of lime-cream. This dust, you will observe, is not the gritty, grey dust of the street but the fluffy brown dust of the house, showing that it has been hung up indoors most of the time; while the marks of moisture upon the inside are proof positive that the wearer perspired very freely, and could therefore, hardly be in the best of training.'

'But his wife – you said that she had ceased to love him.'

'This hat has not been brushed for weeks. When I see you, my dear Watson, with a week's accumulation of dust upon your hat, and when your wife allows you to go out in such a state, I shall fear that you also have been unfortunate enough to lose your wife's affection.'

'But he might be a bachelor.'

'Nay, he was bringing home the goose as a peace-offering to his wife. Remember the card upon the bird's leg.'

'You have an answer to everything. But how on earth do you deduce that the gas is not laid on in his house?'

'One tallow stain, or even two, might come by chance; but when I see no less than five, I think that there can be little doubt that the individual must be brought into frequent contact with burning tallow – walks upstairs at night probably with his hat in one hand and a guttering candle in the other. Anyhow, he never got tallow-stains from a gas-jet. Are you satisfied?'

'Well, it is very ingenious,' said I, laughing; 'but since, as you said just now, there has been no crime committed, and no harm done save the loss of a goose, all this seems to be rather a waste of energy.'

Sherlock Holmes had opened his mouth to reply, when the door flew open, and Peterson, the commissionaire, rushed into the apartment with flushed cheeks and the face of a man who is dazed with astonishment.

'The goose, Mr Holmes! The goose, sir!' he gasped.

'Eh? What of it, then? Has it returned to life and flapped off through the kitchen window?' Holmes twisted himself round upon the sofa to get a fairer view of the man's excited face.

'See here, sir! See what my wife found in its crop!' He held out his hand and displayed upon the centre of the palm a brilliantly scintillating blue stone, rather smaller than a bean in size, but of such purity and radiance that it twinkled like an electric point in the dark hollow of his hand.

Sherlock Holmes sat up with a whistle. 'By Jove, Peterson!' said he, 'this is treasure trove indeed. I suppose you know what you have got?'

'A diamond, sir? A precious stone. It cuts into glass as though it were putty.'

'It's more than a precious stone. It is *the* precious stone.'

'Not the Countess of Morcar's blue carbuncle!' I ejaculated.

'Precisely so. I ought to know its size and shape, seeing that I have read the advertisement about it in *The Times* every day lately. It is absolutely unique, and its value can only be conjectured, but the reward offered of £1000 is certainly not within a twentieth part of the market price.'

'A thousand pounds! Great Lord of mercy!' The commissionaire plumped down into a chair and stared from one to the other of us.

'That is the reward, and I have reason to know that there are sentimental considerations in the background which would induce the Countess to part with half her fortune if she could but recover the gem.'

'It was lost, if I remember aright, at the Hotel Cosmopolitan,' I remarked.

'Precisely so, on December 22nd, just five days ago. John Horner, a plumber, was accused of having abstracted it from the lady's jewel-case. The evidence against him was so strong that the case has been referred to the Assizes. I have some account of the matter here, I believe.' He rummaged amid his newspapers, glancing over the dates, until at last he smoothed one out, doubled it over, and read the following paragraph:

'Hotel Cosmopolitan Jewel Robbery. John Horner, 26,

plumber, was brought up upon the charge of having upon the 22nd inst., abstracted from the jewel-case of the Countess of Morcar the valuable gem known as the blue carbuncle. James Ryder, upper-attendant at the hotel, gave his evidence to the effect that he had shown Horner up to the dressing-room of the Countess of Morcar upon the day of the robbery in order that he might solder the second bar of the grate, which was loose. He had remained with Horner some little time, but had finally been called away. On returning, he found that Horner had disappeared, that the bureau had been forced open, and that the small morocco casket in which, as it afterwards transpired, the Countess was accustomed to keep her jewel, was lying empty upon the dressing-table. Ryder instantly gave the alarm, and Horner was arrested the same evening; but the stone could not be found either upon his person or in his rooms. Catherine Cusack, maid to the Countess, deposed to having heard Ryder's cry of dismay on discovering the robbery, and to having rushed into the room, where she found matters as described by the last witness. Inspector Bradstreet, B division, gave evidence as to the arrest of Horner, who struggled frantically, and protested his innocence in the strongest terms. Evidence of a previous conviction for robbery having been given against the prisoner, the magistrate refused to deal summarily with the offence, but referred it to the Assizes. Horner, who had shown signs of intense emotion during the proceedings, fainted away at the conclusion and was carried out of court.

'Hum! So much for the police-court,' said Holmes

thoughtfully, tossing aside the paper. 'The question for us now to solve is the sequence of events leading from a rifled jewel-case at one end to the crop of a goose in Tottenham Court Road at the other. You see, Watson, our little deductions have suddenly assumed a much more important and less innocent aspect. Here is the stone; the stone came from the goose, and the goose came from Mr Henry Baker, the gentleman with the bad hat and all the other characteristics with which I have bored you. So now we must set ourselves very seriously to finding this gentleman and ascertaining what part he has played in this little mystery. To do this, we must try the simplest means first, and these lie undoubtedly in an advertisement in all the evening papers. If this fail, I shall have recourse to other methods.'

'What will you say?'

'Give me a pencil and that slip of paper. Now, then:

'Found at the corner of Goodge Street, a goose and a black felt hat. Mr Henry Baker can have the same by applying at 6.30 this evening at 221B, Baker Street.

That is clear and concise.'

'Very. But will he see it?'

'Well, he is sure to keep an eye on the papers, since, to a poor man, the loss was a heavy one. He was clearly so scared by his mischance in breaking the window and by the approach of Peterson that he thought of nothing but flight, but since then he must have bitterly regretted the impulse which caused him to drop his bird. Then, again, the introduction of his name will cause him to see it, for everyone who knows him will direct his attention to it. Here you are, Peterson, run down to the advertising agency and have this put in the evening papers.'

'In which, sir?'

'Oh, in the *Globe, Star, Pall Mall, St James's, Evening News Standard, Echo*, and any others that occur to you.'

'Very well, sir. And this stone?'

'Ah, yes, I shall keep the stone. Thank you. And, I say, Peterson, just buy a goose on your way back and leave it here with me, for we must have one to give to this gentleman in place of the one which your family is now devouring.'

When the commissionaire had gone, Holmes took up the stone and held it against the light. 'It's a bonny thing,' said he. 'Just see how it glints and sparkles. Of course it is a nucleus and focus of crime. Every good stone is. They are the devil's pet baits. In the larger and older jewels every facet may stand for a bloody deed. This stone is not yet twenty years old. It was found in the banks of the Amoy River in southern China and is remarkable in having every characteristic of the carbuncle, save that it is blue in shade instead of ruby red. In spite of its youth, it has already a sinister history. There have been two murders, a vitriol-throwing, a suicide, and several robberies brought about for the sake of this forty-grain weight of crystallized charcoal. Who would think that so pretty a toy would be a purveyor to the gallows and the prison? I'll lock it up in my strong box now and drop a line to the Countess to say that we have it.'

'Do you think that this man Horner is innocent?'

'I cannot tell.'

'Well, then, do you imagine that this other one, Henry Baker, had anything to do with the matter?'

'It is, I think, much more likely that Henry Baker is an absolutely innocent man, who had no idea that the bird which he was carrying was of considerably more value than if it were made of solid gold. That, however, I shall determine by a very simple test if we have an answer to our advertisement.'

'And you can do nothing until then?'

'Nothing.'

'In that case I shall continue my professional round. But I shall come back in the evening at the hour you have mentioned, for I should like to see the solution of so tangled a business.'

'Very glad to see you. I dine at seven. There is a woodcock, I believe. By the way, in view of recent occurrences, perhaps I ought to ask Mrs Hudson to examine its crop.'

I had been delayed at a case, and it was a little

after half-past six when I found myself in Baker Street once more. As I approached the house I saw a tall man in a Scotch bonnet with a coat which was buttoned up to his chin waiting outside in the bright semicircle which was thrown from the fanlight. Just as I arrived the door was opened, and we were shown up together to Holmes's room.

'Mr Henry Baker, I believe,' said he, rising from his armchair and greeting his visitor with the easy air of geniality which he could so readily assume. 'Pray take this chair by the fire, Mr Baker. It is a cold night, and I observe that your circulation is more adapted for summer than for winter. Ah, Watson, you have just come at the right time. Is that your hat, Mr Baker?'

'Yes, sir, that is undoubtedly my hat.'

He was a large man with rounded shoulders, a massive head, and a broad, intelligent face, sloping down to a pointed beard of grizzled brown. A touch of red in nose and cheeks, with a slight tremor of his extended hand, recalled Holmes's surmise as to his habits. His rusty black frock-coat was buttoned right up in front, with the collar turned up, and his lank wrists protruded from his sleeves without a sign of cuff or shirt. He spoke in a slow staccato fashion, choosing his words with care, and gave the impression generally of a man of learning and letters who had had ill-usage at the hands of fortune.

'We have retained these things for some days,'

said Holmes, 'because we expected to see an advertisement from you giving your address. I am at a loss to know now why you did not advertise.'

Our visitor gave a rather shame-faced laugh. 'Shillings have not been so plentiful with me as they once were,' he remarked. 'I had no doubt that the gang of roughs who assaulted me had carried off both my hat and the bird. I did not care to spend more money in a hopeless attempt at recovering them.'

'Very naturally. By the way, about the bird, we were compelled to eat it.'

'To eat it!' Our visitor half rose from his chair in his excitement.

'Yes, it would have been of no use to anyone had we not done so. But I presume that this other goose upon the sideboard, which is about the same weight and perfectly fresh, will answer your purpose equally well?'

'Oh, certainly, certainly,' answered Mr Baker with a sigh of relief.

'Of course, we still have the feathers, legs, crop, and so on of your own bird, so if you wish –'

The man burst into a hearty laugh. 'They might be useful to me as relics of my adventure,' said he, 'but beyond that I can hardly see what use the *disjecta membra* of my late acquaintance are going to be to me. No, sir, I think that, with your permission, I will confine my attentions to the excellent bird which I perceive upon the sideboard.'

Sherlock Holmes glanced sharply across at me with a slight shrug of his shoulders.

'There is your hat, then, and there your bird,' said he. 'By the way, would it bore you to tell me where you got the other one from? I am somewhat of a fowl fancier, and I have seldom seen a better grown goose.'

'Certainly, sir,' said Baker, who had risen and tucked his newly gained property under his arm. 'There are a few of us who frequent the Alpha Inn, near the Museum – we are to be found in the Museum itself during the day, you understand. This year our good host, Windigate by name, instituted a goose club, by which, on consideration of some few pence every week, we were each to receive a bird at Christmas. My pence were duly paid, and the rest is familiar to you. I am much indebted to you, sir, for a Scotch bonnet is fitted neither to my years nor my gravity.' With a comical pomposity of manner he bowed solemnly to both of us and strode off upon his way.

'So much for Mr Henry Baker,' said Holmes when he had closed the door behind him. 'It is quite certain that he knows nothing whatever about the matter. Are you hungry, Watson?'

'Not particularly.'

'Then I suggest that we turn our dinner into a supper and follow up this clue while it is still hot.'

'By all means.'

It was a bitter night, so we drew on our ulsters and wrapped cravats about our throats. Outside, the stars were shining coldly in a cloudless sky, and the breath of the passers-by blew out into smoke like so many pistol shots. Our footfalls rang out crisply and loudly as we swung through the doctors' quarter, Wimpole Street, Harley Street, and so through Wigmore Street into Oxford Street. In a quarter of an hour we were in Bloomsbury at the Alpha Inn, which is a small public-house at the corner of one of the streets which runs down into Holborn. Holmes pushed open the door of the private bar and ordered two glasses of beer from the ruddy-faced, white-aproned landlord.

'Your beer should be excellent if it is as good as your geese,' said he.

'My geese!' the man seemed surprised.

'Yes. I was speaking only half an hour ago to Mr Henry Baker, who was a member of your goose club.'

'Ah! yes, I see. But you see, sir, them's not *our* geese.'

'Indeed! Whose, then?'

'Well, I got the two dozen from a salesman in Covent Garden.'

'Indeed? I know some of them. Which was it?'

'Breckinridge is his name.'

'Ah! I don't know him. Well, here's your good health, landlord, and prosperity to your house. Good-night.'

'Now for Mr Breckinridge,' he continued, but-toning up his coat as we came out into the frosty air. 'Remember, Watson, that though we have so homely a thing as a goose at one end of this chain, we have at the other a man who will certainly get seven years' penal servitude unless we can establish his innocence. It is possible that our inquiry may but confirm his guilt; but, in any case, we have a line of investigation which has been missed by the police, and which a singular chance has placed in our hands. Let us follow it out to the bitter end. Faces to the south, then, and quick march!'

We passed across Holborn, down Endell Street, and so through a zigzag of slums to Covent Garden Market. One of the largest stalls bore the name of Breckinridge upon it, and the proprietor, a horsy-looking man, with a sharp face and trim side-whiskers, was helping a boy to put up the shutters.

'Good-evening. It's a cold night,' said Holmes.

The salesman nodded and shot a questioning glance at my companion.

'Sold out of geese, I see,' continued Holmes, pointing at the bare slabs of marble.

'Let you have five hundred tomorrow morning.'

'That's no good.'

'Well, there are some on the stall with the gas-flare.'

'Ah, but I was recommended to you.'

'Who by?'

'The landlord of the Alpha.'

'Oh, yes; I sent him a couple of dozen.'

'Fine birds they were, too. Now where did you get them from?'

To my surprise the question provoked a burst of anger from the salesman.

'Now, then, mister,' said he, with his head cocked and his arms akimbo, 'what are you driving at? Let's have it straight, now.'

'It is straight enough. I should like to know who sold you the geese which you supplied to the Alpha.'

'Well, then, I shan't tell you. So now!'

'Oh, it is a matter of no importance; but I don't know why you should be so warm over such a trifle.'

'Warm! You'd be as warm, maybe, if you were as pestered as I am. When I pay good money for a good article there should be an end of the business; but it's "Where are the geese?" and "Who did you sell the geese to?" and "What will you take for the geese?" One would think they were the only geese in the world, to hear the fuss that is made over them.'

'Well, I have no connection with any other people who have been making inquiries,' said Holmes carelessly. 'If you won't tell us the bet is off, that is all. But I'm always ready to back my opinion on a matter of fowls, and I have a fiver on it that the bird I ate is country bred.'

'Well, then, you've lost your fiver, for it's town bred,' snapped the salesman.

'It's nothing of the kind.'

'I say it is.'

'I don't believe it.'

'D'you think you know more about fowls than I, who have handled them ever since I was a nipper? I tell you, all those birds that went to the Alpha were town bred.'

'You'll never persuade me to believe that.'

'Will you bet, then?'

'It's merely taking your money, for I know that I am right. But I'll have a sovereign on with you, just to teach you not to be obstinate.'

The salesman chuckled grimly. 'Bring me the books, Bill,' said he.

The small boy brought round a small thin volume and a great greasy-backed one, laying them out together beneath the hanging lamp.

'Now then, Mr Cocksure,' said the salesman, 'I thought that I was out of geese, but before I finish you'll find that there is still one left in my shop. You see this little book?'

'Well?'

'That's the list of the folk from whom I buy. D'you see? Well, then, here on this page are the country folk, and the numbers after their names are where their accounts are in the big ledger. Now, then! You see this other page in red ink? Well, that is a list of my town suppliers. Now, look at that third name. Just read it out to me.'

'Mrs Oakshott, 117, Brixton Road – 249,' read Holmes.

'Quite so. Now turn that up in the ledger.'

Holmes turned to the page indicated. 'Here you are, "Mrs Oakshott, 117, Brixton Road, egg and poultry supplier."'

'Now, then, what's the last entry?'

'"December 22nd. Twenty-four geese at 7s. 6d."'

'Quite so. There you are. And underneath?'

'"Sold to Mr Windigate of the Alpha, at 12s."'

'What have you to say now?'

Sherlock Holmes looked deeply chagrined. He drew a sovereign from his pocket and threw it down upon the slab, turning away with the air of a man whose disgust is too deep for words. A few yards off he stopped under a lamp-post and laughed in the hearty, noiseless fashion which was peculiar to him.

'When you see a man with whiskers of that cut and the "Pink 'un" protruding out of his pocket, you can always draw him by a bet,' said he. 'I daresay that if I had put £100 down in front of him, that man would not have given me such complete information as was drawn from him by the idea that he was doing me on a wager. Well, Watson, we are, I fancy, nearing the end of our quest, and the only point which remains to be determined is whether we should go on to this Mrs Oakshott tonight, or whether we should reserve it for tomorrow. It is clear from what that surly fellow said that there are others besides ourselves who are anxious about the matter, and I should –'

His remarks were suddenly cut short by a loud hubbub which broke out from the stall which we had just left. Turning round we saw a little rat-faced fellow standing in the centre of the circle of yellow light which was thrown by the swinging lamp, while Breckinridge, the salesman, framed in the door of his stall, was shaking his fists fiercely at the cringing figure.

'I've had enough of you and your geese,' he shouted. 'I wish you were all at the devil together. If you come pestering me any more with your silly talk I'll set the dog at you. You bring Mrs Oakshott here and I'll answer her, but what have you to do with it? Did I buy the geese off you?'

'No; but one of them was mine all the same,' whined the little man.

'Well, then, ask Mrs Oakshott for it.'

'She told me to ask you.'

'Well, you can ask the King of Proosia, for all I care. I've had enough of it. Get out of this!' He rushed fiercely forward, and the inquirer flitted away into the darkness.

'Ha! this may save us a visit to Brixton Road,' whispered Holmes. 'Come with me, and we will see what is to be made of this fellow.' Striding through the scattered knots of people who lounged round the flaring stalls, my companion speedily overtook the little man and touched him upon the shoulder. He sprang round, and I could see in the gas-light that every vestige of colour had been driven from his face.

'Who are you, then? What do you want?' he asked in a quavering voice.

'You will excuse me,' said Holmes blandly, 'but I could not help overhearing the questions which you put to the salesman just now. I think that I could be of assistance to you.'

'You? Who are you? How could you know anything of the matter?'

'My name is Sherlock Holmes. It is my business to know what other people don't know.'

'But you can know nothing of this?'

'Excuse me, I know everything of it. You are endeavouring to trace some geese which were sold by Mrs Oakshott, of Brixton Road, to a salesman named Breckinridge, by him in turn to Mr Windigate, of the Alpha, and by him to his club, of which Mr Henry Baker is a member.'

'Oh, sir, you are the very man whom I have longed to meet,' cried the little fellow with outstretched hands and quivering fingers. 'I can hardly explain to you how interested I am in this matter.'

Sherlock Holmes hailed a four-wheeler which was passing. 'In that case we had better discuss it in a cosy room rather than in this wind-swept market-place,' said he. 'But pray tell me, before we go farther, who it is that I have the pleasure of assisting.'

The man hesitated for an instant. 'My name is John Robinson,' he answered with a sidelong glance.

'No, no; the real name,' said Holmes sweetly. 'It is always awkward doing business with an alias.'

A flush sprang to the white cheeks of the stranger. 'Well, then,' said he, 'my real name is James Ryder.'

'Precisely so. Head attendant at the Hotel Cosmopolitan. Pray step into the cab, and I shall soon be able to tell you everything which you would wish to know.'

The little man stood glancing from one to the other of us with half-frightened, half-hopeful eyes, as one who is not sure whether he is on the verge of a windfall or of a catastrophe. Then he stepped into the cab, and in half an hour we were back in the sitting-room at Baker Street. Nothing had been said during our drive, but the high, thin breathing of our new companion, and the claspings and unclaspings of his hands, spoke of the nervous tension within him.

'Here we are!' said Holmes cheerily as we filed into the room. 'The fire looks very seasonable in this weather. You look cold, Mr Ryder. Pray take the basket-chair. I will just put on my slippers before we settle this little matter of yours. Now, then! You want to know what became of those geese?'

'Yes, sir.'

'Or rather, I fancy, of that goose. It was one bird, I imagine, in which you were interested – white, with a black bar across the tail.'

Ryder quivered with emotion. 'Oh, sir,' he cried, 'can you tell me where it went to?'

'It came here.'

'Here?'

'Yes, and a most remarkable bird it proved. I don't wonder that you should take an interest in it. It laid an egg after it was dead – the bonniest, brightest little blue egg that ever was seen. I have it here in my museum.'

Our visitor staggered to his feet and clutched the mantelpiece with his right hand. Holmes unlocked his strong-box and held up the blue carbuncle, which shone out like a star, with a cold, brilliant, many-pointed radiance. Ryder stood glaring with a drawn face, uncertain whether to claim or to disown it.

'The game's up, Ryder,' said Holmes quietly. 'Hold up, man, or you'll be into the fire! Give him an arm back into his chair, Watson. He's not got blood enough to go in for felony with impunity. Give him a dash of brandy. So! Now he looks a little more human. What a shrimp it is, to be sure!'

For a moment he had staggered and nearly fallen, but the brandy brought a tinge of colour into his cheeks, and he sat staring with frightened eyes at his accuser.

'I have almost every link in my hands, and all the proofs which I could possibly need, so there is little which you need tell me. Still, that little may as well be cleared up to make the case complete.

You had heard, Ryder, of this blue stone of the Countess of Morcar's?'

'It was Catherine Cusack who told me of it,' said he in a crackling voice.

'I see – her ladyship's waiting-maid. Well, the temptation of sudden wealth so easily acquired was too much for you, as it has been for better men before you; but you were not very scrupulous in the means you used. It seems to me, Ryder, that there is the making of a very pretty villain in you. You knew that this man Horner, the plumber, had been concerned in some such matter before, and that suspicion would rest the more readily upon him. What did you do, then? You made some small job in my lady's room – you and your confederate Cusack – and you managed that he should be the man sent for. Then, when he had left, you rifled the jewel-case, raised the alarm, and had this unfortunate man arrested. You then –'

Ryder threw himself down suddenly upon the rug and clutched at my companion's knees. 'For God's sake, have mercy!' he shrieked. 'Think of my father! of my mother! It would break their hearts. I never went wrong before! I never will again. I swear it. I'll swear it on a Bible. Oh, don't bring it into court! For Christ's sake, don't!'

'Get back into your chair!' said Holmes sternly. 'It is very well to cringe and crawl now, but you thought little enough of this poor Horner in the dock for a crime of which he knew nothing.'

'I will fly, Mr Holmes. I will leave the country, sir. Then the charge against him will break down.'

'Hum! We will talk about that. And now let us hear a true account of the next act. How came the stone into the goose, and how came the goose into the open market? Tell us the truth, for there lies your only hope of safety.'

Ryder passed his tongue over his parched lips. 'I will tell you it just as it happened, sir,' said he. 'When Horner had been arrested, it seemed to me that it would be best for me to get away with the stone at once, for I did not know at what moment the police might not take it into their heads to search me and my room. There was no place about the hotel where it would be safe. I went out, as if on some commissions, and I made for my sister's house. She had married a man named Oakshott, and lived in Brixton Road, where she fattened fowls for the market. All the way there every man I met seemed to me to be a policeman or a detective; and, for all that it was a cold night, the sweat was pouring down my face before I came to the Brixton Road. My sister asked me what was the matter, and why I was so pale; but I told her that I had been upset by the jewel robbery at the hotel. Then I went into the back yard and smoked a pipe, and wondered what it would be best to do.

'I had a friend once called Maudsley, who went to the bad, and had just been serving his time in

Pentonville. One day he had met me, and fell into talk about the ways of thieves, and how they could get rid of what they stole. I knew that he would be true to me, for I knew one or two things about him; so I made up my mind to go right on to Kilburn, where he lived, and take him into my confidence. He would show me how to turn the stone into money. But how to get to him in safety? I thought of the agonies I had gone through in coming from the hotel. I might at any moment be seized and searched, and there would be the stone in my waistcoat pocket. I was leaning against the wall at the time and looking at the geese which were waddling about round my feet, and suddenly an idea came into my head which showed me how I could beat the best detective that ever lived.

'My sister had told me some weeks before that I might have the pick of her geese for a Christmas present, and I knew that she was always as good as her word. I would take my goose now, and in it I would carry my stone to Kilburn. There was a little shed in the yard, and behind this I drove one of the birds – a fine big one, white, with a barred tail. I caught it, and, prying its bill open, I thrust the stone down its throat as far as my finger could reach. The bird gave a gulp, and I felt the stone pass along its gullet and down into its crop. But the creature flapped and struggled, and out came my sister to know what was the matter. As I turned to speak to her the brute broke loose and fluttered off among the others.

'"Whatever were you doing with that bird, Jem?"' says she.

'"Well," said I, "you said you'd give me one for Christmas, and I was feeling which was the fattest."

'"Oh," says she, "we've set yours aside for you – Jem's bird, we call it. It's the big white one over yonder. There's twenty-six of them, which makes one for you, and one for us, and two dozen for the market."

'"Thank you, Maggie," says I; "but if it is all the same to you, I'd rather have that one I was handling just now."

'"The other is a good three pound heavier," said she, "and we fattened it expressly for you."

'"Never mind. I'll have the other, and I'll take it now," said I.

'"Oh, just as you like," said she, a little huffed. "Which is it you want, then?"

'"That white one with the barred tail, right in the middle of the flock."

'"Oh, very well. Kill it and take it with you."

'Well, I did what she said, Mr Holmes, and I carried the bird all the way to Kilburn. I told my pal what I had done, for he was a man that it was easy to tell a thing like that to. He laughed until he choked, and we got a knife and opened the goose. My heart turned to water, for there was no sign of the stone, and I knew that some terrible mistake had occurred. I left the bird, rushed back to my sister's, and hurried into the back yard. There was not a bird to be seen there.

'"Where are they all, Maggie?" I cried.

'"Gone to the dealer's, Jem."

'"Which dealer's?"

'"Breckinridge, of Covent Garden."

'"But was there another with a barred tail?" I asked, "the same as the one I chose?"

'"Yes, Jem; there were two barred-tailed ones, and I could never tell them apart."

'Well, then, of course I saw it all, and I ran off as hard as my feet would carry me to this man Breckinridge; but he had sold the lot at once, and not one word would he tell me as to where they had gone. You heard him yourselves tonight. Well, he has always answered me like that. My sister thinks that I am going mad. Sometimes I think that I am myself. And now – and now I am myself a branded thief, without ever having touched the wealth for which I sold my character. God help me! God help me!' He burst into convulsive sobbing, with his face buried in his hands.

There was a long silence, broken only by his heavy breathing, and by the measured tapping of Sherlock Holmes's finger-tips upon the edge of the table. Then my friend rose and threw open the door.

'Get out!' said he.

'What, sir! Oh, Heaven bless you!'

'No more words. Get out!'

And no more words were needed. There was a

rush, a clatter upon the stairs, the bang of a door, and the crisp rattle of running footfalls from the street.

'After all, Watson,' said Holmes, reaching up his hand for his clay pipe, 'I am not retained by the police to supply their deficiencies. If Horner were in danger it would be another thing; but this fellow will not appear against him, and the case must collapse. I suppose that I am commuting a felony, but it is just possible that I am saving a soul. This fellow will not go wrong again; he is too terribly frightened. Send him to jail now, and you make him a jail-bird for life. Besides, it is the season of forgiveness. Chance has put in our way a most singular and whimsical problem, and its solution is its own reward. If you will have the goodness to touch the bell, Doctor, we will begin another investigation, in which also a bird will be the chief feature.'

THE MUSGRAVE RITUAL

An anomaly which often struck me in the character of my friend Sherlock Holmes was that, although in his methods of thought he was the neatest and most methodical of mankind, and although also he affected a certain quiet primness of dress, he was none the less in his personal habits one of the most untidy men that ever drove a fellow-lodger to distraction. Not that I am in the least conventional in that respect myself. The rough-and-tumble work in Afghanistan, coming on the top of the natural Bohemianism of disposition, has made me rather more lax than befits a medical man. But with me there is a limit, and when I find a man who keeps his cigars in the coal-scuttle, his tobacco in the toe end of a Persian slipper, and his unanswered correspondence transfixed by a jack-knife into the very centre of his wooden mantelpiece, then I begin to give myself virtuous airs. I have always held, too, that pistol practice should be distinctly an open-air pastime; and when Holmes, in one of his queer humours, would sit in an armchair with his hair-trigger and a hundred Boxer cartridges and proceed to adorn the opposite wall with a patriotic V. R. done in bullet-pocks, I felt strongly that neither the atmosphere nor the appearance of our room was improved by it.

Our chambers were always full of chemicals and of criminal relics which had a way of wandering into unlikely positions, and of turning up in the butter-dish or in even less desirable places. But his papers were my great crux. He had a horror of destroying documents, especially those which were connected with his past cases, and yet it was only once in every year or two that he would muster energy to docket and arrange them; for, as I have mentioned somewhere in these incoherent memoirs, the outbursts of passionate energy when he performed the remarkable feats with which his name is associated were followed by reactions of lethargy during which he would lie about with his violin and his books, hardly moving save from the sofa to the table. Thus month after month his papers accumulated until every corner of the room was stacked with bundles of manuscript which were on no account to be burned, and which could not be put away save by their owner. One winter's night, as we sat together by the fire, I ventured to suggest to him that, as he had finished pasting extracts into his commonplace book, he might employ the next two hours in making our room a little more habitable. He could not deny the justice of my request, so with a rather rueful face he went off to his bedroom, from which he returned presently pulling a large tin box behind him. This he placed in the middle of the floor, and, squatting down upon a stool in front of it, he threw back the lid. I could see that it was already a third full of bundles of paper tied up with red tape into separate packages.

'There are cases enough here, Watson,' said he, looking at me with mischievous eyes. 'I think that if you knew all that I had in this box you would ask me to pull some out instead of putting others in.'

'These are the records of your early work, then?' I asked. 'I have often wished that I had notes of those cases.'

'Yes, my boy, these were all done prematurely before my biographer had come to glorify me.' He lifted bundle after bundle in a tender, caressing sort of way. 'They are not all successes, Watson,' said he. 'But there are some pretty little problems among them. Here's the record of the Tarleton murders, and the case of Vamberry, the wine merchant, and the adventure of the old Russian woman, and the singular affair of the aluminium crutch, as well as a full account of Ricoletti of the club-foot, and his abominable wife. And here – ah, now, this really is something a little *recherché*.'

He dived his arm down to the bottom of the chest and brought up a small wooden box with a sliding lid such as children's toys are kept in. From within he produced a crumpled piece of paper, an old-fashioned brass key, a peg of wood with a ball of string attached to it, and three rusty old discs of metal.

'Well, my boy, what do you make of this lot?' he asked, smiling at my expression.

'It is a curious collection.'

'Very curious, and the story that hangs round it will strike you as being more curious still.'

'These relics have a history, then?'

'So much so that they *are* history.'

'What do you mean by that?'

Sherlock Holmes picked them up one by one and laid them along the edge of the table. Then he reseated himself in his chair and looked them over with a gleam of satisfaction in his eyes.

'These,' said he, 'are all that I have left to remind me of the adventure of the Musgrave Ritual.'

I had heard him mention the case more than once, though I had never been able to gather the details. 'I should be so glad', said I, 'if you would give me an account of it.'

'And leave the litter as it is?' he cried mischievously. 'Your tidiness won't bear much strain, after all, Watson. But I should be glad that you should add this case to your annals, for there are points in it which make it quite unique in the criminal records of this or, I believe, of any other country. A collection of my trifling achievements would certainly be incomplete which contained no account of this very singular business.

'You may remember how the affair of the *Gloria Scott*, and my conversation with the unhappy man whose fate I told you of, first turned my attention in the direction of the profession which has become my life's work. You see me now when my name has become known far and wide, and when I am generally recognized both by the public and by the official force as being a final court of appeal in doubtful cases. Even when you knew me first, at the time of the affair which you have commemorated in "A Study in Scarlet," I had already established a considerable, though not a very lucrative, connection. You can hardly realize, then, how difficult I found it at first, and how long I had to wait before I succeeded in making any headway.

'When I first came up to London I had rooms in Montague Street, just round the corner from the British Museum, and there I waited, filling in my too abundant leisure time by studying all those branches of science which might make me more efficient. Now and again cases came in my way, principally through the introduction of old fellow-students, for during my last years at the university there was a good deal of talk there about myself and my methods. The third of these cases was that of the Musgrave Ritual, and it is to the interest which was aroused by that singular chain of events, and the large issues which proved to be at stake, that I trace my first stride towards the position which I now hold.

'Reginald Musgrave had been in the same college as myself, and I had some slight acquaintance with him. He was not generally popular among the undergraduates, though it always seemed to me that what was set down as pride was really an attempt to cover extreme natural diffidence. In appearance he was a man of an exceedingly aristocratic type, thin, high-nosed, and large-eyed, with languid and yet courtly manners. He was indeed a scion of one of the very oldest families in the kingdom, though his branch was a cadet one which had separated from the northern Musgraves some time in the sixteenth century and had established itself in western Sussex, where the Manor House of Hurlstone is perhaps the oldest inhabited building in the county. Something of his birthplace seemed to cling to the man, and I never looked at his pale, keen face or the poise of his head without associating him with grey archways and mullioned windows and all the venerable wreckage of a feudal keep. Once or twice we drifted into talk, and I can remember that more than once he expressed a keen interest in my methods of observation and inference.

'For four years I had seen nothing of him until one morning he walked into my room in Montague Street. He had changed little, was dressed like a young man of fashion – he was always a bit of a dandy – and preserved the same quiet, suave manner which had formerly distinguished him.

'"How has all gone with you, Musgrave?" I asked after we had cordially shaken hands.

'"You probably heard of my poor father's death," said he; "he was carried off about two years ago. Since then I have of course had the Hurlstone estate to manage, and as I am member of my district as well, my life has been a busy one. But I understand, Holmes, that you are turning to practical ends those powers with which you used to amaze us?"

'"Yes," said I, "I have taken to living by my wits."

'"I am delighted to hear it, for your advice at present would be exceedingly valuable to me. We have had some very strange doings at Hurlstone, and the police have been able to throw no light upon the matter. It is really the most extraordinary and inexplicable business."

'You can imagine with what eagerness I listened to him, Watson, for the very chance for which I had been panting during all those months of inaction seemed to have come within my reach. In my inmost heart I believed that I could succeed where others failed, and now I had the opportunity to test myself.

'"Pray let me have the details," I cried.

'Reginald Musgrave sat down opposite to me and lit the cigarette which I had pushed towards him.

'"You must know", said he, "that though I am a bachelor, I have to keep up a considerable staff of servants at Hurlstone, for it is a rambling old place and takes a good deal of looking after. I preserve, too, and in the pheasant months I usually have a house-party, so that it would not do to be short-handed. Altogether there are eight maids, the cook, the butler, two footmen, and a boy. The garden and the stables of course have a separate staff.

'"Of these servants the one who had been longest in our service was Brunton, the butler. He was a young schoolmaster out of place when he was first taken up by my father, but he was a man of great energy and character, and he soon became quite invaluable in the household. He was a well-grown, handsome man, with a splendid forehead, and though he has been with us for twenty years he cannot be more than forty now. With his personal advantages and his extraordinary gifts – for he can speak several languages and play nearly every musical instrument – it is wonderful that he should have been satisfied so long in such a position, but I suppose that he was comfortable and lacked energy to make any change. The butler of Hurlstone is always a thing that is remembered by all who visit us.

'"But this paragon has one fault. He is a bit of a Don Juan, and you can imagine that for a man like him it is not a very difficult part to play in a quiet country district. When he was married it was all right, but since he has been a widower we have had no end of trouble with him. A few months ago we were in hopes that he was about to settle down again, for he became engaged to Rachel Howells, our second housemaid; but he has thrown her over since then and taken up with Janet Tregellis, the daughter of the head game-keeper. Rachel – who is a very good girl, but of an excitable Welsh temperament – had a sharp touch of brain-fever and goes about the house now – or did until yesterday – like a black-eyed shadow of her former self. That was our first drama at Hurlstone; but a second one came to drive it from our minds, and it was prefaced by the disgrace and dismissal of butler Brunton.

'"This was how it came about. I have said that the man was intelligent, and this very intelligence has caused his ruin, for it seems to have led to an insatiable curiosity about things which did not in the least concern him. I had no idea of the lengths to which this would carry him until the merest accident opened my eyes to it.

'"I have said that the house is a rambling one. One day last week – on Thursday night, to be more exact – I found that I could not sleep, having foolishly taken a cup of strong *café noir* after my dinner. After struggling against it until two in the morning, I felt that it was quite hopeless, so I rose and lit the candle with the intention of continuing a novel which I was reading. The book, however, had been left in the billiard-room, so I pulled on my dressing-gown and started off to get it.

'"In order to reach the billiard-room I had to descend a flight of stairs and then to cross the head of a passage which led to the library and the gun-room. You can imagine my surprise when, as I looked down this corridor, I saw a glimmer of light coming from the open door of the library. I had myself extinguished the lamp and closed the door before coming to bed. Naturally my first thought was of burglars. The corridors at Hurlstone have their walls largely decorated with trophies of old weapons. From one of these I picked a battle-axe, and then, leaving my candle behind me, I crept on tiptoe down the passage and peeped in at the open door.

'"Brunton, the butler, was in the library. He was sitting, fully dressed, in an easy-chair, with a slip of paper which looked like a map upon his knees, and his forehead sunk forward upon his hand in deep thought. I stood dumb with astonishment, watching him from the darkness. A small taper on the edge of the table shed a feeble light which sufficed to show me that he was fully dressed. Suddenly, as I looked, he rose from his chair, and, walking over to a bureau at the side, he unlocked it and drew out one of the drawers. From this he took a paper, and, returning to his seat, he flattened it out beside the taper on the edge of the table and began to study it with minute attention. My indignation at this calm examination of our family documents overcame me so far that I took a step forward, and Brunton, looking up, saw me standing in the doorway. He sprang to his feet, his face turned livid with fear, and he thrust into his breast the chart-like paper which he had been originally studying.

"'"So!' said I. 'This is how you repay the trust which we have reposed in you. You will leave my service tomorrow.'

"'"He bowed with the look of a man who is utterly crushed and slunk past me without a word. The taper was still on the table, and by its light I glanced to see what the paper was which Brunton had taken from the bureau. To my surprise it was nothing of any importance at all, but simply a copy of the questions and answers in the singular old observance called the Musgrave Ritual. It is a sort of ceremony peculiar to our family, which each Musgrave for centuries past has gone through on his coming of age – a thing of private interest, and perhaps of some little importance to the archaeologist, like our own blazonings and charges, but of no practical use whatever."

"'"We had better come back to the paper afterwards," said I.

"'"If you think it really necessary," he answered with some hesitation. "To continue my statement, however: I relocked the bureau, using the key which Brunton had left, and I had turned to go when I was surprised to find that the butler had returned, and was standing before me.

"'"'Mr Musgrave, sir,' he cried in a voice which was hoarse with emotion, 'I can't bear disgrace, sir. I've always been proud above my station in life, and disgrace would kill me. My blood will be on your head, sir – it will, indeed – if you drive me to despair. If you cannot keep me after what has passed, then for God's sake let me give you notice and leave in a month, as if of my own free will. I could stand that, Mr Musgrave, but not to be cast out before all the folk that I know so well.'

'"'You don't deserve much consideration, Brunton,' I answered. 'Your conduct has been most infamous. However, as you have been a long time in the family, I have no wish to bring public disgrace upon you. A month, however, is too long. Take yourself away in a week, and give what reason you like for going.'

'"'Only a week, sir?' he cried in a despairing voice. 'A fortnight – say at least a fortnight!'

'"'A week,' I repeated, 'and you may consider yourself to have been very leniently dealt with.'

'"He crept away, his face sunk upon his breast, like a broken man, while I put out the light and returned to my room.

'"For two days after this Brunton was most assiduous in his attention to his duties. I made no allusion to what had passed and waited with some curiosity to see how he would cover his disgrace. On the third morning, however, he did not appear, as was his custom, after breakfast to receive my instructions for the day. As I left the dining-room I happened to meet Rachel Howells, the maid. I have told you that she had only recently recovered from an illness and was looking so wretchedly pale and wan that I remonstrated with her for being at work.

'"'You should be in bed,' I said. 'Come back to your duties when you are stronger.'

'"'She looked at me with so strange an expression that I began to suspect that her brain was affected.

'"'I am strong enough, Mr Musgrave,' said she.

'"'We will see what the doctor says,' I answered. 'You must stop work now, and when you go downstairs just say that I wish to see Brunton.'

'"'The butler is gone,' said she.

'"'Gone! Gone where?'

'"'He is gone. No one has seen him. He is not in his room. Oh, yes, he is gone, he is gone!' She fell back against the wall with shriek after shriek of laughter, while I, horrified at this sudden hysterical attack, rushed to the bell to summon help. The girl was taken to her room, still screaming and sobbing, while I made inquiries about Brunton. There was no doubt about it that he had disappeared. His bed had not been slept in, he had been seen by no one since he had retired to his room the night before, and yet it was difficult to see how he could have left the house, as both windows and doors were found to be fastened in the morning. His clothes, his watch, and even his money were in his room, but the black suit which he usually wore was missing. His slippers, too, were gone, but his boots were left behind. Where then could butler Brunton have gone in the night, and what could have become of him now?

'"Of course we searched the house from cellar to garret, but there was no trace of him. It is, as I have said, a labyrinth of an old house, especially the original wing, which is now practically uninhabited; but we ransacked every room and cellar without discovering the least sign of the missing man. It was incredible to me that he could have gone away leaving all his property behind him, and yet where could he be? I called in the local police, but without success. Rain had fallen on the night before, and we examined the lawn and the paths all round the house, but in vain. Matters were in this state, when a new development quite drew our attention away from the original mystery.

'"For two days Rachel Howells had been so ill, sometimes delirious, sometimes hysterical, that a nurse had been employed to sit up with her at night. On the third night after Brunton's disappearance, the nurse, finding her patient sleeping nicely, had dropped into a nap in the armchair, when she woke in the early morning to find the bed empty, the window open, and no signs of the invalid. I was instantly aroused, and, with the two footmen, started off at once in search of the missing girl. It was not difficult to tell the direction which she had taken, for, starting from under her window, we could follow her footmarks easily across the lawns to the edge of the mere, where they vanished close to the gravel path which leads out of the grounds. The lake there is eight feet deep, and you can imagine our feelings when we saw that the trail of the poor demented girl came to an end at the edge of it.

'"Of course, we had the drags at once and set to work to recover the remains, but no trace of the body could we find. On the other hand, we brought to the surface an object of a most unexpected kind. It was a linen bag which contained within it a mass of old rusted and discoloured metal and several dull-coloured pieces of pebble or glass. This strange find was all that we could get from the mere, and, although we made every possible search and inquiry yesterday, we know nothing of the fate either of Rachel Howells or of Richard Brunton. The county police are at their wit's end, and I have come up to you as a last resource."

'You can imagine, Watson, with what eagerness I listened to this extraordinary sequence of events, and endeavoured to piece them together, and to devise some common thread upon which they might all hang. The butler was gone. The maid was gone. The maid had loved the butler, but had afterwards had cause to hate him. She was of Welsh blood, fiery and passionate. She had been terribly excited immediately after his disappearance. She had flung into the lake a bag containing some curious contents. These were all factors which had to be taken into consideration, and yet none of them got quite to the heart of the matter. What was the starting-point of this chain of events? There lay the end of this tangled line.

'"I must see that paper, Musgrave," said I, "which this butler of yours thought it worth his while to consult, even at the risk of the loss of his place."

'"It is rather an absurd business, this ritual of ours," he answered. "But it has at least the saving grace of antiquity to excuse it. I have a copy of the questions and answers here if you care to run your eye over them."

'He handed me the very paper which I have here, Watson, and this is the strange catechism to which each Musgrave had to submit when he came to man's estate. I will read you the questions and answers as they stand.

'"Whose was it?"

'"His who is gone."

'"Who shall have it?"

'"He who will come."

'"Where was the sun?"

'"Over the oak."

'"Where was the shadow?"

'"Under the elm."

'"How was it stepped?"

'"North by ten and by ten, east by five and by five, south by two and by two, west by one and by one, and so under."

'"What shall we give for it?"

' "All that is ours."

' "Why should we give it?"

' "For the sake of the trust."

' "The original has no date, but is in the spelling of the middle of the seventeenth century," remarked Musgrave. "I am afraid, however, that it can be of little help to you in solving this mystery."

' "At least," said I, "it gives us another mystery, and one which is even more interesting than the first. It may be that the solution of the one may prove to be the solution of the other. You will excuse me, Musgrave, if I say that your butler appears to me to have been a very clever man, and to have had a clearer insight than ten generations of his masters."

' "I hardly follow you," said Musgrave. "The paper seems to me to be of no practical importance."

' "But to me it seems immensely practical, and I fancy that Brunton took the same view. He had probably seen it before that night on which you caught him."

' "It is very possible. We took no pains to hide it."

' "He simply wished, I should imagine, to refresh his memory upon that last occasion. He had, as I understand, some sort of map or chart which he was comparing with the manuscript, and which he thrust into his pocket when you appeared."

' "That is true. But what could he have to do

with this old family custom of ours, and what does this rigmarole mean?"

'"I don't think that we should have much difficulty in determining that," said I; "with your permission we will take the first train down to Sussex and go a little more deeply into the matter upon the spot."

'The same afternoon saw us both at Hurlstone. Possibly you have seen pictures and read descriptions of the famous old building, so I will confine my account of it to saying that it is built in the shape of an L, the long arm being the more modern portion, and the shorter the ancient nucleus from which the other has developed. Over the low, heavy-lintelled door, in the centre of this old part, is chiselled the date, 1607, but experts are agreed that the beams and stonework are really much older than this. The enormously thick walls and tiny windows of this part had in the last century driven the family into building the new wing, and the old one was used now as a storehouse and a cellar, when it was used at all. A splendid park with fine old timber surrounds the house, and the lake, to which my client had referred, lay close to the avenue, about two hundred yards from the building.

'I was already firmly convinced, Watson, that there were not three separate mysteries here, but one only, and that if I could read the Musgrave Ritual aright I should hold in my hand the clue which would lead me to the truth concerning both the butler Brunton and the maid Howells. To that then I turned all my energies. Why should this servant be so anxious to master this old formula? Evidently because he saw something in it which had escaped all those generations of country squires, and from which he expected some personal advantage. What was it then, and how had it affected his fate?

'It was perfectly obvious to me, on reading the Ritual, that the measurements must refer to some spot to which the rest of the document alluded, and that if we could find that spot we should be in a fair way towards finding what the secret was which the old Musgraves had thought it necessary to embalm in so curious a fashion. There were two guides given us to start with, an oak and an elm. As to the oak there could be no question at all. Right in front of the house, upon the left-hand side of the drive, there stood a patriarch among oaks, one of the most magnificent trees that I have ever seen.

'"That was there when your Ritual was drawn up," said I as we drove past it.

'"It was there at the Norman Conquest in all probability," he answered. "It has a girth of twenty-three feet."

'Here was one of my fixed points secured.

'"Have you any old elms?" I asked.

'"There used to be a very old one over yonder, but it was struck by lightning ten years ago, and we cut down the stump."

'"You can see where it used to be?"

'"Oh, yes."

'"There are no other elms?"

'"No old ones, but plenty of beeches."

'"I should like to see where it grew."

'We had driven up in a dog-cart, and my client led me away at once, without our entering the house, to the scar on the lawn where the elm had stood. It was nearly midway between the oak and the house. My investigation seemed to be progressing.

'"I suppose it is impossible to find out how high the elm was?" I asked.

'"I can give you it at once. It was sixty-four feet."

'"How do you come to know it?" I asked in surprise.

'"When my old tutor used to give me an exercise in trigonometry, it always took the shape of measuring heights. When I was a lad I worked out every tree and building in the estate."

'This was an unexpected piece of luck. My data were coming more quickly than I could have reasonably hoped.

'"Tell me," I asked, "did your butler ever ask you such a question?"

'Reginald Musgrave looked at me in astonishment. "Now that you call it to my mind," he answered, "Brunton *did* ask me about the height of the tree some months ago in connection with some little argument with the groom."

'This was excellent news, Watson, for it showed me that I was on the right road. I looked up at the sun. It was low in the heavens, and I calculated that in less than an hour it would lie just above the topmost branches of the old oak. One condition mentioned in the Ritual would then be fulfilled. And the shadow of the elm must mean the farther end of the shadow, otherwise the trunk would have been chosen as the guide. I had, then, to find where the far end of the shadow would fall when the sun was just clear of the oak.'

'That must have been difficult, Holmes, when the elm was no longer there.'

'Well, at least I knew that if Brunton could do it, I could also. Besides, there was no real difficulty. I went with Musgrave to his study and whittled myself this peg, to which I tied this long string with a knot at each yard. Then I took two lengths of a fishing-rod, which came to just six feet, and I went back with my client to where the elm had been. The sun was just grazing the top of the oak. I fastened the rod on end, marked out the direction of the shadow, and measured it. It was nine feet in length.

'Of course the calculation now was a simple one. If a rod of six feet threw a shadow of nine, a tree of sixty-four feet would throw one of ninety-six, and the line of the one would of course be the line of the other. I measured out the distance, which brought me almost to the wall of the house, and I thrust a peg into the spot. You can imagine my exultation, Watson, when within two inches of my peg I saw a conical depression in the ground. I knew that it was the mark made by Brunton in his measurements, and that I was still upon his trail.

'From this starting-point I proceeded to step, having first taken the cardinal points by my pocket-compass. Ten steps with each foot took me along parallel with the wall of the house, and again I marked my spot with a peg. Then I carefully paced off five to the east and two to the south. It brought me to the very threshold of the old door. Two steps to the west meant now that I was to go two paces down the stone-flagged passage, and this was the place indicated by the Ritual.

'Never have I felt such a cold chill of disappointment, Watson. For a moment it seemed to me that there must be some radical mistake in my calculations. The setting sun shone full upon the passage floor, and I could see that the old, foot-worn grey stones with which it was paved were firmly cemented together, and had certainly not been moved for many a long year. Brunton had not been at work here. I tapped upon the floor, but it sounded the same all over, and there was no sign of any crack or crevice. But, fortunately, Musgrave, who had begun to appreciate the meaning of my proceedings, and who was now as excited as myself, took out his manuscript to check my calculations.

'"And under," he cried. "You have omitted the 'and under'."

'I had thought that it meant that we were to dig, but now, of course, I saw at once that I was wrong. "There is a cellar under this then?" I cried.

'"Yes, and as old as the house. Down here, through this door."'

'We went down a winding stone stair, and my companion, striking a match, lit a large lantern which stood on a barrel in the corner. In an instant it was obvious that we had at last come upon the true place, and that we had not been the only people to visit the spot recently.

'It had been used for the storage of wood, but the billets, which had evidently been littered over the floor, were now piled at the sides, so as to leave a clear space in the middle. In this space lay a large and heavy flagstone with a rusted iron ring in the centre to which a thick shepherd's-check muffler was attached.

'"By Jove!" cried my client. "That's Brunton's muffler. I have seen it on him and could swear to it. What has the villain been doing here?"

'At my suggestion a couple of the county police were summoned to be present, and I then endeavoured to raise the stone by pulling on the cravat. I could only move it slightly, and it was with the aid of one of the constables that I succeeded at last in carrying it to one side. A black hole yawned beneath into which we all peered, while Musgrave, kneeling at the side, pushed down the lantern.

'A small chamber about seven feet deep and four feet square lay open to us. At one side of this was a squat, brass-bound wooden box, the lid of which was hinged upward, with this curious old-fashioned key projecting from the lock. It was furred outside by a thick layer of dust, and damp and worms had eaten through the wood, so that a crop of livid fungi was growing on the inside of it. Several discs of metal, old coins apparently, such as I hold here, were scattered over the bottom of the box, but it contained nothing else.

'At the moment, however, we had no thought for the old chest, for our eyes were riveted upon that which crouched beside it. It was the figure of a man, clad in a suit of black, who squatted down upon his hams with his forehead sunk upon the edge of the box and his two arms thrown out on each side of it. The attitude had drawn all the stagnant blood to the face, and no man could have recognized that distorted liver-coloured countenance; but his height, his dress, and his hair were all sufficient to show my client, when we had drawn the body up, that it was indeed his missing butler. He had been dead some days, but there was no wound or bruise upon his person to show how he had met his dreadful end. When his body had been carried from the cellar we found ourselves still confronted with a problem which was almost as formidable as that with which we had started.

'I confess that so far, Watson, I had been disappointed in my investigation. I had reckoned upon solving the matter when once I had found the place referred to in the Ritual; but now I was there, and was apparently as far as ever from knowing what it was which the family had concealed with such elaborate precautions. It is true that I had thrown a light upon the fate of Brunton, but now I had to ascertain how that fate had come upon him, and what part had been played in the matter by the woman who had disappeared. I sat down upon a keg in the corner and thought the whole matter carefully over.

'You know my methods in such cases, Watson. I put myself in the man's place, and, having first gauged his intelligence, I try to imagine how I should myself have proceeded under the same circumstances. In this case the matter was simplified by Brunton's intelligence being quite first-rate, so that it was unnecessary to make any allowance for the personal equation, as the astronomers have dubbed it. He knew that something valuable was concealed. He had spotted the place. He found that the stone which covered it was just too heavy for a man to move unaided. What would he do next? He could not get help from outside, even if he had someone whom he could trust, without the unbarring of doors and considerable risk of detection. It was better, if he could, to have his helpmate inside the house. But whom could he ask? This girl had been devoted to him. A man always finds it hard to realize that he may have finally lost a woman's love, however badly he may have treated her. He would try by a few attentions to make his peace with the girl Howells, and then would engage her as his accomplice. Together they would come at night to the cellar, and their united force would suffice to raise the stone. So far I could follow their actions as if I had actually seen them.

'But for two of them, and one a woman, it must have been heavy work, the raising of that stone. A burly Sussex policeman and I had found it no light job. What would they do to assist them? Probably what I should have done myself. I rose and examined carefully the different billets of wood which were scattered round the floor. Almost at once I came upon what I expected. One piece, about three feet in length, had a very marked indentation at one end, while several were flattened at the sides as if they had been compressed by some considerable weight. Evidently, as they had dragged the stone up, they had thrust the chunks of wood into the chink until at last when the opening was large enough to crawl through, they would hold it open by a billet placed lengthwise, which might very well become indented at the lower end, since the whole weight of the stone would press it down on to the edge of this other slab. So far I was still on safe ground.

'And now how was I to proceed to reconstruct this midnight drama? Clearly, only one could fit into the hole, and that one was Brunton. The girl must have waited above. Brunton then unlocked the box, handed up the contents presumably – since they were not to be found – and then – and then what happened?

'What smouldering fire of vengeance had suddenly sprung into flame in this passionate Celtic woman's soul when she saw the man who had wronged her – wronged her, perhaps, far more than we suspected – in her power? Was it a chance that the wood had slipped and that the stone had shut Brunton into what had become his sepulchre? Had she only been guilty of silence as to his fate? Or had some sudden blow from her hand dashed the support away and sent the slab crashing down into its place? Be that as it might, I seemed to see that woman's figure still clutching at her treasure trove and flying wildly up the winding stair, with her ears ringing perhaps with the muffled screams from behind her and with the drumming of frenzied hands against the slab of stone which was choking her faithless lover's life out.

'Here was the secret of her blanched face, her shaken nerves, her peals of hysterical laughter on the next morning. But what had been in the box? What had she done with that? Of course, it must have been the old metal and pebbles which my client had dragged from the mere. She had thrown them in there at the first opportunity to remove the last trace of her crime.

'For twenty minutes I had sat motionless, thinking the matter out. Musgrave still stood with a very pale face, swinging his lantern and peering down into the hole.

'"These are coins of Charles the First," said he, holding out the few which had been in the box; "you see we were right in fixing our date for the Ritual."

'"We may find something else of Charles the First," I cried, as the probable meaning of the first two questions of the Ritual broke suddenly upon me. "Let me see the contents of the bag which you fished from the mere."

'We ascended to his study, and he laid the débris before me. I could understand his regarding it as of small importance when I looked at it, for the metal was almost black and the stones lustreless and dull. I rubbed one of them on my sleeve, however, and it glowed afterwards like a spark in the dark hollow of my hand. The metal work was in the form of a double ring, but it had been bent and twisted out of its original shape.

'"You must bear in mind," said I, "that the royal party made head in England even after the death of the king, and that when they at last fled they probably left many of their most precious possessions buried behind them, with the intention of returning for them in more peaceful times."

'"My ancestor, Sir Ralph Musgrave, was a prominent cavalier and the right-hand man of Charles the Second in his wanderings," said my friend.

'"Ah, indeed!" I answered. "Well now, I think that really should give us the last link that we wanted. I must congratulate you on coming into the possession, though in rather a tragic manner, of a relic which is of great intrinsic value, but of even greater importance as a historical curiosity."

'"What is it, then?" he gasped in astonishment.

'"It is nothing less than the ancient crown of the kings of England."

'"The crown!"

'"Precisely. Consider what the Ritual says. How does it run? 'Whose was it?' 'His who is gone.' That was after the execution of Charles. Then, 'Who shall have it?' 'He who will come.' That was Charles the Second, whose advent was already foreseen. There can, I think, be no doubt that this battered and shapeless diadem once encircled the brows of the royal Stuarts."

'"And how came it in the pond?"

'"Ah, that is a question that will take some time to answer." And with that I sketched out to him the whole long chain of surmise and of proof which I had constructed. The twilight had closed in and the moon was shining brightly in the sky before my narrative was finished.

'"And how was it then that Charles did not get his crown when he returned?" asked Musgrave, pushing back the relic into its linen bag.

'"Ah, there you lay your finger upon the one point which we shall probably never be able to clear up. It is likely that the Musgrave who held the secret died in the interval, and by some oversight left this guide to his descendant without explaining the meaning of it. From that day to this it has been handed down from father to son, until at last it came within reach of a man who tore its secret out of it and lost his life in the venture."

'And that's the story of the Musgrave Ritual, Watson. They have the crown down at Hurlstone – though they had some legal bother and a considerable sum to pay before they were allowed to retain it. I am sure that if you mentioned my name they would be happy to show it to you. Of the woman nothing was ever heard, and the probability is that she got away out of England and carried herself and the memory of her crime to some land beyond the seas.'

The Reigate Puzzle

It was some time before the health of my friend Mr Sherlock Holmes recovered from the strain caused by his immense exertions in the spring of '87. The whole question of the Netherland-Sumatra Company and of the colossal schemes of Baron Maupertuis are too recent in the minds of the public, and are too intimately concerned with politics and finance to be fitting subjects for this series of sketches. They led, however, in an indirect fashion to a singular and complex problem which gave my friend an opportunity of demonstrating the value of a fresh weapon among the many with which he waged his lifelong battle against crime.

On referring to my notes I see that it was upon the fourteenth of April that I received a telegram from Lyons which informed me that Holmes was lying ill in the Hotel Dulong. Within twenty-four hours I was in his sick-room and was relieved to find that there was nothing formidable in his symptoms. Even his iron constitution, however, had broken down under the strain of an investigation which had extended over two months, during which period he had never worked less than fifteen hours a day and had more than once, as he assured me, kept to his task for five days at a stretch. Even the triumphant issue of his labours could not save him from reaction after so terrible an exertion, and at a time when Europe was ringing with his name and when his room was literally ankle-deep with congratulatory telegrams I found him a prey to the blackest depression. Even the knowledge that he had succeeded where the police of three countries had failed, and that he had outmanoeuvred at every point the most accomplished swindler in Europe, was insufficient to rouse him from his nervous prostration.

Three days later we were back in Baker Street together; but it was evident that my friend would be much the better for a change, and the thought of a week of springtime in the country was full of attractions to me also. My old friend, Colonel Hayter, who had come under my professional care in Afghanistan, had now taken a house near Reigate in Surrey and had frequently asked me to come down to him upon a visit. On the last occasion he had remarked that if my friend would only come with me he would be glad to extend his hospitality to him also. A little diplomacy was needed, but when Holmes understood that the establishment was a bachelor one, and that he would be allowed the fullest freedom, he fell in with my plans and a week after our return from Lyons we were under the colonel's roof. Hayter was a fine old soldier who had seen much of the world, and he soon found, as I had expected, that Holmes and he had much in common.

On the evening of our arrival we were sitting in the colonel's gun-room after dinner, Holmes stretched upon the sofa, while Hayter and I looked over his little armory of Eastern weapons.

'By the way,' said he suddenly, 'I think I'll take one of these pistols upstairs with me in case we have an alarm.'

'An alarm!' said I.

'Yes, we've had a scare in this part lately. Old Acton, who is one of our county magnates, had his house broken into last Monday. No great damage done, but the fellows are still at large.'

'No clue?' asked Holmes, cocking his eye at the colonel.

'None as yet. But the affair is a petty one, one of our little country crimes, which must seem too small for your attention, Mr Holmes, after this great international affair.'

Holmes waved away the compliment, though his smile showed that it had pleased him.

'Was there any feature of interest?'

'I fancy not. The thieves ransacked the library and got very little for their pains. The whole place was turned upside down, drawers burst open, and presses ransacked, with the result that an odd volume of Pope's *Homer*, two plated candlesticks, an ivory letter-weight, a small oak barometer, and a ball of twine are all that have vanished.'

'What an extraordinary assortment!' I exclaimed.

'Oh, the fellows evidently grabbed hold of everything they could get.'

Holmes grunted from the sofa.

'The county police ought to make something of that,' said he; 'why, it is surely obvious that –'

But I held up a warning finger.

'You are here for a rest, my dear fellow. For heaven's sake don't get started on a new problem when your nerves are all in shreds.'

Holmes shrugged his shoulders with a glance of comic resignation towards the colonel, and the talk drifted away into less dangerous channels.

It was destined, however, that all my professional caution should be wasted, for next morning the problem obtruded itself upon us in such a way that it was impossible to ignore it, and our country visit took a turn which neither of us could have anticipated. We were at breakfast when the colonel's butler rushed in with all his propriety shaken out of him.

'Have you heard the news, sir?' he gasped. 'At the Cunningham's, sir!'

'Burglary!' cried the colonel, with his coffee-cup in mid-air.

'Murder!'

The colonel whistled. 'By Jove!' said he. 'Who's killed, then? The JP or his son?'

'Neither, sir. It was William the coachman.

Shot through the heart, sir, and never spoke again.'

'Who shot him, then?'

'The burglar, sir. He was off like a shot and got clean away. He'd just broke in at the pantry window when William came on him and met his end in saving his master's property.'

'What time?'

'It was last night, sir, somewhere about twelve.'

'Ah, then, we'll step over afterwards,' said the colonel, coolly settling down to his breakfast again. 'It's a baddish business,' he added when the butler had gone; 'he's our leading man about here, is old Cunningham, and a very decent fellow too. He'll be cut up over this, for the man has been in his service for years and was a good servant. It's evidently the same villains who broke into Acton's.'

'And stole that very singular collection,' said Holmes thoughtfully.

'Precisely.'

'Hum! It may prove the simplest matter in the world, but all the same at first glance this is just a little curious, is it not? A gang of burglars acting in the country might be expected to vary the scene of their operations, and not to crack two cribs in the same district within a few days. When you spoke last night of taking precautions I remember that it passed through my mind that this was probably the last parish in England to which the thief or thieves would be likely to turn their attention – which shows that I have still much to learn.'

'I fancy it's some local practitioner,' said the colonel. 'In that case, of course, Acton's and Cunningham's are just the places he would go for, since they are far the largest about here.'

'And richest?'

'Well, they ought to be, but they've had a law-suit for some years which has sucked the blood out of both of them, I fancy. Old Acton has some claim on half Cunningham's estate, and the lawyers have been at it with both hands.'

'If it's a local villain there should not be much difficulty in running him down,' said Holmes with a yawn. 'All right, Watson, I don't intend to meddle.'

'Inspector Forrester, sir,' said the butler, throwing open the door.

The official, a smart, keen-faced young fellow, stepped into the room. 'Good-morning, Colonel,' said he. 'I hope I don't intrude, but we hear that Mr Holmes of Baker Street is here.'

The colonel waved his hand towards my friend, and the inspector bowed.

'We thought that perhaps you would care to step across, Mr Holmes.'

'The fates are against you, Watson,' said he, laughing. 'We were chatting about the matter when you came in, Inspector. Perhaps you can let us have a few details.' As he leaned back in his chair in the familiar attitude I knew that the case was hopeless.

'We had no clue in the Acton affair. But here we have plenty to go on, and there's no doubt it is the same party in each case. The man was seen.'

'Ah!'

'Yes, sir. But he was off like a deer after the shot that killed poor William Kirwan was fired. Mr Cunningham saw him from the bedroom window, and Mr Alec Cunningham saw him from the back passage. It was quarter to twelve when the alarm broke out. Mr Cunningham had just got into bed, and Mr Alec was smoking a pipe in his dressing-gown. They both heard William, the coachman, calling for help, and Mr Alec ran down to see what was the matter. The back door was open, and as he came to the foot of the stairs he saw two men wrestling together outside. One of them fired a shot, the other dropped, and the murderer rushed across the garden and over the hedge. Mr Cunningham, looking out of his bedroom, saw the fellow as he gained the road, but lost sight of him at once. Mr Alec stopped to see if he could help the dying man, and so the villain got clean away. Beyond the fact that he was a middle-sized man and dressed in some dark stuff, we have no personal clue; but we are making energetic inquiries, and if he is a stranger we shall soon find him out.'

'What was this William doing there? Did he say anything before he died?'

'Not a word. He lives at the lodge with his mother, and as he was a very faithful fellow we imagine that he walked up to the house with the intention of seeing that all was right there. Of course this Acton business has put everyone on their guard. The robber must have just burst open the door – the lock has been forced – when William came upon him.'

'Did William say anything to his mother before going out?'

'She is very old and deaf, and we can get no information from her. The shock has made her half-witted, but I understand that she was never very bright. There is one very important circumstance, however. Look at this!'

He took a small piece of torn paper from a notebook and spread it out upon his knee.

'This was found between the finger and thumb of the dead man. It appears to be a fragment torn from a larger sheet. You will observe that the hour mentioned upon it is the very time at which the poor fellow met his fate. You see that this murderer might have torn the rest of the sheet from him or he might have taken this fragment from the murderer. It reads almost as though it were an appointment.'

Holmes took up the scrap of paper, a facsimile of which is here reproduced.

'Presuming that it is an appointment,' continued the inspector, 'it is of course a conceivable theory that this William Kirwan, though he had the reputation of being an honest man, may have been in league with the thief. He may have met him there, may even have helped him to break in the door, and then they may have fallen out between themselves.'

'This writing is of extraordinary interest,' said Holmes, who had been examining it with intense concentration. 'These are much deeper waters than I had thought.' He sank his head upon his hands, while the inspector smiled at the effect which his case had had upon the famous London specialist.

'Your last remark,' said Holmes presently, 'as to the possibility of there being an understanding between the burglar and the servant, and this being a note of appointment from one to the other, is an ingenious and not entirely impossible supposition. But this writing opens up –' He sank his head into his hands again and remained for some minutes in the deepest thought. When he raised his face again I was surprised to see that his cheek was tinged with colour, and his eyes as bright as before his illness. He sprang to his feet with all his old energy.

'I'll tell you what,' said he, 'I should like to have a quiet little glance into the details of this case. There is something in it which fascinates me extremely. If you will permit me, Colonel, I will leave my friend Watson and you, and I will step round with the inspector to test the truth of one or two little fancies of mine. I will be with you again in half an hour.'

An hour and a half had elapsed before the inspector returned alone.

'Mr Holmes is walking up and down in the field outside,' said he. 'He wants us all four to go up to the house together.'

'To Mr Cunningham's?'

'Yes, sir.'

'What for?'

The inspector shrugged his shoulders. 'I don't quite know, sir. Between ourselves, I think Mr Holmes has not quite got over his illness yet. He's been behaving very queerly, and he is very much excited.'

'I don't think you need alarm yourself,' said I. 'I have usually found that there was method in his madness.'

'Some folk might say there was madness in his method,' muttered the inspector. 'But he's all on fire to start, Colonel, so we had best go out if you are ready.'

We found Holmes pacing up and down in the field, his chin sunk upon his breast, and his hands thrust into his trousers pockets.

'The matter grows in interest,' said he. 'Watson, your country trip has been a distinct success. I have had a charming morning.'

'You have been up to the scene of the crime, I understand,' said the colonel.

'Yes, the inspector and I have made quite a little reconnaissance together.'

'Any success?'

'Well, we have seen some very interesting things. I'll tell you what we did as we walk. First of all, we saw the body of this unfortunate man. He certainly died from a revolver wound as reported.'

'Had you doubted it, then?'

'Oh, it is as well to test everything. Our inspection was not wasted. We then had an interview with Mr Cunningham and his son, who were able to point out the exact spot where the murderer had broken through the garden-hedge in his flight. That was of great interest.'

'Naturally.'

'Then we had a look at this poor fellow's mother. We could get no information from her, however, as she is very old and feeble.'

'And what is the result of your investigations?'

'The conviction that the crime is a very peculiar one. Perhaps our visit now may do something to make it less obscure. I think that we are both agreed, Inspector, that the fragment of paper in the dead man's hand, bearing, as it does, the very hour of his death written upon it, is of extreme importance.'

'It should give a clue, Mr Holmes.'

'It *does* give a clue. Whoever wrote that note was the man who brought William Kirwan out of his bed at that hour. But where is the rest of that sheet of paper?'

'I examined the ground carefully in the hope of finding it,' said the inspector.

'It was torn out of the dead man's hand. Why was someone so anxious to get possession of it? Because it incriminated him. And what would he do with it? Thrust it into his pocket, most likely, never noticing that a corner of it had been left in the grip of the corpse. If we could get the rest of that sheet it is obvious that we should have gone a long way towards solving the mystery.'

'Yes, but how can we get at the criminal's pocket before we catch the criminal?'

'Well, well, it was worth thinking over. Then there is another obvious point. The note was sent to William. The man who wrote it could not have taken it; otherwise, of course, he might have delivered his own message by word of mouth. Who brought the note, then? Or did it come through the post?'

'I have made inquiries,' said the inspector. 'William received a letter by the afternoon post yesterday. The envelope was destroyed by him.'

'Excellent!' cried Holmes, clapping the inspector on the back. 'You've seen the postman. It is a pleasure to work with you. Well, here is the lodge, and if you will come up, Colonel, I will show you the scene of the crime.'

We passed the pretty cottage where the murdered man had lived and walked up an oak-lined avenue to the fine old Queen Anne house, which bears the date of Malplaquet upon the lintel of the door. Holmes and the inspector led us round it until we came to the side gate, which is separated by a stretch of garden from the hedge which lines the road. A constable was standing at the kitchen door.

'Throw the door open, officer,' said Holmes. 'Now, it was on those stairs that young Mr Cunningham stood and saw the two men struggling just where we are. Old Mr Cunningham was at that window – the second on the left – and he saw the fellow get away just to the left of that bush. So did the son. They are both sure of it on account of the bush. Then Mr Alec ran out and knelt beside the wounded man. The ground is very hard, you see, and there are no marks to guide us.' As he spoke two men came down the garden path, from round the angle of the house. The one was an elderly man, with a strong, deep-lined, heavy-eyed face; the other a dashing young fellow, whose bright, smiling expression and showy dress were in strange contrast with the business which had brought us there.

'Still at it, then?' said he to Holmes. 'I thought you Londoners were never at fault. You don't seem to be so very quick, after all.'

'Ah, you must give us a little time,' said Holmes good-humouredly.

'You'll want it,' said young Alec Cunningham. 'Why, I don't see that we have any clue at all.'

'There's only one,' answered the inspector. 'We

thought that if we could only find – Good heavens, Mr Holmes! what is the matter?'

My poor friend's face had suddenly assumed the most dreadful expression. His eyes rolled upward, his features writhed in agony, and with a suppressed groan he dropped on his face upon the ground. Horrified at the suddenness and severity of the attack, we carried him into the kitchen, where he lay back in a large chair and breathed heavily for some minutes. Finally, with a shame-faced apology for his weakness, he rose once more.

'Watson would tell you that I have only just recovered from a severe illness,' he explained. 'I am liable to these sudden nervous attacks.'

'Shall I send you home in my trap?' asked old Cunningham.

'Well, since I am here, there is one point on which I should like to feel sure. We can very easily verify it.'

'What is it?'

'Well, it seems to me that it is just possible that the arrival of this poor fellow William was not before, but after, the entrance of the burglar into the house. You appear to take it for granted that although the door was forced the robber never got in.'

'I fancy that is quite obvious,' said Mr Cunningham gravely. 'Why, my son Alec had not yet gone to bed, and he would certainly have heard anyone moving about.'

'Where was he sitting?'

'I was smoking in my dressing-room.'

'Which window is that?'

'The last on the left, next my father's.'

'Both of your lamps were lit, of course?'

'Undoubtedly.'

'There are some very singular points here,' said Holmes, smiling. 'Is it not extraordinary that a burglar – and a burglar who had some previous experience – should deliberately break into a house at a time when he could see from the lights that two of the family were still afoot?'

'He must have been a cool hand.'

'Well, of course, if the case were not an odd one we should not have been driven to ask you for an explanation,' said young Mr Alec. 'But as to your ideas that the man had robbed the house before William tackled him, I think it a most absurd notion. Wouldn't we have found the place disarranged and missed the things which he had taken?'

'It depends on what the things were,' said Holmes. 'You must remember that we are dealing with a burglar who is a very peculiar fellow, and who appears to work on lines of his own. Look, for example, at the queer lot of things which he took from Acton's – what was it? – a ball of string, a letter-weight, and I don't know what other odds and ends.'

'Well, we are quite in your hands, Mr Holmes,' said old Cunningham. 'Anything which you or the inspector may suggest will most certainly be done.'

'In the first place,' said Holmes, 'I should like you to offer a reward – coming from yourself, for the officials may take a little time before they would agree upon the sum, and these things cannot be done too promptly. I have jotted down the form here, if you would not mind signing it. Fifty pounds was quite enough, I thought.'

'I would willingly give five hundred,' said the JP, taking the slip of paper and the pencil which Holmes handed to him. 'This is not quite correct, however,' he added, glancing over the document.

'I wrote it rather hurriedly.'

'You see you begin, "Whereas, at about a quarter to one on Tuesday morning an attempt was made", and so on. It was at a quarter to twelve, as a matter of fact.'

I was pained at the mistake, for I knew how keenly Holmes would feel any slip of the kind. It was his specialty to be accurate as to fact, but his recent illness had shaken him, and this one little incident was enough to show me that he was still far from being himself. He was obviously embarrassed for an instant, while the inspector raised his eyebrows, and Alec Cunningham burst into a laugh. The old gentleman corrected the mistake, however, and handed the paper back to Holmes.

'Get it printed as soon as possible,' he said; 'I think your idea is an excellent one.'

Holmes put the slip of paper carefully away into his pocketbook.

'And now,' said he, 'it really would be a good thing that we should all go over the house together and make certain that this rather erratic burglar did not, after all, carry anything away with him.'

Before entering, Holmes made an examination of the door which had been forced. It was evident that a chisel or strong knife had been thrust in, and the lock forced back with it. We could see the marks in the wood where it had been pushed in.

'You don't use bars, then?' he asked.

'We have never found it necessary.'

'You don't keep a dog?'

'Yes, but he is chained on the other side of the house.'

'When do the servants go to bed?'

'About ten.'

'I understand that William was usually in bed also at that hour?'

'Yes.'

'It is singular that on this particular night he should have been up. Now, I should be very glad if you would have the kindness to show us over the house, Mr Cunningham.'

A stone-flagged passage, with the kitchens branching away from it, led by a wooden staircase directly to the first floor of the house. It came out upon the landing opposite to a second more ornamental stair which came up from the front hall. Out of this landing opened the drawing-room and several bedrooms, including those of Mr Cunningham and his son. Holmes walked slowly, taking keen note of the architecture of the house. I could tell from his expression that he was on a hot scent, and yet I could not in the least imagine in what direction his inferences were leading him.

'My good sir,' said Mr Cunningham, with some impatience, 'this is surely very unnecessary. That is my room at the end of the stairs, and my son's is the one beyond it. I leave it to your judgement whether it was possible for the thief to have come up here without disturbing us.'

'You must try round and get on a fresh scent, I fancy,' said the son with a rather malicious smile.

'Still, I must ask you to humour me a little further. I should like, for example, to see how far the windows of the bedrooms command the front. This, I understand, is your son's room' – he pushed open the door – 'and that, I presume is the dressing-room in which he sat smoking when the alarm was given. Where does the window of that look out to?' He stepped across the bedroom, pushed open the door, and glanced round the other chamber.

'I hope that you are satisfied now?' said Mr Cunningham tartly.

'Thank you, I think I have seen all that I wished.'

'Then if it is really necessary we can go into my room.'

'If it is not too much trouble.'

The JP shrugged his shoulders and led the way into his own chamber, which was a plainly furnished and commonplace room. As we moved across it in the direction of the window, Holmes fell back until he and I were the last of the group. Near the foot of the bed stood a dish of oranges and a carafe of water. As we passed it Holmes, to my unutterable astonishment, leaned over in front of me and deliberately knocked the whole thing over. The glass smashed into a thousand pieces and the fruit rolled about into every corner of the room.

'You've done it now, Watson,' said he coolly. 'A pretty mess you've made of the carpet.'

I stooped in some confusion and began to pick up the fruit, understanding for some reason my companion desired me to take the blame upon myself. The others did the same and set the table on its legs again.

'Hullo!' cried the inspector, 'where's he got to?'

Holmes had disappeared.

'Wait here an instant,' said young Alec Cunningham. 'The fellow is off his head, in my opinion. Come with me, father, and see where he has got to!'

They rushed out of the room, leaving the inspector, the colonel, and me staring at each other.

''Pon my word, I am inclined to agree with Master Alec,' said the official. 'It may be the effect of this illness, but it seems to me that –'

His words were cut short by a sudden scream of

'Help! Help! Murder!' With a thrill I recognized the voice as that of my friend. I rushed madly from the room on to the landing. The cries, which had sunk down into a hoarse, inarticulate shouting, came from the room which we had first visited. I dashed in, and on into the dressing-room beyond. The two Cunninghams were bending over the prostrate figure of Sherlock Holmes, the younger clutching his throat with both hands, while the elder seemed to be twisting one of his wrists. In an instant the three of us had torn them away from him, and Holmes staggered to his feet, very pale and evidently greatly exhausted.

'Arrest these men, Inspector,' he gasped.

'On what charge?'

'That of murdering their coachman, William Kirwan.'

The inspector stared about him in bewilderment. 'Oh, come now, Mr Holmes,' said he at last, 'I'm sure you don't really mean to –'

'Tut, man, look at their faces!' cried Holmes curtly.

Never certainly have I seen a plainer confession of guilt upon human countenances. The older man seemed numbed and dazed, with a heavy, sullen expression upon his strongly marked face. The son, on the other hand, had dropped all that jaunty, dashing style which had characterized him, and the ferocity of a dangerous wild beast gleamed in his dark eyes and distorted his handsome features. The inspector said nothing, but, stepping to the door, he blew his whistle. Two of his constables came at the call.

'I have no alternative, Mr Cunningham,' said he. 'I trust that this may all prove to be an absurd mistake, but you can see that – Ah, would you? Drop it!' He struck out with his hand, and a revolver which the younger man was in the act of cocking clattered down upon the floor.

'Keep that,' said Holmes, quietly putting his foot upon it; 'you will find it useful at the trial. But this is what we really wanted.' He held up a little crumpled piece of paper.

'The remainder of the sheet!' cried the inspector.

'Precisely.'

'And where was it?'

'Where I was sure it must be. I'll make the whole matter clear to you presently. I think, Colonel, that you and Watson might return now, and I will be with you again in an hour at the furthest. The inspector and I must have a word with the prisoners, but you will certainly see me back at luncheon time.'

Sherlock Holmes was as good as his word, for about one o'clock he rejoined us in the colonel's smoking-room. He was accompanied by a little elderly gentleman, who was introduced to me as the Mr Acton whose house had been the scene of the original burglary.

'I wished Mr Acton to be present while I

demonstrated this small matter to you,' said Holmes, 'for it is natural that he should take a keen interest in the details. I am afraid, my dear Colonel, that you must regret the hour that you took in such a stormy petrel as I am.'

'On the contrary,' answered the colonel warmly, 'I consider it the greatest privilege to have been permitted to study your methods of working. I confess that they quite surpass my expectations, and that I am utterly unable to account for your result. I have not yet seen the vestige of a clue.'

'I am afraid that my explanation may disillusion you, but it has always been my habit to hide none of my methods, either from my friend Watson or from anyone who might take an intelligent interest in them. But, first, as I am rather shaken by the knocking about which I had in the dressing-room, I think that I shall help myself to a dash of your brandy, Colonel. My strength has been rather tried of late.'

'I trust you had no more of those nervous attacks.'

Sherlock Holmes laughed heartily. 'We will come to that in its turn,' said he. 'I will lay an account of the case before you in its due order, showing you the various points which guided me in my decision. Pray interrupt me if there is any inference which is not perfectly clear to you.

'It is of the highest importance in the art of detection to be able to recognize, out of a number of facts, which are incidental and which vital.

Otherwise your energy and attention must be dissipated instead of being concentrated. Now, in this case there was not the slightest doubt in my mind from the first that the key of the whole matter must be looked for in the scrap of paper in the dead man's hand.

'Before going into this, I would draw your attention to the fact that, if Alec Cunningham's narrative was correct, and if the assailant, after shooting William Kirwan, had *instantly* fled, then it obviously could not be he who tore the paper from the dead man's hand. But if it was not he, it must have been Alec Cunningham himself, for by the time that the old man had descended several servants were upon the scene. The point is a simple one, but the inspector had overlooked it because he had started with the supposition that these county magnates had had nothing to do with the matter. Now, I make a point of never having any prejudices, and of following docilely wherever fact may lead me, and so, in the very first stage of the investigation, I found myself looking a little askance at the part which had been played by Mr Alec Cunningham.

'And now I made a very careful examination of the corner of paper which the inspector had submitted to us. It was at once clear to me that it formed part of a very remarkable document. Here it is. Do you not now observe something very suggestive about it?'

'It has a very irregular look,' said the colonel.

'My dear sir,' cried Holmes, 'there cannot be the least doubt in the world that it has been written by two persons doing alternate words. When I draw your attention to the strong *t*'s of "at" and "to", and ask you to compare them with the weak ones of "quarter" and "twelve" you will instantly recognize the fact. A very brief analysis of these four words would enable you to say with the utmost confidence that the "learn" and the "maybe" are written in the stronger hand, and the "what" in the weaker.'

'By Jove, it's as clear as day!' cried the colonel. 'Why on earth should two men write a letter in such a fashion?'

'Obviously the business was a bad one, and one of the men who distrusted the other was determined that, whatever was done, each should have an equal hand in it. Now, of the two men, it is clear that the one who wrote the "at" and "to" was the ringleader.'

'How do you get at that?'

'We might deduce it from the mere character of the one hand as compared with the other. But we have more assured reasons than that for supposing it. If you examine this scrap with attention you will come to the conclusion that the man with the stronger hand wrote all his words first, leaving blanks for the other to fill up. These blanks were not always sufficient, and you can see that the second man had a squeeze to fit his "quarter" in between the "at" and the "to", showing that the latter were already written. The man who wrote all his words first is undoubtedly the man who planned the affair.'

'Excellent!' cried Mr Acton.

'But very superficial,' said Holmes. 'We come now, however, to a point which is of importance. You may not be aware that the deduction of a man's age from his writing is one which has been brought to considerable accuracy by experts. In normal cases one can place a man in his true decade with tolerable confidence. I say normal cases, because ill-health and physical weakness reproduce the signs of old age, even when the invalid is a youth. In this case, looking at the bold, strong hand of the one, and the rather broken-backed appearance of the other, which still retains its legibility although the *t*'s have begun to lose their crossing, we can say that the one was a young man and the other was advanced in years without being positively decrepit.'

'Excellent!' cried Mr Acton again.

'There is a further point, however, which is subtler and of greater interest. There is something in common between these hands. They belong to men who are blood-relatives. It may be most obvious to you in the Greek *e*'s, but to me there are many small points which indicate the same thing. I have no doubt at all that a family mannerism can be traced in these two specimens of writing. I am only, of course, giving you the leading results now of my examination of the paper. There were twenty-three other deductions which would be of more interest to experts than to you. They all tend to deepen the impression upon my mind that the Cunninghams, father and son, had written this letter.

'Having got so far, my next step was, of course, to examine into the details of the crime, and to see how far they would help us. I went up to the house with the inspector and saw all that was to be seen. The wound upon the dead man was, as I was able to determine with absolute confidence, fired from a revolver at the distance of something over four yards. There was no powder blackening on the clothes. Evidently, therefore, Alec Cunningham had lied when he said that the two men were struggling when the shot was fired. Again, both father and son agreed as to the place where the man escaped into the road. At that point, however, as it happens, there is a broadish ditch, moist at the bottom. As there were no indications of boot-marks about this ditch, I was absolutely sure not only that the Cunninghams had again lied but that there had never been any unknown man upon the scene at all.

'And now I have to consider the motive of this singular crime. To get at this, I endeavoured first of all to solve the reason of the original burglary at Mr Acton's. I understood, from something which the colonel told us, that a lawsuit had been going on between you, Mr Acton, and the Cunninghams. Of course, it instantly occurred to me that they had broken into your library with the intention of getting at some document which might be of importance in the case.'

'Precisely so,' said Mr Acton. 'There can be no possible doubt as to their intentions. I have the clearest claim upon half of their present estate, and if they could have found a single paper – which, fortunately, was in the strong-box of my solicitors – they would undoubtedly have crippled our case.'

'There you are,' said Holmes, smiling. 'It was a dangerous, reckless attempt in which I seem to trace the influence of young Alec. Having found nothing, they tried to divert suspicion by making it appear to be an ordinary burglary, to which end they carried off whatever they could lay their hands upon. That is all clear enough, but there was much that was still obscure. What I wanted, above all, was to get the missing part of that note. I was certain that Alec had torn it out of the dead man's hand, and almost certain that he must have thrust it into the pocket of his dressing-gown. Where else could he have put it? The only question was whether it was still there. It was worth an effort to find out, and for that object we all went up to the house.

'The Cunninghams joined us, as you doubtless remember, outside the kitchen door. It was, of course, of the very first importance that they should not be reminded of the existence of this paper, otherwise they would naturally destroy it without delay. The inspector was about to tell them the importance which we attached to it when, by the luckiest chance in the world, I tumbled down in a sort of fit and so changed the conversation.'

'Good heavens!' cried the colonel, laughing, 'do you mean to say all our sympathy was wasted and your fit an imposture?'

'Speaking professionally, it was admirably done,' cried I, looking in amazement at this man who was forever confounding me with some new phase of his astuteness.

'It is an art which is often useful,' said he. 'When I recovered I managed, by a device which had perhaps some little merit of ingenuity, to get old Cunningham to write the word "twelve", so that I might compare it with the "twelve" upon the paper.'

'Oh, what an ass I have been!' I exclaimed.

'I could see that you were commiserating me over my weakness,' said Holmes, laughing. 'I was sorry to cause you the sympathetic pain which I know that you felt. We then went upstairs together, and, having entered the room and seen the dressing-gown hanging up behind the door, I contrived, by upsetting a table, to engage their attention for the moment and slipped back to examine the pockets. I had hardly got the paper, however – which was, as I had expected, in one of them – when the two Cunninghams were on me, and would, I verily believe, have murdered me then and there but for your prompt and friendly aid. As it is, I feel that young man's grip on my throat now, and the father has twisted my wrist round in the effort to get the paper out of my hand. They saw that I must know all about it, you see, and the sudden change from absolute security to complete despair made them perfectly desperate.

'I had a little talk with old Cunningham afterwards as to the motive of the crime. He was tractable enough, though his son was a perfect demon, ready to blow out his own or anybody else's brains if he could have got to his revolver. When Cunningham saw that the case against him was so strong he lost all heart and made a clean breast of everything. It seems that William had secretly followed his two masters on the night when they made their raid upon Mr Acton's and, having thus got them into his power, proceeded, under threats of exposure, to levy blackmail upon them. Mr Alec, however, was a dangerous man to play games of that sort with. It was a stroke of positive genius on his part to see in the burglary scare which was convulsing the countryside an opportunity of plausibly getting rid of the man whom he feared. William was decoyed up and shot, and had they only got the whole of the note and paid a little more attention to detail in their accessories, it is very possible that suspicion might never have been aroused.'

'And the note?' I asked.

If you will only come round
to the east gate you will
will very much surprise you and
be of the greatest service to you and also
to Anne Morrison. But say nothing to anyone
upon the matter

Sherlock Holmes placed the subjoined paper before us.

'It is very much the sort of thing that I expected,' said he. 'Of course, we do not yet know what the relations may have been between Alec Cunningham, William Kirwan, and Annie Morrison. The result shows that the trap was skilfully baited. I am sure that you cannot fail to be delighted with the traces of heredity shown in the *p*'s and in the tails of the *g*'s. The absence of the *i*-dots in the old man's writing is also most characteristic. Watson, I think our quiet rest in the country has been a distinct success, and I shall certainly return much invigorated to Baker Street tomorrow.'

'I am afraid, Watson, that I shall have to go,' said Holmes as we sat down together to our breakfast one morning.

'Go! Where to?'

'To Dartmoor; to King's Pyland.'

I was not surprised. Indeed, my only wonder was that he had not already been mixed up in this extraordinary case, which was the one topic of conversation through the length and breadth of England. For a whole day my companion had rambled about the room with his chin upon his chest and his brows knitted, charging and recharging his pipe with the strongest black tobacco, and absolutely deaf to any of my questions or remarks. Fresh editions of every paper had been sent up by our news agent, only to be glanced over and tossed down into a corner. Yet, silent as he was, I knew perfectly well what it was over which he was brooding. There was but one problem before the public which could challenge his powers of analysis, and that was the singular disappearance of the favourite for the Wessex Cup, and the tragic murder of its trainer. When, therefore, he suddenly announced his intention of setting out for the scene of the drama, it was only what I had both expected and hoped for.

'I should be most happy to go down with you if I should not be in the way,' said I.

'My dear Watson, you would confer a great favour upon me by coming. And I think that your time will not be misspent, for there are points about the case which promise to make it an absolutely unique one. We have, I think, just time to catch our train at Paddington, and I will go further into the matter upon our journey. You would oblige me by bringing with you your very excellent field-glass.'

And so it happened that an hour or so later I found myself in the corner of a first-class carriage flying along en route for Exeter, while Sherlock Holmes, with his sharp, eager face framed in his ear-flapped travelling-cap, dipped rapidly into the bundle of fresh papers which he had procured at Paddington. We had left Reading far behind us before he thrust the last one of them under the seat and offered me his cigar-case.

'We are going well,' said he, looking out of the window and glancing at his watch. 'Our rate at present is fifty-three and a half miles an hour.'

'I have not observed the quarter-mile posts,' said I.

'Nor have I. But the telegraph posts upon this line are sixty yards apart, and the calculation is a simple one. I presume that you have looked into this matter of the murder of John Straker and the disappearance of Silver Blaze?'

'I have seen what the *Telegraph* and the *Chronicle* have to say.

'It is one of those cases where the art of the reasoner should be used rather for the sifting of details than for the acquiring of fresh evidence. The tragedy has been so uncommon, so complete, and of such personal importance to so many people that we are suffering from a plethora of surmise, conjecture, and hypothesis. The difficulty is to detach the framework of fact – of absolute undeniable fact – from the embellishments of theorists and reporters. Then, having established ourselves upon this sound basis, it is our duty to see what inferences may be drawn and what are the special points upon which the whole mystery turns. On Tuesday evening I received telegrams from both Colonel Ross, the owner of the horse, and from Inspector Gregory, who is looking after the case, inviting my co-operation.'

'Tuesday evening!' I exclaimed. 'And this is Thursday morning. Why didn't you go down yesterday?'

'Because I made a blunder, my dear Watson – which is, I am afraid, a more common occurrence than anyone would think who only knew me through your memoirs. The fact is that I could not believe it possible that the most remarkable horse in England could long remain concealed, especially in so sparsely inhabited a place as the north of Dartmoor. From hour to hour yesterday I expected to hear that he had been found, and that his abductor was the murderer of John Straker. When, however, another morning had come and I found that beyond the arrest of young Fitzroy Simpson nothing had been done, I felt that it was time for me to take action. Yet in some ways I feel that yesterday has not been wasted.'

'You have formed a theory, then?'

'At least I have got a grip of the essential facts of the case. I shall enumerate them to you, for nothing clears up a case so much as stating it to another person, and I can hardly expect your co-operation if I do not show you the position from which we start.'

I lay back against the cushions, puffing at my cigar, while Holmes, leaning forward, with his long, thin forefinger checking off the points upon the palm of his left hand, gave me a sketch of the events which had led to our journey.

'Silver Blaze', said he, 'is from the Somomy stock and holds as brilliant a record as his famous ancestor. He is now in his fifth year and has brought in turn each of the prizes of the turf to Colonel Ross, his fortunate owner. Up to the time of the catastrophe he was the first favourite for the Wessex Cup, the betting being three to one on him. He has always, however, been a prime favourite with the racing public and has never yet disappointed them, so that even at those odds enormous sums of money have been laid upon him. It is obvious, therefore, that there were many people who had the strongest interest in preventing Silver Blaze from being there at the fall of the flag next Tuesday.

'The fact was, of course, appreciated at King's Pyland, where the colonel's training-stable is situated. Every precaution was taken to guard the favourite. The trainer, John Straker, is a retired jockey who rode in Colonel Ross's colours before he became too heavy for the weighing-chair. He has served the colonel for five years as jockey and for seven as trainer, and has always shown himself to be a zealous and honest servant. Under him were three lads, for the establishment was a small one, containing only four horses in all. One of these lads sat up each night in the stable, while the others slept in the loft. All three bore excellent characters. John Straker, who is a married man, lived in a small villa about two hundred yards from the stables. He has no children, keeps one maidservant, and is comfortably off. The country round is very lonely, but about half a mile to the north there is a small cluster of villas which have been built by a Tavistock contractor for the use of invalids and others who may wish to enjoy the pure Dartmoor air. Tavistock itself lies two miles to the west, while across the moor, also about two miles distant, is the larger training establishment of Mapleton, which belongs to Lord Backwater and is managed by Silas Brown. In every other direction the moor is a complete wilderness, inhabited only by a few roaming gypsies. Such was the general situation last Monday night when the catastrophe occurred.

'On that evening the horses had been exercised and watered as usual, and the stables were locked up at nine o'clock. Two of the lads walked up to the trainer's house, where they had supper in the kitchen, while the third, Ned Hunter, remained on guard. At a few minutes after nine the maid, Edith Baxter, carried down to the stables his supper, which consisted of a dish of curried mutton. She took no liquid, as there was a water-tap in the stables, and it was the rule that the lad on duty should drink nothing else. The maid carried a lantern with her, as it was very dark and the path ran across the open moor.

'Edith Baxter was within thirty yards of the stables when a man appeared out of the darkness and called to her to stop. As she stepped into the circle of yellow light thrown by the lantern she saw that he was a person of gentlemanly bearing, dressed in a grey suit of tweeds, with a cloth cap. He wore gaiters and carried a heavy stick with a knob to it. She was most impressed, however, by the extreme pallor of his face and by the nervousness of his manner. His age, she thought, would be rather over thirty than under it.

'"Can you tell me where I am?" he asked. "I had almost made up my mind to sleep on the moor when I saw the light of your lantern."

'"You are close to the King's Pyland training stables," said she.

'"Oh, indeed! What a stroke of luck!" he cried. "I understand that a stable-boy sleeps there alone every night. Perhaps that is his supper which you are carrying to him. Now I am sure that you would not be too proud to earn the price of a new dress, would you?" He took a piece of white paper folded up out of his waistcoat pocket. "See that the boy has this tonight, and you shall have the prettiest frock that money can buy."

'She was frightened by the earnestness of his manner and ran past him to the window through which she was accustomed to hand the meals. It was already opened, and Hunter was seated at the small table inside. She had begun to tell him of what had happened when the stranger came up again.

'"Good-evening," said he, looking through the window. "I wanted to have a word with you." The girl has sworn that as he spoke she noticed the corner of the little paper packet protruding from his closed hand.

'"What business have you here?" asked the lad.

'"It's business that may put something into your pocket," said the other. "You've two horses in for the Wessex Cup – Silver Blaze and Bayard. Let me have the straight tip and you won't be a loser. Is it a fact that at the weights Bayard could give the other a hundred yards in five furlongs, and that the stable have put their money on him?"

'"So, you're one of those damned touts!" cried the lad. "I'll show you how we serve them in King's Pyland." He sprang up and rushed across the stable to unloose the dog. The girl fled away to the house, but as she ran she looked back and saw that the stranger was leaning through the window. A minute later, however, when Hunter rushed out with the hound he was gone, and though he ran all round the buildings he failed to find any trace of him.'

'One moment,' I asked. 'Did the stable-boy, when he ran out with the dog, leave the door unlocked behind him?'

'Excellent, Watson, excellent!' murmured my companion. 'The importance of the point struck me so forcibly that I sent a special wire to Dartmoor yesterday to clear the matter up. The boy locked the door before he left it. The window, I may add, was not large enough for a man to get through.

'Hunter waited until his fellow-grooms had returned, when he sent a message to the trainer and told him what had occurred Straker was excited at hearing the account, although he does not seem to have quite realized its true significance. It left him, however, vaguely uneasy, and Mrs Straker, waking at one in the morning, found that he was dressing. In reply to her inquiries, he said that he could not sleep on account of his anxiety about the horses, and that he intended to walk down to the stables to see that all was well. She begged him to remain at home, as she could hear the rain pattering against the window, but in spite of her entreaties he pulled on his large mackintosh and left the house.

'Mrs Straker awoke at seven in the morning to find that her husband had not yet returned. She dressed herself hastily, called the maid, and set off for the stables. The door was open; inside, huddled together upon a chair, Hunter was sunk in a state of absolute stupor, the favourite's stall was empty, and there were no signs of his trainer.

'The two lads who slept in the chaff-cutting loft above the harness-room were quickly aroused. They had heard nothing during the night, for they are both sound sleepers. Hunter was obviously under the influence of some powerful drug, and as no sense could be got out of him, he was left to sleep it off while the two lads and the two women ran out in search of the absentees. They still had hopes that the trainer had for some reason taken out the horse for early exercise, but on ascending the knoll near the house, from which all the neighbouring moors were visible, they not only could see no signs of the missing favourite, but they perceived something which warned them that they were in the presence of a tragedy.

'About a quarter of a mile from the stables John Straker's overcoat was flapping from a furze-bush. Immediately beyond there was a bowl-shaped depression in the moor, and at the bottom of this was found the dead body of the unfortunate trainer. His head had been shattered by a savage blow from some heavy weapon, and he was wounded in the thigh, where there was a long, clean cut, inflicted evidently by some very sharp instrument. It was clear, however, that Straker had defended himself vigorously against his assailants, for in his right hand he held a small knife, which was clotted with blood up to the handle, while in his left he clasped a red and black silk cravat, which was recognized by the maid as having been worn on the preceding evening by the stranger who had visited the stables. Hunter, on recovering from his stupor, was also quite positive as to the ownership of the cravat. He was equally certain that the same stranger had, while standing at the window, drugged his curried mutton, and so deprived the stables of their watch-man. As to the missing horse, there were abundant proofs in the mud which lay at the bottom of the fatal hollow that he had been there at the time of the struggle. But from that morning he has disappeared, and although a large reward has been offered, and all the gypsies of Dartmoor are on the alert, no news has come of him. Finally, an analysis has shown that the remains of his supper left by the stable-lad contained an appreciable quantity of powdered opium, while the people at the house partook of the same dish on the same night without any ill effect.

'Those are the main facts of the case, stripped of all surmise, and stated as baldly as possible. I shall now recapitulate what the police have done in the matter.

'Inspector Gregory, to whom the case has been committed, is an extremely competent officer. Were he but gifted with imagination he might rise to great heights in his profession. On his arrival he promptly found and arrested the man upon whom suspicion naturally rested. There was little difficulty in finding him, for he inhabited one of those villas which I have mentioned. His name, it appears, was Fitzroy Simpson. He was a man of excellent birth and education, who had squandered a fortune upon the turf, and who lived now by doing a little quiet and genteel book-making in the sporting clubs of London. An examination of his betting-book shows that bets to the amount of five thousand pounds had been registered by him against the favourite. On being arrested he volunteered the statement that he had come down to Dartmoor in the hope of getting some information about the King's Pyland horses, and also about Desborough, the second favourite, which was in charge of Silas Brown at the Mapleton stables. He did not attempt to deny that he had acted as described upon the evening before, but declared that he had no sinister designs and had simply wished to obtain first-hand information. When confronted with his cravat he turned very pale and was utterly unable to account for its presence in the hand of the murdered man. His wet clothing showed that he had been out in the storm of the night before, and his stick, which was a penang-lawyer weighted with lead, was just such a weapon as might, by repeated blows, have inflicted the terrible injuries to which the trainer had succumbed. On the other hand, there was no wound upon his person, while the state of Straker's knife would show that one at least of his assailants must bear his mark upon him. There you have it all in a nutshell, Watson, and if you can give me any light I shall be infinitely obliged to you.'

I had listened with the greatest interest to the statement which Holmes, with characteristic clearness, had laid before me. Though most of the facts were familiar to me, I had not sufficiently appreciated their relative importance, nor their connection to each other.

'Is it not possible,' I suggested, 'that the incised wound upon Straker may have been caused by his own knife in the convulsive struggles which follow any brain injury?'

'It is more than possible; it is probable,' said Holmes. 'In that case one of the main points in favour of the accused disappears.'

'And yet,' said I, 'even now I fail to understand what the theory of the police can be.'

'I am afraid that whatever theory we state has very grave objections to it,' returned my companion. 'The police imagine, I take it, that this Fitzroy Simpson, having drugged the lad, and having in some way obtained a duplicate key, opened the stable door and took out the horse, with the intention, apparently, of kidnapping him altogether. His bridle is missing, so that Simpson must have put this on. Then, having left the door open behind him, he was leading the horse away over the moor when he was either met or overtaken by the trainer. A row naturally ensued. Simpson beat out the trainer's brains with his heavy stick without receiving any injury from the small knife which Straker used in self-defence, and then the thief either led the horse on to some secret hiding-place, or else it may have bolted during the struggle, and be now wandering out on the moors. That is the case as it appears to the police, and improbable as it is, all other explanations are more improbable still. However, I shall very quickly test the matter when I am once upon the spot, and until then I cannot really see how we can get much further than our present position.'

It was evening before we reached the little town of Tavistock, which lies, like the boss of a shield, in the middle of the huge circle of Dartmoor. Two gentlemen were awaiting us in the station – the one a tall, fair man with lion-like hair and beard and curiously penetrating light blue eyes; the other a small, alert person, very neat and dapper, in a frock-coat and gaiters, with trim little side-whiskers and an eyeglass. The latter was Colonel Ross, the well-known sportsman; the other, Inspector Gregory; a man who was rapidly making his name in the English detective service.

'I am delighted that you have come down, Mr

Holmes,' said the colonel. 'The inspector here has done all that could possibly be suggested, but I wish to leave no stone unturned in trying to avenge poor Straker and in recovering my horse.'

'Have there been any fresh developments?' asked Holmes.

'I am sorry to say that we have made very little progress,' said the inspector. 'We have an open carriage outside, and as you would no doubt like to see the place before the light fails, we might talk it over as we drive.'

A minute later we were all seated in a comfortable landau and were rattling through the quaint old Devonshire city. Inspector Gregory was full of his case and poured out a stream of remarks, while Holmes threw in an occasional question or interjection. Colonel Ross leaned back with his arms folded and his hat tilted over his eyes, while I listened with interest to the dialogue of the two detectives. Gregory was formulating his theory, which was almost exactly what Holmes had foretold in the train.

'The net is drawn pretty close round Fitzroy Simpson,' he remarked, 'and I believe myself that he is our man. At the same time I recognize that the evidence is purely circumstantial, and that some new development may upset it.'

'How about Straker's knife?'

'We have quite come to the conclusion that he wounded himself in his fall.'

'My friend Dr Watson made that suggestion to

me as we came down. If so, it would tell against this man Simpson.'

'Undoubtedly. He has neither a knife nor any sign of a wound. The evidence against him is certainly very strong. He had a great interest in the disappearance of the favourite. He lies under suspicion of having poisoned the stable-boy; he was undoubtedly out in the storm; he was armed with a heavy stick, and his cravat was found in the dead man's hand. I really think we have enough to go before a jury.'

Holmes shook his head. 'A clever counsel would tear it all to rags,' said he. 'Why should he take the horse out of the stable? If he wished to injure it, why could he not do it there? Has a duplicate key been found in his possession? What chemist sold him the powdered opium? Above all, where could he, a stranger to the district, hide a horse, and such a horse as this? What is his own explanation as to the paper which he wished the maid to give to the stable-boy?'

'He says that it was a ten-pound note. One was found in his purse. But your other difficulties are not so formidable as they seem. He is not a stranger to the district. He has twice lodged at Tavistock in the summer. The opium was probably brought from London. The key, having served its purpose, would be hurled away. The horse may be at the bottom of one of the pits or old mines upon the moor.'

'What does he say about the cravat?'

'He acknowledges that it is his and declares that he has lost it. But a new element has been introduced into the case which may account for his leading the horse from the stable.'

Holmes pricked up his ears.

'We have found traces which show that a party of gypsies encamped on Monday night within a mile of the spot where the murder took place. On Tuesday they were gone. Now, presuming that there was some understanding between Simpson and these gypsies, might he not have been leading the horse to them when he was overtaken, and may they not have him now?'

'It is certainly possible.'

'The moor is being scoured for these gypsies. I have also examined every stable and outhouse in Tavistock, and for a radius of ten miles.'

'There is another training-stable quite close, I understand?'

'Yes, and that is a factor which we must certainly not neglect. As Desborough, their horse, was second in the betting, they had an interest in the disappearance of the favourite. Silas Brown, the trainer, is known to have had large bets upon the event, and he was no friend to poor Straker. We have, however, examined the stables, and there is nothing to connect him with the affair.'

'And nothing to connect this man Simpson with the interests of the Mapleton stables?'

'Nothing at all.'

Holmes leaned back in the carriage, and the conversation ceased. A few minutes later our driver pulled up at a neat little red-brick villa with overhanging eaves which stood by the road. Some distance off, across a paddock, lay a long grey-tiled outbuilding. In every other direction the low curves of the moor, bronze-coloured from the fading ferns, stretched away to the sky-line, broken only by the steeples of Tavistock, and by a cluster of houses away to the westward which marked the Mapleton stables. We all sprang out with the exception of Holmes, who continued to lean back with his eyes fixed upon the sky in front of him, entirely absorbed in his own thoughts. It was only when I touched his arm that he roused himself with a violent start and stepped out of the carriage.

'Excuse me,' said he, turning to Colonel Ross, who had looked at him in some surprise. 'I was day-dreaming.' There was a gleam in his eyes and a suppressed excitement in his manner which convinced me, used as I was to his ways, that his hand was upon a clue, though I could not imagine where he had found it.

'Perhaps you would prefer at once to go on to the scene of the crime, Mr Holmes?' said Gregory.

'I think that I should prefer to stay here a little and go into one or two questions of detail. Straker was brought back here, I presume?'

'Yes, he lies upstairs. The inquest is tomorrow.'

'He has been in your service some years, Colonel Ross?'

'I have always found him an excellent servant.'

'I presume that you made an inventory of what he had in his pockets at the time of his death, Inspector?'

'I have the things themselves in the sitting-room if you would care to see them.'

'I should be very glad.' We all filed into the front room and sat round the central table while the inspector unlocked a square tin box and laid a small heap of things before us. There was a box of vestas, two inches of tallow candle, an ADP brier-root pipe, a pouch of sealskin with half an ounce of long-cut Cavendish, a silver watch with a gold chain, five sovereigns in gold, an aluminum pencil-case, a few papers, and an ivory-handled knife with a very delicate, inflexible blade marked Weiss & Co., London.

'This is a very singular knife,' said Holmes, lifting it up and examining it minutely. 'I presume, as I see bloodstains upon it, that it is the one which was found in the dead man's grasp. Watson, this knife is surely in your line?'

'It is what we call a cataract knife,' said I.

'I thought so. A very delicate blade devised for very delicate work. A strange thing for a man to carry with him upon a rough expedition, especially as it would not shut in his pocket.'

'The tip was guarded by a disc of cork which we found beside his body,' said the inspector.

'His wife tells us that the knife had lain upon the dressing-table, and that he had picked it up as he left the room. It was a poor weapon, but perhaps the best that he could lay his hands on at the moment.'

'Very possibly. How about these papers?'

'Three of them are receipted hay-dealers' accounts. One of them is a letter of instructions from Colonel Ross. This other is a milliner's account for thirty-seven pounds fifteen made out by Madame Lesurier, of Bond Street, to William Derbyshire. Mrs Straker tells us that Derbyshire was a friend of her husband's, and that occasionally his letters were addressed here.'

'Madame Derbyshire had somewhat expensive tastes,' remarked Holmes, glancing down the account. 'Twenty-two guineas is rather heavy for a single costume. However, there appears to be nothing more to learn, and we may now go down to the scene of the crime.'

As we emerged from the sitting-room a woman, who had been waiting in the passage, took a step forward and laid her hand upon the inspector's sleeve. Her face was haggard and thin and eager, stamped with the print of a recent horror.

'Have you got them? Have you found them?' she panted.

'No, Mrs Straker. But Mr Holmes here has come from London to help us, and we shall do all that is possible.'

'Surely I met you in Plymouth at a garden-party some little time ago, Mrs Straker?' said Holmes.

'No, sir; you are mistaken.'

'Dear me! Why, I could have sworn to it. You wore a costume of dove-coloured silk with ostrich-feather trimming.'

'I never had such a dress, sir,' answered the lady.

'Ah, that quite settles it,' said Holmes. And with an apology he followed the inspector outside. A short Walk across the moor took us to the hollow in which the body had been found. At the brink of it was the furze-bush upon which the coat had been hung.

'There was no wind that night, I understand,' said Holmes.

'None, but very heavy rain.'

'In that case the overcoat was not blown against the furze-bush, but placed there.'

'Yes, it was laid across the bush.'

'You fill me with interest. I perceive that the ground has been trampled up a good deal. No doubt many feet have been here since Monday night.'

'A piece of matting has been laid here at the side, and we have all stood upon that.'

'Excellent.'

'In this bag I have one of the boots which Straker wore, one of Fitzroy Simpson's shoes, and a cast horseshoe of Silver Blaze.'

'My dear Inspector, you surpass yourself!'

Holmes took the bag, and, descending into the hollow, he pushed the matting into a more central position. Then stretching himself upon his face and leaning his chin upon his hands, he made a careful study of the trampled mud in front of him. 'Hullo!' said he suddenly. 'What's this?' It was a wax vesta, half burned, which was so coated with mud that it looked at first like a little chip of wood.

'I cannot think how I came to overlook it,' said the inspector with an expression of annoyance.

'It was invisible, buried in the mud. I only saw it because I was looking for it.'

'What! you expected to find it?'

'I thought it not unlikely.'

He took the boots from the bag and compared the impressions of each of them with marks upon the ground. Then he clambered up to the rim of the hollow and crawled about among the ferns and bushes.

'I am afraid that there are no more tracks,' said the inspector. 'I have examined the ground very carefully for a hundred yards in each direction.'

'Indeed!' said Holmes, rising. 'I should not have the impertinence to do it again after what you say. But I should like to take a little walk over the moor before it grows dark that I may know my ground tomorrow, and I think that I shall put this horseshoe into my pocket for luck.'

Colonel Ross, who had shown some signs of impatience at my companion's quiet and systematic method of work, glanced at his watch. 'I wish you would come back with me, Inspector,' said he. 'There are several points on which I should like your advice, and especially as to whether we do not owe it to the public to remove our horse's name from the entries for the cup.'

'Certainly not,' cried Holmes with decision. 'I should let the name stand.'

The colonel bowed. 'I am very glad to have had your opinion, sir,' said he. 'You will find us at poor Straker's house when you have finished your work, and we can drive together into Tavistock.'

He turned back with the inspector, while Holmes and I walked slowly across the moor. The sun was beginning to sink behind the stable of Mapleton, and the long, sloping plain in front of us was tinged with gold, deepening into rich, ruddy browns where the faded ferns and brambles caught the evening light. But the glories of the landscape were all wasted upon my companion, who was sunk in the deepest thought.

'It's this way, Watson,' said he at last. 'We may leave the question of who killed John Straker for the instant and confine ourselves to finding out what has become of the horse. Now, supposing that he broke away during or after the tragedy, where could he have gone to? The horse is a very gregarious creature. If left to himself his instincts would have been either to return to King's Pyland or go over to Mapleton. Why should he run wild upon the moor? He would surely have been seen by now. And why should gypsies kidnap him? These people always clear out when they hear of trouble, for they do not wish to be pestered by the police. They could not hope to sell such a horse. They would run a great risk and gain nothing by taking him. Surely that is clear.'

'Where is he, then?'

'I have already said that he must have gone to King's Pyland or to Mapleton. He is not at King's Pyland. Therefore he is at Mapleton. Let us take that as a working hypothesis and see what it leads us to. This part of the moor, as the inspector remarked, is very hard and dry. But it falls away towards Mapleton, and you can see from here that there is a long hollow over yonder, which must have been very wet on Monday night. If our supposition is correct, then the horse must have crossed that, and there is the point where we should look for his tracks.'

We had been walking briskly during this conversation, and a few more minutes brought us to the hollow in question. At Holmes's request I walked down the bank to the right, and he to the left, but I had not taken fifty paces before I heard him give a shout and saw him waving his hand to me. The track of a horse was plainly outlined in the soft earth in front of him, and the shoe which he took from his pocket exactly fitted the impression.

'See the value of imagination,' said Holmes. 'It is the one quality which Gregory lacks. We imagined what might have happened, acted upon the supposition, and find ourselves justified. Let us proceed.'

We crossed the marshy bottom and passed over a quarter of a mile of dry, hard turf. Again the ground sloped, and again we came on the tracks. Then we lost them for half a mile, but only to pick them up once more quite close to Mapleton. It was Holmes who saw them first, and he stood pointing with a look of triumph upon his face. A man's track was visible beside the horse's.

'The horse was alone before,' I cried.

'Quite so. It was alone before. Hullo, what is this?'

The double track turned sharp off and took the direction of King's Pyland. Holmes whistled, and we both followed along after it. His eyes were on the trail, but I happened to look a little to one side and saw to my surprise the same tracks coming back again in the opposite direction.

'One for you, Watson,' said Holmes when I pointed it out. 'You have saved us a long walk, which would have brought us back on our own traces. Let us follow the return track.'

We had not to go far. It ended at the paving of asphalt which led up to the gates of the Mapleton stables. As we approached, a groom ran out from them.

'We don't want any loiterers about here,' said he.

'I only wished to ask a question,' said Holmes, with his finger and thumb in his waistcoat pocket.

Should I be too early to see your master, Mr Silas Brown, if I were to call at five o'clock tomorrow morning?'

'Bless you, sir, if anyone is about he will be, for he is always the first stirring. But here he is, sir, to answer your questions for himself. No, sir, no, it is as much as my place is worth to let him see me touch your money. Afterwards, if you like.'

As Sherlock Holmes replaced the half-crown which he had drawn from his pocket, a fierce-looking elderly man strode out from the gate with a hunting-crop swinging in his hand.

'What's this, Dawson!' he cried. 'No gossiping! Go about your business! And you, what the devil do you want here?'

'Ten minutes' talk with you, my good sir,' said Holmes in the sweetest of voices.

'I've no time to talk to every gadabout. We want no strangers here. Be off, or you may find a dog at your heels.'

Holmes leaned forward and whispered something in the trainer's ear. He started violently and flushed to the temples.

'It's a lie!' he shouted. 'An infernal lie!'

'Very good. Shall we argue about it here in public or talk it over in your parlour?'

'Oh, come in if you wish to.'

Holmes smiled. 'I shall not keep you more than a few minutes, Watson,' said he. 'Now, Mr Brown, I am quite at your disposal.'

It was twenty minutes, and the reds had all

faded into greys before Holmes and the trainer reappeared. Never have I seen such a change as had been brought about in Silas Brown in that short time. His face was ashy pale, beads of perspiration shone upon his brow, and his hands shook until the hunting-crop wagged like a branch in the wind. His bullying, overbearing manner was all gone too, and he cringed along at my companion's side like a dog with its master.

'Your instructions will be done. It shall all be done,' said he.

'There must be no mistake,' said Holmes, looking round at him. The other winced as he read the menace in his eyes.

'Oh, no, there shall be no mistake. I shall be there. Should I change it first or not?'

Holmes thought a little and then burst out laughing. 'No, don't,' said he, 'I shall write to you about it. No tricks, now, or –'

'Oh, you can trust me, you can trust me!'

'Yes, I think I can. Well, you shall hear from me tomorrow.' He turned upon his heel, disregarding the trembling hand which the other held out to him, and we set off for King's Pyland.

'A more perfect compound of the bully, coward, and sneak than Master Silas Brown I have seldom met with,' remarked Holmes as we trudged along together.

'He has the horse, then?'

'He tried to bluster out of it, but I described to him so exactly what his actions had been upon that morning that he is convinced that I was watching him. Of course you observed the peculiarly square toes in the impressions, and that his own boots exactly corresponded to them. Again, of course no subordinate would have dared to do such a thing. I described to him how, when according to his custom he was the first down, he perceived a strange horse wandering over the moor. How he went out to it, and his astonishment at recognizing, from the white forehead which has given the favourite its name, that chance had put in his power the only horse which could beat the one upon which he had put his money. Then I described how his first impulse had been to lead him back to King's Pyland, and how the devil had shown him how he could hide the horse until the race was over, and how he had led it back and concealed it at Mapleton. When I told him every detail he gave it up and thought only of saving his own skin.'

'But his stables had been searched?'

'Oh, an old horse-faker like him has many a dodge.'

'But are you not afraid to leave the horse in his power now, since he has every interest of injuring it?'

'My dear fellow, he will guard it as the apple of his eye. He knows that his only hope of mercy is to produce it safe.'

'Colonel Ross did not impress me as a man who would be likely to show much mercy in any case.'

'The matter does not rest with Colonel Ross. I follow my own methods and tell as much or as little as I choose. That is the advantage of being unofficial. I don't know whether you observed it, Watson, but the colonel's manner has been just a trifle cavalier to me. I am inclined now to have a little amusement at his expense. Say nothing to him about the horse.'

'Certainly not without your permission.'

'And of course this is all quite a minor point compared to the question of who killed John Straker.'

'And you will devote yourself to that?'

'On the contrary, we both go back to London by the night train.' I was thunderstruck by my friend's words. We had only been a few hours in Devonshire, and that he should give up an investigation which he had begun so brilliantly was quite incomprehensible to me. Not a word more could I draw from him until we were back at the trainer's house. The colonel and the inspector were awaiting us in the parlour.

'My friend and I return to town by the night-express, said Holmes. 'We have had a charming little breath of your beautiful Dartmoor air.'

The inspector opened his eyes, and the colonel's lip curled in a sneer.

So you despair of arresting the murderer of poor Straker,' said he.

Holmes shrugged his shoulders. 'There are certainly grave difficulties in the way,' said he. 'I have every hope, however, that your horse will start upon Tuesday, and I beg that you will have your jockey in readiness. Might I ask for a photograph of Mr John Straker?'

The inspector took one from an envelope and handed it to him.

'My dear Gregory, you anticipate all my wants. If I might ask you to wait here for an instant, I have a question which I should like to put to the maid.'

'I must say that I am rather disappointed in our London consultant,' said Colonel Ross bluntly as my friend left the room. 'I do not see that we are any further than when he came.'

'At least you have his assurance that your horse will run,' said I.

'Yes, I have his assurance,' said the colonel with a shrug of his shoulders. 'I should prefer to have the horse.'

I was about to make some reply in defence of my friend when he entered the room again.

'Now, gentlemen,' said he, 'I am quite ready for Tavistock.'

As we stepped into the carriage one of the stable-lads held the door open for us. A sudden idea seemed to occur to Holmes, for he leaned forward and touched the lad upon the sleeve.

'You have a few sheep in the paddock,' he said. 'Who attends to them?'

'I do, sir.'

'Have you noticed anything amiss with them of late?'

'Well, sir, not of much account, but three of them have gone lame, sir.'

I could see that Holmes was extremely pleased, for he chuckled and rubbed his hands together.

'A long shot, Watson, a very long shot,' said he, pinching my arm. 'Gregory, let me recommend to your attention this singular epidemic among the sheep. Drive on, coachman!'

Colonel Ross still wore an expression which showed the poor opinion which he had formed of my companion's ability, but I saw by the inspector's face that his attention had been keenly aroused.

'You consider that to be important?' he asked.

'Exceedingly so.'

'Is there any point to which you would wish to draw my attention?'

'To the curious incident of the dog in the night-time.'

'The dog did nothing in the night-time.'

'That was the curious incident,' remarked Sherlock Holmes.

Four days later Holmes and I were again in the train, bound for Winchester to see the race for the Wessex Cup. Colonel Ross met us by appointment outside the station, and we drove in his drag to the course beyond the town. His face was grave, and his manner was cold in the extreme.

'I have seen nothing of my horse,' said he.

'I suppose that you would know him when you saw him?' asked Holmes.

The colonel was very angry. 'I have been on the turf for twenty years and never was asked such a question as that before,' said he. 'A child would know Silver Blaze with his white forehead and his mottled off-foreleg.'

'How is the betting?'

'Well, that is the curious part of it. You could have got fifteen to one yesterday, but the price has become shorter and shorter, until you can hardly get three to one now.'

'Hum!' said Holmes. 'Somebody knows something, that is clear.'

As the drag drew up in the enclosure near the grandstand I glanced at the card to see the entries.

Wessex Plate [it ran] 50 sovs. each h ft with 1000 sovs. added, for four and five year olds. Second, £300. Third, £200. New course (one mile and five furlongs).
1. Mr Heath Newton's The Negro. Red cap.
Cinnamon jacket.
2. Colonel Wardlaw's Pugilist. Pink cap. Blue and black jacket.
3. Lord Backwater's Desborough. Yellow cap and sleeves.
4. Colonel Ross's Silver Blaze. Black cap. Red jacket.
5. Duke of Balmoral's Iris. Yellow and black stripes.
6. Lord Singleford's Rasper. Purple cap. Black sleeves.

'We scratched our other one and put all hopes on your word,' said the colonel. 'Why, what is that? Silver Blaze favourite?'

'Five to four against Silver Blaze!' roared the ring. 'Five to four against Silver Blaze! Five to fifteen against Desborough! Five to four on the field!'

'There are the numbers up,' I cried. 'They are all six there.'

'All six there? Then my horse is running,' cried the colonel in great agitation. 'But I don't see him. My colours have not passed.'

'Only five have passed. This must be he.'

As I spoke a powerful bay horse swept out from the weighing enclosure and cantered past us, bearing on its back the well-known black and red of the colonel.

'That's not my horse,' cried the owner. 'That beast has not a white hair upon its body. What is this that you have done, Mr Holmes?'

'Well, well, let us see how he gets on,' said my friend imperturbably. For a few minutes he gazed through my field-glass. 'Capital! An excellent start!' he cried suddenly. 'There they are, coming round the curve!'

From our drag we had a superb view as they came up the straight. The six horses were so close together that a carpet could have covered them, but halfway up the yellow of the Mapleton stable showed to the front. Before they reached us, however, Desborough's bolt was shot, and the colonel's horse, coming away with a rush, passed the post a good six lengths before its rival, the Duke of Balmoral's Iris making a bad third.

'It's my race, anyhow,' gasped the colonel, passing his hand over his eyes. 'I confess that I can make neither head nor tail of it. Don't you think that you have kept up your mystery long enough, Mr Holmes?'

'Certainly, Colonel, you shall know everything. Let us all go round and have a look at the horse together. Here he is,' he continued as we made our way into the weighing enclosure, where only owners and their friends find admittance. 'You have only to wash his face and his leg in spirits of wine, and you will find that he is the same old Silver Blaze as ever.

'You take my breath away!'

'I found him in the hands of a faker and took the liberty of running him just as he was sent over.'

'My dear sir, you have done wonders. The horse looks very fit and well. It never went better in its life. I owe you a thousand apologies for having doubted your ability. You have done me a great service by recovering my horse. You would do me a greater still if you could lay your hands on the murderer of John Straker.'

'I have done so,' said Holmes quietly.

The colonel and I stared at him in amazement. 'You have got him! Where is he, then?'

'He is here.'

'Here! Where?'

'In my company at the present moment.'

The colonel flushed angrily. 'I quite recognize that I am under obligations to you, Mr Holmes,' said he, 'but I must regard what you have just said as either a very bad joke or an insult.'

Sherlock Holmes laughed. 'I assure you that I have not associated you with the crime, Colonel,' said he. 'The real murderer is standing immediately behind you.' He stepped past and laid his hand upon the glossy neck of the thoroughbred.

'The horse!' cried both the colonel and myself.

'Yes, the horse. And it may lessen his guilt if I say that it was done in self-defence, and that John Straker was a man who was entirely unworthy of your confidence. But there goes the bell, and as I stand to win a little on this next race, I shall defer a lengthy explanation until a more fitting time.'

We had the corner of a Pullman car to ourselves that evening as we whirled back to London, and I fancy that the journey was a short one to Colonel Ross as well as to myself as we listened to our companion's narrative of the events which had occurred at the Dartmoor training-stables upon that Monday night, and the means by which he had unravelled them.

'I confess,' said he, 'that any theories which I had formed from the newspaper reports were entirely erroneous. And yet there were indications there, had they not been overlaid by other details which concealed their true import. I went to Devonshire with the conviction that Fitzroy Simpson was the true culprit, although, of course, I saw that the evidence against him was by no means complete. It was while I was in the carriage, just as we reached the trainer's house, that the immense significance of the curried mutton occurred to me. You may remember that I was distrait and remained sitting after you had all alighted. I was marvelling in my own mind how I could possibly have overlooked so obvious a clue.'

'I confess', said the colonel, 'that even now I cannot see how it helps us.'

'It was the first link in my chain of reasoning. Powdered opium is by no means tasteless. The flavour is not disagreeable, but it is perceptible. Were it mixed with any ordinary dish the eater would undoubtedly detect it and would probably eat no more. A curry was exactly the medium which would disguise this taste. By no possible supposition could this stranger, Fitzroy Simpson, have caused curry to be served in the trainer's family that night, and it is surely too monstrous a coincidence to suppose that he happened to come along with powdered opium upon the very night when a dish happened to be served which would disguise the flavour. That is unthinkable. Therefore Simpson becomes eliminated from the case, and our attention centres upon Straker and his wife, the only two people who could have chosen curried mutton for supper that night. The opium was added after the dish was set aside for the stable-boy, for the others had the same for supper with no ill effects. Which of them, then, had access to that dish without the maid seeing them?

'Before deciding that question I had grasped the significance of the silence of the dog, for one true inference invariably suggests others. The Simpson incident had shown me that a dog was kept in the stables, and yet, though someone had been in and had fetched out a horse, he had not barked enough to arouse the two lads in the loft. Obviously the midnight visitor was someone whom the dog knew well.

'I was already convinced, or almost convinced, that John Straker went down to the stables in the dead of the night and took out Silver Blaze. For what purpose? For a dishonest one, obviously, or why should he drug his own stable-boy? And yet I was at a loss to know why. There have been cases before now where trainers have made sure of great sums of money by laying against their own horses through agents and then preventing them from winning by fraud. Sometimes it is a pulling jockey. Sometimes it is some surer and subtler means. What was it here? I hoped that the contents of his pockets might help me to form a conclusion.

'And they did so. You cannot have forgotten the singular knife which was found in the dead man's hand, a knife which certainly no sane man would choose for a weapon. It was, as Dr Watson told us, a form of knife which is used for the most delicate operations known in surgery. And it was to be used for a delicate operation that night. You must know, with your wide experience of turf matters, Colonel Ross, that it is possible to make a slight nick upon the tendons of a horse's ham, and to do it subcutaneously, so as to leave absolutely no trace. A horse so treated would develop a slight lameness, which would be put down to a strain in exercise or a touch of rheumatism, but never to foul play.'

'Villain! Scoundrel!' cried the colonel.

'We have here the explanation of why John Straker wished to take the horse out on to the moor. So spirited a creature would have certainly roused the soundest of sleepers when it felt the prick of the knife. It was absolutely necessary to do it in the open air.'

'I have been blind!' cried the colonel. 'Of course that was why he needed the candle and struck the match.'

'Undoubtedly. But in examining his belongings I was fortunate enough to discover not only the method of the crime but even its motives. As a man of the world, Colonel, you know that men do not carry other people's bills about in their pockets. We have most of us quite enough to do to settle our own. I at once concluded that Straker was leading a double life and keeping a second establishment. The nature of the bill showed that there was a lady in the case, and one who had expensive tastes. Liberal as you are with your servants, one can hardly expect that they can buy twenty-guinea walking dresses for their ladies. I questioned Mrs Straker as to the dress without her knowing it, and, having satisfied myself that it had never reached her, I made a note of the milliner's address and felt that by calling there with Straker's photograph I could easily dispose of the mythical Derbyshire.

'From that time on all was plain. Straker had led out the horse to a hollow where his light would be invisible. Simpson in his flight had dropped his cravat, and Straker had picked it up – with some idea, perhaps, that he might use it in securing the horse's leg. Once in the hollow, he had got behind the horse and had struck a light; but the creature, frightened at the sudden glare, and with the strange instinct of animals feeling that some mischief was intended, had lashed out, and the steel shoe had struck Straker full on the forehead. He had already, in spite of the rain, taken off his overcoat in order to do his delicate task, and so, as he fell, his knife gashed his thigh. Do I make it clear?'

'Wonderful!' cried the colonel. 'Wonderful! You might have been there!'

'My final shot was, I confess, a very long one. It struck me that so astute a man as Straker would not undertake this delicate tendon-nicking without a little practice. What could he practise on? My eyes fell upon the sheep, and I asked a question which, rather to my surprise, showed that my surmise was correct.

'When I returned to London I called upon the milliner, who had recognized Straker as an excellent customer of the name of Derbyshire, who had a very dashing wife, with a strong partiality for expensive dresses. I have no doubt that this woman had plunged him over head and ears in debt, and so led him into this miserable plot.'

'You have explained all but one thing,' cried the colonel. 'Where was the horse?'

'Ah, it bolted, and was cared for by one of your neighbours. We must have an amnesty in that direction, I think. This is Clapham Junction, if I am not mistaken, and we shall be in Victoria in less than ten minutes. If you care to smoke a cigar in our rooms, Colonel, I shall be happy to give you any other details which might interest you.'

THE ADVENTURE OF THE DANCING MEN

Holmes had been seated for some hours in silence with his long, thin back curved over a chemical vessel in which he was brewing a particularly malodorous product. His head was sunk upon his breast, and he looked from my point of view like a strange, lank bird, with dull grey plumage and a black top-knot.

So, Watson,' said he, suddenly, 'you do not propose to invest in South African securities?'

I gave a start of astonishment. Accustomed as I was to Holmes's curious faculties, this sudden intrusion into my most intimate thoughts was utterly inexplicable.

'How on earth do you know that?' I asked.

He wheeled round upon his stool, with a steaming test-tube in his hand, and a gleam of amusement in his deep-set eyes.

'Now, Watson, confess yourself utterly taken aback,' said he.

'I am.'

'I ought to make you sign a paper to that effect.'

'Why?'

'Because in five minutes you will say that it is all so absurdly simple.'

'I am sure that I shall say nothing of the kind.'

'You see, my dear Watson' – he propped his test-tube in the rack, and began to lecture with the air of a professor addressing his class – 'it is not really difficult to construct a series of inferences, each dependent upon its predecessor and each simple in itself. If, after doing so, one simply knocks out all the central inferences and presents one's audience with the starting-point and the conclusion, one may produce a startling, though possibly a meretricious, effect. Now, it was not really difficult, by an inspection of the groove between your left forefinger and thumb, to feel sure that you did *not* propose to invest your small capital in the gold fields.'

'I see no connection.'

'Very likely not; but I can quickly show you a close connection. Here are the missing links of the very simple chain: 1. You had chalk between your left finger and thumb when you returned from the club last night. 2. You put chalk there when you play billiards, to steady the cue. 3. You never play billiards except with Thurston. 4. You told me, four weeks ago, that Thurston had an option on some South African property which would expire in a month, and which he desired you to share with him. 5. Your checkbook is locked in my drawer, and you have not asked for the key. 6. You do not propose to invest your money in this manner.'

'How absurdly simple!' I cried.

'Quite so!' said he, a little nettled. 'Every problem becomes very childish when once it is explained to you. Here is an unexplained one. See what you can make of that, friend Watson.' He tossed a sheet of paper upon the table, and turned once more to his chemical analysis.

I looked with amazement at the absurd hieroglyphics upon the paper.

'Why, Holmes, it is a child's drawing,' I cried.

'Oh, that's your idea!'

'What else should it be?'

'That is what Mr Hilton Cubitt, of Riding Thorpe Manor, Norfolk, is very anxious to know. This little conundrum came by the first post, and he was to follow by the next train. There's a ring at the bell, Watson. I should not be very much surprised if this were he.'

A heavy step was heard upon the stairs, and an instant later there entered a tall, ruddy, clean-shaven gentleman, whose clear eyes and florid cheeks told of a life led far from the fogs of Baker Street. He seemed to bring a whiff of his strong, fresh, bracing, east-coast air with him as he entered. Having shaken hands with each of us, he was about to sit down, when his eye rested upon the paper with the curious markings, which I had just examined and left upon the table.

'Well, Mr Holmes, what do you make of these?' he cried. 'They told me that you were fond of queer mysteries, and I don't think you can find a queerer one than that. I sent the paper on ahead, so that you might have time to study it before I came.'

'It is certainly rather a curious production,' said Holmes. 'At first sight it would appear to be some childish prank. It consists of a number of absurd little figures dancing across the paper upon which they are drawn. Why should you attribute any importance to so grotesque an object?'

'I never should, Mr Holmes. But my wife does. It is frightening her to death. She says nothing, but I can see terror in her eyes. That's why I want to sift the matter to the bottom.'

Holmes held up the paper so that the sunlight shone full upon it. It was a page torn from a notebook. The markings were done in pencil, and ran in this way:

𝆕𝆕𝆕𝆕𝆕𝆕𝆕𝆕𝆕𝆕𝆕𝆕𝆕𝆕

Holmes examined it for some time, and then, folding it carefully up, he placed it in his pocketbook.

'This promises to be a most interesting and unusual case,' said he. 'You gave me a few particulars in your letter, Mr Hilton Cubitt, but I should be very much obliged if you would kindly go over it all again for the benefit of my friend, Dr Watson.'

'I'm not much of a story-teller,' said our visitor,

nervously clasping and unclasping his great, strong hands. 'You'll just ask me anything that I don't make clear. I'll begin at the time of my marriage last year, but I want to say first of all that, though I'm not a rich man, my people have been at Riding Thorpe for a matter of five centuries, and there is no better known family in the county of Norfolk. Last year I came up to London for the Jubilee, and I stopped at a boardinghouse in Russell Square, because Parker, the vicar of our parish, was staying in it. There was an American young lady there – Patrick was the name – Elsie Patrick. In some way we became friends, until before my month was up I was as much in love as man could be. We were quietly married at a registry office, and we returned to Norfolk a married couple. You'll think it very mad, Mr Holmes, that a man of a good old family should marry a wife in this fashion, knowing nothing of her past or of her people, but if you saw her and knew her, it would help you to understand.

'She was very straight about it, was Elsie. I can't say that she did not give me every chance of getting out of it if I wished to do so. "I have had some very disagreeable associations in my life," said she, "I wish to forget all about them. I would rather never allude to the past, for it is very painful to me. If you take me, Hilton, you will take a woman who has nothing that she need be personally ashamed of; but you will have to be content with my word for it, and to allow me to be silent as to all that passed up to the time when I became yours. If these conditions are too hard, then go back to Norfolk, and leave me to the lonely life in which you found me." It was only the day before our wedding that she said those very words to me. I told her that I was content to take her on her own terms, and I have been as good as my word.

'Well, we have been married now for a year, and very happy we have been. But about a month ago, at the end of June, I saw for the first time signs of trouble. One day my wife received a letter from America. I saw the American stamp. She turned deadly white, read the letter, and threw it into the fire. She made no allusion to it afterwards, and I made none, for a promise is a promise, but she has never known an easy hour from that moment. There is always a look of fear upon her face – a look as if she were waiting and expecting. She would do better to trust me. She would find that I was her best friend. But until she speaks, I can say nothing. Mind you, she is a truthful woman, Mr Holmes, and whatever trouble there may have been in her past life it has been no fault of hers. I am only a simple Norfolk squire, but there is not a man in England who ranks his family honour more highly than I do. She knows it well, and she knew it well before she married me. She would never bring any stain upon it – of that I am sure.

'Well, now I come to the queer part of my

story. About a week ago – it was the Tuesday of last week – I found on one of the window-sills a number of absurd little dancing figures like these upon the paper. They were scrawled with chalk. I thought that it was the stable-boy who had drawn them, but the lad swore he knew nothing about it. Anyhow, they had come there during the night. I had them washed out, and I only mentioned the matter to my wife afterwards. To my surprise, she took it very seriously, and begged me if any more came to let her see them. None did come for a week, and then yesterday morning I found this paper lying on the sundial in the garden. I showed it to Elsie, and down she dropped in a dead faint. Since then she has looked like a woman in a dream, half dazed, and with terror always lurking in her eyes. It was then that I wrote and sent the paper to you, Mr Holmes. It was not a thing that I could take to the police, for they would have laughed at me, but you will tell me what to do. I am not a rich man, but if there is any danger threatening my little woman, I would spend my last copper to shield her.'

He was a fine creature, this man of the old English soil – simple, straight, and gentle, with his great, earnest, blue eyes and broad, comely face. His love for his wife and his trust in her shone in his features. Holmes had listened to his story with the utmost attention, and now he sat for some time in silent thought.

'Don't you think, Mr Cubitt,' said he, at last,

'that your best plan would be to make a direct appeal to your wife, and to ask her to share her secret with you?'

Hilton Cubitt shook his massive head.

'A promise is a promise, Mr Holmes. If Elsie wished to tell me she would. If not, it is not for me to force her confidence. But I am justified in taking my own line – and I will.'

'Then I will help you with all my heart. In the first place, have you heard of any strangers being seen in your neighbourhood?'

'No.'

'I presume that it is a very quiet place. Any fresh face would cause comment?'

'In the immediate neighbourhood, yes. But we have several small watering-places not very far away. And the farmers take in lodgers.'

'These hieroglyphics have evidently a meaning. If it is a purely arbitrary one, it may be impossible for us to solve it. If, on the other hand, it is systematic, I have no doubt that we shall get to the bottom of it. But this particular sample is so short that I can do nothing, and the facts which you have brought me are so indefinite that we have no basis for an investigation. I would suggest that you return to Norfolk, that you keep a keen lookout, and that you take an exact copy of any fresh dancing men which may appear. It is a thousand pities that we have not a reproduction of those which were done in chalk upon the window-sill. Make a discreet inquiry also as to any strangers in the neighbourhood. When you have collected some fresh evidence, come to me again. That is the best advice which I can give you, Mr Hilton Cubitt. If there are any pressing fresh developments, I shall be always ready to run down and see you in your Norfolk home.'

The interview left Sherlock Holmes very thoughtful, and several times in the next few days I saw him take his slip of paper from his notebook and look long and earnestly at the curious figures inscribed upon it. He made no allusion to the affair, however, until one afternoon a fortnight or so later. I was going out when he called me back.

'You had better stay here, Watson.'

'Why?'

'Because I had a wire from Hilton Cubitt this morning. You remember Hilton Cubitt, of the dancing men? He was to reach Liverpool Street at one-twenty. He may be here at any moment. I gather from this wire that there have been some new incidents of importance.'

We had not long to wait, for our Norfolk squire came straight from the station as fast as a hansom could bring him. He was looking worried and depressed, with tired eyes and a lined forehead.

'It's getting on my nerves, this business, Mr Holmes,' said he, as he sank, like a wearied man, into an armchair. 'It's bad enough to feel that you are surrounded by unseen, unknown folk, who have some kind of design upon you, but when, in addition to that, you know that it is just killing your wife by inches, then it becomes as much as flesh and blood can endure. She's wearing away under it – just wearing away before my eyes.'

'Has she said anything yet?'

'No, Mr Holmes, she has not. And yet there have been times when the poor girl has wanted to speak, and yet could not quite bring herself to take the plunge. I have tried to help her, but I daresay I did it clumsily, and scared her from it. She has spoken about my old family, and our reputation in the county, and our pride in our unsullied honour, and I always felt it was leading to the point, but somehow it turned off before we got there.'

'But you have found out something for yourself?'

'A good deal, Mr Holmes. I have several fresh dancing-men pictures for you to examine, and, what is more important, I have seen the fellow.'

'What, the man who draws them?'

'Yes, I saw him at his work. But I will tell you everything in order. When I got back after my visit to you, the very first thing I saw next morning was a fresh crop of dancing men. They had been drawn in chalk upon the black wooden door of the tool-house, which stands beside the lawn in full view of the front windows. I took an exact copy, and here it is.' He unfolded a paper and laid it upon the table. Here is a copy of the hieroglyphics:

'Excellent!' said Holmes. 'Excellent! Pray continue.'

'When I had taken the copy, I rubbed out the marks, but, two mornings later, a fresh inscription had appeared. I have a copy of it here':

Holmes rubbed his hands and chuckled with delight.

'Our material is rapidly accumulating,' said he.

'Three days later a message was left scrawled upon paper, and placed under a pebble on the sundial. Here it is. The characters are, as you see, exactly the same as the last one. After that I determined to lie in wait, so I got out my revolver and I sat up in my study, which overlooks the lawn and garden. About two in the morning I was seated by the window, all being dark save for the moonlight outside, when I heard steps behind me, and there was my wife in her dressing-gown. She implored me to come to bed. I told her frankly that I wished to see who it was who played such absurd tricks upon us. She answered that it was some senseless practical joke, and that I should not take any notice of it.

'"If it really annoys you, Hilton, we might go and travel, you and I, and so avoid this nuisance."

'"What, be driven out of our own house by a

practical joker?" said I. "Why, we should have the whole county laughing at us."

'"Well, come to bed," said she, "and we can discuss it in the morning."

'Suddenly, as she spoke, I saw her white face grow whiter yet in the moonlight, and her hand tightened upon my shoulder. Something was moving in the shadow of the tool-house. I saw a dark, creeping figure which crawled round the corner and squatted in front of the door. Seizing my pistol, I was rushing out, when my wife threw her arms round me and held me with convulsive strength. I tried to throw her off, but she clung to me most desperately. At last I got clear, but by the time I had opened the door and reached the house the creature was gone. He had left a trace of his presence, however, for there on the door was the very same arrangement of dancing men which had already twice appeared, and which I have copied on that paper. There was no other sign of the fellow anywhere, though I ran all the time, for when I examined the door again in the morning, he had scrawled some more of his pictures under the line which I had already seen.'

'Have you that fresh drawing?'

'Yes, it is very short, but I made a copy of it, and here it is.'

Again he produced a paper. The new dance was in this form:

'Tell me,' said Holmes – and I could see by his eyes that he was much excited – 'was this a mere addition to the first or did it appear to be entirely separate?'

'It was on a different panel of the door.'

'Excellent! This is far the most important of all for our purpose. It fills me with hopes. Now, Mr Hilton Cubitt, please continue your most interesting statement.'

'I have nothing more to say, Mr Holmes, except that I was angry with my wife that night for having held me back when I might have caught the skulking rascal. She said that she feared that I might come to harm. For an instant it had crossed my mind that perhaps what she really feared was that *he* might come to harm, for I could not doubt that she knew who this man was, and what he meant by these strange signals. But there is a tone in my wife's voice, Mr Holmes, and a look in her eyes which forbid doubt, and I am sure that it was indeed my own safety that was in her mind. There's the whole case, and now I want your advice as to what I ought to do. My own inclination is to put half a dozen of my farm lads in the shrubbery, and when this fellow comes again to give him such a hiding that he will leave us in peace for the future.'

'I fear it is too deep a case for such simple remedies,' said Holmes. 'How long can you stay in London?'

'I must go back today. I would not leave my

wife alone all night for anything. She is very nervous, and begged me to come back.'

'I daresay you are right. But if you could have stopped, I might possibly have been able to return with you in a day or two. Meanwhile you will leave me these papers, and I think that it is very likely that I shall be able to pay you a visit shortly and to throw some light upon your case.'

Sherlock Holmes preserved his calm professional manner until our visitor had left us, although it was easy for me, who knew him so well, to see that he was profoundly excited. The moment that Hilton Cubitt's broad back had disappeared through the door my comrade rushed to the table, laid out all the slips of paper containing dancing men in front of him, and threw himself into an intricate and elaborate calculation. For two hours I watched him as he covered sheet after sheet of paper with figures and letters, so completely absorbed in his task that he had evidently forgotten my presence. Sometimes he was making progress and whistled and sang at his work; sometimes he was puzzled, and would sit for long spells with a furrowed brow and a vacant eye. Finally he sprang from his chair with a cry of satisfaction, and walked up and down the room rubbing his hands together. Then he wrote a long telegram upon a cable form. 'If my answer to this is as I hope, you will have a very pretty case to add to your collection, Watson,' said he. 'I expect that we shall be able to go down to Norfolk tomorrow, and to take our friend some very definite news as to the secret of his annoyance.'

I confess that I was filled with curiosity, but I was aware that Holmes liked to make his disclosures at his own time and in his own way, so I waited until it should suit him to take me into his confidence.

But there was a delay in that answering telegram, and two days of impatience followed, during which Holmes pricked up his ears at every ring of the bell. On the evening of the second there came a letter from Hilton Cubitt. All was quiet with him, save that a long inscription had appeared that morning upon the pedestal of the sundial. He enclosed a copy of it, which is here reproduced:

Holmes bent over this grotesque frieze for some minutes, and then suddenly sprang to his feet with an exclamation of surprise and dismay. His face was haggard with anxiety.

'We have let this affair go far enough,' said he. 'Is there a train to North Walsham tonight?'

I turned up the timetable. The last had just gone.

'Then we shall breakfast early and take the very first in the morning,' said Holmes. 'Our presence is most urgently needed. Ah! here is our expected cablegram. One moment, Mrs Hudson, there may be an answer. No, that is quite as I expected. This message makes it even more essential that we should not lose an hour in letting Hilton Cubitt know how matters stand, for it is a singular and a dangerous web in which our simple Norfolk squire is entangled.'

So, indeed, it proved, and as I come to the dark conclusion of a story which had seemed to me to be only childish and bizarre, I experience once again the dismay and horror with which I was filled. Would that I had some brighter ending to communicate to my readers, but these are the chronicles of fact, and I must follow to their dark crisis the strange chain of events which for some days made Riding Thorpe Manor a household word through the length and breadth of England.

We had hardly alighted at North Walsham, and mentioned the name of our destination, when the station-master hurried towards us. 'I suppose that you are the detectives from London?' said he.

A look of annoyance passed over Holmes's face.

'What makes you think such a thing?'

'Because Inspector Martin from Norwich has just passed through. But maybe you are the surgeons. She's not dead – or wasn't by last accounts. You may be in time to save her yet – though it be for the gallows.'

Holmes's brow was dark with anxiety.

'We are going to Riding Thorpe Manor,' said

he, 'but we have heard nothing of what has passed there.'

'It's a terrible business,' said the stationmaster. 'They are shot, both Mr Hilton Cubitt and his wife. She shot him and then herself – so the servants say. He's dead and her life is despaired of. Dear, dear, one of the oldest families in the county of Norfolk, and one of the most honoured.'

Without a word Holmes hurried to a carriage, and during the long seven miles' drive he never opened his mouth. Seldom have I seen him so utterly despondent. He had been uneasy during all our journey from town, and I had observed that he had turned over the morning papers with anxious attention, but now this sudden realization of his worst fears left him in a blank melancholy. He leaned back in his seat, lost in gloomy speculation. Yet there was much around to interest us, for we were passing through as singular a countryside as any in England, where a few scattered cottages represented the population of today, while on every hand enormous square-towered churches bristled up from the flat green landscape and told of the glory and prosperity of old East Anglia. At last the violet rim of the German Ocean appeared over the green edge of the Norfolk coast, and the driver pointed with his whip to two old brick and timber gables which projected from a grove of trees. 'That's Riding Thorpe Manor,' said he.

As we drove up to the porticoed front door, I observed in front of it, beside the tennis lawn, the black toolhouse and the pedestalled sundial with which we had such strange associations. A dapper little man, with a quick, alert manner and a waxed moustache, had just descended from a high dog-cart. He introduced himself as Inspector Martin, of the Norfolk Constabulary, and he was considerably astonished when he heard the name of my companion.

'Why, Mr Holmes, the crime was only committed at three this morning. How could you hear of it in London and get to the spot as soon as I?'

'I anticipated it. I came in the hope of preventing it.'

'Then you must have important evidence, of which we are ignorant, for they were said to be a most united couple.'

'I have only the evidence of the dancing men,' said Holmes. 'I will explain the matter to you later. Meanwhile, since it is too late to prevent this tragedy, I am very anxious that I should use the knowledge which I possess in order to ensure that justice be done. Will you associate me in your investigation, or will you prefer that I should act independently?'

'I should be proud to feel that we were acting together, Mr Holmes,' said the inspector, earnestly.

'In that case I should be glad to hear the evidence and to examine the premises without an instant of unnecessary delay.'

Inspector Martin had the good sense to allow my friend to do things in his own fashion, and contented himself with carefully noting the results. The local surgeon, an old, white-haired man, had just come down from Mrs Hilton Cubitt's room, and he reported that her injuries were serious, but not necessarily fatal. The bullet had passed through the front of her brain, and it would probably be some time before she could regain consciousness. On the question of whether she had been shot or had shot herself, he would not venture to express any decided opinion. Certainly the bullet had been discharged at very close quarters. There was only the one pistol found in the room, two barrels of which had been emptied. Mr Hilton Cubitt had been shot through the heart. It was equally conceivable that he had shot her and then himself, or that she had been the criminal, for the revolver lay upon the floor midway between them.

'Has he been moved?' asked Holmes.

'We have moved nothing except the lady. We could not leave her lying wounded upon the floor.'

'How long have you been here, Doctor?'

'Since four o'clock.'

'Anyone else?'

'Yes, the constable here.'

'And you have touched nothing?'

'Nothing.'

'You have acted with great discretion. Who sent for you?'

'The housemaid, Saunders.'

'Was it she who gave the alarm?'

'She and Mrs King, the cook.'

'Where are they now?'

'In the kitchen, I believe.'

'Then I think we had better hear their story at once.'

The old hall, oak-panelled and high-windowed, had been turned into a court of investigation. Holmes sat in a great, old-fashioned chair, his inexorable eyes gleaming out of his haggard face. I could read in them a set purpose to devote his life to this quest until the client whom he had failed to save should at last be avenged. The trim Inspector Martin, the old, grey-headed country doctor, myself, and a stolid village policeman made up the rest of that strange company.

The two women told their story clearly enough. They had been aroused from their sleep by the sound of an explosion, which had been followed a minute later by a second one. They slept in adjoining rooms, and Mrs King had rushed in to Saunders. Together they had descended the stairs. The door of the study was open, and a candle was burning upon the table. Their master lay upon his face in the centre of the room. He was quite dead. Near the window his wife was crouching, her head leaning against the wall. She was horribly wounded, and the side of her face was red with blood. She breathed heavily, but was incapable of saying anything. The passage, as well as the room, was full of smoke and the smell of powder. The window was certainly shut and fastened upon the inside. Both women were positive upon the point. They had at once sent for the doctor and for the constable. Then, with the aid of the groom and the stable-boy, they had conveyed their injured mistress to her room. Both she and her husband had occupied the bed. She was clad in her dress – he in his dressing-gown, over his night-clothes. Nothing had been moved in the study. So far as they knew, there had never been any quarrel between husband and wife. They had always looked upon them as a very united couple.

These were the main points of the servants' evidence. In answer to Inspector Martin, they were clear that every door was fastened upon the inside, and that no one could have escaped from the house. In answer to Holmes, they both remembered that they were conscious of the smell of powder from the moment that they ran out of their rooms upon the top floor. 'I commend that fact very carefully to your attention,' said Holmes to his professional colleague. 'And now I think that we are in a position to undertake a thorough examination of the room.'

The study proved to be a small chamber, lined on three sides with books, and with a writing-table facing an ordinary window, which looked out upon the garden. Our first attention was given to the body of the unfortunate squire, whose huge frame lay stretched across the room. His disordered dress showed that he had been hastily aroused from sleep. The bullet had been fired at him from the front, and had remained in his body, after penetrating the heart. His death had certainly been instantaneous and painless. There was no powder-marking either upon his dressing-gown or on his hands. According to the country surgeon, the lady had stains upon her face, but none upon her hand.

'The absence of the latter means nothing, though its presence may mean everything,' said Holmes. 'Unless the powder from a badly fitting cartridge happens to spurt backward, one may fire many shots without leaving a sign. I would suggest that Mr Cubitt's body may now be removed. I suppose, Doctor, you have not recovered the bullet which wounded the lady?'

'A serious operation will be necessary before that can be done. But there are still four cartridges in the revolver. Two have been fired and two wounds inflicted, so that each bullet can be accounted for.'

'So it would seem,' said Holmes. 'Perhaps you can account also for the bullet which has so obviously struck the edge of the window?'

He had turned suddenly, and his long, thin finger was pointing to a hole which had been drilled right through the lower window-sash, about an inch above the bottom.

'By George!' cried the inspector. 'How ever did you see that?'

'Because I looked for it.'

'Wonderful!' said the country doctor. 'You are certainly right, sir. Then a third shot has been fired, and therefore a third person must have been present. But who could that have been, and how could he have got away?'

'That is the problem which we are now about to solve,' said Sherlock Holmes. 'You remember, Inspector Martin, when the servants said that on leaving their room they were at once conscious of a smell of powder, I remarked that the point was an extremely important one?'

'Yes, sir; but I confess I did not quite follow you.'

'It suggested that at the time of the firing, the window as well as the door of the room had been open. Otherwise the fumes of powder could not have been blown so rapidly through the house. A draught in the room was necessary for that. Both door and window were only open for a very short time, however.'

'How do you prove that?'

'Because the candle was not guttered.'

'Capital! cried the inspector. 'Capital!'

'Feeling sure that the window had been open at the time of the tragedy, I conceived that there might have been a third person in the affair, who stood outside this opening and fired through it. Any shot directed at this person might hit the sash. I looked, and there, sure enough, was the bullet mark!'

'But how came the window to be shut and fastened?'

'The woman's first instinct would be to shut and fasten the window. But, hallo! what is this?'

It was a lady's handbag which stood upon the study table – a trim little handbag of crocodile-skin and silver. Holmes opened it and turned the contents out. There were twenty fifty-pound notes of the Bank of England, held together by an india-rubber band – nothing else.

'This must be preserved, for it will figure in the trial,' said Holmes, as he handed the bag with its contents to the inspector. 'It is now necessary that we should try to throw some light upon this third bullet, which has clearly, from the splintering of the wood, been fired from inside the room. I should like to see Mrs King, the cook, again. You said, Mrs King, that you were awakened by a *loud* explosion. When you said that, did you mean that it seemed to you to be louder than the second one?'

'Well, sir, it wakened me from my sleep, so it is hard to judge. But it did seem very loud.'

'You don't think that it might have been two shots fired almost at the same instant?'

'I am sure I couldn't say, sir.'

'I believe that it was undoubtedly so. I rather think, Inspector Martin, that we have now ex-hausted all that this room can teach us. If you will kindly step round with me, we shall see what fresh evidence the garden has to offer.'

A flower-bed extended up to the study window, and we all broke into an exclamation as we approached it. The flowers were trampled down, and the soft soil was imprinted all over with footmarks. Large, masculine feet they were, with peculiarly long, sharp toes. Holmes hunted about among the grass and leaves like a retriever after a wounded bird. Then, with a cry of satisfaction, he bent forward and picked up a little brazen cylinder.

'I thought so,' said he; 'the revolver had an ejector, and here is the third cartridge. I really think, Inspector Martin, that our case is almost complete.'

The country inspector's face had shown his intense amazement at the rapid and masterful progress of Holmes's investigation. At first he had shown some disposition to assert his own position, but now he was overcome with admiration, and ready to follow without question wherever Holmes led.

'Whom do you suspect?' he asked.

'I'll go into that later. There are several points in this problem which I have not been able to explain to you yet. Now that I have got so far, I had best proceed on my own lines, and then clear the whole matter up once and for all.'

'Just as you wish, Mr Holmes, so long as we get our man.'

'I have no desire to make mysteries, but it is impossible at the moment of action to enter into long and complex explanations. I have the threads of this affair all in my hand. Even if this lady should never recover consciousness, we can still reconstruct the events of last night, and ensure that justice be done. First of all, I wish to know whether there is any inn in this neighbourhood known as "Elrige's"?'

The servants were cross-questioned, but none of them had heard of such a place. The stable-boy threw a light upon the matter by remembering that a farmer of that name lived some miles off, in the direction of East Ruston.

'Is it a lonely farm?'

'Very lonely, sir.'

'Perhaps they have not heard yet of all that happened here during the night?'

'Maybe not, sir.'

Holmes thought for a little, and then a curious smile played over his face.

Saddle a horse, my lad,' said he. 'I shall wish you to take a note to Elrige's Farm.'

He took from his pocket the various slips of the dancing men. With these in front of him, he worked for some time at the study-table. Finally he handed a note to the boy, with directions to put it into the hands of the person to whom it was addressed, and especially to answer no questions of any sort which might be put to him. I saw the outside of the note, addressed in straggling, irregular characters, very unlike Holmes's usual precise hand. It was consigned to Mr Abe Slaney, Elrige's Farm, East Ruston, Norfolk.

'I think, Inspector,' Holmes remarked, 'that you would do well to telegraph for an escort, as, if my calculations prove to be correct, you may have a particularly dangerous prisoner to convey to the county jail. The boy who takes this note could no doubt forward your telegram. If there is an afternoon train to town, Watson, I think we should do well to take it, as I have a chemical analysis of some interest to finish, and this investigation draws rapidly to a close.'

When the youth had been dispatched with the note, Sherlock Holmes gave his instructions to the servants. If any visitor were to call asking for Mrs Hilton Cubitt, no information should be given as to her condition, but he was to be shown at once into the drawing-room. He impressed these points upon them with the utmost earnestness. Finally he led the way into the drawing-room, with the remark that the business was now out of our hands, and that we must while away the time as best we might until we could see what was in store for us. The doctor had departed to his patients, and only the inspector and myself remained.

'I think that I can help you to pass an hour in an interesting and profitable manner,' said Holmes, drawing his chair up to the table, and spreading out in front of him the various papers upon which were recorded the antics of the dancing men. 'As to you, friend Watson, I owe you every atonement for having allowed your natural curiosity to remain so long unsatisfied. To you, Inspector, the whole incident may appeal as a remarkable professional study. I must tell you, first of all, the interesting circumstances connected with the previous consultations which Mr Hilton Cubitt has had with me in Baker Street.' He then shortly recapitulated the facts which have already been recorded. 'I have here in front of me these singular productions, at which one might smile, had they not proved themselves to be the forerunners of so terrible a tragedy. I am fairly familiar with all forms of secret writings, and am myself the author of a trifling monograph upon the subject, in which I analyse one hundred and sixty separate ciphers, but I confess that this is entirely new to me. The object of those who invented the system has apparently been to conceal that these characters convey a message, and to give the idea that they are the mere random sketches of children.

'Having once recognized, however, that the symbols stood for letters, and having applied the rules which guide us in all forms of secret writings, the solution was easy enough. The first message submitted to me was so short that it was impossible for me to do more than to say, with some confidence, that the symbol ⸸ stood for E. As you are aware, E is the most common letter in the English alphabet, and it predominates to so marked an extent that even in a short sentence one would expect to find it most often. Out of fifteen symbols in the first message, four were the same, so it was reasonable to set this down as E. It is true that in some cases the figure was bearing a flag, and in some cases not, but it was probable, from the way in which the flags were distributed, that they were used to break the sentence up into words. I accepted this as a hypothesis, and noted that E was represented by 𝕏

'But now came the real difficulty of the inquiry. The order of the English letters after E is by no means well marked, and any preponderance which may be shown in an average of a printed sheet may be reversed in a single short sentence. Speaking roughly, T, A, O, I, N, S, H, R, D, and L are the numerical order in which letters occur; but T, A, O, and I are very nearly abreast of each other, and it would be an endless task to try each combination until a meaning was arrived at. I therefore waited for fresh material. In my second interview with Mr Hilton Cubitt he was able to give me two other short sentences and one message, which appeared – since there was no flag – to be a single word. Here are the symbols. Now, in the single word I have already got the two E's coming second and fourth in a word of five letters. It might be 'sever', or 'lever', or 'never'. There can be no question that the latter as a reply to an appeal is far the most probable, and the circumstances pointed to its being a reply written by the lady. Accepting it as correct, we are now able to say that the symbols ⚡ stand respectively for N, V, and R. 'Even now I was in considerable difficulty, but a happy thought put me in possession of several other letters. It occurred to me that if these appeals came, as I expected, from someone who had been intimate with the lady in her early life, a combination which contained two E's with three letters between might very well stand for the name 'ELSIE'. On examination I found that such a combination formed the termination of the message which was three times repeated. It was certainly some appeal to 'Elsie'. In this way I had got my L, S, and I. But what appeal could it be? There were only four letters in the word which preceded 'Elsie', and it ended in E. Surely the word must be 'COME'. I tried all other four letters ending in E, but could find none to fit the case. So now I was in possession of C, O, and M and I was in a position to attack the first message once more, dividing it into words and putting dots for each symbol which was still unknown. So treated, it worked out in this fashion:

.M . ERE . . E SL. NE.

'Now the first letter *can* only be A, which is a most useful discovery, since it occurs no fewer than three times in this short sentence, and the H is also apparent in the second word. Now it becomes:

AM HERE A. E SLANE.

Or, filling in the obvious vacancies in the name:

AM HERE ABE SLANEY.

I had so many letters now that I could proceed with considerable confidence to the second message, which worked out in this fashion:

A. ELRI. ES.

Here I could only make sense by putting T and G for the missing letters, and supposing that the name was that of some house or inn at which the writer was staying.'

Inspector Martin and I had listened with the utmost interest to the full and clear account of how my friend had produced results which had led to so complete a command over our difficulties.

'What did you do then, sir?' asked the inspector.

'I had every reason to suppose that this Abe Slaney was an American, since Abe is an American contraction, and since a letter from America had been the starting-point of all the trouble. I had also every cause to think that there was some criminal secret in the matter. The lady's allusions to her past, and her refusal to take her husband into her confidence, both pointed in that direction. I therefore cabled to my friend, Wilson Hargreave, of the New York Police Bureau, who has more than once made use of my knowledge of London crime. I asked him whether the name of Abe Slaney was known to him. Here is his reply: 'The most dangerous crook in Chicago'. On the very evening upon which I had his answer, Hilton Cubitt sent me the last message from Slaney. Working with known letters, it took this form:

ELSIE. RE. ARE TO MEET THY GO.

The addition of a P and a D completed a message which showed me that the rascal was proceeding from persuasion to threats, and my knowledge of the crooks of Chicago prepared me to find that he might very rapidly put his words into action. I at once came to Norfolk with my friend and colleague, Dr Watson, but, unhappily, only in time to find that the worst had already occurred.'

'It is a privilege to be associated with you in the handling of a case,' said the inspector, warmly. 'You will excuse me, however, if I speak frankly to you. You are only answerable to yourself, but I have to answer to my superiors. If this Abe Slaney, living at Elrige's, is indeed the murderer, and if he has made his escape while I am seated here, I should certainly get into serious trouble.'

'You need not be uneasy. He will not try to escape.'

'How do you know?'

'To fly would be a confession of guilt.'

'Then let us go to arrest him.'

'I expect him here every instant.'

'But why should he come?'

'Because I have written and asked him.'

'But this is incredible, Mr Holmes! Why should he come because you have asked him? Would not such a request rather rouse his suspicions and cause him to fly?'

'I think I have known how to frame the letter,' said Sherlock Holmes. 'In fact, if I am not very much mistaken, here is the gentleman himself coming up the drive.'

A man was striding up the path which led to the door. He was a tall, handsome, swarthy fellow, clad in a suit of grey flannel, with a Panama hat, a bristling black beard, and a great, aggressive hooked nose, and flourishing a cane as he walked. He swaggered up the path as if the place belonged to him, and we heard his loud, confident peal at the bell.

'I think, gentlemen,' said Holmes, quietly, 'that we had best take up our position behind the door. Every precaution is necessary when dealing with such a fellow. You will need your handcuffs, Inspector. You can leave the talking to me.'

We waited in silence for a minute – one of those minutes which one can never forget. Then the door opened and the man stepped in. In an instant Holmes clapped a pistol to his head, and Martin slipped the handcuffs over his wrists. It was all done so swiftly and deftly that the fellow was helpless before he knew that he was attacked. He glared from one to the other of us with a pair of blazing black eyes. Then he burst into a bitter laugh.

'Well, gentlemen, you have the drop on me this time. I seem to have knocked up against something hard. But I came here in answer to a letter from Mrs Hilton Cubitt. Don't tell me that she is in this? Don't tell me that she helped to set a trap for me?'

'Mrs Hilton Cubitt was seriously injured, and is at death's door.'

The man gave a hoarse cry of grief, which rang through the house.

'You're crazy!' he cried, fiercely. 'It was he that was hurt, not she. Who would have hurt little Elsie? I may have threatened her – God forgive me! – but I would not have touched a hair of her pretty head. Take it back – you! Say that she is not hurt!'

'She was found, badly wounded, by the side of her dead husband.'

He sank with a deep groan on to the settee, and buried his face in his manacled hands. For five minutes he was silent. Then he raised his face once more, and spoke with the cold composure of despair.

'I have nothing to hide from you, gentlemen,' said he. 'If I shot the man he had his shot at me, and there's no murder in that. But if you think I could have hurt that woman, then you don't know either me or her. I tell you, there was never a man in this world loved a woman more than I loved' her. I had a right to her. She was pledged to me years ago. Who was this Englishman that he should come between us? I tell you that I had the first right to her, and that I was only claiming my own.'

'She broke away from your influence when she found the man that you are,' said Holmes sternly. 'She fled from America to avoid you, and she married an honourable gentleman in England. You dogged her and followed her and made her life a misery to her, in order to induce her to abandon the husband whom she loved and respected in order to fly with you, whom she feared and hated. You have ended by bringing about the death of a noble man and driving his wife to suicide. That is your record in this business, Mr Abe Slaney, and you will answer for it to the law.'

'If Elsie dies, I care nothing what becomes of me,' said the American. He opened one of his hands, and looked at a note crumpled up in his palm. 'See here, mister,' he cried, with a gleam of suspicion in his eyes, 'you're not trying to scare me over this, are you? If the lady is hurt as bad as you say, who was it that wrote this note?' He tossed it forward on to the table.

'I wrote it, to bring you here.'

'You wrote it? There was no one on earth out-side the Joint who knew the secret of the dancing men. How came you to write it?'

'What one man can invent another can dis-cover,' said Holmes. 'There is a cab coming to convey you to Norwich, Mr Slaney. But, mean-while, you have time to make some small repara-tion for the injury you have wrought. Are you aware that Mrs Hilton Cubitt has herself lain under grave suspicion of the murder of her hus-band, and that it was only my presence here, and the knowledge which I happened to possess, which has saved her from the accusation? The least that you owe her is to make it clear to the whole world that she was in no way, directly or indirectly, responsible for his tragic end.'

'I ask nothing better,' said the American. 'I guess the very best case I can make for myself is the absolute naked truth.'

'It is my duty to warn you that it will be used against you,' cried the inspector, with the magnifi-cent fair play of the British criminal law.

Slaney shrugged his shoulders.

'I'll chance that,' said he. 'First of all, I want you gentlemen to understand that I have known this lady since she was a child. There were seven of us in a gang in Chicago, and Elsie's father was the boss of the Joint. He was a clever man, was old Patrick. It was he who invented that writing, which would pass as a child's scrawl unless you just happened to have the key to it. Well, Elsie learned some of our ways, but she couldn't stand the business, and she had a bit of honest money of her own, so she gave us all the slip and got away to London. She had been engaged to me, and she would have married me, I believe, if I had taken over another profession, but she would have nothing to do with anything on the cross. It was only after her marriage to this Englishman that I was able to find out where she was. I wrote to her, but got no answer. After that I came over, and, as letters were no use, I put my messages where she could read them.

'Well, I have been here a month now. I lived in that farm, where I had a room down below, and could get in and out every night, and no one the wiser. I tried all I could to coax Elsie away. I knew that she read the messages, for once she wrote an answer under one of them. Then my temper got the better of me, and I began to threaten her. She sent me a letter then, imploring me to go away, and saying that it would break her heart if any scandal should come upon her husband. She said that she would come down when her husband was asleep at three in the morning, and speak with me through the end window, if I would go away afterwards and leave her in peace. She came down and brought money with her, trying to bribe me to go. This made me mad, and I caught her arm and tried to pull her through the window. At that moment in rushed the husband with his revolver in his hand. Elsie had sunk down upon the floor, and we were face to face. I was heeled also, and I held up my gun to scare him off and let me get away. He fired and missed me. I pulled off almost at the same instant, and down he dropped. I made away across the garden, and as I went I heard the window shut behind me. That's God's truth, gentlemen, every word of it; and I heard no more about it until that lad came riding up with a note which made me walk in here, like a jay, and give myself into your hands.'

A cab had driven up whilst the American had been talking. Two uniformed policemen sat inside. Inspector Martin rose and touched his prisoner on the shoulder.

'It is time for us to go.'

'Can I see her first?'

'No, she is not conscious. Mr Sherlock Holmes, I only hope that, if ever again I have an important case, I shall have the good fortune to have you by my side.'

We stood at the window and watched the cab drive away. As I turned back, my eye caught the pellet of paper which the prisoner had tossed upon the table. It was the note with which Holmes had decoyed him.

'See if you can read it, Watson,' said he, with a smile.

It contained no word, but this little line of dancing men:

'If you use the code which I have explained,' said Holmes, 'you will find that it simply means "Come here at once." I was convinced that it was an invitation which he would not refuse, since he could never imagine that it could come from anyone but the lady. And so, my dear Watson, we have ended by turning the dancing men to good when they have so often been the agents of evil, and I think that I have fulfilled my promise of giving you something unusual for your notebook. Three-forty is our train, and I fancy we should be back in Baker Street for dinner.'

Only one word of epilogue. The American, Abe Slaney, was condemned to death at the winter assizes at Norwich, but his penalty was changed to penal servitude in consideration of mitigating circumstances, and the certainty that Hilton Cubitt had fired the first shot. Of Mrs Hilton Cubitt I only know that I have heard she recovered entirely, and that she still remains a widow, devoting her whole life to the care of the poor and to the administration of her husband's estate.

The Adventure of the Six Napoleons

It was no very unusual thing for Mr Lestrade, of Scotland Yard, to look in upon us of an evening, and his visits were welcome to Sherlock Holmes, for they enabled him to keep in touch with all that was going on at the police headquarters. In return for the news which Lestrade would bring, Holmes was always ready to listen with attention to the details of any case upon which the detective was engaged, and was able occasionally, without any active interference, to give some hint or suggestion drawn from his own vast knowledge and experience.

On this particular evening, Lestrade had spoken of the weather and the newspapers. Then he had fallen silent, puffing thoughtfully at his cigar. Holmes looked keenly at him.

'Anything remarkable on hand?' he asked.

'Oh, no, Mr Holmes – nothing very particular.'

'Then tell me about it.'

Lestrade laughed.

'Well, Mr Holmes, there is no use denying that there is something on my mind. And yet it is such an absurd business, that I hesitated to bother you about it. On the other hand, although it is trivial, it is undoubtedly queer, and I know that you have a taste for all that is out of the common. But, in my opinion, it comes more in Dr Watson's line than ours.'

'Disease?' said I.

'Madness, anyhow. And a queer madness, too. You wouldn't think there was anyone living at this time of day who had such a hatred of Napoleon the First that he would break any image of him that he could see.'

Holmes sank back in his chair.

'That's no business of mine,' said he.

'Exactly. That's what I said. But then, when the man commits burglary in order to break images which are not his own, that brings it away from the doctor and on to the policeman.'

Holmes sat up again.

'Burglary! This is more interesting. Let me hear the details.'

Lestrade took out his official notebook and refreshed his memory from its pages.

'The first case reported was four days ago,' said he. 'It was at the shop of Morse Hudson, who has a place for the sale of pictures and statues in the Kennington Road. The assistant had left the front shop for an instant, when he heard a crash, and hurrying in he found a plaster bust of Napoleon, which stood with several other works of art upon the counter, lying shivered into fragments. He rushed out into the road, but, although several passersby declared that they had noticed a man run out of the shop, he could neither see anyone nor could he find any means of identifying the rascal. It seemed to be one of those senseless acts of hooliganism which occur from time to time, and it was reported to the constable on the beat as such. The plaster cast was not worth more than a few shillings, and the whole affair appeared to be too childish for any particular investigation.

'The second case, however, was more serious, and also more singular. It occurred only last night.

'In Kennington Road, and within a few hundred yards of Morse Hudson's shop, there lives a well-known medical practitioner, named Dr Barnicot, who has one of the largest practices upon the south side of the Thames. His residence and principal consulting-room is at Kennington Road, but he has a branch surgery and dispensary at Lower Brixton Road, two miles away. This Dr Barnicot is an enthusiastic admirer of Napoleon, and his house is full of books, pictures, and relics of the French Emperor. Some little time ago he purchased from Morse Hudson two duplicate plaster casts of the famous head of Napoleon by the French sculptor, Devine. One of these he placed in his hall in the house at Kennington Road, and the other on the mantelpiece of the surgery at Lower Brixton. Well, when Dr Barnicot came down this morning he was astonished to find that his house had been burgled during the night, but that nothing had been taken save the plaster head from the hall. It had been carried out and had been dashed savagely against the garden wall, under which its splintered fragments were discovered.'

Holmes rubbed his hands.

'This is certainly very novel,' said he.

'I thought it would please you. But I have not got to the end yet. Dr Barnicot was due at his surgery at twelve o'clock, and you can imagine his amazement when, on arriving there, he found that the window had been opened in the night, and that the broken pieces of his second bust were strewn all over the room. It had been smashed to atoms where it stood. In neither case were there any signs which could give us a clue as to the criminal or lunatic who had done the mischief. Now, Mr Holmes, you have got the facts.'

'They are singular, not to say grotesque,' said Holmes. 'May I ask whether the two busts smashed in Dr Barnicot's rooms were the exact duplicates of the one which was destroyed in Morse Hudson's shop?'

'They were taken from the same mould.'

'Such a fact must tell against the theory that the man who breaks them is influenced by any general hatred of Napoleon. Considering how many hundreds of statues of the great Emperor must exist in London, it is too much to suppose such a coincidence as that a promiscuous iconoclast should chance to begin upon three specimens of the same bust.'

'Well, I thought as you do,' said Lestrade. 'On the other hand, this Morse Hudson is the purveyor of busts in that part of London, and these three were the only ones which had been in his shop for years. So, although, as you say, there are many hundreds of statues in London, it is very probable that these three were the only ones in that district. Therefore, a local fanatic would begin with them. What do you think, Dr Watson?'

'There are no limits to the possibilities of monomania,' I answered. 'There is the condition which the modern French psychologists have called the "*idée fixé*", which may be trifling in character, and accompanied by complete sanity in every other way. A man who had read deeply about Napoleon, or who had possibly received some hereditary family injury through the great war, might conceivably form such an *idée fixe* and under its influence be capable of any fantastic outrage.'

'That won't do, my dear Watson,' said Holmes, shaking his head, 'for no amount of *idée fixe* would enable your interesting monomaniac to find out where these busts were situated.'

'Well, how do *you* explain it?'

'I don't attempt to do so. I would only observe that there is a certain method in the gentleman's eccentric proceedings. For example, in Dr Barnicot's hall, where a sound might arouse the family, the bust was taken outside before being broken, whereas in the surgery, where there was less danger of an alarm, it was smashed where it stood. The affair seems absurdly trifling, and yet I dare call nothing trivial when I reflect that some of my most classic cases have had the least promising commencement. You will remember, Watson, how the dreadful business of the Abernetty family was first brought to my notice by the depth which the parsley had sunk into the butter upon a hot day. I can't afford, therefore, to smile at your three broken busts, Lestrade, and I shall be very much obliged to you if you will let me hear of any fresh development of so singular a chain of events.'

The development for which my friend had asked came in a quicker and an infinitely more tragic form than he could have imagined. I was still dressing in my bedroom next morning, when there was a tap at the door and Holmes entered, a telegram in his hand. He read it aloud:

'Come instantly, 131 Pitt Street, Kensington.

LESTRADE.'

'What is it, then?' I asked.

'Don't know – may be anything. But I suspect it is the sequel of the story of the statues. In that case our friend the image-breaker has begun operations in another quarter of London. There's coffee on the table, Watson, and I have a cab at the door.'

In half an hour we had reached Pitt Street, a quiet little backwater just beside one of the briskest currents of London life. No. 131 was one of a row, all flat-chested, respectable, and most unromantic dwellings. As we drove up, we found the railings in front of the house lined by a curious crowd. Holmes whistled.

'By George! it's attempted murder at the least. Nothing less will hold the London message-boy. There's a deed of violence indicated in that fellow's round shoulders and outstretched neck. What's this, Watson? The top steps swilled down and the other ones dry. Footsteps enough, anyhow! Well, well, there's Lestrade at the front window, and we shall soon know all about it.'

The official received us with a very grave face and showed us into a sitting-room, where an exceedingly unkempt and agitated elderly man, clad in a flannel dressing-gown, was pacing up and down. He was introduced to us as the owner of the house – Mr Horace Harker, of the Central Press Syndicate.

'It's the Napoleon bust business again,' said Lestrade. 'You seemed interested last night, Mr Holmes, so I thought perhaps you would be glad to be present now that the affair has taken a very much graver turn.'

'What has it turned to, then?'

'To murder. Mr Harker, will you tell these gentlemen exactly what has occurred?'

The man in the dressing-gown turned upon us with a most melancholy face.

'It's an extraordinary thing,' said he, 'that all my life I have been collecting other people's news, and now that a real piece of news has come my own way I am so confused and bothered that I can't put two words together. If I had come in here as a journalist, I should have interviewed myself and had two columns in every evening paper. As it is, I am giving away valuable copy by telling my story over and over to a string of different people, and I can make no use of it myself. However, I've heard your name, Mr Sherlock Holmes, and if you'll only explain this queer business, I shall be paid for my trouble in telling you the story.'

Holmes sat down and listened.

'It all seems to centre round that bust of Napoleon which I bought for this very room about four months ago. I picked it up cheap from Harding Brothers, two doors from the High Street Station. A great deal of my journalistic work is done at night, and I often write until the early morning. So it was today. I was sitting in my den, which is at the back of the top of the house, about three o'clock, when I was convinced that I heard some sounds downstairs. I listened, but they were not repeated, and I concluded that they came from outside. Then suddenly, about five minutes later, there came a most horrible yell – the most dreadful sound, Mr Holmes, that ever I heard. It will ring in my ears as long as I live. I sat frozen with horror for a minute or two. Then I seized the poker and went downstairs. When I entered this room I found the window wide open, and I at once observed that the bust was gone from the mantelpiece. Why any burglar should take such a thing passes my understanding, for it was only a plaster cast and of no real value whatever.

'You can see for yourself that anyone going out through that open window could reach the front doorstep by taking a long stride. This was clearly what the burglar had done, so I went round and opened the door. Stepping out into the dark, I nearly fell over a dead man, who was lying there. I ran back for a light, and there was the poor fellow, a great gash in his throat and the whole place swimming in blood. He lay on his back, his knees drawn up, and his mouth horribly open. I shall see him in my dreams. I had just time to blow on my police-whistle, and then I must have fainted, for I knew nothing more until I found the policeman standing over me in the hall.'

'Well, who was the murdered man?' asked Holmes.

'There's nothing to show who he was,' said Lestrade. 'You shall see the body at the mortuary, but we have made nothing of it up to now. He is a tall man, sunburned, very powerful, not more than thirty. He is poorly dressed, and yet does not appear to be a labourer. A horn-handled clasp knife was lying in a pool of blood beside him. Whether it was the weapon which did the deed, or whether it belonged to the dead man, I do not know. There was no name on his clothing, and nothing in his pockets save an apple, some string, a shilling map of London, and a photograph. Here it is.'

It was evidently taken by a snapshot from a small camera. It represented an alert, sharp-featured simian man, with thick eyebrows and a very peculiar projection of the lower part of the face, like the muzzle of a baboon.

'And what became of the bust?' asked Holmes, after a careful study of this picture.

'We had news of it just before you came. It has been found in the front garden of an empty house in Campden House Road. It was broken into fragments. I am going round now to see it. Will you come?'

'Certainly. I must just take one look round.' He examined the carpet and the window. 'The fellow had either very long legs or was a most active man,' said he. 'With an area beneath, it was no mean feat to reach that window-ledge and open that window. Getting back was comparatively simple. Are you coming with us to see the remains of your bust, Mr Harker?'

The disconsolate journalist had seated himself at a writing-table.

'I must try and make something of it, said he, 'though I have no doubt that the first editions of the evening papers are out already with full details. It's like my luck! You remember when the stand fell at Doncaster? Well, I was the only journalist in the stand, and my journal the only one that had no account of it, for I was too shaken to write it. And now I'll be too late with a murder done on my own doorstep.'

As we left the room, we heard his pen travelling shrilly over the foolscap.

The spot where the fragments of the bust had been found was only a few hundred yards away. For the first time our eyes rested upon this presentment of the great emperor, which seemed to raise such frantic and destructive hatred in the mind of the unknown. It lay scattered, in splintered shards, upon the grass. Holmes picked up several of them and examined them carefully. I was convinced, from his intent face and his purposeful manner, that at last he was upon a clue.

'Well?' asked Lestrade.

Holmes shrugged his shoulders.

'We have a long way to go yet,' said he. 'And yet – and yet – well, we have some suggestive facts to act upon. The possession of this trifling bust was worth more, in the eyes of this strange criminal, than a human life. This is one point. Then there is the singular fact that he did not break it in the house, or immediately outside the house, if to break it was his sole object.'

'He was rattled and bustled by meeting this other fellow. He hardly knew what he was doing.'

'Well, that's likely enough. But I wish to call your attention very particularly to the position of this house, in the garden of which the bust was destroyed.'

Lestrade looked about him.

'It was an empty house, and so he knew that he would not be disturbed in the garden.'

'Yes, but there is another empty house farther up the street which he must have passed before he came to this one. Why did he not break it there, since it is evident that every yard that he carried it increased the risk of someone meeting him?'

'I give it up,' said Lestrade.

Holmes pointed to the street lamp above our heads.

'He could see what he was doing here, and he could not there. That was his reason.'

'By Jove! that's true,' said the detective. 'Now that I come to think of it, Dr Barnicot's bust was broken not far from his red lamp. Well, Mr Holmes, what are we to do with that fact?'

'To remember it – to docket it. We may come on something later which will bear upon it. What steps do you propose to take now, Lestrade?'

'The most practical way of getting at it, in my opinion, is to identify the dead man. There should be no difficulty about that. When we have found who he is and who his associates are, we should have a good start in learning what he was doing in

Pitt Street last night, and who it was who met him and killed him on the doorstep of Mr Horace Harker. Don't you think so?'

'No doubt; and yet it is not quite the way in which I should approach the case.'

'What would you do then?'

'Oh, you must not let me influence you in any way. I suggest that you go on your line and I on mine. We can compare notes afterwards, and each will supplement the other.'

'Very good,' said Lestrade.

'If you are going back to Pitt Street, you might see Mr Horace Harker. Tell him for me that I have quite made up my mind, and that it is certain that a dangerous homicidal lunatic, with Napoleonic delusions, was in his house last night. It will be useful for his article.'

Lestrade stared.

'You don't seriously believe that?'

Holmes smiled.

'Don't I? Well, perhaps I don't. But I am sure that it will interest Mr Horace Harker and the subscribers of the Central Press Syndicate. Now, Watson, I think that we shall find that we have a long and rather complex day's work before us. I should be glad, Lestrade, if you could make it convenient to meet us at Baker Street at six o'clock this evening. Until then I should like to keep this photograph, found in the dead man's pocket. It is possible that I may have to ask your company and assistance upon a small expedition which will have to be undertaken tonight, if my chain of reasoning should prove to be correct. Until then goodbye and good luck!'

Sherlock Holmes and I walked together to the High Street, where we stopped at the shop of Harding Brothers, whence the bust had been purchased. A young assistant informed us that Mr Harding would be absent until afternoon, and that he was himself a newcomer, who could give us no information. Holmes's face showed his disappointment and annoyance.

'Well, well, we can't expect to have it all our own way, Watson,' he said, at last. 'We must come back in the afternoon, if Mr Harding will not be here until then. I am, as you have no doubt surmised, endeavouring to trace these busts to their source, in order to find if there is not something peculiar which may account for their remarkable fate. Let us make for Mr Morse Hudson, of the Kennington Road, and see if he can throw any light upon the problem.'

A drive of an hour brought us to the picture-dealer's establishment. He was a small, stout man with a red face and a peppery manner.

'Yes, sir. On my very counter, sir,' said he. 'What we pay rates and taxes for I don't know, when any ruffian can come in and break one's goods. Yes, sir, it was I who sold Dr Barnicot his two statues. Disgraceful, sir! A Nihilist plot – that's what I make it. No one but an anarchist would go about breaking statues. Red republicans

– that's what I call 'em. Who did I get the statues from? I don't see what that has to do with it. Well, if you really want to know, I got them from Gelder & Co., in Church Street, Stepney. They are a well-known house in the trade, and have been this twenty years. How many had I? Three – two and one are three – two of Dr Barnicot's, and one smashed in broad daylight on my own counter. Do I know that photograph? No, I don't. Yes, I do, though. Why, it's Beppo. He was a kind of Italian piece-work man, who made himself useful in the shop. He could carve a bit, and gild and frame, and do odd jobs. The fellow left me last week, and I've heard nothing of him since. No, I don't know where he came from nor where he went to. I had nothing against him while he was here. He was gone two days before the bust was smashed.'

'Well, that's all we could reasonably expect from Morse Hudson,' said Holmes, as we emerged from the shop. 'We have this Beppo as a common factor, both in Kennington and in Kensington, so that is worth a ten-mile drive. Now, Watson, let us make for Gelder & Co., of Stepney, the source and origin of the busts. I shall be surprised if we don't get some help down there.'

In rapid succession we passed through the fringe of fashionable London, hotel London, theatrical London, literary London, commercial London, and, finally, maritime London, till we came to a riverside city of a hundred thousand souls, where the tenement houses swelter and reek with the outcasts of Europe. Here, in a broad thoroughfare, once the abode of wealthy City merchants, we found the sculpture works for which we searched. Outside was a considerable yard full of monumental masonry. Inside was a large room in which fifty workers were carving or moulding. The manager, a big blond German, received us civilly and gave a clear answer to all Holmes's questions. A reference to his books showed that hundreds of casts had been taken from a marble copy of Devine's head of Napoleon, but that the three which had been sent to Morse Hudson a year or so before had been half of a batch of six, the other three being sent to Harding Brothers, of Kensington. There was no reason why those six should be different from any of the other casts. He could suggest no possible cause why anyone should wish to destroy them – in fact, he laughed at the idea. Their wholesale price was six shillings, but the retailer would get twelve or more. The cast was taken in two moulds from each side of the face, and then these two profiles of plaster of Paris were joined together to make the complete bust. The work was usually done by Italians, in the room we were in. When finished, the busts were put on a table in the passage to dry, and afterwards stored. That was all he could tell us.

But the production of the photograph had a remarkable effect upon the manager. His face flushed with anger, and his brows knotted over his blue Teutonic eyes.

'Ah, the rascal!' he cried. 'Yes, indeed, I know him very well. This has always been a respectable establishment, and the only time that we have ever had the police in it was over this very fellow. It was more than a year ago now. He knifed another Italian in the street, and then he came to the works with the police on his heels, and he was taken here. Beppo was his name – his second name I never knew. Serve me right for engaging a man with such a face. But he was a good workman – one of the best.'

'What did he get?'

'The man lived and he got off with a year. I have no doubt he is out now, but he has not dared to show his nose here. We have a cousin of his here, and I daresay he could tell you where he is.'

'No, no,' cried Holmes, 'not a word to the cousin – not a word, I beg of you. The matter is very important, and the farther I go with it, the more important it seems to grow. When you referred in your ledger to the sale of those casts I observed that the date was June 3rd of last year. Could you give me the date when Beppo was arrested?'

'I could tell you roughly by the pay-list,' the manager answered. 'Yes,' he continued, after some turning over of pages, 'he was paid last on May 20th.'

'Thank you,' said Holmes. 'I don't think that I

need intrude upon your time and patience any more.' With a last word of caution that he should say nothing as to our researches, we turned our faces westwards once more.

The afternoon was far advanced before we were able to snatch a hasty luncheon at a restaurant. A news-bill at the entrance announced 'Kensington Outrage. Murder by a Madman', and the contents of the paper showed that Mr Horace Harker had got his account into print after all. Two columns were occupied with a highly sensational and flowery rendering of the whole incident. Holmes propped it against the cruet-stand and read it while he ate. Once or twice he chuckled.

'This is all right, Watson,' said he. 'Listen to this:

It is satisfactory to know that there can be no difference of opinion upon this case, since Mr Lestrade, one of the most experienced members of the official force, and Mr Sherlock Holmes, the well-known consulting expert, have each come to the conclusion that the grotesque series of incidents, which have ended in so tragic a fashion, arise from lunacy rather than from deliberate crime. No explanation save mental aberration can cover the facts.

The Press, Watson, is a most valuable institution, if you only know how to use it. And now, if you have quite finished, we will hark back to Kensington and see what the manager of Harding Brothers has to say on the matter.'

The founder of that great emporium proved to be a brisk, crisp little person, very dapper and quick, with a clear head and a ready tongue.

'Yes, sir, I have already read the account in the evening papers. Mr Horace Harker is a customer of ours. We supplied him with the bust some months ago. We ordered three busts of that sort from Gelder & Co., of Stepney. They are all sold now. To whom? Oh, I daresay by consulting our sales book we could very easily tell you. Yes, we have the entries here. One to Mr Harker you see, and one to Mr Josiah Brown, of Laburnum Lodge, Laburnum Vale, Chiswick, and one to Mr Sandeford, of Lower Grove Road, Reading. No, I have never seen this face which you show me in the photograph. You would hardly forget it, would you, sir, for I've seldom seen an uglier. Have we any Italians on the staff? Yes, sir, we have several among our workpeople and cleaners. I daresay they might get a peep at that sales book if they wanted to. There is no particular reason for keeping a watch upon that book. Well, well, it's a very strange business, and I hope that you will let me know if anything comes of your inquiries.'

Holmes had taken several notes during Mr Harding's evidence, and I could see that he was thoroughly satisfied by the turn which affairs were taking. He made no remark, however, save that, unless we hurried, we should be late for our appointment with Lestrade. Sure enough, when we reached Baker Street the detective was already there, and we found him pacing up and down in a fever of impatience. His look of importance showed that his day's work had not been in vain.

'Well?' he asked. 'What luck, Mr Holmes?'

'We have had a very busy day, and not entirely a wasted one,' my friend explained. 'We have seen both the retailers and also the wholesale manufacturers. I can trace each of the busts now from the beginning.'

'The busts!' cried Lestrade. 'Well, well, you have your own methods, Mr Sherlock Holmes, and it is not for me to say a word against them, but I think I have done a better day's work than you. I have identified the dead man.'

'You don't say so?'

'And found a cause for the crime.'

'Splendid!'

'We have an inspector who makes a specialty of Saffron Hill and the Italian Quarter. Well, this dead man had some Catholic emblem round his neck, and that, along with his colour, made me think he was from the South. Inspector Hill knew him the moment he caught sight of him. His name is Pietro Venucci, from Naples, and he is one of the greatest cut-throats in London. He is connected with the Mafia, which, as you know, is a secret political society, enforcing its decrees by murder. Now, you see how the affair begins to clear up. The other fellow is probably an Italian also, and a member of the Mafia. He has broken the rules in some fashion. Pietro is set upon his track. Probably the photograph we found in his pocket is the man himself, so that he may not knife the wrong person. He dogs the fellow, he sees him enter a house, he waits outside for him, and in the scuffle he receives his own death-wound. How is that, Mr Sherlock Holmes?'

Holmes clapped his hands approvingly.

'Excellent, Lestrade, excellent!' he cried. 'But I didn't quite follow your explanation of the destruction of the busts.'

'The busts! You never can get those busts out of your head. After all, that is nothing; petty larceny, six months at the most. It is the murder that we are really investigating, and I tell you that I am gathering all the threads into my hands.'

'And the next stage?'

'Is a very simple one. I shall go down with Hill to the Italian Quarter, find the man whose photograph we have got, and arrest him on the charge of murder. Will you come with us?'

'I think not. I fancy we can attain our end in a simpler way. I can't say for certain, because it all depends – well, it all depends upon a factor which is completely outside our control. But I have great hopes – in fact, the betting is exactly two to one – that if you will come with us tonight I shall be able to help you to lay him by the heels.'

'In the Italian Quarter?'

'No, I fancy Chiswick is an address which is more likely to find him. If you will come with me to Chiswick tonight, Lestrade, I'll promise to go to the Italian Quarter with you tomorrow, and no harm will be done by the delay. And now I think that a few hours' sleep would do us all good, for I do not propose to leave before eleven o'clock, and it is unlikely that we shall be back before morning. You'll dine with us, Lestrade, and then you are welcome to the sofa until it is time for us to start. In the meantime, Watson, I should be glad if you would ring for an express messenger, for I have a letter to send and it is important that it should go at once.'

Holmes spent the evening in rummaging among the files of the old daily papers with which one of our lumber-rooms was packed. When at last he descended, it was with triumph in his eyes, but he said nothing to either of us as to the result of his researches. For my own part, I had followed step by step the methods by which he had traced the various windings of this complex case, and, though I could not yet perceive the goal which we would reach, I understood clearly that Holmes expected this grotesque criminal to make an attempt upon the two remaining busts, one of which, I remembered, was at Chiswick. No doubt the object of our journey was to catch him in the very act, and I could not but admire the cunning with which my friend had inserted a wrong clue in the evening paper, so as to give the fellow the idea that he could continue his scheme with impunity. I was not surprised when Holmes suggested that I should take my revolver with me. He had himself picked up the loaded hunting-crop, which was his favourite weapon.

A four-wheeler was at the door at eleven, and in it we drove to a spot at the other side of Hammersmith Bridge. Here the cabman was directed to wait. A short walk brought us to a secluded road fringed with pleasant houses, each standing in its own grounds. In the light of a street lamp we read 'Laburnum Villa' upon the gate-post of one of them. The occupants had evidently retired to rest, for all was dark save for a fanlight over the hall door, which shed a single blurred circle on to the garden path. The wooden fence which separated the grounds from the road threw a dense black shadow upon the inner side, and here it was that we crouched.

'I fear that you'll have a long wait,' Holmes whispered. 'We may thank our stars that it is not raining. I don't think we can even venture to smoke to pass the time. However, it's a two to one chance that we get something to pay us for our trouble.'

It proved, however, that our vigil was not to be so long as Holmes had led us to fear, and it ended in a very sudden and singular fashion. In an instant, without the least sound to warn us of his coming, the garden gate swung open, and a lithe, dark figure, as swift and active as an ape, rushed up the garden path. We saw it whisk past the light thrown from over the door and disappear against the black shadow of the house. There was a long pause, during which we held our breath, and then a very gentle creaking sound came to our ears. The window was being opened. The noise ceased, and again there was a long silence. The fellow was making his way into the house. We saw the sudden flash of a dark lantern inside the room. What he sought was evidently not there, for again we saw the flash through another blind, and then through another.

'Let us get to the open window. We will nab him as he climbs out,' Lestrade whispered.

But before we could move, the man had emerged again. As he came out into the glimmering patch of light, we saw that he carried something white under his arm. He looked stealthily all around him. The silence of the deserted street reassured him. Turning his back upon us he laid down his burden, and the next instant there was the sound of a sharp tap, followed by a clatter and rattle. The man was so intent upon what he was doing that he never heard our steps as we stole across the grass plot. With the bound of a tiger Holmes was on his back, and an instant later Lestrade and I had him by either wrist, and the handcuffs had been fastened. As we turned him over I saw a hideous, sallow face, with writhing, furious features, glaring up at us, and I knew that it was indeed the man of the photograph whom we had secured.

But it was not our prisoner to whom Holmes was giving his attention. Squatted on the doorstep, he was engaged in most carefully examining that which the man had brought from the house. It was a bust of Napoleon, like the one which we had seen that morning, and it had been broken into similar fragments. Carefully Holmes held each separate shard to the light, but in no way did it differ from any other shattered piece of plaster. He had just completed his examination when the hall lights flew up, the door opened, and the owner of the house, a jovial, rotund figure in shirt and trousers, presented himself.

'Mr Josiah Brown, I suppose?' said Holmes.

'Yes, sir; and you, no doubt, are Mr Sherlock Holmes? I had the note which you sent by the express messenger, and I did exactly what you told me. We locked every door on the inside and awaited developments. Well, I'm very glad to see that you have got the rascal. I hope, gentlemen, that you will come in and have some refreshment.'

However, Lestrade was anxious to get his man into safe quarters, so within a few minutes our cab had been summoned and we were all four upon our way to London. Not a word would our captive say, but he glared at us from the shadow of his matted hair, and once, when my hand seemed within his reach, he snapped at it like a hungry wolf. We stayed long enough at the police-station to learn that a search of his clothing revealed nothing save a few shillings and a long sheath knife, the handle of which bore copious traces of recent blood.

'That's all right,' said Lestrade, as we parted. 'Hill knows all these gentry, and he will give a name to him. You'll find that my theory of the Mafia will work out all right. But I'm sure I am exceedingly obliged to you, Mr Holmes, for the workmanlike way in which you laid hands upon him. I don't quite understand it all yet.'

'I fear it is rather too late an hour for explanations,' said Holmes. 'Besides, there are one or two details which are not finished off, and it is one of these cases which are worth working out to the very end. If you will come round once more to my rooms at six o'clock tomorrow, I think I shall be able to show you that even now you have not grasped the entire meaning of this business, which presents some features which make it absolutely original in the history of crime. If ever I permit you to chronicle any more of my little problems, Watson, I foresee that you will enliven your pages by an account of the singular adventure of the Napoleonic busts.'

When we met again next evening, Lestrade was furnished with much information concerning our prisoner. His name, it appeared, was Beppo, second name unknown. He was a well-known ne'er-do-well among the Italian colony. He had once been a skilful sculptor and had earned an honest living, but he had taken to evil courses and had twice already been in jail – once for a petty theft, and once, as we had already heard, for stabbing a fellow-countryman. He could talk English perfectly well. His reasons for destroying the busts were still unknown, and he refused to answer any questions upon the subject, but the police had discovered that these same busts might very well have been made by his own hands, since he was engaged in this class of work at the establishment of Gelder & Co. To all this information, much of which we already knew, Holmes listened with polite attention, but I, who knew him so well, could clearly see that his thoughts were elsewhere, and I detected a mixture of mingled uneasiness and expectation beneath that mask which he was wont to assume. At last he started in his chair, and his eyes brightened. There had been a ring at the bell. A minute later we heard steps upon the stairs, and an elderly red-faced man with grizzled side-whiskers was ushered in. In his right hand he carried an old-fashioned carpet-bag, which he placed upon the table.

'Is Mr Sherlock Holmes here?'

My friend bowed and smiled. 'Mr Sandeford, of Reading, I suppose?' said he.

'Yes, sir, I fear that I am a little late, but the trains were awkward. You wrote to me about a bust that is in my possession.'

'Exactly.'

'I have your letter here. You said, "I desire to possess a copy of Devine's Napoleon, and am prepared to pay you ten pounds for the one which is in your possession." Is that right?'

'Certainly.'

'I was very much surprised at your letter, for I could not imagine how you knew that I owned such a thing.'

'Of course you must have been surprised, but the explanation is very simple. Mr Harding, of Harding Brothers, said that they had sold you their last copy, and he gave me your address.'

'Oh, that was it, was it? Did he tell you what I paid for it?'

'No, he did not.'

'Well, I am an honest man, though not a very rich one. I only gave fifteen shillings for the bust, and I think you ought to know that before I take ten pounds from you.'

'I am sure the scruple does you honour, Mr Sandeford. But I have named that price, so I intend to stick to it.'

'Well, it is very handsome of you, Mr Holmes. I brought the bust up with me, as you asked me to do. Here it is!' He opened his bag, and at last we saw placed upon our table a complete specimen of that bust which we had already seen more than once in fragments.

Holmes took a paper from his pocket and laid a ten-pound note upon the table.

'You will kindly sign that paper, Mr Sandeford, in the presence of these witnesses. It is simply to say that you transfer every possible right that you ever had in the bust to me. I am a methodical man, you see, and you never know what turn events might take afterwards. Thank you, Mr

Sandeford; here is your money, and I wish you a very good evening.'

When our visitor had disappeared, Sherlock Holmes's movements were such as to rivet our attention. He began by taking a clean white cloth from a drawer and laying it over the table. Then he placed his newly acquired bust in the centre of the cloth. Finally, he picked up his hunting-crop and struck Napoleon a sharp blow on the top of the head. The figure broke into fragments, and Holmes bent eagerly over the shattered remains. Next instant, with a loud shout of triumph he held up one splinter, in which a round, dark object was fixed like a plum in a pudding.

'Gentlemen,' he cried, 'let me introduce you to the famous black pearl of the Borgias.'

Lestrade and I sat silent for a moment, and then, with a spontaneous impulse, we both broke out clapping, as at the well-wrought crisis of a play. A flush of colour sprang to Holmes's pale cheeks, and he bowed to us like the master dramatist who receives the homage of his audience. It was at such moments that for an instant he ceased to be a reasoning machine, and betrayed his human love for admiration and applause. The same singularly proud and reserved nature which turned away with disdain from popular notoriety was capable of being moved to its depths by spontaneous wonder and praise from a friend.

'Yes, gentlemen,' said he, 'it is the most famous pearl now existing in the world, and it has been my good fortune, by a connected chain of inductive reasoning, to trace it from the Prince of Colonna's bedroom at the Dacre Hotel, where it was lost, to the interior of this, the last of the six busts of Napoleon which were manufactured by Gelder & Co., of Stepney. You will remember, Lestrade, the sensation caused by the disappearance of this valuable jewel, and the vain efforts of the London police to recover it. I was myself consulted upon the case, but I was unable to throw any light upon it. Suspicion fell upon the maid of the Princess, who was an Italian, and it was proved that she had a brother in London, but we failed to trace any connection between them. The maid's name was Lucretia Venucci, and there is no doubt in my mind that this Pietro who was murdered two nights ago was the brother. I have been looking up the dates in the old files of the paper, and I find that the disappearance of the pearl was exactly two days before the arrest of Beppo, for some crime of violence – an event which took place in the factory of Gelder & Co., at the very moment when these busts were being made. Now you clearly see the sequence of events, though you see them, of course, in the inverse order to the way in which they presented themselves to me. Beppo had the pearl in his possession. He may have stolen it from Pietro, he may have been Pietro's confederate, he may have been the go-between of Pietro and his sister. It is of no consequence to us which is the correct solution.

'The main fact is that he *had* the pearl, and at that moment, when it was on his person, he was pursued by the police. He made for the factory in which he worked, and he knew that he had only a few minutes in which to conceal this enormously valuable prize, which would otherwise be found on him when he was searched. Six plaster casts of Napoleon were drying in the passage. One of them was still soft. In an instant Beppo, a skilful workman, made a small hole in the wet plaster, dropped in the pearl, and with a few touches covered over the aperture once more. It was an admirable hiding-place. No one could possibly find it. But Beppo was condemned to a year's imprisonment, and in the meanwhile his six busts were scattered over London. He could not tell which contained his treasure. Only by breaking them could he see. Even shaking would tell him nothing, for as the plaster was wet it was probable that the pearl would adhere to it – as, in fact, it had done. Beppo did not despair, and he conducted his search with considerable ingenuity and perseverance. Through a cousin who works with Gelder, he found out the retail firms who had bought the busts. He managed to find employment with Morse Hudson, and in that way tracked down three of them. The pearl was not there. Then, with the help of some Italian employé, he succeeded in finding out where the other three busts had gone. The first was at Harker's. There he was dogged by his confederate, who held Beppo responsible for the loss of the pearl, and he stabbed him in the scuffle which followed.'

'If he was his confederate, why should he carry his photograph?' I asked.

'As a means of tracing him, if he wished to inquire about him from any third person. That was the obvious reason. Well, after the murder I calculated that Beppo would probably hurry rather than delay his movements. He would fear that the police would read his secret, and so he hastened on before they should get ahead of him. Of course, I could not say that he had not found the pearl in Harker's bust. I had not even concluded for certain that it was the pearl, but it was evident to me that he was looking for something, since he carried the bust past the other houses in order to break it in the garden which had a lamp overlooking it. Since Harker's bust was one in three, the chances were exactly as I told you – two to one against the pearl being inside it. There remained two busts, and it was obvious that he would go for the London one first. I warned the inmates of the house, so as to avoid a second tragedy, and we went down, with the happiest results. By that time, of course, I knew for certain that it was the Borgia pearl that we were after. The name of the murdered man linked the one event with the other. There only remained a single bust – the Reading one – and the pearl must be there. I bought it in your presence from the owner – and there it lies.'

We sat in silence for a moment.

'Well,' said Lestrade, 'I've seen you handle a good many cases, Mr Holmes, but I don't know that I ever knew a more workmanlike one than that. We're not jealous of you at Scotland Yard. No, sir, we are very proud of you, and if you come down tomorrow, there's not a man, from the oldest inspector to the youngest constable, who wouldn't be glad to shake you by the hand.'

'Thank you!' said Holmes. 'Thank you!' and as he turned away, it seemed to me that he was more nearly moved by the softer human emotions than I had ever seen him. A moment later he was the cold and practical thinker once more. 'Put the pearl in the safe, Watson,' said he, 'and get out the papers of the Conk-Singleton forgery case. Goodbye, Lestrade. If any little problem comes your way, I shall be happy, if I can, to give you a hint or two as to its solution.'

The Missing Three-Quarter

We were fairly accustomed to receive weird telegrams at Baker Street, but I have a particular recollection of one which reached us on a gloomy February morning some seven or eight years ago and gave Mr Sherlock Holmes a puzzled quarter of an hour. It was addressed to him, and ran thus:

Please await me. Terrible misfortune. Right wing three-quarter missing. Indispensable tomorrow.
OVERTON

'Strand postmark, and dispatched ten thirty-six,' said Holmes, reading it over and over. 'Mr Overton was evidently considerably excited when he sent it, and somewhat incoherent in consequence. Well, well, he will be here, I dare say, by the time I have looked through *The Times*, and then we shall know all about it. Even the most insignificant problem would be welcome in these stagnant days.'

Things had indeed been very slow with us, and I had learned to dread such periods of inaction, for I knew by experience that my companion's brain was so abnormally active that it was dangerous to leave it without material upon which to work. For years I had gradually weaned him from that drug mania which had threatened once to check his remarkable career. Now I knew that under ordinary conditions he no longer craved for this artificial stimulus; but I was well aware that the fiend was not dead, but sleeping; and I have known that the sleep was a light one and the waking near when in periods of idleness I have seen the drawn look upon Holmes's ascetic face, and the brooding of his deep-set and inscrutable eyes. Therefore I blessed this Mr Overton, whoever he might be, since he had come with his enigmatic message to break that dangerous calm which brought more peril to my friend than all the storms of his tempestuous life.

As we expected, the telegram was soon followed by its sender, and the card of Mr Cyril Overton, of Trinity College, Cambridge, announced the arrival of an enormous young man, sixteen stone of solid bone and muscle, who spanned the doorway with his broad shoulders and looked from one of us to the other with a comely face which was haggard with anxiety.

'Mr Sherlock Holmes?'

My companion bowed.

'I've been down to Scotland Yard, Mr Holmes. I saw Inspector Stanley Hopkins. He advised me to come to you. He said the case, so far as he could see, was more in your line than in that of the regular police.'

'Pray sit down and tell me what is the matter.'

'It's awful, Mr Holmes, simply awful! I wonder my hair isn't grey. Godfrey Staunton – you've heard of him, of course? He's simply the hinge that the whole team turns on. I'd rather spare the two from the pack and have Godfrey for my three-quarter line. Whether it's passing, or tackling, or dribbling, there's no one to touch him; and then, he's got the head and can hold us all together. What am I to do? That's what I ask you, Mr Holmes. There's Moorhouse, first reserve, but he is trained as a half, and he always edges right in on to the scrum instead of keeping out on the touch-line. He's a fine place-kick, it's true, but, then, he has no judgment, ind he can't sprint for nuts. Why, Morton or Johnson, the Oxford fliers, could romp round him. Stevenson is fast enough, but he couldn't drop from the twenty-five line, and a three-quarter who can't either punt or drop isn't worth a place for pace alone. No, Mr Holmes, we are done unless you can help me to find Godfrey Staunton.'

My friend had listened with amused surprise to this long speech, which was poured forth with extraordinary vigour and earnestness, every point being driven home by the slapping of a brawny hand upon the speaker's knee. When our visitor was silent Holmes stretched out his hand and took down letter 'S' of his commonplace book. For once he dug in vain into that mine of varied information.

'There is Arthur H. Staunton, the rising young forger,' said he, 'and there was Henry Staunton, whom I helped to hang, but Godfrey Staunton is a new name to me.'

It was our visitor's turn to look surprised.

'Why, Mr Holmes, I thought you knew things,' said he. 'I suppose, then, if you have never heard of Godfrey Staunton you don't know Cyril Overton?'

Holmes shook his head good-humouredly.

'Great Scott!' cried the athlete. 'Why, I was first reserve for England against Wales, and I've skippered the 'Varsity all this year. But that's nothing. I didn't think there was a soul in England who didn't know Godfrey Staunton, the crack three-quarter, Cambridge, Blackheath, and five Internationals. Good Lord! Mr Holmes, where *have* you lived?'

Holmes laughed at the young giant's naïve astonishment.

'You live in a different world to me, Mr Overton, a sweeter and healthier one. My ramifications stretch out into many sections of society, but never, I am happy to say, into amateur sport, which is the best and soundest thing in England. However, your unexpected visit this morning shows me that even in that world of fresh air and fair play there may be work for me to do; so now, my good sir, I beg you to sit down and to tell me slowly and quietly exactly what it is that has occurred, and how you desire that I should help you.'

Young Overton's face assumed the bothered look of the man who is more accustomed to using his muscles than his wits; but by degrees, with many repetitions and obscurities which I may omit from his narrative, he laid his strange story before us.

'It's this way, Mr Holmes. As I have said, I am the skipper of the Rugger team of Cambridge 'Varsity, and Godfrey Staunton is my best man. Tomorrow we play Oxford. Yesterday we all came up and we settled at Bentley's private hotel. At ten o'clock I went round and saw that all the fellows had gone to roost, for I believe in strict training and plenty of sleep to keep a team fit. I had a word or two with Godfrey before he turned in. He seemed to me to be pale and bothered. I asked him what was the matter. He said he was all right – just a touch of headache. I bade him good night and left him. Half an hour later the porter tells me that a rough-looking man with a beard called with a note for Godfrey. He had not gone to bed, and the note was taken to his room. Godfrey read it and fell back in a chair as if he had been pole-axed. The porter was so scared that he was going to fetch me, but Godfrey stopped him, had a drink of water, and pulled himself together. Then he went downstairs, said a few words to the man who was waiting in the hall, and the two of them went off together. The last that the porter saw of them, they were almost running down the street in the direction of the Strand. This morning

Godfrey's room was empty, his bed had never been slept in, add his things were all just as I had seen them the night before. He had gone off at a moment's notice with this stranger, and no word has come back from him since. I don't believe he will ever come back. He was a sportsman, was Godfrey, down to his marrow, and he wouldn't have stopped his training and let down his skipper if it were not for some cause that was too strong for him. No; I feel as if he were gone for good and we should never see him again.'

Sherlock Holmes listened with the deepest attention to this singular narrative.

'What did you do?' he asked.

'I wired to Cambridge to learn if anything had been heard of him there. I have had an answer. No one has seen him.'

'Could he have got back to Cambridge?'

'Yes, there is a late train – quarter-past eleven.'

'But so far as you can ascertain, he did not take it?'

'No, he has not been seen.'

'What did you do next?'

'I wired to Lord Mount-James.'

'Why to Lord Mount-James?'

'Godfrey is an orphan, and Lord Mount-James is his nearest relative – his uncle, I believe.'

'Indeed. This throws new light upon the matter. Lord Mount-James is one of the richest men in England.'

'So I've heard Godfrey say.'

'And your friend was closely related?'

'Yes, he was his heir, and the old boy is nearly eighty – cram full of gout, too. They say he could chalk his billiard-cue with his knuckles. He never allowed Godfrey a shilling in his life, for he is an absolute miser, but it will all come to him right enough.'

'Have you heard from Lord Mount-James?'

'No.'

'What motive could your friend have in going to Lord Mount-James?'

'Well, something was worrying him the night before, and if it was to do with money it is possible that he would make for his nearest relative who had so much of it, though from all I have heard he would not have much chance of getting it. Godfrey was not fond of the old man. He would not go if he could help it.'

'Well, we can soon determine that. If your friend was going to his relative Lord Mount-James, you have then to explain the visit of this rough-looking fellow at so late an hour, and the agitation that was caused by his coming.'

Cyril Overton pressed his hands to his head. 'I can make nothing of it!' said he.

'Well, well, I have a clear day, and I shall be happy to look into the matter,' said Holmes. 'I should strongly recommend you to make your preparations for your match without reference to this young gentleman. It must, as you say, have been an overpowering necessity which tore him away in such a fashion, and the same necessity is likely to hold him away. Let us step round together to this hotel, and see if the porter can throw any fresh light upon the matter.'

Sherlock Holmes was a past master in the art of putting a humble witness at his ease, and very soon, in the privacy of Godfrey Staunton's abandoned room, he had extracted all that the porter had to tell. The visitor of the night before was not a gentleman, neither was he a working man. He was simply what the porter described as a 'medium-looking chap'; a man of fifty, beard grizzled, pale face, quietly dressed. He seemed himself to be agitated. The porter had observed his hand trembling when he had held out the note. Godfrey Staunton had crammed the note into his pocket. Staunton had not shaken hands with the man in the hall. They had exchanged a few sentences, of which the porter had only distinguished the one word 'time'. Then they had hurried off in the manner described. It was just half-past ten by the hall clock.

'Let me see,' said Holmes, seating himself on Staunton's bed 'You are the day porter, are you not?'

'Yes, sir; I go off duty at eleven.'

'The night porter saw nothing, I suppose?' 'No, sir; one theatre party came in late. No one else.' 'Were you on duty all day yesterday?'

'Yes, sir.'

'Did you take any message to Mr Staunton?'

'Yes, sir; one telegram.'

'Ah! that is interesting. What o'clock was this?'

'About six.'

'Where was Mr Staunton when he received it?'

'Here in his room.'

'Were you present when he opened it?'

'Yes, sir; I waited to see if there was an answer.'

'Well, was there?'

'Yes, sir. He wrote an answer.'

'Did you take it?'

'No; he took it himself.'

'But he wrote it in your presence?'

'Yes, sir. I was standing by the door, and he with his back turned at that table. When he had written it he said, "All right, porter, I will take this myself."'

'What did he write it with?'

'A pen, sir.'

'Was the telegraphic form one of these on the table?'

'Yes, sir; it was the top one.'

Holmes rose. Taking the forms, he carried them over to the window and carefully examined that which was uppermost.

'It is a pity he did not write in pencil,' said he, throwing them down again with a shrug of disappointment. 'As you have no doubt frequently observed, Watson, the impression usually goes through – a fact which has dissolved many a happy marriage. However, I can find no trace here. I rejoice, however, to perceive that he wrote with a broad-pointed quill pen, and I can hardly doubt that we will find some impression upon this blotting pad. Ah, yes, surely this is the very thing!'

He tore off a strip of the blotting-paper and turned towards us the following hieroglyphic:

Cyril Overton was much excited. 'Hold it to the glass,' he cried.

'That is unnecessary,' said Holmes. 'The paper is thin, and the reverse will give the message. There it is.' He turned it over, and we read:

'So that is the tail end of the telegram which Godfrey Staunton dispatched within a few hours of his disappearance. There are at least six words of the message which have escaped us; but what remains – "Stand by us for God's sake!" – proves that this young man saw a formidable danger which approached him, and from which someone else could protect him. "*Us*", mark you! Another person was involved. Who should it be but the pale-faced, bearded man who seemed himself in so nervous a state? What then, is the connection between Godfrey Staunton and the bearded man?

And what is the third source from which each of them sought for help against pressing danger? Our inquiry has already narrowed down to than.'

'We have only to find to whom that telegram is addressed,' I suggested.

'Exactly, my dear Watson. Your reflection, though profound, had already crossed my mind. But I dare say it may have come to your notice that if you walk into a post-office and demand to see the counterfoil of another man's message there may be some disinclination on the part of the officials to oblige you. There is so much red tape in these matters! However, I have no doubt that with a little delicacy and finesse the end may be attained. Meanwhile, I should like in your presence, Mr Overton, to go through these papers which have been left upon the table.'

There were a number of letters, bills, and note-books, which Holmes turned over and examined with quick, nervous fingers and darting, penetrating eyes. 'Nothing here,' he said at last. 'By the way, I suppose your friend was a healthy young fellow – nothing amiss with him?'

'Sound as a bell.'

'Have you ever known him ill?'

'Not a day. He has been laid up with a hack, and once he slipped his knee cap, but that was nothing.'

'Perhaps he was not so strong as you suppose. I should think he may have had some secret trouble.

With your assent I will put one or two of these papers in my pocket, in case they should bear upon our future inquiry.'

'One moment, one moment!' cried a querulous voice, and we looked up to find a queer little old man jerking and twitching in the doorway. He was dressed in rusty black, with a very broad-brimmed top-hat and a loose white necktie – the whole effect being that of a very rustic parson or of an undertaker's mute. Yet, in spite of his shabby and even absurd appearance, his voice had a sharp crackle, and his manner a quick intensity which commanded attention.

'Who are you, sir, and by what right do you touch this gentleman's papers?' be asked.

'I am a private detective, and I am endeavouring to explain his disappearance.'

'Oh, you are, are you? And who instructed you, eh?'

'This gentleman, Mr Staunton's friend, was referred to me by Scotland Yard.'

'Who are you, sir?'

'I am Cyril Overton.'

'Then it is you who sent me a telegram. My name is Lord Mount-James. I came round as quickly as the Bayswater bus would bring me. So you have instructed a detective?'

'Yes, sir.'

'And are you prepared to meet the cost?'

'I have no doubt, sir, that my friend Godfrey, when we find him, will be prepared to do that.'

'But if he is never found, eh? Answer me that!'

'In that case no doubt his family –'

'Nothing of the sort, sir!' screamed the little man. 'Don't look to me for a penny – not a penny! You understand that, Mr Detective! I am all the family that this young man has got, and I tell you that I am not responsible. If he has any expectations it is due to the fact that I have never wasted money, and I do not propose to begin to do so now. As to those papers with which you are making so free, I may tell you that in case there should be anything of any value among them you will be held strictly to account for what you do with them.'

'Very good, sir,' said Sherlock Holmes. 'May I ask in the meanwhile whether you have yourself any theory to account for this young man's disappearance?'

'No, sir, I have not. He is big enough and old enough to look after himself, and if he is so foolish as to lose himself I entirely refuse to accept the responsibility of hunting for him.'

'I quite understand your position,' said Holmes, with a mischievous twinkle in his eyes. 'Perhaps you don't quite understand mine. Godfrey Staunton appears to have been a poor man. If he has been kidnapped it could not have been for anything which he himself possesses. The fame of your wealth has gone abroad, Lord Mount-James, and it is entirely possible that a gang of thieves has secured your nephew in order to gain from him some information as to your house, your habits, and your treasure.'

The face of our unpleasant little visitor turned as white as his neckcloth.

'Heavens, sir, what an idea! I never thought of such villainy! What inhuman rogues there are in the world! But Godfrey is a fine lad – a staunch lad. Nothing would induce him to give his old uncle away. I'll have the plate moved over to the bank this evening. In the meantime spare no pains, Mr Detective. I beg you to leave no stone unturned to bring him safely back. As to money, well, so far as a fiver, or even a tenner, goes, you can always look to me.'

Even in his chastened frame of mind the noble miser could give us no information which could help us, for he knew little of the private life of his nephew. Our only clue lay in the truncated telegram, and with a copy of this in his hand Holmes set forth to find a second link for his chain. We had shaken off Lord Mount-James, and Overton had gone to consult with the other members of his team over the misfortune which had befallen them. There was a telegraph office at a short distance from the hotel. We halted outside it.

'It's worth trying, Watson,' said Holmes. 'Of course, with a warrant we could demand to see the counterfoils, but we have not reached that stage yet. I don't suppose they remember faces in so busy a place. Let us venture it.'

'I am sorry to trouble you,' said he in his blandest manner to the young woman behind the grating; 'there is some small mistake about a telegram I sent yesterday. I have had no answer, and I very much fear that I must have omitted to put my name at the end. Could you tell me if this was so?'

The young lady turned over a sheaf of counterfoils.

'What o'clock was it?' she asked.

'A little after six.'

'Whom was it to?'

Holmes put his finger to his lips and glanced at me. 'The last words in it were "for God's sake",' he whispered confidentially; 'I am very anxious at getting no answer.'

The young woman separated one of the forms.

'This is it. There is no name,' said she, smoothing it out upon the counter.

'Then that, of course, accounts for my getting no answer,' said Holmes. 'Dear me, how very stupid of me, to be sure! Good morning, miss, and many thanks for having relieved my mind.' He chuckled and rubbed his hands when we found ourselves in the street once more.

'Well?' I asked.

'We progress, my dear Watson, we progress. I had seven different schemes for getting a glimpse of that telegram, but I could hardly hope to succeed the very first time.'

'And what have you gained?'

'A starting-point for our investigation.' He hailed a cab. 'King's Cross Station,' said he.

'We have a journey, then?'

'Yes, I think we must run down to Cambridge together. All the indications seem to point in that direction.'

'Tell me,' I asked as we rattled up Gray's Inn Road, 'have you any suspicion yet as to the cause of the disappearance? I don't think that among all our cases I have known one where the motives were more obscure. Surely you don't really imagine that he may be kidnapped in order to give information against his wealthy uncle?'

'I confess, my dear Watson, that that does not appeal to me as a very probable explanation. It struck me, however, as being the one which was most likely to interest that exceedingly unpleasant old person.'

'It certainly did that. But what are your alternatives?'

'I could mention several. You must admit that it is curious and suggestive that this incident should occur on the eve of this important match, and should involve the only man whose presence seems essential to the success of the side. It may, of course, be coincidence, but it is interesting. Amateur sport is free from betting, but a good deal of outside betting goes on among the public, and it is possible that it might be worth someone's while to get at a player as the ruffians of the Turf get at a racehorse. There is one explanation. A second very obvious one is that this young man really is the heir of a great property, however modest his means may be at present, and it is not impossible that a plot to hold him for ransom might be concocted.'

'These theories take no account of the telegram.'

'Quite true, Watson. The telegram still remains the only solid thing with which we have to deal, and we must not permit our attention to wander away from it. It is to gain light upon the purpose of this telegram that we are now upon our way to Cambridge. The path of our investigation is at present obscure, but I shall be very surprised if before evening we have not cleared it up or made a considerable advance along it.'

It was already dark when we reached the old University city. Holmes took a cab at the station, and ordered the man to drive to the house of Dr Leslie Armstrong. A few minutes later we had stopped at a large mansion in the busiest thorough-fare. We were shown in, and after a long wait were admitted into the consulting-room, where we found the doctor seated behind his table.

It argues the degree in which I had lost touch with my profession that the name of Leslie Armstrong was unknown to me. Now I am aware that he is not only one of the heads of the medical school of the University, but a thinker of European reputation in more than one branch of science. Yet even without knowing his brilliant record one could not fail to be impressed by a mere glance at the man – the square, massive face, the brooding eyes under the thatched brows, and the granite moulding of the inflexible jaw. A man of deep character, a man with an alert mind, grim, ascetic, self-contained, formidable – so I read Dr Leslie Armstrong. He held my friend's card in his hand, and he looked up with no very pleased expression upon his dour features.

'I have heard your name, Mr Sherlock Holmes, and I am aware of your profession, one of which I by no means approve.'

'In that, doctor, you will find yourself in agreement with every criminal in the country,' said my friend quietly.

'So far as your efforts are directed towards the suppression of crime, sir, they must have the support of every reasonable member of the community, though I cannot doubt that the official machinery is amply sufficient for the purpose. Where your calling is more open to criticism is when you pry into the secrets of private individuals, when you rake up family matters which are better hidden, and when you incidentally waste the time of men who are more busy than yourself. At the present moment, for example, I should be writing a treatise instead of conversing with you.'

'No doubt, doctor; and yet the conversation may prove more important than the treatise. Incidentally I may tell you that we are doing the reverse of what you very justly blame, and that we are endeavouring to prevent anything like public exposure of private matters which must necessarily follow when once the case is fairly in the hands of the official police. You may look upon me simply as an irregular pioneer who goes in front of the regular force of the country. I have come to ask you about Mr Godfrey Staunton.'

'What about him?'

'You know him, do you not?'

'He is an intimate friend of mine.'

'You are aware that he has disappeared?'

'Ah, indeed!' There was no change of expression in the rugged features of the doctor.

'He left his hotel last night. He has not been heard of.'

'No doubt he will return.'

'Tomorrow is the 'Varsity football match.'

'I have no sympathy with these childish games. The young man's fate interests me deeply, since I know him and like him. The football match does not come within my horizon at all.'

'I claim your sympathy, then, in my investigation of Mr Staunton's fate. Do you know where he is?'

'Certainly not.'

'You have not seen him since yesterday?'

'No, I have not.'

'Was Mr Staunton a healthy man?'

'Absolutely.'

'Did you ever know him ill?'

'Never.'

Holmes popped a sheet of paper before the doctor's eyes. 'Then perhaps you will explain this receipted bill for thirteen guineas, paid by Mr Godfrey Staunton last month to Dr Leslie Armstrong, of Cambridge. I picked it out from among the papers upon his desk.'

The doctor flushed with anger.

'I do not feel that there is any reason why I should render an explanation to you, Mr Holmes.'

Holmes replaced the bill in his notebook.

'If you prefer a public explanation it must come sooner or later,' said he. 'I have already told you that I can hush up that which others will be bound to publish, and you would really be wiser to take me into your complete confidence.'

'I know nothing about it.'

'Did you hear from Mr Staunton in London?'

'Certainly not.'

'Dear me, dear me! – the post office again!' Holmes sighed wearily. 'A most urgent telegram was dispatched to you from London by Godfrey Staunton at six-fifteen yesterday evening – a telegram which is undoubtedly associated with his disappearance – and yet you have not had it. It is most culpable. I shall certainly go down to the office here and register a complaint.'

Dr Leslie Armstrong sprang up from behind his desk, and his dark face was crimson with fury.

'I'll trouble you to walk out of my house, sir,' said he. 'You can tell your employer, Lord

Mount-James, that I do not wish to have anything to do either with him or with his agents. No, sir, not another word!' He rang the bell furiously. 'John, show these gentlemen out.' A pompous butler ushered us severely to the door, and we found ourselves in the street. Holmes burst out laughing.

'Dr Leslie Armstrong is certainly a man of energy and character,' said he 'I have not seen a man who, if he turned his talents that way, was more calculated to fill the gap left by the illustrious Moriarty. And now, my poor Watson, here we are, stranded and friendless, in this inhospitable town, which we cannot leave without abandoning our case. This little inn just opposite Armstrong's house is singularly adapted to our needs. If you would engage a front room and purchase the necessaries for the night, I may have time to make a few inquiries.'

These few inquiries proved to be, however, to be a more lengthy proceeding than Holmes had imagined, for he did not return to the inn until nearly nine o clock. He was pale and dejected, stained with dust, and exhausted with hunger and fatigue. A cold supper was ready upon the table, and when his needs were satisfied and his pipe alight he was ready to take that half-comic and wholly philosophic view which was natural to him when his affairs were going awry. The sound of carriage wheels caused him to rise and glance out of the window. A brougham and pair of greys under the glare of a gas-lamp stood before the doctor's door.

'It's been out three hours,' said Holmes; 'started at half-past six, and here it is back again. That gives a radius of ten or twelve miles, and he does it once, or sometimes twice, a day.'

'No unusual thing for a doctor in practice.'

'But Armstrong is not really a doctor in practice. He is a lecturer and a consultant, but he does not care for general practice, which distracts him from his literary work. Why, then, does he make these long journeys, which must be exceedingly irksome to him, and who is it that he visits?'

'His coachman —'

'My dear Watson, can you doubt that it was to him that I first applied? I do not know whether it came from his own innate depravity or from the promptings of his master, but he was rude enough to set a dog at me. Neither dog nor man liked the look of my stick, however, and the matter fell through. Relations were strained after that, and further inquiries out of the question. All that I have learned I got from a friendly native in the yard of our own inn. It was he who told me of the doctor's habits and of his daily journey. At that instant, to give point to his words, the carriage came round to the door.'

'Could you not follow it?'

'Excellent, Watson! You are scintillating this evening. The idea did cross my mind. There is, as you may have observed, a bicycle shop next to our inn. Into this I rushed, engaged a bicycle, and was able to get started before the carriage was quite out of sight. I rapidly overtook it, and then, keeping at a discreet distance of a hundred yards or so, I followed its lights until we were clear of the town. We had got well out on the country road when a somewhat mortifying incident occurred. The carriage stopped, the doctor alighted, walked swiftly back to where I had also halted, and told me in an excellent sardonic fashion that he feared the road was narrow, and that he hoped his carriage did not impede the passage of my bicycle. Nothing could have been more admirable than his way of putting it. I at once rode past the carriage, and, keeping to the main road, I went on for a few miles, and then halted in a convenient place to see if the carriage passed. There was no sign of it, however, and so it became evident that it had turned down one of several side-roads which I had observed. I rode back, but again saw nothing of the carriage, and now, as you perceive, it has returned after me. Of course, I had at the outset no particular reason to connect these journeys with the disappearance of Godfrey Staunton, and was only inclined to investigate them on the general grounds that everything which concerns Dr Armstrong is at present of interest to us; but, now that I find he keeps so keen a lookout upon anyone who may follow him on these excursions, the affair appears more important, and I shall not be satisfied until I have made the matter clear.'

'We can follow him tomorrow.'

'Can we? It is not so easy as you seem to think. You are not familiar with Cambridgeshire scenery, are you? It does not lend itself to concealment. All this country that I passed over tonight is as flat and clean as the palm of your hand, and the man we are following is no fool, as he very clearly showed tonight. I have wired to Overton to let us know any fresh London developments at this address, and in the meantime we can only concentrate our attention upon Dr Armstrong, whose name the obliging young lady at the office allowed me to read upon the counterfoil of Staunton's urgent message. He knows where that young man is – to that I'll swear – and if he knows, then it must be our fault if we cannot manage to know also. At present it must be admitted that the odd trick is in his possession, and, as you are aware, Watson, it is not my habit to leave the game in that condition.'

And yet the next day brought us no nearer to the solution of the mystery. A note was handed in after breakfast, which Holmes passed across to me with a smile.

Sir [it ran] – I can assure you that you are wasting your time in dogging my movements. I have, as you discovered last night, a window at the back of my brougham, and if you desire a twenty-mile ride which will lead you to the spot from which you started, you have only to follow me. Meanwhile, I can inform you that no spying upon me can in any way help Mr Godfrey Staunton, and I am convinced that the best service you can do to that gentleman is to return at once to London and to report to your employer that you are unable to trace him. Your time in Cambridge will certainly be wasted.

Yours faithfully,

LESLIE ARMSTRONG

'An outspoken, honest antagonist is the doctor,' said Holmes. 'Well, well, he excites my curiosity, and I must really know more before I leave him.'

'His carriage is at his door now,' said I. 'There he is stepping into it. I saw him glance up at our window as he did so. Suppose I try my luck upon the bicycle?'

'No, no, my dear Watson! With all respect for your natural acumen, I do not think that you are quite a match for the worthy doctor. I think that possibly I can attain our end by some independent explorations of my own. I am afraid that I must leave you to your own devices, as the appearance of *two* inquiring strangers upon a sleepy country-side might excite more gossip than I care for. No doubt you will find some sights to amuse you in this venerable city, and I hope to bring back a more favourable report to you before evening.'

Once more, however, my friend was destined to be disappointed. He came back at night weary and unsuccessful.

'I have had a blank day, Watson. Having got the doctor's general direction, I spent the day in visiting all the villages upon that side of Cambridge, and comparing notes with publicans and other local news agencies. I have covered some ground: Chesterton, Histon, Waterbeach, and Oakington have each been explored, and have each proved disappointing. The daily appearance of a brougham and pair could hardly have been overlooked in such sleepy hollows. The doctor has scored once more. Is there a telegram for me?'

'Yes; I opened it. Here it is: "Ask for Pompey from Jeremy Dixon, Trinity College." I don't understand it.'

'Oh, it is clear enough. It is from our friend Overton, and is in answer to a question from me. I'll just send round a note to Mr Jeremy Dixon, and then I have no doubt that our luck will turn. By the way, is there any news of the match?'

'Yes, the local evening paper has an excellent account in its last edition. Oxford won by a goal and two tries. The last sentences of the description say: "The defeat of the Light Blues may be entirely attributed to the unfortunate absence of the crack International, Godfrey Staunton, whose want was felt at every instant of the game. The lack of combination in the three-quarter line and their weakness both in attack and defence more than neutralized the efforts of a heavy and hard-working pack."'

'Then our friend Overton's forebodings have been justified,' said Holmes. 'Personally I am in agreement with Dr Armstrong, and football does not come within my horizon. Early to bed tonight, Watson, for I foresee that tomorrow may be an eventful day.'

I was horrified by my first glimpse of Holmes next morning, for he sat by the fire holding his tiny hypodermic syringe. I associated that with the single weakness of his nature, and I feared the worst when I saw it glittering in his hand. He laughed at my expression of dismay, and laid it upon the table.

'No, no, my dear fellow, there is no cause for alarm. It is not upon this occasion the instrument of evil, but it will rather prove to be the key which will unlock our mystery. On this syringe I base all my hopes. I have just returned from a small scouting expedition, and everything is favourable. Eat a good breakfast, Watson, for I propose to get upon Dr Armstrong's trail today, and once on it I will not stop for rest or food until I run him to his burrow.'

'In that case,' said I, 'we had best carry our breakfast with us, for he is making an early start. His carriage is at the door.'

'Never mind. Let him go. He will be clever if he can drive where I cannot follow him. When you have finished come downstairs with me, and I will introduce you to a detective who is a very eminent specialist in the work that lies before us.'

When we descended I followed Holmes into the

stableyard, where he opened the door of a loose-box and led out a squat lop-eared, white-and-tan dog, something between a beagle and a foxhound.

'Let me introduce you to Pompey,' said he. 'Pompey is the pride of the local draghounds, no very great flier, as his build will show, but a staunch hound on a scent. Well, Pompey, you may not be fast, but I expect you will be too fast for a couple of middle-aged London gentlemen, so I will take the liberty of fastening this leather leash to your collar. Now, boy, come along, and show what you can do.' He led him across to the doctor's door. The dog sniffed round for an instant, and then with a shrill whine of excitement started off down the street, tugging at his leash in his efforts to go faster. In half an hour we were clear of the town and hastening down a country road.

'What have you done, Holmes?' I asked.

'A threadbare and venerable device, but useful upon occasion. I walked into the doctor's yard this morning and shot my syringe full of aniseed over the hind wheel. A draghound will follow aniseed from here to John o' Groats, and our friend Armstrong would have to drive through the Cam before he would shake Pompey off his trail. Oh, the cunning rascal! This is how he gave me the slip the other night.'

The dog had suddenly turned out of the main road into a grass-grown lane. Half a mile farther this opened into another broad road, and the trail turned hard to the right in the direction of the town, which we had just quitted. The road took a sweep to the south of the town and continued in the opposite direction to that in which we started.

'This detour has been entirely for our benefit, then?' said Holmes. 'No wonder that my inquiries among those villages led to nothing. The doctor has certainly played the game for all it is worth, and one would like to know the reason for such elaborate deception. This should be the village of Trumpington to the right of us. And, by Jove! here is the brougham coming round the corner! Quick, Watson, quick, or we are done!'

He sprang through a gate into a field, dragging the reluctant Pompey after him. We had hardly got under the shelter of the hedge when the carriage rattled past. I caught a glimpse of Dr Armstrong within, his shoulders bowed, his head sunk on his hands, the very image of distress. I could tell by my companion's graver face that he also had seen.

'I fear there is some dark ending to our quest,' said he. 'It cannot be long before we know it. Come, Pompey! Ah, it is the cottage in the field.'

There could be no doubt that we had reached the end of our journey. Pompey ran about and whined eagerly outside the gate, where the marks of the brougham's wheels were still to be seen. A footpath led across to the lonely cottage. Holmes tied the dog to the hedge, and we hastened onwards. My friend knocked at the little rustic door, and knocked again without response. And yet the cottage was not deserted, for a low sound came to our ears – a kind of drone of misery and despair, which was indescribably melancholy. Holmes paused irresolute, and then he glanced back at the road which we had just traversed. A brougham was coming down it, and there could be no mistaking those grey horses.

'By Jove, the doctor is coming back!' cried Holmes. 'That settles it. We are bound to see what it means before he comes.'

He opened the door, and we stepped into the hall. The droning sound swelled louder upon our ears, until it became one long, deep wail of distress. It came from upstairs. Holmes darted up, and I followed him. He pushed open a half-closed door, and we both stood appalled at the sight before us.

A woman, young and beautiful, was lying dead upon the bed. Her calm, pale face, with dim, wide-opened blue eyes, looked upwards from amid a great tangle of golden hair. At the foot of the bed, half sitting, half kneeling, his face buried in the clothes, was a young man, whose frame was racked by his sobs. So absorbed was he by his bitter grief that he never looked up until Holmes's hand was on his shoulder.

'Are you Mr Godfrey Staunton?'

'Yes, yes; I am – but you are too late. She is dead.'

The man was so dazed that he could not be made to understand that we were anything but doctors who had been sent to his assistance. Holmes was endeavouring to utter a few words of consolation, and to explain the alarm which had been caused to his friends by his sudden disappearance, when there was a step upon the stairs, and there was the heavy, stern, questioning face of Dr Armstrong at the door.

'So, gentlemen,' said he, 'you have attained your end, and have certainly chosen a particularly delicate moment for your intrusion. I would not brawl in the presence of death, but I can assure you that if I were a younger man your monstrous conduct would not pass with impunity.'

'Excuse me, Dr Armstrong, I think we are a little at cross purposes,' said my friend with dignity. 'If you could step downstairs with us we may each be able to give some light to the other upon this miserable affair.'

A minute later the grim doctor and ourselves were in the sitting-room below.

'Well, sir?' said he.

'I wish you to understand, in the first place, that I am not employed by Lord Mount-James, and that my sympathies in this matter are entirely against that nobleman. When a man is lost it is my duty to ascertain his fate, but having done so the matter ends so far as I am concerned; and so long as there is nothing criminal, I am much more anxious to hush up private scandals than to give them publicity. If, as I imagine, there is no breach of the law in this matter, you can absolutely depend upon my discretion and my co-operation in keeping the facts out of the papers!'

Dr Armstrong took a quick step forward and wrung Holmes by the hand.

'You are a good fellow,' said he. 'I had misjudged you. I thank heaven that my compunction at leaving poor Staunton all alone in this plight caused me to turn my carriage back, and so to make your acquaintance. Knowing as much as you do, the situation is very easily explained. A year ago Godfrey Staunton lodged in London for a time, and became passionately attached to his landlady's daughter, whom he married. She was as good as she was beautiful, and as intelligent as she was good. No man need be ashamed of such a wife. But Godfrey was heir to this crabbed old nobleman, and it was quite certain that the news of his marriage would have been the end of his inheritance. I knew the lad well, and I loved him for his many excellent qualities. I did all I could to help him to keep things straight. We did our very best to keep the thing from everyone, for when once such a whisper gets about it is not long before everyone has heard it. Thanks to this lonely cottage and his own discretion, Godfrey has up to now succeeded. Their secret was known to no one save to me and to one excellent servant who has at present gone for assistance to Trumpington. But at last there came a terrible blow in the shape of dangerous illness to his wife. It was consumption of the most virulent kind. The poor boy was half crazed with grief, and yet he had to go to London to play this match, for he could not get out of it without explanations which would expose the secret. I tried to cheer him up by a wire, and he sent me one in reply imploring me to do all I could. This was the telegram which you appear in some inexplicable way to have seen. I did not tell him how urgent the danger was, for I knew that he could do no good here, but I sent the truth to the girl's father, and he very injudiciously communicated it to Godfrey. The result was that he came straight away in a state bordering on frenzy, and has remained in the same state, kneeling at the end of her bed, until this morning death put an end to her sufferings. That is all, Mr Holmes, and I am sure that I can rely upon your discretion and that of your friend.'

Holmes grasped the doctor's hand.

'Come, Watson,' said he, and we passed from that house of grief into the pale sunlight of the winter day.

THE SOLITARY CYCLIST

From the years 1894 to 1901 inclusive, Mr Sherlock Holmes was a very busy man. It is safe to say that there was no public case of any difficulty in which he was not consulted during those eight years, and there were hundreds of private cases, some of them of the most intricate and extraordinary character, in which he played a prominent part. Many startling successes and a few unavoidable failures were the outcome of this long period of continuous work. As I have preserved very full notes of all these cases, and was myself personally engaged in many of them, it may be imagined that it is no easy task to know which I should select to lay before the public. I shall, however, preserve my former rule, and give the preference to those cases which derive their interest not so much from the brutality of the crime as from the ingenuity and dramatic quality of the solution. For this reason I will now lay before the reader the facts connected with Miss Violet Smith, the solitary cyclist of Charlington, and the curious sequel of our investigation, which culminated in unexpected tragedy. It is true that the circumstances did not permit of any striking illustration of those powers for which my friend was famous, but there were some points about the case which made it stand out in those long records of crime from which I gather the material for these little narratives.

On referring to my notebook for the year 1895, I find that it was upon Saturday, April 23rd, that we first heard of Miss Violet Smith. Her visit was, I remember, extremely unwelcome to Holmes, for he was immersed at the moment in a very abstruse and complicated problem concerning the peculiar persecution to which John Vincent Harden, the well-known tobacco millionaire, had been subjected. My friend, who loved above all things precision and concentration of thought, resented anything which distracted his attention from the matter in hand. And yet without harshness, which was foreign to his nature, it was impossible to refuse to listen to the story of the young and beautiful woman, tall, graceful and queenly, who presented herself at Baker Street late in the evening and implored his assistance and advice. It was vain to urge that his time was already fully occupied, for the young lady had come with the determination to tell her story, and it was evident that nothing short of force could get her out of the room until she had done so. With a resigned air and a somewhat weary smile, Holmes begged the beautiful intruder to take a seat and to inform us what it was that was troubling her.

'At least it cannot be your health,' said he, as his keen eyes darted over her; 'so ardent a bicyclist must be full of energy.'

She glanced down in surprise at her own feet, and I observed the slight roughening of the side of the sole caused by the friction of the edge of the pedal.

'Yes, I bicycle a good deal, Mr Holmes, and that has something to do with my visit to you today.'

My friend took the lady's ungloved hand and examined it with as close an attention and as little sentiment as a scientist would show to a specimen.

'You will excuse me, I am sure. It is my business,' said he, as he dropped it. 'I nearly fell into the error of supposing that you were typewriting. Of course, it is obvious that it is music. You observe the spatulate finger end, Watson, which is common to both professions? There is a spirituality about the face, however' – he gently turned it towards the light – 'which the typewriter does not generate. This lady is a musician.'

'Yes, Mr Holmes, I teach music.'

'In the country, I presume, from your complexion.'

'Yes, sir; near Farnham, on the borders of Surrey.'

'A beautiful neighbourhood, and full of the most interesting associations. You remember, Watson, that it was near there that we took Archie

Stamford, the forger. Now, Miss Violet, what has happened to you near Farnham, on the borders of Surrey?'

The young lady, with great clearness and composure, made the following curious statement:

'My father is dead, Mr Holmes. He was James Smith, who conducted the orchestra at the old Imperial Theatre. My mother and I were left without a relation in the world except one uncle, Ralph Smith, who went to Africa twenty-five years ago, and we have never had a word from him since. When Father died we were left very poor, but one day we were told that there was an advertisement in *The Times* inquiring for our whereabouts. You can imagine how excited we were, for we thought that someone had left us a fortune. We went at once to the lawyer whose name was given in the paper. There we met two gentlemen, Mr Carruthers and Mr Woodley, who were home on a visit from South Africa. They said that my uncle was a friend of theirs, that he died some months before in poverty in Johannesburg, and that he had asked them with his last breath to hunt up his relations and see that they were in no want. It seemed strange to us that Uncle Ralph, who took no notice of us when he was alive, should be so careful to look after us when he was dead; but Mr Carruthers explained that the reason was that my uncle had just heard of the death of his brother, and so felt responsible for our fate.'

'Excuse me,' said Holmes; 'when was this interview?'

'Last December – four months ago.'

'Pray proceed.'

'Mr Woodley seemed to me to be a most odious person. He was forever making eyes at me – a coarse, puffy-faced, red-moustached young man, with his hair plastered down on each side of his forehead. I thought that he was perfectly hateful – and I was sure that Cyril would not wish me to know such a person.'

'Oh, Cyril is his name!' said Holmes, smiling.

The young lady blushed and laughed.

'Yes, Mr Holmes; Cyril Morton, an electrical engineer, and we hope to be married at the end of the Summer. Dear me, how *did* I get talking about him? What I wished to say was that Mr Woodley was perfectly odious, but that Mr Carruthers, who was a much older man, was more agreeable. He was a dark, sallow, clean-shaven, silent person; but he had polite manners and a pleasant smile. He inquired how we were left, and on finding that we were very poor he suggested that I should come and teach music to his only daughter, aged ten. I said that I did not like to leave my mother, on which he suggested that I should go home to her every weekend, and he offered me a hundred a year, which was certainly splendid pay. So it ended by my accepting, and I went down to Chiltern Grange, about six miles from Farnham. Mr Carruthers was a widower, but he had engaged a lady-housekeeper, a very respectable, elderly person, called Mrs Dixon, to look after his establishment. The child was a dear, and everything promised well. Mr Carruthers was very kind and very musical, and we had most pleasant evenings together. Every weekend I went home to my mother in town.

'The first flaw in my happiness was the arrival of the red-moustached Mr Woodley. He came for a visit of a week, and oh, it seemed three months to me! He was a dreadful person, a bully to everyone else, but to me something infinitely worse. He made odious love to me, boasted of his wealth, said that if I married him I would have the finest diamonds in London, and finally, when I would have nothing to do with him, he seized me in his arms one day after dinner – he was hideously strong – and he swore that he would not let me go until I had kissed him. Mr Carruthers came in, and tore him off from me, on which he turned upon his own host, knocking him down and cutting his face open. That was the end of his visit, as you can imagine. Mr Carruthers apologized to me next day, and assured me that I should never be exposed to such an insult again. I have not seen Mr Woodley since.

'And now, Mr Holmes, I come at last to the special thing which has caused me to ask your advice today. You must know that every Saturday forenoon I ride on my bicycle to Farnham Station in order to get the 12.22 to town. The road from

Chiltern Grange is a lonely one, and at one spot it is particularly so, for it lies for over a mile between Charlington Heath upon one side and the woods which lie round Charlington Hall upon the other. You could not find a more lonely tract of road anywhere, and it is quite rare to meet so much as a cart, or a peasant, until you reach the high-road near Crooksbury Hill. Two weeks ago I was passing this place when I chanced to look back over my shoulder, and about two hundred yards behind me I saw a man, also on a bicycle. He seemed to be a middle-aged man, with a short, dark beard. I looked back before I reached Farnham, but the man was gone, so I thought no more about it. But you can imagine how surprised I was, Mr Holmes, when on my return on the Monday I saw the same man on the same stretch of road. My astonishment was increased when the incident occurred again, exactly as before; on the following Saturday and Monday. He always kept his distance, and did not molest me in any way, but still it certainly was very odd. I mentioned it to Mr Carruthers, who seemed interested in what I said, and told me that he had ordered a horse and trap, so that in future I should not pass over these lonely roads without some companion.

'The horse and trap were to have come this week, but for some reason they were not delivered, and again I had to cycle to the station. That was this morning. You can think that I looked out when I came to Charlington Heath, and there, sure enough, was the man, exactly as he had been the two weeks before. He always kept so far from me that I could not clearly see his face, but it was certainly someone whom I did not know. He was dressed in a dark suit with a cloth cap. The only thing about his face that I could clearly see was his dark beard. Today I was not alarmed, but I was filled with curiosity, and I determined to find out who he was and what he wanted. I slowed down my machine, but he slowed down his. Then I stopped altogether, but he stopped also. Then I laid a trap for him. There is a sharp turning of the road, and I pedalled very quickly round this, and then I stopped and waited. I expected him to shoot round and pass me before he could stop. But he never appeared. Then I went back and looked round the corner. I could see a mile of road, but he was not on it. To make it the more extraordinary there was no side-road at this point down which he could have gone.'

Holmes chuckled and rubbed his hands.

'This case certainly presents some features of its own,' said he. 'How much time elapsed between your turning the corner and your discovery that the road was clear?'

'Two or three minutes.'

'Then he could not have retreated down the road, and you say that there are no side-roads?'

'None.'

'Then he certainly took a footpath on one side or the other.'

'It could not have been on the side of the heath or I should have seen him.'

'So by the process of exclusion we arrive at the fact that he made his way towards Charlington Hall, which, as I understand, is situated in its own grounds on one side of the road. Anything else?'

'Nothing, Mr Holmes, save that I was so perplexed that I felt I should not be happy until I had seen you and had your advice.'

Holmes sat in silence for some little time.

'Where is the gentleman to whom you are engaged?' he asked at last.

'He is in the Midland Electric Company, at Coventry.'

'He would not pay you a surprise visit?'

'Oh, Mr Holmes! As if I should not know him!'

'Have you had any other admirers?'

'Several before I knew Cyril.'

'And since?'

'There was this dreadful man, Woodley, if you can call him an admirer.'

'No one else?'

Our fair client seemed a little confused.

'Who was he?' asked Holmes.

'Oh, it may be a mere fancy of mine; but it has seemed to me sometimes that my employer, Mr Carruthers, takes a great deal of interest in me. We are thrown rather together. I play his accompaniments in the evening. He has never said anything. He is a perfect gentleman. But a girl always knows.'

'Ha!' Holmes looked grave. 'What does he do for a living?'

'He is a rich man.'

'No carriages or horses?'

'Well, at least he is fairly well-to-do. But he goes into the City two or three times a week. He is deeply interested in South African gold shares.'

'You will let me know any fresh development, Miss Smith. I am very busy just now, but I will find time to make some inquiries into your case. In the meantime, take no step without letting me know. Goodbye, and I trust that we shall have nothing but good news from you.'

'It is part of the settled order of Nature that such a girl should have followers,' said Holmes, as he pulled at his meditative pipe, 'but for choice not on bicycles in lonely country roads. Some secretive lover, beyond all doubt. But there are curious and suggestive details about the case, Watson.'

'That he should appear only at that point?'

'Exactly. Our first effort must be to find who are the tenants of Charlington Hall. Then, again, how about the connection between Carruthers and Woodley, since they appear to be men of such different types? How came they *both* to be so keen upon looking up Ralph Smith's relations? One more point. What sort of a *ménage* is it which pays double the market price for a governess, but does not keep a horse although six miles from the station? Odd, Watson – very odd.'

'You will go down?'

'No, my dear fellow, *you* will go down. This may be some trifling intrigue, and I cannot break my other important research for the sake of it. On Monday you will arrive early at Farnham; you will conceal yourself near Charlington Heath; you will observe these facts for yourself, and act as your own judgement advises. Then, having inquired as to the occupants of the Hall, you will come back to me and report. And now, Watson, not another word of the matter until we have a few solid stepping stones on which we may hope to get across to our solution.'

We had ascertained from the lady that she went down upon the Monday by the train which leaves Waterloo at 9.50, so I started early and caught the 9.13. At Farnham Station I had no difficulty in being directed to Charlington Heath. It was impossible to mistake the scene of the young lady's adventure, for the road runs between the open heath on one side, and an old yew hedge upon the other, surrounding a park which is studded with magnificent trees. There was a main gateway of lichen studded stone, each side-pillar surmounted by mouldering heraldic emblems; but besides this central carriage drive I observed several points where there were gaps in the hedge and paths leading through them. The house was invisible from the road, but the surroundings all spoke of gloom and decay.

The heath was covered with golden patches of

flowering gorse, gleaming magnificently in the light of the bright spring sunshine. Behind one of these clumps I took up my position, so as to command both the gateway of the Hall and a long stretch of the road upon either side. It had been deserted when I left it, but now I saw a cyclist riding down it from the opposite direction to that in which I had come. He was clad in a dark suit, and I saw that he had a black beard. On reaching the end of the Charlington grounds he sprang from his machine and led it through a gap in the hedge, disappearing from my view.

A quarter of an hour passed and then a Second cyclist appeared. This time it was the young lady coming from the station. I saw her look about her as she came to the Charlington hedge. An instant later the man emerged from his hiding place, sprang upon his bicycle, and followed her. In all the broad landscape those were the only moving figures, the graceful girl sitting very straight upon her machine and the man behind her bending low over his handle-bar, with a curiously furtive suggestion in every movement. She looked back at him and slowed her pace. He slowed also. She stopped. He at once stopped, too, keeping two hundred yards behind her. Her next movement was as unexpected as it was spirited. She suddenly whisked her wheels round and dashed straight at him! He was as quick as she, however, and darted off in desperate flight. Presently she came back up the road again, her head haughtily in the air, not deigning to take further notice of her silent attendant. He had turned also, and still kept his distance until the curve of the road hid them from my sight.

I remained in my hiding-place, and it was well that I did so, for presently the man reappeared, cycling slowly back. He turned in at the Hall gates and dismounted from his machine. For some minutes I could see him standing among the trees. His hands were raised, and he seemed to be settling his necktie. Then he mounted his bicycle and rode away from me down the drive towards the Hall. I ran across the heath and peered through the trees. Far away I could catch glimpses of the old grey building with its bristling Tudor chimneys, but the drive ran through a dense shrubbery, and I saw no more of my man.

However, it seemed to me that I had done a fairly good morning's work, and I walked back in high Spirits to Farnham. The local house agent could tell me nothing about Charlington Hall, and referred me to a well known firm in Pall Mall. There I halted on my way home, and met with courtesy from the representative. No, I could not have Charlington Hall for the Summer. I was just too late. It had been let about a month ago. Mr Williamson was the name of the tenant. He was a respectable elderly gentleman. The polite agent was afraid he could say no more, as the affairs of his clients were not matters which he could discuss.

Mr Sherlock Holmes listened with attention to the long report which I was able to present to him that evening, but it did not elicit that word of curt praise which I had hoped for and should have valued. On the contrary, his austere face was even more severe than usual as he commented upon the things that I had done and the things that I had not.

'Your hiding-place, my dear Watson, was very faulty. You should have been behind the hedge; then you would have had a close view of this interesting person. As it is you were some hundreds of yards away, and can tell me even less than Miss Smith. She thinks she does not know the man; I am convinced she does. Why, otherwise, should he be so desperately anxious that she should not get so near him as to see his features? You describe him as bending over the handle-bar. Concealment again, you see. You really have done remarkably badly. He returns to the house, and you want to find out who he is. You come to a London house agent!'

'What should I have done?' I cried, with some heat.

'Gone to the nearest public house. That is the centre of country gossip. They would have told you every name, from the master to the scullery-maid. Williamson! It conveys nothing to my mind. If he is an elderly man he is not this active cyclist who springs away from that athletic young lady's pursuit. What have we gained by your expedition?

The knowledge that the girl's story is true. I never doubted it. That there is a connection between the cyclist and the Hall. I never doubted that either. That the Hall is tenanted by Williamson. Who's the better for that? Well, well, my dear sir, don't look so depressed. We can do little more until next Saturday, and in the meantime I may make one or two inquiries myself.'

Next morning we had a note from Miss Smith, recounting shortly and accurately the very incidents which I had seen, but the pith of the letter lay in the postscript:

I am sure that you will respect my confidence, Mr Holmes, when I tell you that my place here has become difficult owing to the fact that my employer has proposed marriage to me. I am convinced that his feelings are most deep and most honourable. At the same time my promise is, of course, given. He took my refusal very seriously, but also very gently. You can understand, however, that the situation is a little strained.

'Our young friend seems to be getting into deep waters,' said Holmes thoughtfully, as he finished the letter. 'The case certainly presents more features of interest and more possibility of development than I had originally thought. I should be none the worse for a quiet, peaceful day in the country, and I am inclined to run down this afternoon and test one or two theories which I have formed.'

Holmes's quiet day in the country had a singular termination, for he arrived at Baker Street late in the evening with a cut lip and a discoloured lump upon his forehead, besides a general air of dissipation which would have made his own person the fitting object of a Scotland Yard investigation. He was immensely tickled by his own adventures, and laughed heartily as he recounted them.

'I get so little active exercise that it is always a treat,' said he. 'You are aware that I have some proficiency in the good old British sport of boxing. Occasionally it is of service. Today, for example, I should have come to very ignominious grief without it.'

I begged him to tell me what had occurred.

'I found that country pub which I had already recommended to your notice, and there I made my discreet inquiries. I was in the bar, and a garrulous landlord was giving me all that I wanted. Williamson is a white bearded man, and he lives alone with a small staff of servants at the Hall. There is some rumour that he is or has been a clergyman; but one or two incidents of his short residence at the Hall struck me as peculiarly un-ecclesiastical. I have already made some inquiries at a clerical agency, and they tell me that there *was* a man of that name in orders whose career has been a singularly dark one. The landlord further informed me that there are usually weekend visitors – "a warm lot, sir" – at the Hall, and especially one gentleman with a red moustache, Mr Woodley by name, who was always there. We had got as far as this when who should walk in but the gentleman himself, who had been drinking his beer in the taproom, and had heard the whole conversation. Who was I? What did I want? What did I mean by asking questions? He had a fine flow of language, and his adjectives were very vigorous. He ended a string of abuse by a vicious backhander, which I failed to entirely avoid. The next few minutes were delicious. It was a straight left against a slogging ruffian. I emerged as you see me. Mr Woodley went home in a cart. So ended my country trip, and it must be confessed that, however enjoyable, my day on the Surrey border has not been much more profitable than your own.'

The Thursday brought us another letter from our client:

You will not be surprised, Mr Holmes (said she), to hear that I am leaving Mr Carruthers' employment. Even the high pay cannot reconcile me to the discomforts of my situation. On Saturday I come up to town, and I do not intend to return. Mr Carruthers has got a trap, and so the dangers of the lonely road, if there ever were any dangers, are now over.

As to the special cause of my leaving, it is not merely the strained situation with Mr Carruthers, but it is the reappearance of that odious man, Mr Woodley. He was always hideous, but he looks more awful than ever now, for he appears to have had an accident and he is much disfigured. I saw him out of the window, but I am glad to say I did not meet him. He had a long talk with Mr Carruthers, who seemed much excited afterwards. Woodley must be staying in the neighbour-hood, for he did not sleep here, and yet I caught a glimpse of him again this morning slinking about in the shrubbery. I would sooner have a savage wild animal loose about the place. I loathe and fear him more than I can say. How *can* Mr Carruthers endure such a creature for a moment? However, all my troubles will be over on Saturday.

'So I trust, Watson, so I trust,' said Holmes gravely. 'There is some deep intrigue going on round that little woman, and it is our duty to see that no one molests her upon that last journey. I think, Watson, that we must spare time to run down together on Saturday morning, and make sure that this curious and inconclusive investigation has no untoward ending.'

I confess that I had not up to now taken a very serious view of the case, which had seemed to me rather grotesque and bizarre than dangerous. That a man should lie in wait for and follow a very handsome woman is no unheard-of thing, and if he had so little audacity that he not only dared not address her, but even fled from her approach, he was not a very formidable assailant. The ruffian Woodley was a very different person, but, except on the one occasion, he had not molested our client, and now he visited the house of Carruthers without intruding upon her presence. The man on the bicycle was doubtless a member of those weekend parties at the Hall of which the publican had spoken; but who he was or what he wanted was as obscure as ever. It was the severity of Holmes's manner and the fact that he slipped a revolver into his pocket before leaving our rooms which impressed me with the feeling that tragedy might prove to lurk behind this curious train of events.

A rainy night had been followed by a glorious morning, and the heath-covered countryside, with the glowing clumps of flowering gorse, seemed all the more beautiful to eyes which were weary of the duns and drabs and slate-greys of London. Holmes and I walked along the broad, sandy road inhaling the fresh morning air, and rejoicing in the music of the birds and the fresh breath of the spring. From a rise of the road on the shoulder of Crooksbury Hill we could see the grim Hall bristling out from amidst the ancient oaks, which, old as they were, were still younger than the building which they surrounded. Holmes pointed down the long tract of road which wound, a reddish-yellow band, between the brown of the heath and the budding green of the woods. Far away, a black dot, we could see a vehicle moving in our direction. Holmes gave an exclamation of impatience.

'I had given a margin of half an hour,' said he. 'If that is her trap she must be making for the earlier train. I fear, Watson, that she will be past Charlington before we can possibly meet her.'

From the instant that we passed the rise we could no longer see the vehicle, but we hastened onwards at such a pace that my sedentary life began to tell upon me, and I was compelled to fall behind. Holmes, however, was always in training, for he had inexhaustible stores of nervous energy upon which to draw. His springy step never slowed, until suddenly, when he was a hundred yards in front of me, he halted, and I saw him throw up his hand with a gesture of grief and despair. At the same instant an empty dog-cart, the horse cantering, the reins trailing, appeared round the curve of the road and rattled swiftly towards us.

'Too late, Watson; too late!' cried Holmes, as I ran panting to his side. 'Fool that I was not to allow for the earlier train! It's abduction, Watson – abduction! Murder! Heaven knows what! Block the road! Stop the horse! That's right. Now jump in, and let us see if I can repair the consequences of my own blunder.'

We had sprung into the dog-cart, and Holmes, after turning the horse, gave it a sharp cut with a whip, and we flew back along the road. As we turned the curve the whole stretch of road between the Hall and the heath was opened up. I grasped Holmes's arm.

'That's the man!' I gasped.

A solitary cyclist was coming towards us. His head was down and his shoulders rounded as he put every ounce of energy that he possessed on to the pedals. He was flying like a racer. Suddenly he raised his bearded face, saw us close to him, and pulled up, springing from his machine. That coal-black beard was in singular contrast to the pallor of his face, and his eyes were as bright as if he had a fever. He stared at us and at the dog-cart. Then a look of amazement came over his face.

'Halloa! Stop there!' he shouted, holding his bicycle to block our road. 'Where did you get that dog-cart? Pull up, man!' he yelled, drawing a pistol from his side pocket. 'Pull up, I say, or, by George, I'll put a bullet into your horse!'

Holmes threw the reins into my lap and sprang down from the cart.

'You're the man we want to see. Where is Miss Violet Smith?' he said in his quick, clear way.

'That's what I am asking you. You're in her dog-cart. You ought to know where she is.'

'We met the dog-cart on the road. There was no one in it. We drove back to help the young lady.'

'Good Lord! Good Lord! What shall I do?' cried the stranger, in an ecstasy of despair. 'They've got her, that hell-hound Woodley and the blackguard parson. Come, man, come, if you really are her friend. Stand by me and we'll save her, if I have to leave my carcass in Charlington Wood.'

He ran distractedly, his pistol in his hand, towards a gap in the hedge. Holmes followed him, and I, leaving the horse grazing beside the road, followed Holmes.

'This is where they came through,' said he, pointing to the marks of several feet upon the muddy path. 'Halloa! Stop a minute! Who's this in the bush?'

It was a young fellow about seventeen, dressed like an ostler, with leather cords and gaiters. He lay upon his back, his knees drawn up, a terrible cut upon his head. He was insensible, but alive. A glance at his wound told me that it had not penetrated the bone.

'That's Peter, the groom,' cried the stranger. 'He drove her. The beasts have pulled him off and clubbed him. Let him lie; we can't do him any good, but we may save her from the worst fate that can befall a woman.

We ran frantically down the path, which wound among the trees. We had reached the shrubbery which surrounded the house when Holmes pulled up.

'They didn't go to the house. Here are their marks on the left – here, beside the laurel bushes! Ah, I said so!'

As he spoke a woman's shrill scream – a scream which vibrated with a frenzy of horror – burst from the thick green clump of bushes in front of us. It ended suddenly on its highest note with a choke and gurgle.

'This way! This way! They are in the bowling alley,' cried the stranger, darting through the bushes. 'Ah, the cowardly dogs! Follow me, gentle-men! Too late! too late! by the living Jingo!'

We had broken suddenly into a lovely glade of green-sward surrounded by ancient trees. On the farther side of it, under the shadow of a mighty oak, there stood a singular group of three people. One was a woman, our client, drooping and faint, a handkerchief round her mouth. Opposite her stood a brutal, heavy-faced, red-moustached young man, his gaitered legs parted wide, one arm akimbo, the other waving a riding-crop, his whole attitude suggestive of a triumphant bravado. Be-tween them an elderly, grey-bearded man, wearing a short surplice over a light tweed suit, had evi-dently just completed the wedding service, for he pocketed his Prayer Book as we appeared, and slapped the sinister bridegroom upon the back in jovial congratulation.

'They're married!' I gasped.

'Come on!' cried our guide; 'come on!' He rushed across the glade, Holmes and I at his heels. As we approached, the lady staggered against the trunk of the tree for support. William-son, the ex-clergyman, bowed to us with mock politeness, and the bully Woodley advanced with a shout of brutal and exultant laughter.

'You can take your beard off, Bob,' said he. 'I know you right enough. Well, you and your pals have just come in time for me to be able to introduce you to Mrs Woodley.'

Our guide's answer was a singular one. He

snatched off the dark beard which had disguised him and threw it on the ground, disclosing a long, sallow, clean-shaven face below it. Then he raised his revolver and covered the young ruffian, who was advancing upon him with his dangerous riding-crop swinging in his hand.

'Yes,' said our ally, 'I *am* Bob Carruthers, and I'll see this woman righted if I have to swing for it. I told you what I'd do if you molested her, and, by the Lord, I'll be as good as my word!'

'You're too late. She's my wife!'

'No, she's your widow.'

His revolver cracked, and I saw the blood spurt from the front of Woodley's waistcoat. He spun round with a scream and fell upon his back, his hideous red face turning suddenly to a dreadful mottled pallor. The old man, still clad in his surplice, burst into such a string of foul oaths as I have never heard, and pulled out a revolver of his own, but before he could raise it he was looking down the barrel of Holmes's weapon.

'Enough of this,' said my friend coldly. 'Drop that pistol! Watson, pick it up! Hold it to his head! Thank you. You, Carruthers, give me that revolver. We'll have no more violence. Come, hand it over!'

'Who are you, then?'

'My name is Sherlock Holmes.'

'Good Lord!'

'You have heard of me, I see. I will represent the official police until their arrival. Here, you!'

he shouted to the frightened groom, who had appeared at the edge of the glade. 'Come here. Take this note as hard as you can ride to Farnham.' He scribbled a few words upon a leaf from his notebook. 'Give it to the superintendent at the police-station. Until he comes, I must detain you all under my personal custody.'

The strong, masterful personality of Holmes dominated the tragic scene, and all were equally puppets in his hands. Williamson and Carruthers found themselves carrying the wounded Woodley into the house, and I gave my arm to the frightened girl. The injured man was laid on his bed, and at Holmes's request I examined him. I carried my report to where he sat in the old tapestry-hung dining-room with his two prisoners before him.

'He will live,' said I.

'What!' cried Carruthers, springing out of his chair. 'I'll go upstairs and finish him first. Do you tell me that the girl, that angel, is to be tied to Roaring Jack Woodley for life?'

'You need not concern yourself about that,' said Holmes. 'There are two very good reasons why she should under no circumstances be his wife. In the first place, we are very safe in questioning Mr Williamson's right to solemnize a marriage.'

'I have been ordained,' cried the old rascal.

'And also unfrocked.'

'Once a clergyman, always a clergyman.'

'I think not. How about the licence?'

'We had a licence for the marriage. I have it here in my pocket.'

'Then you got it by a trick. But in any case a forced marriage is no marriage, but it is a very serious felony, as you will discover before you have finished. You'll have time to think the point out during the next ten years or so, unless I am mistaken. As to you, Carruthers, you would have done better to keep your pistol in your pocket.'

'I begin to think so, Mr Holmes; but when I thought of all the precaution I had taken to shield this girl – for I loved her, Mr Holmes, and it is the only time that ever I knew what love was – it fairly drove me mad to think that she was in the power of the greatest brute and bully in South Africa, a man whose name is a holy terror from Kimberley to Johannesburg. Why, Mr Holmes, you'll hardly believe it, but ever since that girl has been in my employment I never once let her go past this house, where I knew these rascals were lurking, without following her on my bicycle just to see that she came to no harm. I kept my distance from her, and I wore a beard so that she should not recognize me, for she is a good and high-spirited girl, and she wouldn't have stayed in my employment long if she had thought that I was following her about the country roads.'

'Why didn't you tell her of her danger?'

'Because then, again, she would have left me, and I couldn't bear to face that. Even if she couldn't love me it was a great deal to me just to see her dainty form about the house, and to hear the sound of her voice.'

'Well,' said I, 'you call that love, Mr Carruthers, but I should call it selfishness.'

'Maybe the two things go together. Anyhow, I couldn't let her go. Besides, with this crowd about, it was well that she should have someone near to look after her. Then when the cable came I knew they were bound to make a move.'

'What cable?'

Carruthers took a telegram from his pocket.

'That's it!' said he. It was short and concise:

THE OLD MAN IS DEAD

'Hum!' said Holmes. 'I think I see how things worked, and I can understand how this message would, as you say, bring them to a head. But while we wait, you might tell me what you can.'

The old reprobate with the surplice burst into a volley of bad language.

'By Heaven,' said he, 'if you squeal on us, Bob Carruthers, I'll serve you as you served Jack Woodley! You can bleat about the girl to your heart's content, for that's your own affair, but if you round on your pals to this plain-clothes copper it will be the worst day's work that ever you did.'

'Your reverence need not be excited,' said Holmes, lighting a cigarette. 'The case is clear enough against you, and all I ask is a few details for my private curiosity. However, if there's any difficulty in your telling me I'll do the talking, and then you will see how far you have a chance of holding back your secrets. In the first place, three of you came from South Africa on this game – you, Williamson, you, Carruthers, and Woodley.'

'Lie number one,' said the old man; 'I never saw either of them until two months ago, and I have never been in Africa in my life, so you can put that in your pipe and smoke it, Mr Busybody Holmes!'

'What he says is true,' said Carruthers.

'Well, well, two of you came over. His reverence is our own home-made article. You had known Ralph Smith in South Africa. You had reason to believe he would not live long. You found out that his niece would inherit his fortune. How's that – eh?'

Carruthers nodded, and Williamson swore.

'She was next-of-kin, no doubt, and you were aware that the old fellow would make no will.'

'Couldn't read or write,' said Carruthers.

'So you came over, the two of you, and hunted up the girl. The idea was that one of you was to marry her, and the other have a share of the plunder. For some reason Woodley was chosen as the husband. Why was that?'

'We played cards for her on the voyage. He won.'

'I see. You got the young lady into your service, and there Woodley was to do the courting. She recognized the drunken brute that he was, and would have nothing to do with him. Meanwhile, your arrangement was rather upset by the fact that you had yourself fallen in love with the lady. You could no longer bear the idea of this ruffian owning her.'

'No, by George, I couldn't!'

'There was a quarrel between you. He left you in a rage, and began to make his own plans independently of you.

'It strikes me, Williamson, there isn't very much that we can tell this gentleman,' cried Carruthers, with a bitter laugh. 'Yes, we quarrelled, and he knocked me down. I am level with him on that, anyhow. Then I lost sight of him. That was when he picked up with this outcast padre here. I found that they had set up housekeeping together at this place on the line that she had to pass the station. I kept my eye on her after that, for I knew there was some devilry in the wind. I saw them from time to time, for I was anxious to know what they were after. Two days ago Woodley came up to my house with this cable, which showed that Ralph Smith was dead. He asked me if I would stand by the bargain. I said I would not. He asked me if I would marry the girl myself and give him a share. I said I would willingly do so, but that she would not have me. He said, "Let us get her married first, and after a week or two she may see things a bit different." I said I would have nothing to do with violence. So he went off cursing, like the foul-mouthed blackguard that he was, and swearing that he would have her yet. She was leaving me this weekend, and I had got a trap to take her to the station, but I was so uneasy in my mind that I followed her on my bicycle. She had got a start, however, and before I could catch her the mischief was done. The first thing I knew about it was when I saw you two gentlemen driving back in her dog-cart.'

Holmes rose and tossed the end of his cigarette into the grate. 'I have been very obtuse, Watson,' said he. 'When in your report you said that you had seen the cyclist as you thought arrange his necktie in the shrubbery, that alone should have told me all. However, we may congratulate ourselves upon a curious and in some respects a unique case. I perceive three of the county constabulary in the drive, and I am glad to see that the little ostler is able to keep pace with them; so it is likely that neither he nor the interesting bridegroom will be permanently damaged by their morning's adventures. I think, Watson, that in your medical capacity you might wait upon Miss Smith and tell her that if she is sufficiently recovered we shall be happy to escort her to her mother's home. If she is not quite convalescent you will find that a hint that we were about to telegraph to a young electrician in the Midlands would probably complete the cure. As to you, Mr Carruthers, I think that you have done what you could to make amends for your share in an evil plot. There is my card, sir, and if my evidence can be of help to you in your trial it shall be at your disposal.'

In the whirl of our incessant activity it has often been difficult for me, as the reader has probably observed, to round off my narratives, and to give those final details which the curious might expect. Each case has been the prelude to another, and the crisis once over, the actors have passed for ever out of our busy lives. I find, however, a short note at the end of my manuscripts dealing with this case, in which I have put it upon record that Miss Violet Smith did indeed inherit a large fortune, and that she is now the wife of Cyril Morton, the senior partner of Morton and Kennedy, the famous Westminster electricians. Williamson and Woodley were both tried for abduction and assault, the former getting seven years and the latter ten. Of the fate of Carruthers I have no record, but I am sure that his assault was not viewed very gravely by the Court, since Woodley had the reputation of being a most dangerous ruffian, and I think that a few months were sufficient to satisfy the demands of justice.

CHARLES AUGUSTUS MILVERTON

It is years since the incidents of which I speak took place, and yet it is with diffidence that I allude to them. For a long time, even with the utmost discretion and reticence, it would have been impossible to make the facts public; but now the principal person concerned is beyond the reach of human law, and with due suppression the story may be told in such fashion as to injure no one. It records an absolutely unique experience in the career both of Mr Sherlock Holmes and of myself. The reader will excuse me if I conceal the date or any other fact by which he might trace the actual occurrence.

We had been out for one of our evening rambles, Holmes and I, and had returned about six o'clock on a cold, frosty winter's evening. As Holmes turned up the lamp the light fell upon a card on the table. He glanced at it, and then, with an ejaculation of disgust, threw it on the floor. I picked it up and read:

CHARLES AUGUSTUS MILVERTON
APPLEDORE TOWERS
HAMPSTEAD
Agent

'Who is he?' I asked.

'The worst man in London,' Holmes answered, as he sat down and stretched his legs before the fire. 'Is anything on the back of the card?'

I turned it over.

'Will call at 6.30 – C. A. M.,' I read.

'Hum! He's about due. Do you feel a creeping, shrinking sensation, Watson, when you stand before the serpents in the Zoo and see the slithery, gliding, venomous creatures, with their deadly eyes and wicked, flattened faces? Well, that's how Milverton impresses me. I've had to do with fifty murderers in my career, but the worst of them never gave me the repulsion which I have for this fellow. And yet I can't get out of doing business with him – indeed, he is here at my invitation.'

'But who is he?'

'I'll tell you, Watson. He is the king of all the blackmailers. Heaven help the man, and still more the woman, whose secret and reputation come into the power of Milverton. With a smiling face and a heart of marble he will squeeze and squeeze until he has drained them dry. The fellow is a genius in his way, and would have made his mark in some more savoury trade. His method is as follows: he allows it to be known that he is prepared to pay very high sums for letters which compromise people of wealth or position. He receives these wares not only from treacherous valets or maids, but frequently from genteel ruffians who have gained the confidence and affection of trusting women. He deals with no niggard hand. I happen to know that he paid seven hundred pounds to a footman for a note two lines in length, and that the ruin of a noble family was the result. Everything which is in the market goes to Milverton, and there are hundreds in this great city who turn white at his name. No one knows where his grip may fall, for he is far too rich and far too cunning to work from hand to mouth. He will hold a card back for years in order to play it at the moment when the stake is best worth winning. I have said that he is the worst man in London, and I would ask you how could one compare the ruffian who in hot blood bludgeons his mate with this man, who methodically and at his leisure tortures the soul and wrings the nerves in order to add to his already swollen money-bags?'

I had seldom heard my friend speak with such intensity of feeling.

'But surely,' said I, 'the fellow must be within the grasp of the law?'

'Technically, no doubt, but practically not. What would it profit a woman, for example, to get him a few months' imprisonment if her own ruin must immediately follow? His victims dare not hit back. If ever he blackmailed an innocent person, then, indeed, we should have him; but he is as cunning as the Evil One. No, no; we must find other ways to fight him.'

'And why is he here?'

'Because an illustrious client has placed her

piteous case in my hands. It is the Lady Eva Brackwell, the most beautiful *débutante* of last season. She is to be married in a fortnight to the Earl of Dovercourt. This fiend has several imprudent letters – imprudent, Watson, nothing worse – which were written to an impecunious young squire in the country. They would suffice to break off the match. Milverton will send the letters to the earl unless a large sum of money is paid him. I have been commissioned to meet him, and – to make the best terms I can.'

At that instant there was a clatter and a rattle in the street below. Looking down I saw a stately carriage and pair, the brilliant lamps gleaming on the glossy haunches of the noble chestnuts. A footman opened the door, and a small, stout man in a shaggy astrakhan overcoat descended. A minute later he was in the room.

Charles Augustus Milverton was a man of fifty, with a large, intellectual head, a round, plump, hairless face, a perpetual frozen smile, and two keen grey eyes, which gleamed brightly from behind broad, golden-rimmed glasses. There was something of Mr Pickwick's benevolence in his appearance, marred only by the insincerity of the fixed smile and by the hard glitter of those restless and penetrating eyes. His voice was as smooth and suave as his countenance, as he advanced with a plump little hand extended, murmuring his regret for having missed us at his first visit.

Holmes disregarded the outstretched hand and

looked at him with a face of granite. Milverton's smile broadened; he shrugged his shoulders, removed his overcoat, folded it with great deliberation over the back of a chair, and then took a seat.

'This gentleman,' said he, with a wave in my direction. 'Is it discreet? Is it right?'

'Dr Watson is my friend and partner.'

'Very good, Mr Holmes. It is only in your client's interests that I protested. The matter is so very delicate –'

'Dr Watson has already heard of it.'

'Then we can proceed to business. You say that you are acting for Lady Eva. Has she empowered you to accept my terms?'

'What are your terms?'

'Seven thousand pounds.'

'And the alternative?'

'My dear sir, it is painful to me to discuss it; but if the money is not paid on the 14th there certainly will be no marriage on the 18th.' His insufferable smile was more complacent than ever. Holmes thought for a little.

'You appear to me,' he said at last, 'to be taking matters too much for granted. I am, of course, familiar with the contents of these letters. My client will certainly do what I may advise. I shall counsel her to tell her future husband the whole story and to trust to his generosity.'

Milverton chuckled.

'You evidently do not know the earl,' said he.

From the baffled look upon Holmes's face I could clearly see that he did.

'What harm is there in the letters?' he asked.

'They are sprightly – very sprightly,' Milverton answered. 'The lady was a charming correspondent. But I can assure you that the Earl of Dovercourt would fail to appreciate them. However, since you think otherwise, we will let it rest at that. It is purely a matter of business. If you think that it is in the best interests of your client that these letters should be placed in the hands of the earl, then you would indeed be foolish to pay so large a sum of money to regain them.' He rose and seized his astrakhan coat.

Holmes was grey with anger and mortification.

'Wait a little,' he said. 'You go too fast. We would certainly make every effort to avoid scandal in so delicate a matter.'

Milverton relapsed into his chair.

'I was sure that you would see it in that light,' he purred.

'At the same time,' Holmes continued, 'Lady Eva is not a wealthy woman. I assure you that two thousand pounds would be a drain upon her resources, and that the sum you name is utterly beyond her power. I beg, therefore, that you will moderate your demands, and that you will return the letters at the price I indicate, which is, I assure you, the highest that you can get.'

Milverton's smile broadened and his eyes twinkled humorously.

'I am aware that what you say is true about the lady's resources,' said he. 'At the same time, you must admit that the occasion of a lady's marriage is a very suitable time for her friends and relatives to make some little effort upon her behalf. They may hesitate as to an acceptable wedding present. Let me assure them that this little bundle of letters would give more joy than all the candelabra and butter-dishes in London.'

'It is impossible,' said Holmes.

'Dear me, dear me, how unfortunate!' cried Milverton, taking out a bulky pocket-book. 'I cannot help thinking that ladies are ill-advised in not making an effort. Look at this!' He held up a little note with a coat-of-arms upon the envelope. 'That belongs to – well, perhaps it is hardly fair to tell the name until tomorrow morning. But at that time it will be in the hands of the lady's husband. And all because she will not find a beggarly sum which she could get in an hour by turning her diamonds into paste. It *is* such a pity. Now, you remember the sudden end of the engagement be-tween the Honourable Miss Miles and Colonel Dorking? Only two days before the wedding there was a paragraph in the *Morning Post* to say that it was all off. And why? It is almost incredible, but the absurd sum of twelve hundred pounds would have settled the whole question. Is it not pitiful? And there I find you, a man of sense, boggling about terms when your client's future and honour are at stake. You surprise me, Mr Holmes.'

'What I say is true,' Mr Holmes answered. 'The money cannot be found. Surely it is better for you to take the substantial sum which I offer than to ruin this woman's career, which can profit you in no way?'

'There you make a mistake, Mr Holmes. An exposure would profit me indirectly to a considerable extent. I have eight or ten similar cases maturing. If it was circulated among them that I had made a severe example of the Lady Eva I should find all of them much more open to reason. You see my point?'

Holmes sprang from his chair.

'Get behind him, Watson. Don't let him out! Now, sir, let us see the contents of that notebook.'

Milverton had glided as quick as a rat to the side of the room, and stood with his back against the wall.

'Mr Holmes, Mr Holmes!' he said, turning the front of his coat and exhibiting the butt of a large revolver, which projected from the inside pocket. 'I have been expecting you to do something original. This has been done so often, and what good has ever come from it? I assure you that I am armed to the teeth, and I am perfectly prepared to use my weapon, knowing that the law will support me. Besides, your supposition that I would bring the letters here in a notebook is entirely mistaken. I would do nothing so foolish. And now, gentlemen, I have one or two little interviews this evening, and it is a long drive to Hampstead.' He stepped forward, took up his coat, laid his hand on his revolver, and turned to the door. I picked up a chair, but Holmes shook his head, and I laid it down again. With a bow, a smile, and a twinkle Milverton was out of the room, and a few moments after we heard the slam of the carriage door and the rattle of the wheels as he drove away.

Holmes sat motionless by the fire, his hands buried deep in his trouser pockets, his chin sunk upon his breast, his eyes fixed upon the glowing embers. For half an hour he was silent and still. Then, with the gesture of a man who has taken his decision, he sprang to his feet and passed into his bedroom. A little later a rakish young workman with a goatee beard and a swagger lit his clay pipe at the lamp before descending into the street. 'I'll be back some time, Watson,' said he, and vanished into the night. I understood that he had opened his campaign against Charles Augustus Milverton; but I little dreamed the strange shape which that campaign was destined to take.

For some days Holmes came and went at all hours in this attire, but beyond a remark that his time was spent at Hampstead, and that it was not wasted, I knew nothing of what he was doing. At last, however, on a wild, tempestuous evening, when the wind screamed and rattled against the windows, he returned from his last expedition, and, having removed his disguise, he sat before the fire and laughed heartily in his silent, inward fashion.

'You would not call me a marrying man, Watson?'

'No, indeed!'

'You will be interested to hear that I am engaged.'

'My dear fellow! I congrat –'

'To Milverton's housemaid.'

'Good heavens, Holmes!'

'I wanted information, Watson.'

'Surely you have gone too far?'

'It was a most necessary step. I am a plumber with a rising business, Escott by name. I have walked out with her each evening, and I have talked with her. Good heavens, those talks! However, I have got all I wanted. I know Milverton's house as I know the palm of my hand.'

'But the girl, Holmes?'

He shrugged his shoulders.

'You can't help it, my dear Watson. You must play your cards as best you can when such a stake is on the table. However, I rejoice to say that I have a hated rival who will certainly cut me out the instant that my back is turned. What a splendid night it is!'

'You like this weather?'

'It suits my purpose. Watson, I mean to burgle Milverton's house tonight.'

I had a catching of the breath, and my skin went cold at the words, which were slowly uttered in a tone of concentrated resolution. As a flash of lightning in the night shows up in an instant every detail of a wide landscape, so at one glance I seemed to see every possible result of such an action – the detection, the capture, the honoured career ending in irreparable failure and disgrace, my friend himself lying at the mercy of the odious Milverton.

'For Heaven's sake, Holmes, think what you are doing!' I cried.

'My dear fellow, I have given it every consideration. I am never precipitate in my actions, nor would I adopt so energetic and indeed so dangerous a course if any other were possible. Let us look at the matter clearly and fairly. I suppose that you will admit that the action is morally justifiable, though technically criminal. To burgle his house is no more than to forcibly take his pocket-book – an action in which you were prepared to aid me.

I turned it over in my mind.

'Yes,' I said; 'it is morally justifiable so long as our object is to take no articles save those which are used for an illegal purpose.'

'Exactly. Since it is morally justifiable, I have only to consider the question of personal risk. Surely a gentleman should not lay much stress upon this when a lady is in most desperate need of his help?'

'You will be in such a false position.'

'Well, that is part of the risk. There is no other possible way of regaining these letters. The unfortunate lady has not the money, and there are none of her people in whom she could confide. Tomorrow is the last day of grace, and unless we can get the letters tonight this villain will be as good as his word, and will bring about her ruin. I must, therefore, abandon my client to her fate, or I must play this last card. Between ourselves, Watson, it's a Sporting duel between this fellow Milverton and me. He had, as you saw, the best of the first exchanges, but my self-respect and my reputation are concerned to fight it to a finish.'

'Well, I don't like it; but I suppose it must be,' said I. 'When do we start?'

'You are not coming.'

'Then you are not going,' said I. 'I give you my word of honour – and I never broke it in my life – that I will take a cab straight to the police-station and give you away unless you let me share this adventure with you.'

'You can't help me.'

'How do you know that? You can't tell what may happen. Anyway, my resolution is taken. Other people besides you have self-respect and even reputations.'

Holmes had looked annoyed, but his brow cleared, and he clapped me on the shoulder.

'Well, well, my dear fellow, be it so. We have shared the same room for some years, and it would be amusing if we ended by sharing the same cell. You know, Watson, I don't mind confessing to you that I have always had an idea that I would have made a highly efficient criminal.

This is the chance of my lifetime in that direction. See here!' He took a neat little leather case out of a drawer, and opening it he exhibited a number of shining instruments. 'This is a first-class, up-to-date burgling kit, with nickel-plated jemmy, diamond-tipped glass cutter, adaptable keys, and every modern improvement which the march of civilization demands. Here, too, is my dark lantern. Everything is in order. Have you a pair of silent shoes?'

'I have rubber-soled tennis shoes.'

'Excellent. And a mask?'

'I can make a couple out of black silk.'

'I can see that you have a strong natural turn for this sort of thing. Very good; so you make the masks. We shall have some cold supper before we start. It is now nine-thirty. At eleven we shall drive as far as Church Row. It is a quarter of an hour's walk from there to Appledore Towers. We shall be at work before midnight. Milverton is a heavy sleeper, and retires punctually at ten-thirty. With any luck we should be back here by two, with the Lady Eva's letters in my pocket.'

Holmes and I put on our dress-clothes, so that we might appear to be two theatre-goers homeward bound. In Oxford Street we picked up a hansom and drove to an address in Hampstead. Here we paid off our cab, and with our greatcoats buttoned up – for it was bitterly cold, and the wind seemed to blow through us – we walked along the edge of the Heath.

'It's a business that needs delicate treatment,' said Holmes. 'These documents are contained in a safe in the fellow's study, and the study is the ante-room of his bedchamber. On the other hand, like all these stout, little men who do themselves well, he is a plethoric sleeper. Agatha – that's my fiancée – says it is a joke in the servants' hall that it's impossible to wake the master. He has a secretary who is devoted to his interests and never budges from the study all day. That's why we are going at night. Then he has a beast of a dog which roams the garden. I met Agatha late the last two evenings, and she locks the brute up so as to give me a clear run. This is the house, this big one in its own grounds. Through the gate – now to the right among the laurels. We might put on our masks here, I think. You see, there is not a glimmer of light in any of the windows, and everything is working splendidly.'

With our black silk face-coverings, which turned us into two of the most truculent figures in London, we stole up to the silent, gloomy house. A sort of tiled veranda extended along one side of it, lined by several windows and two doors.

'That's his bedroom,' Holmes whispered. 'This door opens straight into the study. It would suit us best, but it is bolted as well as locked, and we should make too much noise getting in. Come round here. There's a greenhouse which opens into the drawing-room.'

The place was locked, but Holmes removed a

circle of glass and turned the key from the inside. An instant afterwards he had closed the door behind us, and we had become felons in the eyes of the law. The thick warm air of the conservatory and the rich, choking fragrance of exotic plants took us by the throat. He seized my hand in the darkness and led me swiftly past banks of shrubs which brushed against our faces. Holmes had re-markable powers, carefully cultivated, of seeing in the dark. Still holding my hand in one of his, he opened a door, and I was vaguely conscious that we had entered a large room in which a cigar had been smoked not long before. He felt his way among the furniture, opened another door, and closed it behind us. Putting out my hand I felt several coats hanging from the wall, and I under-stood that I was in a passage. We passed along it, and Holmes very gently opened a door upon the right-hand side. Something rushed out at us, and my heart sprang into my mouth, but I could have laughed when I realized that it was the cat. A fire was burning in this new room, and again the air was heavy with tobacco smoke. Holmes entered on tiptoe, waited for me to follow, and then very gently closed the door. We were in Milverton's study, and a *portière* at the farther side showed the entrance to his bedroom.

It was a good fire, and the room was illuminated by it. Near the door I saw the gleam of an elec-tric switch, but it was unnecessary, even if it had been safe, to turn it on. At one side of the fireplace was a heavy curtain, which covered the bay window we had seen from outside. On the other side was the door which communicated with the veranda. A desk stood in the centre, with a turning chair of shining red leather. Opposite was a large bookcase, with a marble bust of Athene on the top. In the corner between the bookcase and the wall there stood a tall green safe, the firelight flashing back from the polished brass knobs upon its face. Holmes stole across and looked at it. Then he crept to the door of the bedroom, and stood with slanting head listening intently. No sound came from within. Meanwhile it had struck me that it would be wise to secure our retreat through the outer door, so I examined it. To my amazement it was neither locked nor bolted! I touched Holmes on the arm, and he turned his masked face in that direction. I saw him start, and he was evidently as surprised as I.

'I don't like it,' he whispered, putting his lips to my very ear. 'I can't quite make it out. Anyhow, we have no time to lose.'

'Can I do anything?'

'Yes; stand by the door. If you hear anyone come, bolt it on the inside, and we can get away as we came. If they come the other way, we can get through the door if our job is done, or hide behind these window curtains if it is not. Do you understand?'

I nodded and stood by the door. My first feeling

of fear had passed away, and I thrilled now with a keener zest than I had ever enjoyed when we were the defenders of the law instead of its defiers. The high object of our mission, the consciousness that it was unselfish and chivalrous, the villainous character of our opponent, all added to the sporting interest of the adventure. Far from feeling guilty, I rejoiced and exulted in our dangers. With a glow of admiration I watched Holmes unrolling his case of instruments and choosing his tool with the calm, scientific accuracy of a surgeon who performs a delicate operation. I knew that the opening of safes was a particular hobby with him, and I understood the joy which it gave him to be confronted with this green and gold monster, the dragon which held in its maw the reputations of many fair ladies. Turning up the cuffs of his dress-coat – he had placed his overcoat on a chair – Holmes laid out two drills, a jemmy, and several skeleton keys. I stood at the centre door with my eyes glancing at each of the others, ready for any emergency; though, indeed, my plans were somewhat vague as to what I should do if we were interrupted. For half an hour Holmes worked with concentrated energy, laying down one tool, picking up another, handling each with the strength and delicacy of the trained mechanic. Finally I heard a click, the broad green door swung open, and inside I had a glimpse of a number of paper packets, each tied, sealed, and inscribed. Holmes picked one out, but it was hard to read by the flickering fire, and he drew out his little dark lantern, for it was too dangerous, with Milverton in the next room, to switch on the electric light. Suddenly I saw him halt, listen intently, and then in an instant he had swung the door of the safe to, picked up his coat, stuffed his tools into the pockets, and darted behind the window curtain, motioning me to do the same.

It was only when I had joined him there that I heard what had alarmed his quicker senses. There was a noise somewhere within the house. A door slammed in the distance. Then a confused, dull murmur broke itself into the measured thud of heavy footsteps rapidly approaching. They were in the passage outside the room. They paused at the door. The door opened. There was a sharp snick as the electric light was turned on. The door closed once more, and the pungent reek of a strong cigar was borne to our nostrils. Then the footsteps continued backwards and forwards, backwards and forwards, within a few yards of us. Finally, there was a creak from a chair, and the footsteps ceased. Then a key clicked in a lock, and I heard the rustle of papers. So far I had not dared to look out, but now I gently parted the division of the curtains in front of me and peeped through. From the pressure of Holmes's shoulder against mine I knew that he was sharing my observations. Right in front of us, and almost within our reach, was the broad, rounded back of Milverton. It was evident that we had entirely miscalculated his movements, that he had never been to his bed-room, but that he had been sitting up in some smoking or billiard-room in the farther wing of the house, the windows of which we had not seen. His broad, grizzled head, with its shining patch of baldness, was in the immediate fore-ground of our vision. He was leaning far back in the red leather chair, his legs outstretched, a long black cigar projecting at an angle from his mouth. He wore a semi-military smoking-jacket, claret-coloured, with a black velvet collar. In his hand he held a long legal document, which he was reading in an indolent fashion, blowing rings of tobacco smoke from his lips as he did so. There was no promise of a speedy departure in his com-posed bearing and his comfortable attitude.

I felt Holmes's hand steal into mine and give me a reassuring shake, as if to say that the situation was within his powers, and that he was easy in his mind. I was not sure whether he had seen what was only too obvious from my position – that the door of the safe was imperfectly closed, and that Milverton might at any moment observe it. In my own mind I had determined that if I were sure, from the rigidity of his gaze, that it had caught his eye, I would at once spring out, throw my great-coat over his head, pinion him, and leave the rest to Holmes. But Milverton never looked up. He was languidly interested by the papers in his hand, and page after page was turned as he followed the argument of the lawyer. At least, I thought, when he has finished the document and the cigar he will go to his room; but before he had reached the end of either there came a remarkable development which turned our thoughts into quite another channel.

Several times I had observed that Milverton looked at his watch, and once he had risen and sat down again, with a gesture of impatience. The idea, however, that he might have an appointment at so strange an hour never occurred to me until a faint sound reached my ears from the veranda outside. Milverton dropped his papers and sat rigid in his chair. The sound was repeated, and then there came a gentle tap at the door. Milverton rose and opened it.

'Well,' said he curtly, 'you are nearly half an hour late.'

So this was the explanation of the unlocked door and of the nocturnal vigil of Milverton. There was the gentle rustle of a woman's dress. I had closed the slit between the curtains as Milverton's face turned in our direction, but now I ventured very carefully to open it once more. He had resumed his seat, the cigar still projecting at an insolent angle from the corner of his mouth. In front of him, in the full glare of the electric light, there stood a tall, slim, dark woman, a veil over her face, a mantle drawn round her chin. Her breath came quick and fast and every inch of the lithe figure was quivering with strong emotion.

'Well,' said Milverton, 'you've made me lose a

good night's rest, my dear. I hope you'll prove worth it. You couldn't come any other time – eh?'

The woman shook her head.

'Well, if you couldn't you couldn't. If the countess is a hard mistress you have your chance to get level with her now. Bless the girl, what are you shivering about? That's right! Pull yourself together! Now, let us get down to business.' He took a note from the drawer of his desk. 'You say that you have five letters which compromise the Countess d'Albert. You want to sell them. I want to buy them. So far so good. It only remains to fix a price. I should want to inspect the letters, of course. If they are really good specimens – Great heavens, is it you?'

The woman without a word had raised her veil and dropped the mantle from her chin. It was a dark, handsome, clear-cut face which confronted Milverton, a face with a curved nose, strong, dark eyebrows, shading hard, glittering eyes, and a straight, thin-lipped mouth set in a dangerous smile.

'It is I,' she said – 'the woman whose life you have ruined.'

Milverton laughed, but fear vibrated in his voice. 'You were so very obstinate,' said he. 'Why did you drive me to such extremities? I assure you I wouldn't hurt a fly of my own accord, but every man has his business, and what was I to do? I put the price well within your means. You would not pay.'

'So you sent the letters to my husband, and he – the noblest gentleman that ever lived, a man whose boots I was never worthy to lace – he broke his gallant heart and died. You remember that last night when I came through that door I begged and prayed you for mercy, and you laughed in my face as you are trying to laugh now, only your coward heart cannot keep your lips from twitching? Yes; you never thought to see me here again, but it was that night which taught me how I could meet you face to face, and alone. Well, Charles Milverton, what have you to say?'

'Don't imagine that you can bully me,' said he, rising to his feet. 'I have only to raise my voice, and I could call my servants and have you arrested. But I will make allowance for your natural anger. Leave the room at once as you came, and I will say no more.'

The woman stood with her hand buried in her bosom, and the same deadly smile on her thin lips.

'You will ruin no more lives as you have ruined mine. You will wring no more hearts as you wrung mine. I will free the world of a poisonous thing. Take that, you hound, and that! – and that! – and that! – and that!'

She had drawn a little gleaming revolver, and emptied barrel after barrel into Milverton's body, the muzzle within two feet of his shirt-front. He shrank away, and then fell forward upon the table, coughing furiously and clawing among the papers. Then he staggered to his feet, received another shot, and rolled upon the floor. 'You've done me,' he cried, and lay still. The woman looked at him intently and ground her heel into his upturned face. She looked again, but there was no sound or movement. I heard a sharp rustle, the night air blew into the heated room, and the avenger was gone.

No interference upon our part could have saved the man from his fate; but as the woman poured bullet after bullet into Milverton's shrinking body, I was about to spring out, when I felt Holmes's cold, strong grasp upon my wrist. I understood the whole argument of that firm, restraining grip – that it was no affair of ours; that justice had overtaken a villain; that we had our own duties and our own objects which were not to be lost sight of. But hardly had the woman rushed from the room when Holmes, with swift, silent steps, was over at the other door. He turned the key in the lock. At the same instant we heard voices in the house and the sound of hurrying feet. The revolver shots had roused the household. With perfect coolness Holmes slipped across to the safe, filled his two arms with bundles of letters, and poured them all into the fire. Again and again he did it, until the safe was empty. Someone turned the handle and beat upon the outside of the door. Holmes looked swiftly round. The letter which had been the messenger of death for Milverton lay, all mottled with his blood, upon the table. Holmes tossed it in among the blazing papers. Then he drew the key from the outer door, passed through after me, and locked it on the outside. 'This way, Watson,' said he; 'we can scale the garden wall in this direction.'

I could not have believed that an alarm could have spread so swiftly. Looking back, the huge house was one blaze of light. The front door was open, and figures were rushing down the drive. The whole garden was alive with people, and one fellow raised a view-halloa as we emerged from the veranda and followed hard at our heels. Holmes seemed to know the ground perfectly, and he threaded his way swiftly among a plantation of small trees, I close at his heels, and our foremost pursuer panting behind us. It was a six-foot wall which barred our path, but he sprang to the top and over. As I did the same I felt the hand of the man behind me grab my ankle; but I kicked myself free, and scrambled over a glass-strewn coping. I fell upon my face among some bushes; but Holmes had me on my feet in an instant, and together we dashed away across the huge expanse of Hampstead Heath. We had run two miles, I suppose, before Holmes at last halted and listened intently. All was absolutely silent behind us. We had shaken off our pursuers, and were safe.

We had breakfasted and were smoking our morning pipe, on the day after the remarkable experience which I have recorded, when Mr Lestrade, of Scotland Yard, very solemn and impressive, was ushered into our modest sitting-room.

'Good morning, Mr Holmes,' said he – 'good morning. May I ask if you are very busy just now?'

'Not too busy to listen to you.'

'I thought that, perhaps, if you had nothing particular on hand, you might care to assist us in a most remarkable case which occurred only last night at Hampstead.'

'Dear me!' said Holmes. 'What was that?'

'A murder – a most dramatic and remarkable murder. I know how keen you are upon these things, and I would take it as a great favour if you would step down to Appledore Towers and give us the benefit of your advice. It is no ordinary crime. We have had our eyes upon this Mr Milverton for some time, and, between ourselves, he was a bit of a villain. He is known to have held papers which he used for blackmailing purposes. These papers have all been burned by the murderers. No article of value was taken, as it is probable that the criminals were men of good position, whose sole object was to prevent social exposure.'

'Criminals!' exclaimed Holmes. 'Plural!'

'Yes, there were two of them. They were, as nearly as possible, captured red-handed. We have their footmarks, we have their description; it's ten to one that we trace them. The first fellow was a bit too active, but the second was caught by the under-gardener, and only got away after a struggle. He was a middle-sized, strongly built man – square jaw, thick neck, moustache, a mask over his eyes.'

'That's rather vague,' said Sherlock Holmes. 'Why, it might be a description of Watson!'

'It's true,' said the inspector, with much amusement. 'It might be a description of Watson.'

'Well, I am afraid I can't help you, Lestrade,' said Holmes. 'The fact is that I knew this fellow Milverton, that I considered him one of the most dangerous men in London, and that I think there are certain crimes which the law cannot touch, and which therefore, to some extent, justify private revenge. No, it's no use arguing. I have made up my mind. My sympathies are with the criminals rather than with the victim, and I will not handle this case.'

Holmes had not said one word to me about the tragedy which we had witnessed, but I observed all the morning that he was in the most thoughtful mood, and he gave me the impression, from his vacant eyes and his abstracted manner, of a man who is striving to recall something to his memory. We were in the middle of our lunch, when he suddenly sprang to his feet. 'By Jove, Watson! I've got it!' he cried. 'Take your hat! Come with me!' He hurried at his top speed down Baker Street and along Oxford Street, until we had almost reached Regent Circus. Here on the left hand there stands a shop window filled with photographs of the celebrities and beauties of the day. Holmes's eyes fixed themselves upon one of them, and following his gaze I saw the picture of a regal and stately lady in Court dress, with a high diamond tiara upon her noble head. I looked at that delicately curved nose, at the marked eyebrows, at the straight mouth, and the strong little chin beneath it. Then I caught my breath as I read the time-honoured title of the great nobleman and statesman whose wife she had been. My eyes met those of Holmes, and he put his finger to his lips as we turned away from the window.

Black Peter

I have never known my friend to be in better form,
both mental and physical, than in the year '95. His
increasing fame had brought with it an immense
practice, and I should be guilty of an indiscretion
if I were even to hint at the identity of some of the
illustrious clients who crossed our humble threshold in Baker Street. Holmes, however, like all
great artists, lived for his art's sake, and, save in
the case of the Duke of Holdernesse, I have seldom
known him claim any large reward for his inestim-
able services. So unworldly was he – or so capri-
cious – that he frequently refused his help to the
powerful and wealthy where the problem made no
appeal to his sympathies, while he would devote
weeks of most intense application to the affairs of
some humble client whose case presented those
strange and dramatic qualities which appealed to
his imagination and challenged his ingenuity.

In this memorable year '95 a curious and incon-
gruous succession of cases had engaged his attention, ranging from his famous investigation of the
sudden death of Cardinal Tosca – an inquiry
which was carried out by him at the express desire

of his Holiness the Pope – down to his arrest of Wilson, the notorious canary-trainer, which removed a plague-spot from the East End of London. Close on the heels of these two famous cases came the tragedy of Woodman's Lee, and the very obscure circumstances which surrounded the death of Captain Peter Carey. No record of the doings of Mr Sherlock Holmes would be complete which did not include some account of this very unusual affair.

During the first week of July my friend had been absent so often and so long from our lodgings that I knew he had something on hand. The fact that several rough-looking men called during that time and inquired for Captain Basil made me understand that Holmes was working somewhere under one of the numerous disguises and names with which he concealed his own formidable identity. He had at least five small refuges in different parts of London in which he was able to change his personality. He said nothing of his business to me, and it was not my habit to force a confidence. The first positive sign which he gave me of the direction which his investigation was taking was an extraordinary one. He had gone out before breakfast, and I had sat down to mine, when he strode into the room, his hat upon his head, and a huge barb-headed spear tucked like an umbrella under his arm.

'Good gracious, Holmes!' I cried. 'You don't mean to say that you have been walking about London with that thing?'

'I drove to the butcher's and back.'

'The butcher's?'

'And I return with an excellent appetite. There can be no question, my dear Watson, of the value of exercise before breakfast. But I am prepared to bet that you will not guess the form that my exercise has taken.'

'I will not attempt it.'

He chuckled as he poured out the coffee.

'If you could have looked into Allardyce's back shop you would have seen a dead pig swung from a hook in the ceiling, and a gentleman in his shirt-sleeves furiously stabbing at it with this weapon. I was that energetic person, and I have satisfied myself that by no exertion of my strength can I transfix the pig with a single blow. Perhaps you would care to try?'

'Not for worlds. But why were you doing this?'

'Because it seemed to me to have an indirect bearing upon the mystery of Woodman's Lee. Ah, Hopkins, I got your wire last night, and I have been expecting you. Come and join us.'

Our visitor was an exceedingly alert man, thirty years of age, dressed in a quiet tweed suit, but retaining the erect bearing of one who was accustomed to official uniform. I recognized him at once as Stanley Hopkins, a young police inspector for whose future Holmes had high hopes, while he in turn professed the admiration and respect of a pupil for the scientific methods of the famous amateur. Hopkins's brow was clouded and he sat down with an air of deep dejection.

'No, thank you, sir. I breakfasted before I came round. I spent the night in town, for I came up yesterday to report.'

'And what had you to report?'

'Failure, sir – absolute failure.'

'You have made no progress?'

'None.'

'Dear me! I must have a look at the matter.'

'I wish to heavens that you would, Mr Holmes. It's my first big chance, and I am at my wits' end. For goodness' sake come down and lend me a hand.'

'Well, well, it happens that I have already read all the available evidence, including the report of the inquest, with some care. By the way, what do you make of that tobacco-pouch found on the scene of the crime? Is there no clue there?'

Hopkins looked surprised.

'It was the man's own pouch, sir. His initials were inside it. And it was of sealskin – and he was an old sealer.'

'But he had no pipe.'

'No, sir, we could find no pipe: indeed, he smoked very little. And yet he might have kept some tobacco for his friends.'

'No doubt. I only mention it because if I had been handling the case I should have been inclined to make that the starting point of my investigation. However, my friend Dr Watson knows nothing of this matter, and I should be none the worse for hearing the sequence of events once more. Just give us some short sketch of the essentials.'

Stanley Hopkins drew a slip of paper from his pocket.

'I have a few dates here which will give you the career of the dead man, Captain Peter Carey. He was born in '45 – fifty years of age. He was a most daring and successful seal and whale fisher. In 1883 he commanded the steam sealer *Sea Unicorn*, of Dundee. He had then had several successful voyages in succession, and in the following year, 1884, he retired. After that he travelled for some years, and finally he bought a small place called Woodman's Lee, near Forest Row, in Sussex. There he has lived for six years, and there he died just a week ago today.

'There were some most singular points about the man. In ordinary life he was a strict Puritan – a silent, gloomy fellow. His household consisted of his wife, his daughter, aged twenty, and two female servants. These last were continually changing, for it was never a very cheery situation, and sometimes it became past all bearing. The man was an intermittent drunkard, and when he had the fit on him he was a perfect fiend. He has been known to drive his wife and his daughter out of doors in the middle of the night, and flog them through the park until the whole village outside the gates was aroused by their screams.

'He was summoned once for a savage assault upon the old vicar, who had called upon him to remonstrate with him upon his conduct. In short, Mr Holmes, you would go far before you found a more dangerous man than Peter Carey, and I have heard that he bore the same character when he commanded his ship. He was known in the trade as Black Peter, and the name was given him, not only on account of his swarthy features and the colour of his huge beard, but for the humours which were the terror of all around him. I need not say that he was loathed and avoided by every one of his neighbours, and that I have not heard one single word of sorrow about his terrible end.

'You must have read in the account of the inquest about the man's cabin, Mr Holmes; but perhaps your friend here has not heard of it. He had built himself a wooden outhouse – he always called it "the cabin" – a few hundred yards from his house, and it was here that he slept every night. It was a little, single-roomed hut, sixteen feet by ten. He kept the key in his pocket, made his own bed, cleaned it himself, and allowed no other foot to cross the threshold. There are small windows on each side, which were covered by curtains, and never opened. One of these windows was turned towards the high-road, and when the light burned in it at night the folk used to point it out to each other, and wonder what Black Peter was doing in there. That's the window, Mr Holmes, which gave us one of the few bits of positive evidence that came out at the inquest.

'You remember that a stonemason, named Slater, walking from Forest Row about one o'clock in the morning – two days before the murder –

stopped as he passed the grounds and looked at the square of light still shining among the trees. He swears that the shadow of a man's head turned sideways was clearly visible on the blind, and that this shadow was certainly not that of Peter Carey, whom he knew well. It was that of a bearded man, but the beard was short, and bristled forwards in a way very different from that of the captain. So he says, but he had been two hours in the public-house, and it is some distance from the road to the window. Besides, this refers to the Monday, and the crime was done upon the Wednesday.

'On the Tuesday Peter Carey was in one of his blackest moods, flushed with drink and as savage as a dangerous wild beast. He roamed about the house, and the women ran for it when they heard him coming. Late in the evening he went down to his own hut. About two o'clock the following morning his daughter, who slept with her window open, heard a most fearful yell from that direction, but it was no unusual thing for him to bawl and shout when he was in drink, so no notice was taken. On rising at seven one of the maids noticed that the door of the hut was open, but so great was the terror which the man caused that it was midday before anyone would venture down to see what had become of him. Peeping into the open door, they saw a sight which sent them flying with white faces into the village. Within an hour I was on the spot, and had taken over the case.

'Well, I have fairly steady nerves, as you know,

Mr Holmes, but I give you my word that I got a shake when I put my head into that little house. It was droning like a harmonium with the flies and bluebottles, and the floor and walls were like a slaughterhouse. He had called it a cabin, and a cabin it was, sure enough, for you would have thought that you were in a ship. There was a bunk at one end, a sea-chest, maps and charts, a picture of the *Sea Unicorn*, a line of log-books on a shelf, all exactly as one would expect to find it in a captain's room. And there in the middle of it was the man himself, his face twisted like a lost soul in torment, and his great brindled beard stuck upwards in his agony. Right through his broad breast a steel harpoon had been driven, and it had sunk deep into the wood of the wall behind him. He was pinned like a beetle on a card. Of course, he was quite dead, and had been so from the instant that he uttered that last yell of agony.

'I know your methods, Sir, and I applied them. Before I permitted anything to be moved I examined most carefully the ground outside, and also the floor of the room. There were no footmarks.'

'Meaning that you saw none?'

'I assure you, sir, that there were none.'

'My good Hopkins, I have investigated many crimes, but I have never yet seen one which was committed by a flying creature. As long as the criminal remains upon two legs so long must there be some indentation, some abrasion, some trifling displacement which can be detected by the scientific searcher. It is incredible that this blood-be-spattered room contained no trace which could have aided us. I understand, however, from the inquest that there were some objects which you failed to overlook?'

The young inspector winced at my companion's ironical comments.

'I was a fool not to call you in at the time, Mr Holmes. However, that's past praying for now. Yes, there were several objects in the room which called for special attention. One was the harpoon with which the deed was committed. It had been snatched down from a rack on the wall. Two others remained there, and there was a vacant place for the third. On the stock was engraved "SS *Sea Unicorn*, Dundee". This seemed to establish that the crime had been done in a moment of fury, and that the murderer had seized the first weapon which came in his way. The fact that the crime was committed at two in the morning, and yet Peter Carey was fully dressed, suggested that he had an appointment with the murderer, which is borne out by the fact that a bottle of rum and two dirty glasses stood upon the table.'

'Yes,' said Holmes; 'I think that both inferences are permissible. Was there any other spirit but rum in the room?'

'Yes; there was a tantalus containing brandy and whisky on the sea-chest. It is of no importance to us, however, since the decanters were full and it had therefore not been used.'

'For all that its presence has some significance,' said Holmes. 'However, let us hear some more about the objects which do seem to you to bear upon the case.'

'There was this tobacco-pouch upon the table.'

'What part of the table?'

'It lay in the middle. It was of coarse sealskin – the straight-haired skin, with a leather thong to bind it. Inside was "P. C." on the flap. There was half an ounce of strong ship's tobacco in it.'

'Excellent! What more?'

Stanley Hopkins drew from his pocket a drab-covered note-book. The outside was rough and worn, the leaves were discoloured. On the first page were written the initials 'J. H. N.', and the date '1883'. Holmes laid it on the table and examined it in his minute way, while Hopkins and I gazed over each shoulder. On the second page were printed the letters 'C. P. R.', and then came several sheets of numbers. Another heading was Argentine, another Costa Rica, and another San Paulo, each with pages of signs and figures after it.

'What do you make of these?' asked Holmes.

'They appear to be lists of Stock Exchange securities. I thought that "J. H. N." were the initials of a broker, and that "C. P. R." may have been his client.'

'Try Canadian Pacific Railway,' said Holmes.

Stanley Hopkins swore between his teeth, and struck his thigh with his clenched hand.

'What a fool I have been!' he cried. 'Of course it is as you say. Then "J. H. N." are the only initials we have to solve. I have already examined the old Stock Exchange lists, and I can find no one in 1883 either in the House or among the outside brokers whose initials correspond with these. Yet I feel that the clue is the most important one that I hold. You will admit, Mr Holmes, that there is a possibility that these initials are those of the second person who was present – in other words, of the murderer. I would also urge that the introduction into the case of a document relating to large masses of valuable securities gives us for the first time some indication of a motive for the crime.'

Sherlock Holmes's face showed that he was thoroughly taken aback by this new development.

'I must admit both your points,' said he. 'I confess that the notebook, which did not appear at the inquest, modifies any views which I may have formed. I had come to a theory of the crime in which I can find no place for this. Have you endeavoured to trace any of the securities here mentioned?'

'Inquiries are now being made at the offices, but I fear that the complete register of the stock-holders of these South American concerns is in South America, and that some weeks must elapse before we can trace the shares.'

Holmes had been examining the cover of the notebook with his magnifying lens.

'Surely there is some discoloration here,' said he.

'Yes, sir, it is a blood-stain. I told you that I picked the book off the floor.'

'Was the blood-stain above or below?'

'On the side next to the boards.'

'Which proves, of course, that the book was dropped after the crime was committed.'

'Exactly, Mr Holmes. I appreciated that point, and I conjectured that it was dropped by the murderer on his hurried flight. It lay near the door.'

'I suppose that none of these securities have been found among the property of the dead man?'

'No, sir.'

'Have you any reason to suspect robbery?'

'No, sir. Nothing seemed to have been touched.'

'Dear me, it is certainly a very interesting case. Then there was a knife, was there not?'

'A sheath-knife, still in its sheath. It lay at the feet of the dead man. Mrs Carey had identified it as being her husband's property.'

Holmes was lost in thought for some time.

'Well,' said he at last, 'I suppose I shall have to come out and have a look at it.'

Stanley Hopkins gave a cry of joy.

'Thank you, sir. That will indeed be a weight off my mind.'

Holmes shook his finger at the inspector.

'It would have been an easier task a week ago,'

said he. 'But even now my visit may not be entirely fruitless. Watson, if you can spare the time, I should be very glad of your company. If you will call a four-wheeler, Hopkins, we shall be ready to start for Forest Row in a quarter of an hour.'

Alighting at the small wayside station, we drove for some miles through the remains of widespread woods, which were once part of that great forest which for so long held the Saxon invaders at bay – the impenetrable 'weald', for sixty years the bulwark of Britain. Vast sections of it have been cleared, for this is the seat of the first ironworks of the country, and the trees have been felled to smelt the ore. Now the richer fields of the North have absorbed the trade, and nothing save these ravaged groves and great scars in the earth show the work of the past. Here in a clearing upon the green slope of a hill stood a long, low stone house, approached by a curving drive running through the fields. Nearer the road, and surrounded on three sides by bushes, was a small outhouse, one window and the door facing in our direction. It was the scene of the murder.

Stanley Hopkins led us first to the house, where he introduced us to a haggard, grey-haired woman, the widow of the murdered man, whose gaunt and deep-lined face, with the furtive look of terror in the depths of her red-rimmed eyes, told of the years of hardship and ill-usage which she had endured. With her was her daughter, a pale, fair-haired girl, whose eyes blazed defiantly at us as she told us that she was glad that her father was dead, and that she blessed the hand which had struck him down. It was a terrible household that Black Peter Carey had made for himself, and it was with a sense of relief that we found ourselves in the sunlight again and making our way along the path which had been worn across the fields by the feet of the dead man.

The outhouse was the simplest of dwellings, wooden-walled, single-roofed, one window beside the door, and one on the farther side. Stanley Hopkins drew the key from his pocket, and had stooped to the lock, when he paused with a look of attention and surprise upon his face.

'Someone has been tampering with it,' he said.

There could be no doubt of the fact. The wood-work was cut, and the scratches showed white through the paint, as if they had been that instant done. Holmes had been examining the window.

'Someone has tried to force this also. Whoever it was has failed to make his way in. He must have been a very poor burglar.'

'This is a most extraordinary thing,' said the inspector; 'I could swear that these marks were not here yesterday evening.'

'Some curious person from the village, perhaps,' I suggested.

'Very unlikely. Few of them would dare to set foot in the grounds, far less try to force their way into the cabin. What do you think of it, Mr Holmes?'

'I think that fortune is very kind to us.'

'You mean that the person will come again?'

'It is very probable. He came expecting to find the door open. He tried to get in with the blade of a very small penknife. He could not manage it. What would he do?'

'Come again next night with a more useful tool.'

'So I should say. It will be our fault if we are not there to receive him. Meanwhile, let me see the inside of the cabin.'

The traces of the tragedy had been removed, but the furniture of the little room still stood as it had been on the night of the crime. For two hours, with the most intense concentration, Holmes examined every object in turn, but his face showed that his quest was not a successful one. Once only he paused in his patient investigation.

'Have you taken anything off this shelf, Hopkins?'

'No; I have moved nothing.'

'Something has been taken. There is less dust in this corner of the shelf than elsewhere. It may have been a book lying on its side. It may have been a box. Well, well, I can do nothing more. Let us walk in these beautiful woods, Watson, and give a few hours to the birds and the flowers. We shall meet you here later, Hopkins, and see if we can come to closer quarters with the gentleman who has paid this visit in the night.'

It was past eleven o'clock when we formed our little ambuscade. Hopkins was for leaving the door of the hut open, but Holmes was of the opinion that this would rouse the suspicions of the stranger. The lock was a perfectly simple one, and only a strong blade was needed to push it back. Holmes also suggested that we should wait, not inside the hut, but outside it among the bushes which grew round the farther window. In this way we should be able to watch our man if he struck a light, and see what his object was in this stealthy nocturnal visit.

It was a long and melancholy vigil, and yet it brought with it something of the thrill which the hunter feels when he lies beside the water-pool and waits for the coming of the thirsty beast of prey. What savage creature was it which might steal upon us out of the darkness? Was it a fierce tiger of crime, which could only be taken fighting hard with flashing fang and claw, or would it prove to be some skulking jackal, dangerous only to the weak and unguarded? In absolute silence we crouched amongst the bushes, waiting for whatever might come. At first the steps of a few belated villagers, or the sound of voices from the village, lightened our vigil; but one by one these interruptions died away, and an absolute stillness fell upon us; save for the chimes of the distant church, which told us of the progress of the night, and for the rustle and whisper of a fine rain falling amid the foliage which roofed us in.

Half-past two had chimed, and it was the darkest hour which precedes the dawn, when we all started as a low but sharp click came from the direction of the gate. Someone had entered the drive. Again there was a long silence, and I had begun to fear that it was a false alarm, when a stealthy step was heard upon the other side of the hut, and a moment later a metallic scraping and clicking. The man was trying to force the lock! This time his skill was greater or his tool was better, for there was a sudden snap and the creak of the hinges. Then a match was struck, and next instant the steady light from a candle filled the interior of the hut. Through the gauze curtain our eyes were all riveted upon the scene within.

The nocturnal visitor was a young man, frail and thin, with a black moustache which intensified the deadly pallor of his face. He could not have been much above twenty years of age. I have never seen any human being who appeared to be in such a pitiable fright, for his teeth were visibly chattering, and he was shaking in every limb. He was dressed like a gentleman, in Norfolk jacket and knickerbockers, with a cloth cap upon his head. We watched him staring round with frightened eyes. Then he laid the candle-end upon the table and disappeared from our view into one of the corners. He returned with a large book, one of the log-books which formed a line upon the shelves. Leaning on the table, he rapidly turned over the leaves of this volume until he came to the entry which he sought. Then, with an angry gesture of his clenched hand, he closed the book, replaced it in the corner, and put out the light. He had hardly turned to leave the hut when Hopkins's hand was on the fellow's collar, and I heard his loud gasp of terror as he understood that he was taken. The candle was relit, and there was our wretched captive shivering and cowering in the grasp of the detective. He sank down upon the sea-chest, and looked helplessly from one of us to the other.

'Now, my fine fellow,' said Stanley Hopkins, 'who are you, and what do you want here?'

The man pulled himself together and faced us with an effort at self-composure.

'You are detectives, I suppose?' said he. 'You imagine I am connected with the death of Captain Peter Carey. I assure you that I am innocent.'

'We'll see about that,' said Hopkins. 'First of all, what is your name?'

'It is John Hopley Neligan.'

I saw Holmes and Hopkins exchange a quick glance.

'What are you doing here?'

'Can I speak confidentially?'

'No, certainly not.'

'Why should I tell you?'

'If you have no answer it may go badly with you at the trial.'

The young man winced.

'Well, I will tell you,' he said. 'Why should I

not? And yet I hate to think of this old scandal gaining a new lease of life. Did you ever hear of Dawson & Neligan?'

I could see from Hopkins's face that he never had; but Holmes was keenly interested.

'You mean the West Country bankers,' said he. 'They failed for a million, ruined half the county families of Cornwall, and Neligan disappeared.'

'Exactly. Neligan was my father.'

At last we were getting something positive, and yet it seemed a long gap between an absconding banker and Captain Peter Carey pinned against the wall with one of his own harpoons. We all listened intently to the young man's words.

'It was my father who was really concerned. Dawson had retired. I was only ten years of age at the time, but I was old enough to feel the shame and horror of it all. It has always been said that my father stole all the securities and fled. It is not true. It was his belief that if he were given time in which to realize them all would be well, and every creditor paid in full. He started in his little yacht for Norway just before the warrant was issued for his arrest. I can remember that last night when he bade farewell to my mother. He left us a list of the securities he was taking, and he swore that he would come back with his honour cleared, and that none who had trusted him would suffer. Well, no word was ever heard from him again. Both the yacht and he vanished utterly. We believed, my mother and I, that he and it, with the securities that he had taken with him, were at the bottom of the sea. We had a faithful friend, however, who is a business man, and it was he who discovered some time ago that some of the securities which my father had with him have reappeared on the London market. You can imagine our amazement. I spent months in trying to trace them, and at last, after many doublings and difficulties, I discovered that the original seller had been Captain Peter Carey, the owner of this hut.

'Naturally I made some inquiries about the man. I found that he had been in command of a whaler which was due to return from the Arctic seas at the very same time when my father was crossing to Norway. The autumn of that year was a stormy one and there was a long succession of southerly gales. My father's yacht may well have been blown to the north, and there met by Captain Peter Carey's ship. If that were so, what had become of my father? In any case, if I could prove from Peter Carey's evidence how these securities came on the market, it would be a proof that my father had not sold them, and that he had no view to personal profit when he took them.

'I came down to Sussex with the intention of seeing the captain, but it was at this moment that his terrible death occurred. I read at the inquest a description of his cabin, in which it stated that the old log-books of his vessel were preserved in it. It struck me that if I could see what occurred in the month of August, 1883, on board the *Sea Unicorn*,

I might settle the mystery of my father's fate. I tried last night to get at these log-books, but was unable to open the door. Tonight I tried again, and succeeded; but I find that the pages which deal with that month have been torn from the book. It was at that moment I found myself a prisoner in your hands.'

'Is that all?' asked Hopkins.

'Yes, that is all.' His eyes shifted as he said it.

'You have nothing else to tell us?'

He hesitated.

'No there is nothing.'

'You have not been here before last night?'

'No.'

'Then how do you account for *that*?' cried Hopkins, as he held up the damning notebook, with the initials of our prisoner on the first leaf, and the blood-stain on the cover.

The wretched man collapsed. He sank his face in his hands and trembled all over.

'Where did you get it?' he groaned. 'I did not know. I thought I had lost it at the hotel.'

'That is enough,' said Hopkins sternly. 'Whatever else you have to say you must say in court. You will walk down with me now to the police-station. Well, Mr Holmes, I am very much obliged to you and to your friend for coming down to help me. As it turns out your presence was unnecessary, and I would have brought the case to this successful issue without you; but none the less I am very grateful. Rooms have been reserved for you at the

Brambletye Hotel, so we can all walk down to the village together.'

'Well, Watson, what do you think of it?' asked Holmes as we travelled back next morning.

'I can see that you are not satisfied.'

'Oh, yes, my dear Watson, I am perfectly satisfied. At the same time Stanley Hopkins's methods do not commend themselves to me. I am disappointed in Stanley Hopkins. I had hoped for better things from him. One should always look for a possible alternative and provide against it. It is the first rule of criminal investigation.'

'What, then, is the alternative?'

'The line of investigation which I have myself been pursuing. It may give nothing. I cannot tell. But at least I shall follow it to the end.'

Several letters were waiting for Holmes at Baker Street. He snatched one of them up, opened it, and burst out into a triumphant chuckle of laughter.

'Excellent, Watson. The alternative develops. Have you telegraph forms? Just write a couple of messages for me: "Sumner, Shipping Agent, Ratcliff Highway. Send three men on, to arrive ten tomorrow morning. – Basil." That's my name in those parts. The other is "Inspector Stanley Hopkins, 46 Lord Street, Brixton. Come breakfast tomorrow at nine-thirty. Important. Wire if unable to come. – Sherlock Holmes." There, Watson, this infernal case had haunted me for ten days. I hereby banish it completely from my presence. Tomorrow I trust that we shall hear the last of it for ever.'

Sharp at the hour named Inspector Stanley Hopkins appeared, and we sat down together to the excellent breakfast which Mrs Hudson had prepared. The young detective was in high spirits at his success.

'You really think that your solution must be correct?' asked Holmes.

'I could not imagine a more complete case.'

'It did not seem to me conclusive.'

'You astonish me, Mr Holmes. What more could one ask for?'

'Does your explanation cover every point?'

'Undoubtedly. I find that young Neligan arrived at the Brambletye Hotel on the very day of the crime. He came on the pretence of playing golf. His room was on the ground floor, and he could get out when he liked. That very night he went down to Woodman's Lee, saw Peter Carey at the hut, quarrelled with him, and killed him with the harpoon. Then, horrified by what he had done, he fled out of the hut, dropping the notebook which he had brought with him in order to question Peter Carey about these different securities. You may have observed that some of them were marked with ticks, and the others – the great majority – were not. Those which are ticked have been traced on the London market; but the others presumably were still in the possession of Carey, and young Neligan, according to his own account, was anxious to recover them in order to do the right thing by his father's creditors. After his flight he did not dare to approach the hut again for some time; but at last he forced himself to do so in order to obtain the information which he needed. Surely that is all simple and obvious?'

Holmes smiled and shook his head.

'It seems to me to have only one drawback, Hopkins, and that is that it is intrinsically impossible. Have you tried to drive a harpoon through a body? No? Tut, tut, my dear sir, you must really pay attention to these details. My friend Watson could tell you that I spent a whole morning in that exercise. It is no easy matter, and requires a strong and practised arm. But this blow was delivered with such violence that the head of the weapon sank deep into the wall. Do you imagine that this anaemic youth was capable of so frightful an assault? Is he the man who hob-nobbed in rum and water with Black Peter in the dead of the night? Was it his profile that was seen on the blind two nights before? No, no, Hopkins; it is another and a more formidable person for whom we must seek.'

The detective's face had grown longer and longer during Holmes's speech. His hopes and his ambitions were all crumbling about him. But he would not abandon his position without a struggle.

'You can't deny that Neligan was present that night, Mr Holmes. The book will prove that. I fancy that I have evidence enough to satisfy a jury, even if you are able to pick a hole in it. Besides, Mr Holmes, I have laid my hand upon *my* man. As to this terrible person of yours, where is he?'

'I rather fancy that he is on the stair,' said Holmes serenely. 'I think, Watson, that you would do well to put that revolver where you can reach it.' He rose, and laid a written paper upon a side-table. 'Now we are ready,' said he.

There had been some talking in gruff voices outside, and now Mrs Hudson opened the door to say that there were three men inquiring for Captain Basil.

'Show them in one by one,' said Holmes.

The first who entered was a little ribston-pippin of a man, with ruddy cheeks and fluffy white side-whiskers. Holmes had drawn a letter from his pocket.

'What name?' he asked.

'James Lancaster.'

'I am sorry, Lancaster, but the berth is full. Here is half a sovereign for your trouble. Just step into this room and wait there for a few minutes.'

The second man was a long, dried-up creature, with lank hair and sallow cheeks. His name was Hugh Pattins. He also received his dismissal, his half-sovereign, and the order to wait.

The third applicant was a man of remarkable appearance. A fierce, bulldog face was framed in a tangle of hair and beard, and two bold dark eyes

gleamed behind the cover of thick, tufted, overhung eyebrows. He saluted and stood sailor-
fashion, turning his cap round in his hands.

'Your name?' asked Holmes.

'Patrick Cairns.'

'Harpooner?'

'Yes, sir. Twenty-six voyages.'

'Dundee, I suppose?'

'Yes, sir.'

'And ready to start with an exploring ship?'

'Yes, sir.'

'What wages?'

'Eight pounds a month.'

'Could you start at once?'

'As soon as I get my kit.'

'Have you your papers?'

'Yes, sir.' He took a sheaf of worn and greasy
forms from his pocket. Holmes glanced over them
and returned them.

'You are just the man I want,' said he. 'Here's
the agreement on the side-table. If you sign it the
whole matter will be settled.'

The seaman lurched across the room and took
up the pen.

'Shall I sign here?' he asked, stooping over the
table.

Holmes leaned over his shoulder and passed
both hands over his neck.

'This will do,' said he.

I heard a click of steel and a bellow like an
enraged bull. The next instant Holmes and the

seaman were rolling on the ground together. He was a man of such gigantic strength that, even with the handcuffs which Holmes had so deftly fastened upon his wrist, he would have quickly overpowered my friend had Hopkins and I not rushed to his rescue. Only when I pressed the cold muzzle of the revolver to his temple did he at last understand that resistance was vain. We lashed his ankles with cord and rose breathless from the struggle.

'I must really apologize, Hopkins,' said Sherlock Holmes; 'I fear that the scrambled eggs are cold. However, you will enjoy the rest of your breakfast all the better, will you not, for the thought that you have brought your case to a triumphant conclusion?'

Stanley Hopkins was speechless with amazement.

'I don't know what to say, Mr Holmes,' he blurted out at last, with a very red face. 'It seems to me that I have been making a fool of myself from the beginning. I understand now, what I should never have forgotten, that I am the pupil and you are the master. Even now I see what you have done, but I don't know how you did it, or what it signifies.'

'Well, well,' said Holmes good-humouredly. 'We all learn by experience, and your lesson this time is that you should never lose sight of the alternative. You were so absorbed in young Neligan that you could not spare a thought to Patrick Cairns, the true murderer of Peter Carey.'

The hoarse voice of the seaman broke in on our conversation.

'See here, mister,' said he, 'I make no complaint of being man-handled in this fashion, but I would have you call things by their right names. You say I murdered Peter Carey; I say I *killed* Peter Carey, and there's all the difference. Maybe you don't believe what I say. Maybe you think I am just slinging you a yarn.'

'Not at all,' said Holmes. 'Let us hear what you have to say.

'It's soon told, and, by the Lord, every word of it is truth. I knew Black Peter, and when he pulled out his knife I whipped a harpoon through him sharp, for I knew that it was him or me. That's how he died. You can call it murder. Anyhow, I'd as soon die with a rope round my neck as with Black Peter's knife in my heart.'

'How came you there?' asked Holmes.

'I'll tell it you from the beginning. Just sit me up a little so I can speak easy. It was in '83 that it happened – August of that year. Peter Carey was master of the *Sea Unicorn*, and I was spare harpooner. We were coming out of the ice-pack on our way home, with head winds and a week's southerly gale, when we picked up a little craft that had been blown north. There was one man on her – a landsman. The crew had thought she would founder, and had made for the Norwegian coast in the dinghy. I guess they were all drowned. Well, we took him on board, this man, and he and the skipper had some long talks in the cabin. All the baggage we took off with him was one tin box. So far as I know the man's name was never mentioned, and on the second night he disappeared as if he had never been. It was given out that he had either thrown himself overboard or fallen overboard in the heavy weather that we were having. Only one man knew what had happened to him, and that was me, for with my own eyes I saw the skipper tip up his heels and put him over the rail in the middle watch of a dark night, two days before we sighted the Shetland lights.

'Well, I kept my knowledge to myself and waited to see what would come of it. When we got back to Scotland it was easily hushed up, and nobody asked any questions. A stranger died by an accident, and it was nobody's business to inquire. Shortly after Peter Carey gave up the sea, and it was long years before I could find where he was. I guessed that he had done the deed for the sake of what was in that tin box, and that he could afford now to pay me well for keeping my mouth shut.

'I found out where he was through a sailor man that had met him in London, and down I went to squeeze him. The first night he was reasonable enough, and was ready to give me what would make me free of the sea for life. We were to fix it all two nights later. When I came I found him three-parts drunk and in a vile temper. We sat down and we drank and we yarned about old times, but the more he drank the less I liked the look on his face. I spotted that harpoon upon the wall, and I thought I might need it before I was through. Then at last he broke out at me spitting and cursing, with murder in his eyes and a great clasp-knife in his hand. He had not time to get it from the sheath before I had the harpoon through him. Heavens! what a yell he gave; and his face gets between me and my sleep! I stood there, with his blood splashing round me, and I waited for a bit; but all was quiet, so I took heart once more. I looked round, and there was the tin box on a shelf. I had as much right to it as Peter Carey, anyhow, so I took it with me and left the hut. Like a fool I left my baccy-pouch upon the table.

'Now I'll tell you the queerest part of the whole story. I had hardly got outside the hut when I heard someone coming, and I hid among the bushes. A man came slinking along, went into the hut, gave a cry as if he had seen a ghost, and legged it as hard as he could run until he was out of sight. Who he was or what he wanted is more than I can tell. For my part, I walked ten miles, got a train at Tunbridge Wells, and so reached London, and no one the wiser.

'Well, when I came to examine the box I found there was no money in it, and nothing but papers that I would not dare to sell. I had lost my hold on Black Peter, and was stranded in London without a shilling. There was only my trade left. I saw these advertisements about harpooners and high wages, so I went to the shipping agents, and they sent me here. That's all I know, and I say again that if I killed Black Peter, the law should give me thanks, for I saved them the price of a hempen rope.'

'A very clear statement,' said Holmes, rising and lighting his pipe. 'I think, Hopkins, that you should lose no time in conveying your prisoner to a place of safety. This room is not well adapted for a cell, and Mr Patrick Cairns occupies too large a portion of our carpet.'

'Mr Holmes,' said Hopkins, 'I do not know how to express my gratitude. Even now I do not understand how you attained this result.'

'Simply by having the good fortune to get the right clue from the beginning. It is very possible that if I had known about this notebook it might have led away my thoughts, as it did yours. But all I heard pointed in the one direction. The amazing strength, the skill in the use of the harpoon, the rum and water, the sealskin tobacco-pouch, with the coarse tobacco – all these pointed to a seaman, and one who had been a whaler. I was convinced that the initials "P. C." upon the pouch were a coincidence, and not those of Peter Carey, since he seldom smoked, and no pipe was found in his cabin. You remember that I asked whether whisky and brandy were in the cabin. You said they were. How many landsmen are there who would drink rum when they could get these other spirits? Yes, I was certain it was a seaman.'

'And how did you find him?'

'My dear sir, the problem had become a very simple one. If it were a seaman, it could only be a seaman who had been with him on the *Sea Unicorn*. So far as I could learn, he had sailed in no other ship. I spent three days in wiring to Dundee, and at the end of that time I had ascertained the names of the crew of the *Sea Unicorn* in 1883. When I found Patrick Cairns among the harpooners my research was nearing its end. I argued that the man was probably in London, and that he would desire to leave the country for a time. I therefore spent some days in the East End, devised an Arctic expedition, put forward tempting terms for harpooners who would serve under Captain Basil – and behold the result!'

'Wonderful!' cried Hopkins. 'Wonderful!'

'You must obtain the release of young Neligan as soon as possible,' said Holmes. 'I confess that I think you owe him some apology. The tin box must be returned to him, but of course, the securities which Peter Carey has sold are lost for ever. There's the cab, Hopkins, and you can remove your man. If you want me for the trial, my address and that of Watson will be somewhere in Norway – I'll send particulars later.'

The Golden Pince-Nez

When I look at the three massive manuscript volumes which contain our work for the year 1894 I confess that it is very difficult for me, out of such a wealth of material, to select the cases which are most interesting in themselves and at the same time most conducive to a display of those peculiar powers for which my friend was famous. As I turn over the pages I see my notes upon the repulsive story of the red leech and the terrible death of Crosby the banker. Here also I find an account of the Addleton tragedy and the singular contents of the ancient British barrow. The famous Smith-Mortimer succession case comes also within this period, and so does the tracking and arrest of Huret, the Boulevard assassin – an exploit which won for Holmes an autograph letter of thanks from the French President and the Order of the Legion of Honour. Each of these would furnish a narrative, but on the whole I am of opinion that none of them unite so many singular points of interest as the episode of Yoxley Old Place, which includes, not only the lamentable death of young Willoughby Smith, but also those subsequent developments which threw so curious a light upon the causes of the crime.

It was a wild, tempestuous night towards the close of November. Holmes and I sat together in silence all the evening, he engaged with a powerful lens deciphering the remains of the original inscription upon a palimpsest, I deep in a recent treatise upon surgery. Outside the wind howled down Baker Street, while the rain beat fiercely against the windows. It was strange there in the very depths of the town, with ten miles of man's handiwork on every side of us, to feel the iron grip of Nature, and to be conscious that to the huge elemental forces all London was no more than the molehills that dot the fields. I walked to the window and looked out on the deserted street. The occasional lamps gleamed on the expanse of muddy road and shining pavement. A single cab was splashing its way from the Oxford Street end.

'Well, Watson, it's as well we have not to turn out tonight,' said Holmes, laying aside his lens and rolling up the palimpsest. 'I've done enough for one sitting. It is trying work for the eyes. So far as I can make out, it is nothing more exciting than an Abbey's accounts dating from the second half of the fifteenth century. Halloa! halloa! halloa! What's this?'

Amid the droning of the wind there had come the stamping of a horse's hoofs and the long grind of a wheel as it rasped against the kerb. The cab which I had seen had pulled up at our door.

'What can he want?' I ejaculated, as a man stepped out of it.

'Want! He wants us. And we, my poor Watson, want overcoats and cravats and goloshes, and every aid that man ever invented to fight the weather. Wait a bit, though! There's the cab off again! There's hope yet. He'd have kept it if he had wanted us to come. Run down, my dear fellow, and open the door, for all virtuous folk have been long in bed.'

When the light of the hall lamp fell upon our midnight visitor, I had no difficulty in recognizing him. It was young Stanley Hopkins, a promising detective, in whose career Holmes had several times shown a very practical interest.

'Is he in?' he asked eagerly.

'Come up, my dear sir,' said Holmes's voice from above. 'I hope you have no designs upon us on such a night as this.'

The detective mounted the stairs, and our lamp gleamed upon his shining waterproof. I helped him out of it, while Holmes knocked a blaze out of the logs in the grate.

'Now, my dear Hopkins, draw up and warm your toes,' said he. 'Here's a cigar, and the doctor has a prescription containing hot water and a lemon which is good medicine on a night like this. It must be something important which has brought you out in such a gale.'

'It is indeed, Mr Holmes. I've had a bustling afternoon, I promise you. Did you see anything of the Yoxley case in the latest editions?'

'I've seen nothing later than the fifteenth century today.'

'Well, it was only a paragraph, and all wrong at that, so you have not missed anything. I haven't let the grass grow under my feet. It's down in Kent, seven miles from Chatham and three from the railway line. I was wired for at three-fifteen, reached Yoxley Old Place at five, conducted my investigation, was back at Charing Cross by the last train and straight to you by cab.'

'Which means, I suppose, that you are not quite clear about your case?'

'It means that I can make neither head nor tail of it. So far as I can see, it is just as tangled a business as ever I handled, and yet at first it seemed so simple that one couldn't go wrong. There's no motive, Mr Holmes. That's what bothers me – I can't put my hand on a motive. Here's a man dead – there's no denying that – but, so far as I can see, no reason on earth why anyone should wish him harm.'

Holmes lit his cigar and leaned back in his chair.

'Let us hear about it,' said he.

'I've got my facts pretty clear,' said Stanley Hopkins. 'All I want now is to know what they all mean. The story, so far as I can make it out, is like this. Some years ago this country house, Yoxley Old Place, was taken by an elderly man, who gave the name of Professor Coram. He was an invalid, keeping his bed half the time, and the other half hobbling round the house with a stick, or being pushed about the grounds by the gardener in a bathchair. He was well-liked by the few neighbours who called upon him, and he has the reputation down there of being a very learned man. His household used to consist of an elderly housekeeper, Mrs Marker, and of a maid, Susan Tarlton. These have both been with him since his arrival, and they seem to be women of excellent character. The professor is writing a learned book, and he found it necessary about a year ago to engage a secretary. The first two that he tried were not successes; but the third, Mr Willoughby Smith, a very young man straight from the University, seems to have been just what his employer wanted. His work consisted in writing all the morning to the professor's dictation, and he usually spent the evening in hunting up references and passages which bore upon the next day's work. This Willoughby Smith has nothing against him either as a boy at Uppingham or as a young man at Cambridge. I have seen his testimonials, and from the first he was a decent, quiet, hardworking fellow, with no weak spot in him at all. And yet this is the lad who has met his death this morning in the professor's study under circumstances which can point only to murder.'

The wind howled and screamed at the windows. Holmes and I drew closer to the fire while the young inspector slowly and point by point developed his singular narrative.

'If you were to search all England,' said he, 'I

don't suppose you could find a household more self-contained or free from outside influences. Whole weeks would pass and not one of them go past the garden gate. The professor was buried in his work and existed for nothing else. Young Smith knew nobody in the neighbourhood, and lived very much as his employer did. The women had nothing to take them from the house. Mortimer, the gardener, who wheels the bathchair, is an Army pensioner – an old Crimean man of excellent character. He does not live in the house, but in a three-roomed cottage at the other end of the garden. Those are the only people that you would find within the grounds of Yoxley Old Place. At the same time, the gate of the garden is a hundred yards from the main London to Chatham road. It opens with a latch, and there is nothing to prevent anyone from walking in.

'Now I will give you the evidence of Susan Tarlton, who is the only person who can say anything positive about the matter. It was in the forenoon, between eleven and twelve. She was engaged at the moment in hanging some curtains in the upstairs front bedroom. Professor Coram was still in bed, for when the weather is bad he seldom rises before midday. The housekeeper was busied with some work in the back of the house. Willoughby Smith had been in his bedroom, which he uses as a sitting-room; but the maid heard him at that moment pass along the passage and descend to the study immediately below her.

She did not see him, but she says that she could not be mistaken in his quick, firm tread. She did not hear the study door close, but a minute or so later there was a dreadful cry in the room below. It was a wild, hoarse scream, so strange and un-natural that it might have come either from a man or a woman. At the same instant there was a heavy thud, which shook the whole house, and then all was silence. The maid stood petrified for a moment, and then, recovering her courage, she ran downstairs. The study door was shut, and she opened it. Inside young Mr Willoughby Smith was stretched upon the floor. At first she could see no injury, but as she tried to raise him she saw that blood was pouring from the under side of his neck. It was pierced by a very small but very deep wound, which had divided the carotid artery. The instrument with which the injury had been in-flicted lay upon the carpet beside him. It was one of those small sealing-wax knives to be found on old-fashioned writing-tables, with an ivory handle and a stiff blade. It was part of the fittings of the professor's own desk.

'At first the maid thought that young Smith was already dead, but on pouring some water from the carafe over his forehead, he opened his eyes for an instant. "The professor," he murmured – "it was she." The maid is prepared to swear that those were the exact words. He tried desperately to say something else, and he held his right hand up in the air. Then he fell back dead.

'In the meantime the housekeeper had also arrived upon the scene, but she was just too late to catch the young man's dying words. Leaving Susan with the body, she hurried to the professor's room. He was sitting up in bed, horribly agitated, for he had heard enough to convince him that something terrible had occurred. Mrs Marker is prepared to swear that the professor was still in his night clothes, and, indeed, it was impossible for him to dress without the help of Mortimer, whose orders were to come at twelve o'clock. The professor declares that he heard the distant cry, but that he knows nothing more. He can give no explanation of the young man's last words, "The professor – it was she," but imagines that they were the outcome of delirium. He believes that Willoughby Smith had not an enemy in the world, and can give no reason for the crime. His first action was to send Mortimer, the gardener, for the local police. A little later the chief constable sent for me. Nothing was moved before I got there, and strict orders were given that no one should walk upon the paths leading to the house. It was a splendid chance of putting your theories into practice, Mr Sherlock Holmes. There was really nothing wanting.'

'Except Mr Sherlock Holmes!' said my companion, with a somewhat bitter smile. 'Well, let us hear about it. What sort of job did you make of it?'

'I must ask you first, Mr Holmes, to glance at this rough plan, which will give you a general idea

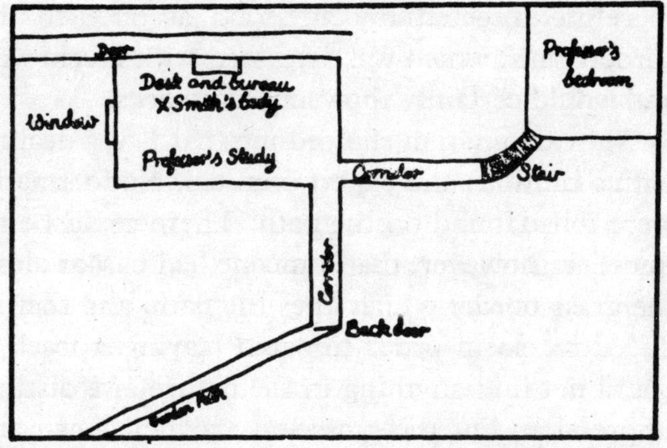

of the position of the professor's study and the various points of the case. It will help you in following my investigations.'

He unfolded the rough chart, which I here reproduce, and he laid it across Holmes's knee. I rose, and, standing behind Holmes, I studied it over his shoulder.

'It is very rough of course, and it only deals with the points which seem to me to be essential. All the rest you will see later for yourself. Now, first of all, presuming that the assassin entered the house, how did he or she come in? Undoubtedly by the garden path and the back door, from which there is direct access to the study. Any other way would have been exceedingly complicated. The escape must also have been made along that line, for of the two other exits from the room one was blocked by Susan as she ran downstairs, and the other leads straight to the professor's bedroom. I therefore directed my attention at once to the garden path, which was saturated with recent rain and would certainly show any footmarks.

'My examination showed me that I was dealing with a cautious and expert criminal. No footmarks were to be found on the path. There could be no question, however, that someone had passed along the grass border which lines the path, and that he had done so in order to avoid leaving a track. I could not find anything in the nature of a distinct impression, but the grass was trodden down and someone had undoubtedly passed. It could only have been the murderer since neither the gardener nor anyone else had been there that morning, and the rain had only begun during the night.'

'One moment,' said Holmes. 'Where does this path lead to?'

'To the road.'

'How long is it?'

'A hundred yards or so.'

'At the point where the path passes through the gate you could surely pick up the tracks?'

'Unfortunately the path was tiled at that point.'

'Well, on the road itself?'

'No; it was all trodden into mire.'

'Tut-tut! Well, then, these tracks upon the grass – were they coming or going?'

'It was impossible to say. There was never any outline.'

'A large foot or a small?'

'You could not distinguish.'

Holmes gave an ejaculation of impatience. 'It has been pouring rain and blowing a hurricane ever since,' said he. 'It will be harder to read now than the palimpsest. Well, well, it can't be helped. What did you do, Hopkins, after you had made certain that you had made certain of nothing?'

'I think I made certain of a good deal, Mr Holmes. I knew that someone had entered the house cautiously from without. I next examined the corridor. It is lined with coconut matting, and had taken no impression of any kind. This brought me into the study itself. It is a scantily furnished room. The main article is a large writing-table with a fixed bureau. This bureau consists of a double column of drawers with a central small cupboard between them. The drawers were open, the cupboard locked. The drawers, it seems, were always open, and nothing of value was kept in them. There were some papers of importance in the cupboard, but there were no signs that this had been tampered with, and the professor assures me that nothing was missing. It is certain that no robbery had been committed.

'I come now to the body of the young man. It was found near the bureau, and just to the left of it, as marked upon that chart. The stab was on the right side of the neck and from behind forwards, so that it is almost impossible that it could have been self-inflicted.'

'Unless he fell upon the knife,' said Holmes.

'Exactly. The idea crossed my mind. But we

found the knife some feet away from the body, so that seems impossible. Then, of course, there are the man's own dying words. And, finally, there was this very important piece of evidence which was found clasped in the dead man's right hand.'

From his pocket Stanley Hopkins drew a small paper packet. He unfolded it, and disclosed a golden pince-nez, with two broken ends of black silk cord dangling from the end of it. 'Willoughby Smith had excellent sight,' he added. 'There can be no question that this was snatched from the face or the person of the assassin.'

Sherlock Holmes took the glasses into his hand and examined them with the utmost attention and interest. He held them on his nose, endeavoured to read through them, went to the window and stared up the street with them, looked at them most minutely in the full light of the lamp, and finally, with a chuckle, seated himself at the table and wrote a few lines upon a sheet of paper, which he tossed across to Stanley Hopkins.

'That's the best I can do for you,' said he. 'It may prove to be of some use.

The astonished detective read the note aloud. It ran as follows:

Wanted, a woman of good address, attired like a lady. She has a remarkably thick nose, with eyes which are set close upon either side of it. She has a puckered forehead, a peering expression and probably rounded shoulders. There are indications that she has had recourse to an optician at least twice during the last few months. As her glasses are of remarkable strength, and as opticians are not very numerous, there should he no difficulty in tracing her.

Holmes smiled at the astonishment of Hopkins, which must have been reflected upon my features.

'Surely my deductions are simplicity itself,' said he. 'It would be difficult to name any articles which afford a finer field for inference than a pair of glasses, especially so remarkable a pair as these. That they belong to a woman I infer from their delicacy, and also, of course, from the last words of the dying man. As to her being a person of refinement and well dressed, they are, as you perceive, handsomely mounted in solid gold, and it is inconceivable that anyone who wore such glasses could be slatternly in other respects. You will find that the clips are too wide for your nose, showing that the lady's nose was very broad at the base. This sort of nose is usually a short and coarse one, but there are a sufficient number of exceptions to prevent me from being dogmatic or from insisting upon this point in my description. My own face is a narrow one, and yet I find that I cannot get my eyes into the centre, or near the centre, of these glasses. Therefore, the lady's eyes are set very near to the sides of the nose. You will perceive, Watson, that the glasses are concave and of unusual strength. A lady whose vision has been so extremely contracted all her life is sure to have the physical characteristics of such vision, which are seen in the forehead, the eyelids, and the shoulders.'

'Yes,' I said, 'I can follow each of your arguments. I confess, however, that I am unable to understand how you arrive at the double visit to the optician.'

Holmes took the glasses into his hand.

'You will perceive,' he said, 'that the clips are lined with tiny bands of cork to soften the pressure upon the nose. One of these is discoloured and worn to some slight extent, but the other is new. Evidently one has fallen off and been replaced. I should judge that the older of them has not been there more than a few months. They exactly correspond, so I gather that the lady went back to the same establishment for the second.'

'By George, it's marvellous!' cried Hopkins, in an ecstasy of admiration. 'To think that I had all that evidence in my hand and never knew it! I had intended, however, to go the round of the London opticians.'

'Of course you would. Meanwhile, have you anything more to tell us about the case?'

'Nothing, Mr Holmes. I think that you know as much as I do now – probably more. We have had inquiries made as to any stranger seen on the country roads or at the railway station. We have heard of none. What beats me is the utter want of all object in the crime. Not a ghost of a motive can anyone suggest.'

'Ah! there I am not in a position to help you. But I suppose you want us to come out tomorrow?'

'If it is not asking too much, Mr Holmes. There's a train from Charing Cross to Chatham at six in the morning, and we should be at Yoxley Old Place between eight and nine.'

'Then we shall take it. Your case has certainly some features of great interest, and I shall be delighted to look into it. Well, it's nearly one, and we had best get a few hours' sleep. I dare say you can manage all right on the sofa in front of the fire. I'll light my spirit-lamp and give you a cup of coffee before we start.'

The gale had blown itself out next day, but it was a bitter morning when we started upon our journey. We saw the cold winter sun rise over the dreary marshes of the Thames and the long, sullen reaches of the river, which I shall ever associate with our pursuit of the Andaman Islander in the earlier days of our career. After a long and weary journey we alighted at a small station some miles from Chatham. While a horse was being put into a trap at the local inn we snatched a hurried breakfast and so we were all ready for business when we at last arrived at Yoxley Old Place. A constable met us at the garden gate.

'Well, Wilson, any news?'

'No, sir, nothing.'

'No reports of any stranger seen?'

'No, sir. Down at the station they are certain that no stranger either came or went yesterday.'

'Have you had inquiries made at inns and lodgings?'

'Yes, sir; there is no one that we cannot account for.'

'Well, it's only a reasonable walk to Chatham. Anyone might stay there, or take a train without being observed. This is the garden path of which I spoke, Mr Holmes. I'll pledge my word there was no mark on it yesterday.'

'On which side were the marks on the grass?'

'This side, sir. This narrow margin of grass between the path and the flower-bed. I can't see the traces now, but they were clear to me then.'

'Yes, yes; someone has passed along,' said Holmes, stooping over the grass border. 'Our lady must have picked her steps carefully, must she not, since on the one side she would leave a track on the path, and on the other an even clearer one on the soft bed?'

'Yes, sir, she must have been a cool hand.'

I saw an intent look pass over Holmes's face.

'You say that she must have come back this way?'

'Yes, sir; there is no other.'

'On this strip of grass?'

'Certainly, Mr Holmes.'

'Hum! It was a very remarkable performance – very remarkable. Well, I think we have exhausted the path. Let us go farther. This garden door is usually kept open, I suppose? Then this visitor had nothing to do but to walk in. The idea of murder was not in her mind, or she would have provided herself with some sort of weapon, instead of having to pick this knife off the writing-table. She advanced along this corridor, leaving no traces upon the coconut matting. Then she found herself in this study. How long was she there? We have no means of judging.'

'Not more than a few minutes, sir. I forgot to tell you that Mrs Marker, the housekeeper, had been in there tidying not very long before – about a quarter of an hour she says.'

'Well, that gives us a limit. Our lady enters this room, and what does she do? She goes over to the writing-table. What for? Not for anything in the drawers. If there had been anything worth her taking it would surely have been locked up. No; it was for something in that wooden bureau. Halloa! what is that scratch upon the face of it? Just hold a match, Watson. Why did you not tell me of this, Hopkins?'

The mark which he was examining began upon the brasswork on the right-hand side of the key-hole, and extended for about four inches, where it had scratched the varnish from the surface.

'I noticed it, Mr Holmes. But you'll always find scratches round a keyhole.'

'This is recent – quite recent. See how the brass shines where it is cut. An old scratch would be the same colour as the surface. Look at it through my lens. There's the varnish, too, like earth on each side of a furrow. Is Mrs Marker there?'

A sad-faced, elderly woman came into the room. 'Did you dust this bureau yesterday morning?'

'Yes, sir.'

'Did you notice this scratch?'

'No, sir, I did not.'

'I am sure you did not, for a duster would have swept away these shreds of varnish. Who has the key of this bureau?'

'The professor keeps it on his watch-chain.'

'Is it a simple key?'

'No, sir; it is a Chubb's key.'

'Very good. Mrs Marker, you can go. Now we are making a little progress. Our lady enters the room, advances to the bureau, and either opens it or tries to do so. While she is thus engaged young Willoughby Smith enters the room. In her hurry to withdraw the key she makes this scratch upon the door. He seizes her, and she, snatching up the nearest object, which happens to be this knife, strikes at him in order to make him let go his hold. The blow is a fatal one. He falls and she escapes, either with or without the object for which she has come. Is Susan the maid there? Could anyone have got away through that door after the time that you heard the cry, Susan?'

'No, sir; it is impossible. Before I got down the stair I'd have seen anyone in the passage. Besides, the door never opened, for I would have heard it.'

'That settles this exit. Then no doubt the lady

went out the way she came. I understand that this other passage leads only to the professor's room. There is no exit that way?'

'No, sir.'

'We shall go down it and make the acquaintance of the professor. Halloa, Hopkins! this is very important, very important indeed. The professor's corridor is also lined with coconut matting.'

'Well, sir, what of that?'

'Don't you see any bearing upon the case? Well, well, I don't insist upon it. No doubt I am wrong. And yet it seems to me to be suggestive. Come with me and introduce me.'

We passed down the passage, which was of the same length as that which led to the garden. At the end was a short flight of steps ending in a door. Our guide knocked, and then ushered us into the professor's bedroom. It was a very large chamber, lined with innumerable volumes, which had overflowed from the shelves and lay in piles in the corners, or were stacked all round at the base of the cases. The bed was in the centre of the room, and in it, propped up with pillows, was the owner of the house. I have seldom seen a more remarkable-looking person. It was a gaunt, aquiline face which was turned towards us, with piercing dark eyes, which lurked in deep hollows under overhung and tufted brows. His hair and beard were white, save that the latter was curiously stained with yellow around his mouth. A cigarette glowed amid the tangle of white hair, and the air of the room was fetid with stale tobacco smoke. As he held out his hand to Holmes I perceived that it also was stained yellow with nicotine.

'A smoker, Mr Holmes?' said he, speaking well-chosen English with a curious little mincing accent. 'Pray take a cigarette. And you, sir? I can recommend them, for I have them especially prepared by Ionides of Alexandria. He sends me a thousand at a time, and I grieve to say that I have to arrange for a fresh supply every fortnight. Bad, Sir, very bad; but an old man has few pleasures. Tobacco and my work – that is all that is left to me.'

Holmes had lit a cigarette, and was shooting little darting glances all over the room.

'Tobacco and my work, but now only tobacco,' the old man exclaimed. 'Alas, what a fatal interruption! Who could have foreseen such a terrible catastrophe? So estimable a young man! I assure you that after a few months' training he was an admirable assistant. What do you think of the matter, Mr Holmes?'

'I have not yet made up my mind.'

'I shall indeed be indebted to you if you can throw a light where all is so dark to us. To a poor bookworm and invalid like myself such a blow is paralysing. I seem to have lost the faculty of thought. But you're a man of action – you are a man of affairs. It is part of the everyday routine of your life. You can preserve your balance in every emergency. We are fortunate indeed in having you at our side.'

Holmes was pacing up and down on one side of the room whilst the old professor was talking. I observed that he was smoking with extraordinary rapidity. It was evident that he shared our host's liking for the fresh Alexandrian cigarettes.

'Yes, sir, it is a crushing blow,' said the old man. 'That is my *magnum opus* – the pile of papers on the side-table yonder. It is my analysis of the documents found in the Coptic monasteries of Syria and Egypt, a work which will cut deep at the very foundation of revealed religion. With my enfeebled health I do not know whether I shall ever be able to complete it now that my assistant has been taken from me. Dear me, Mr Holmes, why, you are even a quicker smoker than I am myself.'

Holmes smiled.

'I am a connoisseur,' said he, taking another cigarette from the box – his fourth – and lighting it from the stub of that which he had finished. 'I will not trouble you with any lengthy cross-examination, Professor Coram, since I gather that you were in bed at the time of the crime and could know nothing about it. I would only ask this – What do you imagine that this poor fellow meant by his last words; "The professor – it was she?"'

The professor shook his head.

'Susan is a country girl,' said he, 'and you know the incredible stupidity of that class. I fancy that the poor fellow murmured some incoherent, delirious words, and that she twisted them into this meaningless message.'

'I see. You have no explanation yourself of the tragedy?'

'Possibly an accident; possibly – I only breathe it among ourselves – a suicide. Young men have their hidden troubles – some affair of the heart, perhaps, which we have never known. It is a more probable supposition than murder.'

'But the eyeglasses?'

'Ah! I am only a student – a man of dreams. I cannot explain the practical things of life. But still, we are aware, my friend, that love-gages may take strange shapes. By all means take another cigarette. It is a pleasure to see anyone appreciate them so. A fan, a glove, glasses – who knows what article may be carried as a token or treasured when a man puts an end to his life? This gentleman speaks of footsteps on the grass; but, after all, it is easy to be mistaken on such a point. As to the knife, it might well be thrown far from the unfortunate man as he fell. It is possible that I speak as a child, but to me it seems that Willoughby Smith has met his fate by his own hand.'

Holmes seemed struck by the theory thus put forward, and he continued to walk up and down for some time, lost in thought and consuming cigarette after cigarette.

'Tell me, Professor Coram,' he said at last, 'what is in that cupboard in the bureau?'

'Nothing that would help a thief. Family papers, letters from my poor wife, diplomas of Universities which have done me honour. Here is the key. You can look for yourself.'

Holmes picked up the key and looked at it for an instant; then he handed it back.

'No; I hardly think that it would help me,' said he. 'I should prefer to go quietly down to your garden and turn the whole matter over in my head. There is something to be said for the theory of suicide which you have put forward. We must apologize for having intruded upon you, Professor Coram, and I promise that we won't disturb you until after lunch. At two o'clock we will come again and report to you anything which may have happened in the interval.'

Holmes was curiously distrait, and we walked up and down the garden path for some time in silence.

'Have you a clue?' I asked at last.

'It depends upon those cigarettes that I smoked,' said he. 'It is possible that I am utterly mistaken. The cigarettes will show me.'

'My dear Holmes,' I exclaimed, 'how on earth –'

'Well, well, you may see for yourself. If not, there's no harm done. Of course, we always have the optician clue to fall back upon, but I take a short cut when I can get it. Ah, here is the good Mrs Marker! Let us enjoy five minutes of instructive conversation with her.'

I may have remarked before that Holmes had, when he liked, a peculiarly ingratiating way with women, and that he very readily established terms of confidence with them. In half the time which he had named he had captured the housekeeper's goodwill, and was chatting with her as if he had known her for years.

'Yes, Mr Holmes, it is as you say, sir. He does smoke something terrible. All day and sometimes all night, sir. I've seen that room of a morning – well, sir, you'd have thought it was a London fog. Poor young Mr Smith, he was a smoker also, but not as bad as the professor. His health – well, I don't know that it's better nor worse for the smoking.'

'Ah,' said Holmes, 'but it kills the appetite.'

'Well, I don't know about that, sir.'

'I suppose the professor eats hardly anything?'

'Well, he is variable. I'll say that for him.'

'I'll wager he took no breakfast this morning, and won't face his lunch after all the cigarettes I saw him consume.'

'Well, you're out there, sir, as it happens, for he ate a remarkably big breakfast this morning. I don't know when I've known him make a better one, and he's ordered a good dish of cutlets for his lunch. I'm surprised myself, for since I came into that room yesterday and saw young Mr Smith lying there on the floor I couldn't bear to look at food. Well, it takes all sorts to make a world, and the professor hasn't let it take his appetite away.'

We loitered the morning away in the garden. Stanley Hopkins had gone down to the village to look into some rumours of a strange woman who had been seen by some children on the Chatham road the previous morning. As to my friend, all his usual energy seemed to have deserted him. I had never known him handle a case in such a half-hearted fashion. Even the news brought back by

Hopkins that he had found the children and that they had undoubtedly seen a woman exactly corresponding with Holmes's description, and wearing either spectacles or eye-glasses, failed to rouse any sign of keen interest. He was more attentive when Susan, who waited upon us at lunch, volunteered the information that she believed Mr Smith had been out for a walk yesterday morning, and that he had only returned half an hour before the tragedy occurred. I could not myself see the bearing of this incident, but I clearly perceived that Holmes was weaving it into the general scheme which he had formed in his brain. Suddenly he sprang from his chair, and glanced at his watch. 'Two o'clock, gentlemen,' said he. 'We must go up and have it out with our friend the professor.'

The old man had just finished his lunch, and certainly his empty dish bore evidence to the good appetite with which his housekeeper had credited him. He was, indeed, a weird figure as he turned his white mane and his glowing eyes towards us. The eternal cigarette smouldered in his mouth. He had been dressed and was seated in an armchair by the fire.

'Well, Mr Holmes, have you solved this mystery yet?' He shoved the large tin of cigarettes which stood on a table beside him towards my companion. Holmes stretched out his hand at the same moment, and between them they tipped the box over the edge. For a minute or two we were all on our knees retrieving stray cigarettes from impossible places. When we rose again I observed that Holmes's eyes were shining and his cheeks tinged with colour. Only at a crisis have I seen those battle-signals flying.

'Yes,' said he, 'I have solved it.'

Stanley Hopkins and I stared in amazement. Something like a sneer quivered over the gaunt features of the old professor.

'Indeed! In the garden?'

'No, here.'

'Here! When?'

'This instant.'

'You are surely joking, Mr Sherlock Holmes. You compel me to tell you that this is too serious a matter to be treated in such a fashion.'

'I have forged and tested every link of my chain, Professor Coram, and I am sure that it is sound. What your motives are, or what exact part you play in this strange business, I am not yet able to say. In a few minutes I shall probably hear it from your own lips. Meanwhile, I will reconstruct what is past for your benefit, so that you may know the information which I still require.

'A lady yesterday entered your study. She came with the intention of possessing herself of certain documents which were in your bureau. She had a key of her own. I have had an opportunity of examining yours, and I do not find that slight discoloration which the scratch made upon the varnish would have produced. You were not an accessory, therefore, and she came, so far as I can read the evidence, without your knowledge to rob you.'

The professor blew a cloud from his lips.

'This is most interesting and instructive,' said he. 'Have you no more to add? Surely, having traced this lady so far, you can also say what has become of her.'

'I will endeavour to do so. In the first place, she was seized by your Secretary, and stabbed him in order to escape. This catastrophe I am inclined to regard as an unhappy accident, for I am convinced that the lady had no intention of inflicting so grievous an injury. An assassin does not come unarmed. Horrified by what she had done, she rushed wildly away from the scene of the tragedy. Unfortunately for her she had lost her glasses in the scuffle, and as she was extremely short-sighted she was really helpless without them. She ran down a corridor, which she imagined to be that by which she had come – both were lined with coconut matting – and it was only when it was too late that she understood that she had taken the wrong passage and that her retreat was cut off behind her. What was she to do? She could not go back. She could not remain where she was. She must go on. She went on. She mounted a stair, pushed open a door, and found herself in your room.'

The old man sat with his mouth open staring wildly at Holmes. Amazement and fear were stamped upon his expressive features. Now, with an effort, he shrugged his shoulders and burst into insincere laughter.

'All very fine, Mr Holmes,' said he. 'But there is one little flaw in a splendid theory. I was myself in my room, and I never left it during the day.'

'I am aware of that, Professor Coram.'

'And you mean to say that I could lie upon that bed and not be aware that a woman had entered my room?'

'I never said so. You *were* aware of it. You spoke with her. You recognized her. You aided her to escape.'

Again the professor burst into high-keyed laughter. He had risen to his feet, and his eyes glowed like embers.

'You are mad!' he cried. 'You are talking insanely. I helped her to escape? Where is she now?'

'She is there,' said Holmes, and he pointed to a high bookcase in the corner of the room.

I saw the old man throw up his arms, a terrible convulsion passed over his grim face, and he fell back in his chair. At the same instant the bookcase at which Holmes pointed swung round upon a hinge, and a woman rushed out into the room.

'You are right,' she cried, in a strange foreign voice. 'You are right! I am here.'

She was brown with the dust and draped with the cobwebs which had come from the walls of her hiding-place. Her face, too, was streaked with grime, and at the best she could never have been handsome, for she had the exact physical characteristics which Holmes had divined, with, in addition, a long and obstinate chin. What with her natural blindness, and what with the change from dark to light, she stood as one dazed, blinking about her to see where and who we were. And yet, in spite of all these disadvantages, there was a certain nobility in the woman's bearing, a gallantry in the defiant chin and in the upraised head, which compelled something of respect and admiration. Stanley Hopkins had laid his hand upon her arm and claimed her as his prisoner, but she waved him aside gently, and yet with an over-mastering dignity which compelled obedience. The old man lay back in his chair, with a twitching face, and stared at her with brooding eyes.

'Yes, sir, I am your prisoner,' she said. 'From where I stood I could hear everything, and I know that you have learned the truth. I confess it all. It was I who killed the young man. But you are right, you who say that it was an accident. I did not even know that it was a knife which I held in my hand, for in my despair I snatched anything from the table and struck at him to make him let me go. It is the truth that I tell.'

'Madame,' said Holmes, 'I am sure that it is the truth. I fear that you are far from well.'

She had turned a dreadful colour, the more ghastly under the dark dust-streaks upon her face. She seated herself on the side of the bed; then she resumed.

'I have only a little time here,' she said, 'but I

would have you to know the whole truth. I am this man's wife. He is not an Englishman. He is a Russian. His name I will not tell.'

For the first time the old man stirred. 'God bless you, Anna!' he cried. 'God bless you!'

She cast a look of the deepest disdain in his direction. 'Why should you cling so hard to that wretched life of yours, Sergius?' said she. 'It has done harm to many and good to none – not even to yourself. However, it is not for me to cause the frail thread to be snapped before God's time. I have enough already upon my soul since I crossed the threshold of this cursed house. But I must speak, or I shall be too late.

'I have said, gentlemen, that I am this man's wife. He was fifty and I a foolish girl of twenty when we married. It was in a city of Russia, a University – I will not name the place.'

'God bless you, Anna!' murmured the old man again.

'We were reformers – revolutionists – Nihilists, you understand. He and I and many more. Then there came a time of trouble, a police officer was killed, many were arrested, evidence was wanted, and in order to save his own life and to earn a great reward my husband betrayed his own wife and his companions. Yes; we were all arrested upon his confession. Some of us found our way to the gallows and some to Siberia. I was among these last, but my term was not for life. My husband came to England with his ill-gotten gains, and has lived in quiet ever since, knowing well that if the Brotherhood knew where he was not a week would pass before justice would be done.'

The old man reached out a trembling hand and helped himself to a cigarette. 'I am in your hands, Anna,' said he. 'You were always good to me.'

'I have not yet told you the height of his villainy!' said she. 'Among our comrades of the Order there was one who was the friend of my heart. He was noble, unselfish, loving – all that my husband was not. He hated violence. We were all guilty – if that is guilt – but he was not. He wrote for ever dissuading me from such a course. These letters would have saved him. So would my diary, in which from day to day I had entered both my feelings towards him and the view which each of us had taken. My husband found and kept both diary and letters. He hid them, and he tried hard to swear away the young man's life. In this he failed, but Alexis was sent a convict to Siberia, where now, at this moment, he works in a salt mine. Think of that, you villain, you villain; now, now, at this very moment, Alexis, a man whose name you are not worthy to speak, works and lives like a slave, and yet I have your life in my hands and I let you go!'

'You were always a noble woman, Anna,' said the old man, puffing at his cigarette.

She had risen, but she fell back again with a little cry of pain.

'I must finish,' she said. 'When my term was

over I set myself to get the diary and letters, which if sent to the Russian Government, would procure my friend's release. I knew that my husband had come to England. After months of searching I discovered where he was. I knew that he still had the diary, for when I was in Siberia I had a letter from him once reproaching me and quoting some passages from its pages. Yet I was sure that with his revengeful nature he would never give it to me of his own free will. I must get it for myself. With this object I engaged an agent from a private detective firm, who entered my husband's house as secretary – it was your second secretary, Sergius, the one who left you so hurriedly. He found that papers were kept in the cupboard, and he got an impression of the key. He would not go farther. He furnished me with a plan of the house, and he told me that in the forenoon the study was always empty, as the secretary was employed up here. So at last I took my courage in both hands and I came down to get the papers for myself. I succeeded, but at what a cost!

'I had just taken the papers and was locking the cupboard when the young man seized me. I had seen him already that morning. He had met me in the road, and I had asked him to tell me where Professor Coram lived, not knowing that he was in his employ.'

'Exactly! Exactly!' said Holmes. 'The secretary came back and told his employer of the woman he had met. Then in his last breath he tried to send a message that it was she – the she whom he had just discussed with him.'

'You must let me speak,' said the woman, in an imperative voice, and her face contracted as if in pain. 'When he had fallen I rushed from the room, chose the wrong door, and found myself in my husband's room. He spoke of giving me up. I showed him that if he did so his life was in my hands. If he gave me to the law I could give him to the Brotherhood. It was not that I wished to lie for my own sake, but it was that I desired to accomplish my purpose. He knew that I would do what I said – that his own fate was involved in mine. For that reason, and for no other, he shielded me. He thrust me into that dark hiding-place, a relic of old days, known only to himself. He took his meals in his own room, and so was able to give me part of his food. It was agreed that when the police left the house I should slip away by night and come back no more. But in some way you have read our plans.' She tore from the bosom of her dress a small packet. 'These are my last words,' said she; 'here is the packet which will save Alexis. I confide it to your honour and to your love of justice. Take it! You will deliver it at the Russian Embassy. Now I have done my duty, and –'

'Stop her!' cried Holmes. He had bounded across the room and had wrenched a small phial from her hand.

'Too late!' she said, sinking back on the bed.

'Too late! I took the poison before I left my hiding-place. My head swims! I am going! I charge you, sir, to remember the packet.'

'A simple case, and yet in some ways an instructive one,' Holmes remarked as we travelled back to town. 'It hinged from the outset upon the pince-nez. But for the fortunate chance of the dying man having seized these I am not sure that we could ever have reached our solution. It was clear to me from the strength of the glasses that the wearer must have been very blind and helpless when deprived of them. When you asked me to believe that she walked along a narrow strip of grass without once making a false step I remarked, as you may remember, that it was a noteworthy performance. In my mind, I set it down as an impossible performance, save in the unlikely case that she had a second pair of glasses. I was forced, therefore, to seriously consider the hypothesis that she had remained within the house. On perceiving the similarity of the two corridors, it became clear that she might very easily have made such a mistake, and in that case it was evident that she must have entered the professor's room. I was keenly on the alert, therefore, for whatever would bear out this supposition, and I examined the room narrowly for anything in the shape of a hiding-place. The carpet seemed continuous and firmly nailed, so I dismissed the idea of a trap-door. There might well be a recess behind the books. As you are aware, such devices are common in old libraries. I observed that books were piled on the floor at all other points, but that one bookcase was left clear. This, then, might be the door. I could see no marks to guide me, but the carpet was of a dun colour, which lends itself very well to examination. I therefore smoked a great number of those excellent cigarettes, and I dropped the ash all over the space in front of the suspected bookcase. It was a simple trick, but exceedingly effective. I then went downstairs, and I ascertained in your presence, Watson, without your quite perceiving the drift of my remarks, that Professor Coram's consumption of food had increased – as one would expect when he is supplying a second person. We then ascended to the room again, when, by upsetting the cigarette-box, I obtained a very excellent view of the floor, and was able to see quite clearly, from the traces upon the cigarette ash, that the prisoner had, in our absence, come out from her retreat. Well, Hopkins, here we are at Charing Cross, and I congratulate you on having brought your case to a successful conclusion. You are going to headquarters, no doubt. I think, Watson, you and I will drive together to the Russian Embassy.'

We have had some dramatic entrances and exits upon our small stage at Baker Street, but I cannot recollect anything more sudden and startling than the first appearance of Dr Thorneycroft Huxtable, MA, PH.D., etc. His card, which seemed too small to carry the weight of his academic distinctions, preceded him by a few seconds, and then he entered himself – so large, so pompous, and so dignified that he was the very embodiment of self-possession and solidity. And yet his first action when the door had closed behind him was to stagger against the table, whence he slipped down upon the floor, and there was that majestic figure prostrate and insensible upon our bearskin hearthrug.

We had sprung to our feet, and for a few moments we stared in silent amazement at this ponderous piece of wreckage, which told of some sudden and fatal storm far out on the ocean of life. Then Holmes hurried with a cushion for his head, and I with brandy for his lips. The heavy white face was seamed with lines of trouble, the hanging pouches under the closed eyes were leaden in colour, the loose mouth drooped dolorously at the corners, the rolling chins were unshaven. Collar and shirt bore the grime of a long journey, and the hair bristled unkempt from the well-shaped head. It was a sorely stricken man who lay before us.

'What is it, Watson?' asked Holmes.

'Absolute exhaustion – possibly mere hunger and fatigue,' said I, with my finger on the thready pulse, where the stream of life trickled thin and small.

'Return ticket from Mackleton, in the North of England,' said Holmes, drawing it from the watch-pocket. 'It is not twelve o'clock yet. He has certainly been an early starter.'

The puckered eyelids had begun to quiver, and now a pair of vacant grey eyes looked up at us. An instant later the man had scrambled on to his feet, his face crimson with shame.

'Forgive this weakness, Mr Holmes; I have been a little overwrought. Thank you, if I might have a glass of milk and a biscuit I have no doubt that I should be better. I came personally, Mr Holmes, in order to ensure that you would return with me. I feared that no telegram would convince you of the absolute urgency of the case.'

'When you are quite restored –'

'I am quite well again. I cannot imagine how I came to be so weak. I wish you, Mr Holmes, to come to Mackleton with me by the next train.'

My friend shook his head.

'My colleague, Dr Watson, could tell you that

we are very busy at present. I am retained in this case of the Ferrers Documents, and the Abergavenny murder is coming up for trial. Only a very important issue could call me from London at present.'

'Important!' Our visitor threw up his hands. 'Have you heard nothing of the abduction of the only son of the Duke of Holdernesse?'

'What! the late Cabinet Minister?'

'Exactly. We had tried to keep it out of the papers, but there was some rumour in the *Globe* last night. I thought it might have reached your ears.'

Holmes shot out his long, thin arm and picked out Volume 'H' in his encyclopaedia of reference.

'"Holdernesse, sixth Duke, KG, PC" – half the alphabet! "Baron Beverley, Earl of Carston" – dear me, what a list! "Lord-Lieutenant of Hallamshire since 1900. Married Edith, daughter of Sir Charles Appledore, 1888. Heir and only child, Lord Saltire. Owns about two hundred and fifty thousand acres. Minerals in Lancashire and Wales. Address: Carlton House Terrace; Holdernesse Hall, Hallamshire; Carston Castle, Bangor, Wales. Lord of the Admiralty, 1872 Chief Secretary of State for – " Well, well, this man is certainly one of the greatest subjects of the Crown!'

'The greatest and perhaps the wealthiest. I am aware, Mr Holmes, that you take a very high line in professional matters, and that you are prepared to work for the work's sake. I may tell you, however, that his Grace has already intimated that a cheque for five thousand pounds will be handed over to the person who can tell him where his son is, and another thousand to him who can name the man, or men, who have taken him.'

'It is a princely offer,' said Holmes. 'Watson, I think that we shall accompany Dr Huxtable back to the North of England. And now, Dr Huxtable, when you have consumed that milk you will kindly tell me what has happened, when it happened, how it happened, and, finally, what Dr Thorneycroft Huxtable, of the Priory School, near Mackleton, has to do with the matter, and why he comes three days after an event – the state of your chin gives the date – to ask for my humble services.'

Our visitor had consumed his milk and biscuits. The light had come back to his eyes and the colour to his cheeks as he set himself with great vigour and lucidity to explain the situation.

'I must inform you, gentlemen, that the Priory is a preparatory school, of which I am the founder and principal. *Huxtable's Sidelights on Horace* may possibly recall my name to your memories. The Priory is, without exception, the best and most select preparatory school in England. Lord Leverstoke, the Earl of Blackwater, Sir Cathcart Soames – they all have entrusted their sons to me. But I felt that my school had reached its zenith when, three weeks ago, the Duke of Holdernesse sent Mr James Wilder, his secretary, with the intimation that young Lord Saltire, ten years old, his only son and heir, was about to be committed to my charge. Little did I think that this would be the prelude to the most crushing misfortune of my life.

'On May 1st the boy arrived, that being the beginning of the summer term. He was a charming youth, and he soon fell into our ways. I may tell you – I trust that I am not indiscreet; half-confidences are absurd in such a case – that he was not entirely happy at home. It is an open secret that the duke's married life had not been a peaceful one, and the matter had ended in a separation by mutual consent, the duchess taking up her residence in the South of France. This had occurred very shortly before, and the boy's sympathies are known to have been strongly with his mother. He moped after her departure from Holdernesse Hall, and it was for this reason that the duke desired to send him to my establishment. In a fortnight the boy was quite at home with us, and was apparently absolutely happy.

'He was last seen on the night of May 13th – that is, the night of last Monday. His room was on the second floor, and was approached through another larger room in which two boys were sleeping. These boys saw and heard nothing, so that it is certain that young Saltire did not pass out that way. His window was open, and there is a stout ivy plant leading to the ground. We could trace no footmarks below, but it is sure that this is the only possible exit.

'His absence was discovered at seven o'clock on Tuesday morning. His bed had been slept in. He had dressed himself fully before going off in his usual school suit of black Eton jacket and dark grey trousers. There were no signs that anyone had entered the room, and it is quite certain that anything in the nature of cries or a struggle would have been heard, since Caunter, the elder boy in the inner room, is a very light sleeper.

'When Lord Saltire's disappearance was discovered I at once called a roll of the whole establishment – boys, masters, and servants. It was then that we ascertained that Lord Saltire had not been alone in his flight. Heidegger, the German master, was missing. His room was on the second floor, at the farther end of the building, facing the same way as Lord Saltire's. His bed had also been slept in; but he had apparently gone away partly dressed, since his shirt and socks were lying on the floor. He had undoubtedly let himself down by the ivy, for we could see the marks of his feet where he had landed on the lawn. His bicycle was kept in a small shed beside this lawn, and it also was gone.

'He had been with me for two years, and came with the best references; but he was a silent, morose man, not very popular with either masters or boys. No trace could be found of the fugitives, and now on Thursday morning we are as ignorant as we were on Tuesday. Inquiry was, of course, made at once at Holdernesse Hall. It is only a few miles away, and we imagined that in some sudden attack of homesickness he had gone back to his father; but nothing had been heard of him. The duke is greatly agitated – and as to me, you have seen yourselves the state of nervous prostration to which the suspense and the responsibility have reduced me. Mr Holmes, if ever you put forward your full powers, I implore you to do so now, for never in your life could you have a case which is more worthy of them.'

Sherlock Holmes had listened with the utmost intentness to the statement of the unhappy schoolmaster. His drawn brows and the deep furrow between them showed that he needed no exhortation to concentrate all his attention upon a problem which, apart from the tremendous interests involved, must appeal so directly to his love of the complex and the unusual. He now drew out his notebook and jotted down one or two memoranda.

'You have been very remiss in not coming to me sooner,' said he severely. 'You start me on my investigation with a very serious handicap. It is inconceivable, for example, that this ivy and this lawn would have yielded nothing to an expert observer.'

'I am not to blame, Mr Holmes. His Grace was extremely desirous to avoid all public scandal. He was afraid of his family unhappiness being dragged before the world. He has a deep horror of anything of the kind.'

'But there has been some official investigation?'

'Yes, sir, and it has proved most disappointing. An apparent clue was at once obtained, since a boy and a young man were reported to have been seen leaving a neighbouring station by an early train. Only last night we had news that the couple had been hunted down in Liverpool, and they prove to have no connection whatever with the matter in hand. Then it was that in my despair and disappointment, after a sleepless night, I came straight to you by the early train.'

'I suppose the local investigation was relaxed while this false clue was being followed up?'

'It was entirely dropped.'

'So that three days have been wasted. The affair has been most deplorably handled.'

'I feel it, and admit it.'

'And yet the problem should be capable of ultimate solution. I shall be very happy to look into it. Have you been able to trace any connection between the missing boy and this German master?'

'None at all.'

'Was he in the master's class?'

'No; he never exchanged a word with him, so far as I know.'

'That is certainly very singular. Had the boy a bicycle?'

'No.'

'Was any other bicycle missing?'

'No.'

'Is that certain?'

'Quite.'

'Well, now, you do not mean to seriously suggest that this German rode off upon a bicycle in the dead of the night bearing the boy in his arms?'

'Certainly not.'

'Then what is the theory in your mind?'

'The bicycle may have been a blind. It may have been hidden somewhere, and the pair gone off on foot.'

'Quite so; but it seems rather an absurd blind, does it not? Were there other bicycles in this shed?'

'Several.'

'Would he not have hidden a *couple* had he desired to give the idea that they had gone off upon them?'

'I suppose he would.'

'Of course he would. The blind theory won't do. But the incident is an admirable starting-point for an investigation. After all, a bicycle is not an easy thing to conceal or to destroy. One other question. Did anyone call to see the boy on the day before he disappeared?'

'No.

'Did he get any letters?'

'Yes; one letter.'

'From whom?'

'From his father.'

'Do you open the boys' letters?'

'No.'

'How do you know it was from the father?'

'The coat-of-arms was on the envelope, and it was addressed in the duke's peculiar stiff hand. Besides, the duke remembers having written.'

'When had he a letter before that?'

'Not for several days.'

'Had he ever had one from France?'

'No; never.'

'You see the point of my questions, of course. Either the boy was carried off by force or he went of his own free will. In the latter case you would expect that some prompting from outside would be needed to make so young a lad do such a thing. If he has had no visitors, that prompting must have come in letters. Hence I try to find out who were his correspondents.'

'I fear I cannot help much. His only correspondent, so far as I know, was his own father.'

'Who wrote to him on the very day of his disappearance. Were the relations between father and son very friendly?'

'His Grace is never very friendly with anyone. He is completely immersed in large public questions, and is rather inaccessible to all ordinary emotions. But he was always kind to the boy in his own way.

'But the sympathies of the latter were with the mother?'

'Yes.'

'Did he say so?'

'No.'

'The duke, then?'

'Good heavens, no!'

'Then how could you know?'

'I have had some confidential talk with Mr James Wilder, his Grace's secretary. It was he who gave me the information about Lord Saltire's feelings.'

'I see. By the way, that last letter of the duke's – was it found in the boy's room after he was gone?'

'No; he had taken it with him. I think, Mr Holmes, it is time that we were leaving for Euston.'

'I will order a four-wheeler. In a quarter of an hour we shall be at your service. If you are telegraphing home, Mr Huxtable, it would be well to allow the people in your neighbourhood to imagine that the inquiry is still going on in Liverpool, or wherever else that red herring led your pack. In the meantime, I will do a little quiet work at your own doors, and perhaps the scent is not so cold but that two old hounds like Watson and myself may get a sniff of it.'

That evening found us in the cold, bracing atmosphere of the Peak country, in which Dr Huxtable's famous school is situated. It was already dark when we reached it. A card was lying on the hall table, and the butler whispered something to his master, who turned to us with agitation in every heavy feature.

'The duke is here,' said he. 'The duke and Mr

Wilder are in the study. Come, gentlemen, and I will introduce you.

I was, of course, familiar with the pictures of the famous statesman, but the man himself was very different from his representation. He was a tall and stately person, scrupulously dressed, with a drawn, thin face, and a nose which was grotesquely curved and long. His complexion was of a dead pallor, which was more startling by contrast with a long, dwindling beard of vivid red, which flowed down over his white waistcoat, with his watch-chain gleaming through its fringe. Such was the stately presence who looked stonily at us from the centre of Dr Huxtable's hearthrug. Beside him stood a very young man, whom I understood to be Wilder, the private secretary. He was small, nervous, alert, with intelligent, light blue eyes and mobile features. It was he who at once, in an incisive and positive tone, opened the conversation.

'I called this morning, Dr Huxtable, too late to prevent you from starting for London. I learned that your object was to invite Mr Sherlock Holmes to undertake the conduct of this case. His Grace is surprised, Dr Huxtable, that you should have taken such a step without consulting him.'

'When I learned the police had failed –'

'His Grace is by no means convinced that the police have failed.'

'But surely, Mr Wilder –'

'You are well aware, Dr Huxtable, that his

Grace is particularly anxious to avoid all public scandal. He prefers to take as few people as possible into his confidence.'

'The matter can be easily remedied,' said the brow-beaten doctor. 'Mr Sherlock Holmes can return to London by the morning train.'

'Hardly that, Doctor, hardly that,' said Holmes, in his blandest voice. 'This northern air is invigorating and pleasant, so I propose to spend a few days upon your moors, and to occupy my mind as best I may. Whether I have the shelter of your roof or of the village inn is, of course, for you to decide.'

I could see that the unfortunate doctor was in the last stage of indecision, from which he was rescued by the deep, sonorous voice of the red-bearded duke, which boomed out like a dinner-gong.

'I agree with Mr Wilder, Dr Huxtable, that you would have done wisely to consult me. But since Mr Holmes has already been taken into your confidence, it would indeed be absurd that we should not avail ourselves of his services. Far from going to the inn, Mr Holmes, I should be pleased if you would come and stay with me at Holdernesse Hall?'

'I thank your Grace. For the purposes of my investigation I think that it would be wiser for me to remain at the scene of the mystery.'

'Just as you like, Mr Holmes. Any information which Mr Wilder or I can give you is, of course, at your disposal.'

'It will probably be necessary for me to see you at the Hall,' said Holmes. 'I would only ask you now, sir, whether you have formed any explanation in your own mind as to the mysterious disappearance of your son?'

'No, sir, I have not.'

'Excuse me if I allude to that which is painful to you, but I have no alternative. Do you think that the duchess had anything to do with the matter?'

The great minister showed perceptible hesitation.

'I do not think so,' he said at last.

'The other most obvious explanation is that the child has been kidnapped for the purpose of levying ransom. You have not had any demand of the sort?'

'No, sir.'

'One more question, your Grace. I understand that you wrote to your son upon the day when this incident occurred.'

'No! I wrote upon the day before.'

'Exactly. But he received it on that day?'

'Yes.'

'Was there anything in your letter which might have unbalanced him or induced him to take such a step?'

'No, sir, certainly not.'

'Did you post that letter yourself?'

The nobleman's reply was interrupted by his secretary, who broke in with some heat.

'His Grace is not in the habit of posting letters himself,' said he. 'The letter was laid with others upon the study table, and I myself put them in the post-bag.'

'You are sure this one was among them?'

'Yes; I observed it.'

'How many letters did your Grace write that day?'

'Twenty or thirty. I have a large correspondence. But surely this is somewhat irrelevant?'

'Not entirely,' said Holmes.

'For my own part,' the duke continued, 'I have advised the police to turn their attention to the South of France. I have already said that I do not believe that the duchess would encourage so monstrous an action, but the lad had the most wrong-headed opinions, and it is possible that he may have fled to her, aided and abetted by this German. I think, Dr Huxtable, that we will now return to the Hall.'

I could see that there were other questions which Holmes would have wished to put; but the nobleman's abrupt manner showed that the interview was at an end. It was evident that to his intensely aristocratic nature this discussion of his intimate family affairs with a stranger was most abhorrent, and that he feared lest every fresh question would throw a fiercer light into the discreetly shadowed corners of his ducal history.

When the nobleman and his secretary had left, my friend flung himself at once with characteristic eagerness into the investigation.

The boy's chamber was carefully examined, and yielded nothing save the absolute conviction that it was only through the window that he could have escaped. The German master's room and effects gave no further clue. In his case a trailer of ivy had given way under his weight, and we saw by the light of a lantern the mark on the lawn where his heels had come down. That one dent in the short green grass was the only material witness left of this inexplicable nocturnal flight.

Sherlock Holmes left the house alone, and only returned after eleven. He had obtained a large ordnance map of the neighbourhood, and this he brought into my room, where he laid it out on the bed, and, having balanced the lamp in the middle of it, he began to smoke over it, and occasionally to point out objects of interest with the reeking amber of his pipe.

'This case grows upon me, Watson,' said he. 'There are decidedly some points of interest in connection with it. In this early stage I want you to realize these geographical features, which may have a good deal to do with our investigation.

'Look at this map. This dark square is the Priory School. I'll put a pin in it. Now, this line is the main road. You see that it runs east and west past the school, and you see also there is no side-road for a mile either way. If these two folk passed away by road it was *this* road.'

'Exactly.'

'By a singular and happy chance we are able to

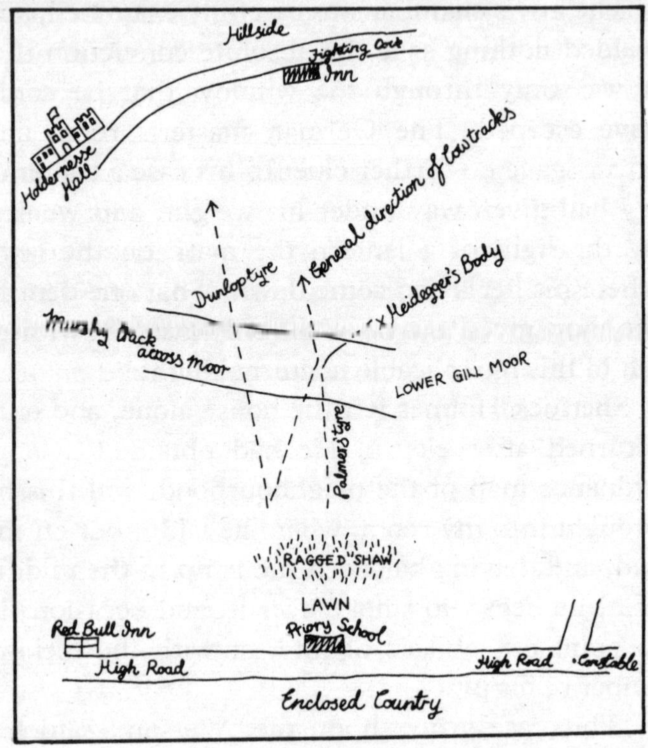

some extent to check what passed along this road during the night in question. At this point, where my pipe is now resting, a country constable was on duty from twelve to six. It is, as you perceive, the first crossroad on the east side. This man declares that he was not absent from his post for an instant, and he is positive that neither boy nor man could have gone that way unseen. I have spoken with this policeman tonight, and he appears to me to be a perfectly reliable person. That blocks this end. We have now to deal with the other. There is an inn here, the Red Bull, the land-lady of which was ill. She had sent to Mackleton for a doctor, but he did not arrive until morning, being absent at another case. The people at the inn were alert all night, awaiting his coming, and one or other of them seems to have continually had an eye upon the road. They declare that no one passed. If their evidence is good, then we are fortunate enough to be able to block the west, and also to be able to say that the fugitives did *not* use the road at all.'

'But the bicycle?' I objected.

'Quite so. We will come to the bicycle presently. To continue our reasoning: if these people did not go by the road, they must have traversed the country to the north of the house or to the south of the house. That is certain. Let us weigh the one against the other. On the south of the house is, as you perceive, a large district of arable land, cut up into small fields, with stone walls between them. There, I admit that a bicycle is impossible. We can dismiss the idea. We turn to the country on the north. Here there lies a grove of trees, marked as the "Ragged Shaw", and on the farther side stretches a great rolling moor, Lower Gill Moor, extending for ten miles, and sloping gradually upwards. Here, at one side of this wilderness, is Holdernessc Hall, ten miles by road, but only six across the moor. It is a peculiarly desolate plain. A few moor farmers have small holdings, where they rear sheep and cattle. Except these, the plover and the curlew are the only inhabitants until you come to the Chesterfield high-road. There is a church there, you see, a few cottages, and an inn. Beyond that the hills become precipitous. Surely it is here to the north that our quest must lie.'

'But the bicycle?' I persisted.

'Well, well!' said Holmes impatiently. 'A good cyclist does not need a high road. The moor is intersected with paths, and the moon was at the full. Halloa! What is this?'

There was an agitated knock at the door, and an instant afterwards Dr Huxtable was in the room. In his hand he held a blue cricket-cap, with a white chevron on the peak.

'At last we have a clue!' he cried. 'Thank Heaven, at last we are on the dear boy's track! It is his cap.'

'Where was it found?'

'In the van of the gipsies who camped on the moor. They left on Tuesday. Today the police traced them down and examined their caravan. This was found.'

'How do they account for it?'

'They shuffled and lied – said that they found it on the moor on Tuesday morning. They know where he is, the rascals! Thank goodness, they are all safe under lock and key. Either the fear of the law or the duke's purse will certainly get out of them all that they know.'

'So far, so good,' said Holmes, when the doctor had at last left the room. 'It at least bears out the theory that it is on the side of the Lower Gill Moor that we must hope for results. The police have really done nothing locally, save the arrest of these gipsies. Look here, Watson! There is a watercourse across the moor. You see it marked here in the map. In some parts it widens into a morass. This is particularly so in the region between Holdernesse Hall and the school. It is vain to look elsewhere for tracks in this dry weather; but at *that* point there is certainly a chance of some record being left. I will call you early tomorrow morning, and you and I will try if we can to throw some light upon the mystery.'

The day was just breaking when I woke to find the long, thin form of Holmes by my bedside. He was fully dressed, and had apparently already been out.

'I have done the lawn and the bicycle shed,' said he. 'I have also had a ramble through the Ragged Shaw. Now, Watson, there is cocoa ready in the next room. I must beg you to hurry, for we have a great day before us.'

His eyes shone, and his cheek was flushed with the exhilaration of the master workman who sees his work lies ready before him. A very different Holmes, this active, alert man, from the introspective and pallid dreamer of Baker Street. I felt, as I looked upon that supple figure, alive with nervous energy, that it was indeed a strenuous day that awaited us.

And yet it opened in the blackest disappointment.

With high hopes we struck across the peaty, russet moor, intersected with a thousand sheep-paths, until we came to the broad light-green belt which marked the morass between us and Holdernesse. Certainly, if the lad had gone homewards, he must have passed this, and he would not pass it without leaving his trace. But no sign of him or the German could be seen. With a darkening face my friend strode along the margin, eagerly observant of every muddy stain upon the mossy surface. Sheep-marks there were in profusion, and at one place, some miles down, cows had left their tracks. Nothing more.

'Check number one,' said Holmes, looking gloomily over the rolling expanse of the moor. 'There is another morass down yonder, and a narrow neck between. Halloa! halloa! halloa! What have we here?'

We had come on a small black ribbon of pathway. In the middle of it, clearly marked on the sodden soil, was the track of a bicycle.

'Hurrah!' I cried. 'We have it.'

But Holmes was shaking his head, and his face was puzzled and expectant rather than joyous.

'A bicycle certainly, but not *the* bicycle,' said he. 'I am familiar with forty-two different impressions left by tyres. This, as you perceive, is a Dunlop, with a patch upon the outer cover. Heidegger's tyres were Palmers', leaving longitudinal stripes. Aveling, the mathematical master, was sure upon the point. Therefore it is not Heidegger's track.'

'The boy's, then?'

'Possibly, if we could prove a bicycle to have been in his possession. But this we have utterly failed to do. This track, as you perceive, was made by a rider who was going from the direction of the school.'

'Or towards it?'

'No, no, my dear Watson. The more deeply sunk impression is, of course, the hind wheel, upon which the weight rests. You perceive several places where it has passed across and obliterated the more shallow mark of the front one. It was undoubtedly heading away from the school. It may or may not be connected with our inquiry, but we will follow it backwards before we go any farther.'

We did so, and at the end of a few hundred yards lost the tracks as we emerged from the boggy portion of the moor. Following the path backwards, we picked out another spot, where a spring trickled across it. Here, once again, was the mark of the bicycle, though nearly obliterated by the hoofs of cows. After that there was no sign, but the path ran right on into Ragged Shaw, the wood which backed on to the school. From this wood the cycle must have emerged. Holmes sat down on a boulder and rested his chin in his hands. I had smoked two cigarettes before he moved.

'Well, well,' said he at last. 'It is, of course, possible that a cunning man might change the tyre of his bicycle in order to leave unfamiliar tracks. A criminal who was capable of such a thought is a man whom I should be proud to do business with. We will leave this question undecided and hark back to our morass again, for we have left a good deal unexplored.'

We continued our systematic survey of the edge of the sodden portion of the moor, and soon our perseverance was gloriously rewarded.

Right across the lower part of the bog lay a miry path. Holmes gave a cry of delight as he approached it. An impression like a fine bundle of telegraph wires ran down the centre of it. It was the Palmer tyre.

'Here is Herr Heidegger, sure enough!' cried Holmes exultantly. 'My reasoning seems to have been pretty sound, Watson.'

'I congratulate you.

'But we have a long way still to go. Kindly walk clear of the path. Now let us follow the trail. I fear that it will not lead very far.'

We found, however, as we advanced, that this portion of the moor was intersected with soft patches, and, though we frequently lost sight of the track, we always succeeded in picking it up once more.

'Do you observe,' said Holmes, 'that the rider is now undoubtedly forcing the pace? There can be no doubt of it. Look at this impression, where you get both tyres clear. The one is as deep as the other. That can only mean that the rider is throwing his weight on to the handle-bar as a man does when he is sprinting. By Jove! he has had a fall.'

There was a broad irregular smudge covering some yards of the track. Then there were a few footmarks, and the tyre reappeared once more.

'A side-slip,' I suggested.

Holmes held up a crumpled branch of flowering gorse. To my horror I perceived that the yellow blossoms were all dabbled with crimson. On the path, too, and among the heather were dark stains of clotted blood.

'Bad!' said Holmes. 'Bad! Stand clear, Watson! Not an unnecessary footstep! What do I read here? He fell wounded, he stood up, he re-mounted, he proceeded. But there is no other track. Cattle on this side-path. He was surely not gored by a bull? Impossible! But I see no traces of anyone else. We must push on, Watson. Surely, with stains as well as the track to guide us, he cannot escape us now.'

Our search was not a very long one. The tracks of the tyre began to curve fantastically upon the wet and shining path. Suddenly, as I looked ahead, the gleam of metal caught my eye from amid the thick gorse bushes. Out of them we dragged a bicycle, Palmer-tyred, one pedal bent, and the whole front of it horribly smeared and slobbered with blood. On the other side of the bushes a shoe was projecting. We ran round, and there lay the unfortunate rider. He was a tall man, full bearded, with spectacles, one glass of which had been knocked out. The cause of his death was a frightful blow upon the head, which had crushed in part of his skull. That he could have gone on after receiving such an injury said much for the vitality and courage of the man. He wore shoes, but no socks, and his open coat disclosed a night-shirt beneath it. It was undoubtedly the German master.

Holmes turned the body over reverently, and examined it with great attention. He then sat in deep thought for a time, and I could see by his ruffled brow that this grim discovery had not, in his opinion, advanced us much in our inquiry.

'It is a little difficult to know what to do, Watson,' said he, at last. 'My own inclinations are to push this inquiry on, for we have already lost so much time that we cannot afford to waste another hour. On the other hand, we are bound to inform the police of this discovery, and to see that this poor fellow's body is looked after.'

'I could take a note back.'

'But I need your company and assistance. Wait a bit! There is a fellow cutting peat up yonder. Bring him over here, and he will guide the police.'

I brought the peasant across, and Holmes dispatched the frightened man with a note to Dr Huxtable.

'Now, Watson,' said he, 'we have picked up two clues this morning. One is the bicycle with the Palmer tyre, and we see what that has led to. The other is the bicycle with the patched Dunlop. Before we start to investigate that, let us try to realize what we *do* know, so as to make the most of it, and to separate the essential from the accidental.

'First of all, I wish to impress upon you that the boy certainly left of his own free will. He got down from his window and he went off, either alone or with someone. That is sure.'

I assented.

'Well, now, let us turn to this unfortunate German master. The boy was fully dressed when he fled. Therefore he foresaw what he would do. But the German went without his socks. He certainly acted on very short notice.'

'Undoubtedly.'

'Why did he go? Because, from his bedroom window, he saw the flight of the boy. Because he wished to overtake him and bring him back. He seized his bicycle, pursued the lad, and in pursuing him met his death.'

'So it would seem.'

'Now I come to the critical part of my argument. The natural action of a man in pursuing a little boy would be to run after him. He would know that he could overtake him. But the German does not do so. He turns to his bicycle. I am told that he was an excellent cyclist. He would not do this if he did not see that the boy had some swift means of escape.'

'The other bicycle.'

'Let us continue our reconstruction. He meets his death five miles from the school – not by a bullet, mark you, which even a lad might conceivably discharge, but by a savage blow dealt by a vigorous arm. The lad, then, *had* a companion in his flight. And the flight was a swift one, since it took five miles before an expert cyclist could overtake them. Yet we survey the ground round the scene of the tragedy. What do we find? A few cattle tracks, nothing more. I took a wide sweep round, and there is no path within fifty yards. Another cyclist could have had nothing to do with the actual murder. Nor were there any human footmarks.'

'Holmes,' I cried, 'this is impossible.'

'Admirable!' he said. 'A most illuminating remark. It *is* impossible as I state it, and therefore I must in some respect have stated it wrong. Yet you saw for yourself. Can you suggest any fallacy?'

'He could not have fractured his skull in a fall?'

'In a morass, Watson?'

'I am at my wits' end.'

'Tut, tut; we have solved some worse problems. At least we have plenty of material, if we can only use it. Come, then, and, having exhausted the Palmer, let us see what the Dunlop with the patched cover has to offer us.'

We picked up the track and followed it onwards for some distance; but soon the moor rose into a long, heather-tufted curve, and we left the water-course behind us. No further help from tracks could be hoped for. At the spot where we saw the last of the Dunlop tyre it might equally have led to Holdernesse Hall, the stately towers of which rose some miles to our left, or to a low, grey village which lay in front of us, and marked the position of the Chesterfield high-road.

As we approached the forbidding and squalid inn, with the Sign of a game-cock above the door, Holmes gave a sudden groan and clutched me by the shoulder to save himself from falling. He had had one of those violent strains of the ankle which leave a man helpless. With difficulty he limped up to the door, where a squat, dark, elderly man was smoking a black clay pipe.

'How are you, Mr Reuben Hayes?' said Holmes.

'Who are you, and how do you get my name so pat?' the countryman answered, with a suspicious flash of a pair of cunning eyes.

'Well, it's printed on the board above your head. It's easy to see a man who is master of his own house. I suppose you haven't such a thing as a carriage in your stables?'

'No; I have not.'

'I can hardly put my foot to the ground.'

'Don't put it to the ground.'

'But I can't walk.'

'Well, then, hop.'

Mr Reuben Hayes's manner was far from gracious, but Holmes took it with admirable good humour.

'Look here, my man,' said he. 'This is really

rather an awkward fix for me. I don't mind how I get on.'

'Neither do I,' said the morose landlord.

'The matter is very important. I would offer you a sovereign for the use of a bicycle.'

The landlord pricked up his ears.

'Where do you want to go?'

'To Holdernesse Hall.'

'Pals of the dook, I suppose?' said the landlord, surveying our mud-stained garments with ironical eyes.

Holmes laughed good-naturedly.

'He'll be glad to see us, anyhow.'

'Why?'

'Because we bring him news of his lost son.'

The landlord gave a very visible start.

'What, you're on his track?'

'He has been heard of in Liverpool. They expect to get him every hour.'

Again a swift change passed over the heavy, unshaven face. His manner was suddenly genial.

'I've less reason to wish the dook well than most men,' said he, 'for I was his headcoachman once, and cruel bad he treated me. It was him that sacked me without a character on the word of a lying corn-chandler. But I'm glad to hear that the young lord was heard of in Liverpool, and I'll help you to take the news to the Hall.'

'Thank you,' said Holmes. 'We'll have some food first. Then you can bring round the bicycle.'

'I haven't got a bicycle.'

Holmes held up a sovereign.

'I tell you, man, that I haven't got one. I'll let you have two horses as far as the Hall.'

'Well, well,' said Holmes, 'we'll talk about it when we've had something to eat.'

When we were left alone in the stone-flagged kitchen it was astonishing how rapidly that sprained ankle recovered. It was nearly nightfall, and we had eaten nothing since early morning, so that we spent some time over our meal. Holmes was lost in thought, and once or twice he walked over to the window and stared earnestly out. It opened on to a squalid courtyard. In the far corner was a smithy, where a grimy lad was at work. On the side were the stables. Holmes had sat down again after one of these excursions, when he suddenly sprang out of his chair with a loud exclamation.

'By Heaven, Watson, I believe that I've got it!' he cried. 'Yes, yes, it must be so. Watson, do you remember seeing any cow-tracks today?'

'Yes, several.'

'Where?'

'Well, everywhere. They were at the morass, and again on the path, and again near where poor Heidegger met his death.'

'Exactly. Well, now, Watson, how many cows did you see on the moor?'

'I don't remember seeing any.'

'Strange, Watson, that we should see tracks all along our line, but never a cow on the whole moor; very strange, Watson, eh?'

'Yes, it is strange.'

'Now, Watson, make an effort; throw your mind back! Can you see those tracks upon the path?'

'Yes, I can.'

'Can you recall that the tracks were sometimes like that, Watson' – he arranged a number of breadcrumbs in this fashion – ::::: – 'and sometimes like this' – :· :· :· :· – 'and occasionally like this' ·· ·· ··

'Can you remember that?'

'No, I cannot.'

'But I can. I could swear to it. However, we will go back at our leisure and verify it. What a blind beetle I have been not to draw my conclusion!'

'And what is your conclusion?'

'Only that it is a remarkable cow which walks, canters, and gallops. By George, Watson, it was no brain of a country publican that thought out such a blind as that! The coast seems to be clear, save for that lad in the smithy. Let us slip out and see what we can see.'

There were two rough-haired, unkempt horses in the tumbledown stable. Holmes raised the hind leg of one of them and laughed loud.

'Old shoes, but newly shod – old shoes, but new nails. This case deserves to be a classic. Let us go across to the smithy.'

The lad continued his work without regarding us. I saw Holmes's eye darting to right and left among the litter of iron and wood, which was scattered about the floor. Suddenly, however, we heard a step behind us, and there was the landlord, his heavy eyebrows drawn down over his savage eyes, his swarthy features convulsed with passion.

He held a short metal-headed stick in his hand, and he advanced in so menacing a fashion that I was right glad to feel the revolver in my pocket.

You infernal spies!' the man cried. 'What are you doing there?'

'Why, Mr Reuben Hayes,' said Holmes coolly, 'one might think that you were afraid of our finding something out.'

The man mastered himself with a violent effort, and his grim mouth loosened into a false laugh, which was more menacing than his frown.

'You're welcome to all you can find out in my smithy,' said he. 'But look here, mister, I don't care for folk poking about my place without my leave, so the sooner you pay your score and get out of this the better I shall be pleased.'

'All right, Mr Hayes – no harm meant,' said Holmes. 'We have been having a look at your horses; but I think I'll walk after all. It's not far, I believe.'

'Not more than two miles to the Hall gates. That's the road to the left.' He watched us with sullen eyes until we had left his premises.

We did not go very far along the road, for Holmes stopped the instant that the curve hid us from the landlord's view.

'We were warm, as the children say, at that

inn,' said he. 'I seem to grow colder every step that I take away from it. No, no; I can't possibly leave it.'

'I am convinced,' said I, 'that this Reuben Hayes knows all about it. A more self-evident villain I never saw.'

'Oh! he impressed you in that way, did he? There are the horses, there is the smithy. Yes, it is an interesting place, this Fighting Cock. I think we shall have another look at it in an unobtrusive way.'

A long, sloping hill-side, dotted with grey lime-stone boulders, stretched behind us. We had turned off the road, and were making our way up the hill, when, looking in the direction of Holder-nesse Hall, I saw a cyclist coming swiftly along.

'Get down, Watson!' cried Holmes, with a heavy hand upon my shoulder. We had hardly sunk from view when the man flew past us on the road. Amid a rolling cloud of dust I caught a glimpse of a pale, agitated face – a face with horror in every lineament, the mouth open, the eyes staring wildly in front. It was like some strange caricature of the dapper James Wilder whom we had seen the night before.

'The duke's secretary!' cried Holmes. 'Come, Watson, let us see what he does.'

We scrambled from rock to rock until in a few moments we had made our way to a point from which we could see the front door of the inn. Wilder's bicycle was leaning against the wall beside it. No one was moving about the house, nor could we catch a glimpse of any faces at the windows. Slowly the twilight crept down as the sun sank behind the high towers of Holdernesse Hall. Then in the gloom we saw the two side-lamps of a trap light up in the stable-yard of the inn, and shortly afterwards heard the rattle of hoofs, as it wheeled out into the road and tore off at a furious pace in the direction of Chesterfield.

'What do you make of that, Watson?' Holmes whispered.

'It looks like a flight.'

'A single man in a dog-cart, so far as I could see. Well, it certainly was not Mr James Wilder, for there he is at the door.'

A red square of light had sprung out of the darkness. In the middle of it was the black figure of the secretary, his head advanced, peering out into the night. It was evident that he was expecting someone. Then at last there were steps in the road, a second figure was visible for an instant against the light, the door shut, and all was black once more. Five minutes later a lamp was lit in a room upon the first floor.

'It seems to be a curious class of custom that is done by the Fighting Cock,' said Holmes.

'The bar is on the other side.'

'Quite so. These are what one may call the private guests. Now, what in the world is Mr James Wilder doing in that den at this hour of night, and who is the companion who comes to meet him there? Come, Watson, we must really take a risk and try to investigate this a little more closely.'

Together we stole down to the road and crept across to the door of the inn. The bicycle still leaned against the wall. Holmes struck a match and held it to the back wheel, and I heard him chuckle as the light fell upon a patched Dunlop tyre. Up above us was the lighted window.

'I must have a peep through that, Watson. If you bend your back and support yourself upon the wall, I think that I can manage.'

An instant later his feet were on my shoulders. But he was hardly up before he was down again.

'Come, my friend,' said he, 'our day's work has been quite long enough. I think that we have gathered all that we can. It's a long walk to the school, and the sooner we get started the better.'

He hardly opened his lips during that weary trudge across the moor, nor would he enter the school when he reached it, but went on to Mackleton Station, whence he could send some telegrams. Late at night I heard him consoling Dr Huxtable, prostrated by the tragedy of his master's death, and later still he entered my room as alert and vigorous as he had been when he started in the morning. 'All goes well, my friend,' said he. 'I promise that before tomorrow evening we shall have reached the solution of the mystery.'

At eleven o'clock next morning my friend and I were walking up the famous yew avenue of Holdernesse Hall. We were ushered through the magnificent Elizabethan doorway and into his Grace's study. There we found Mr James Wilder, demure and courtly, but with some trace of that wild terror of the night before still lurking in his furtive eyes and in his twitching features.

'You have come to see his Grace? I am sorry; but the fact is that the duke is far from well. He has been very much upset by the tragic news. We received a telegram from Dr Huxtable yesterday afternoon, which told us of your discovery.'

'I must see the duke, Mr Wilder.'

'But he is in his room.'

'Then I must go to his room.'

'I believe he is in his bed.'

'I will see him there.'

Holmes's cold and inexorable manner showed the secretary that it was useless to argue with him.

'Very good, Mr Holmes; I will tell him that you are here.'

After half an hour's delay the great nobleman appeared. His face was more cadaverous than ever, his shoulders had rounded, and he seemed to me to be an altogether older man than he had been the morning before. He greeted us with a stately courtesy, and seated himself at his desk, his red beard streaming down on to the table.

'Well, Mr Holmes?' said he.

But my friend's eyes were fixed upon the secretary, who stood by his master's chair.

'I think, your Grace, that I could speak more freely in Mr Wilder's absence.

The man turned a shade paler and cast a malignant glance at Holmes.

'If your Grace wishes –'

'Yes, yes; you had better go. Now, Mr Holmes, what have you to say?'

My friend waited until the door had closed behind the retreating secretary.

'The fact is, your Grace,' said he, 'that my colleague, Dr Watson, and myself had an assurance from Dr Huxtable that a reward had been offered in this case. I should like to have this confirmed from your own lips.'

'Certainly, Mr Holmes.'

'It amounted, if I am correctly informed, to five thousand pounds to anyone who will tell you where your son is?'

'Exactly.'

'And another thousand to the man who will name the person or persons who keep him in custody?'

'Exactly.'

'Under the latter heading is included, no doubt, not only those who may have taken him away, but also those who conspire to keep him in his present position?'

'Yes, yes,' cried the duke impatiently. 'If you do your work well, Mr Sherlock Holmes, you will have no reason to complain of niggardly treatment.'

My friend rubbed his thin hands together with

an appearance of avidity which was a surprise to me, who knew his frugal tastes.

'I fancy that I see your Grace's cheque-book upon the table,' said he. 'I should be glad if you would make me out a cheque for six thousand pounds. It would be as well, perhaps, for you to cross it. The Capital and Counties Bank, Oxford Street branch, are my agents.'

His Grace sat very stern and upright in his chair, and looked stonily at my friend.

'Is this a joke, Mr Holmes? It is hardly a subject for pleasantry.'

'Not at all, your Grace. I was never more earnest in my life.'

'What do you mean, then?'

'I mean that I have earned the reward, I know where your son is, and I know some, at least, of those who are holding him.'

The duke's beard had turned more aggressively red than ever against his ghastly white face.

'Where is he?' he gasped.

'He is, or was last night, at the Fighting Cock Inn, about two miles from your park gate.'

The duke fell back in his chair.

'And whom do you accuse?'

Sherlock Holmes's answer was an astounding one. He stepped swiftly forward and touched the duke upon the shoulder.

'I accuse *you*,' said he. 'And now, your Grace, I'll trouble you for that cheque.'

Never shall I forget the duke's appearance as he

sprang up and clawed with his hands like one who is sinking into an abyss. Then, with an extraordinary effort of aristocratic self-command, he sat down and sank his face in his hands. It was some minutes before he spoke.

'How much do you know?' he asked at last, without raising his head.

'I saw you together last night.'

'Does anyone else besides your friend know?'

'I have spoken to no one.'

The duke took a pen in his quivering fingers and opened his cheque-book.

'I shall be as good as my word, Mr Holmes. I am about to write your cheque, however unwelcome the information which you have gained may be to me. When the offer was first made I little thought the turn which events would take. But you and your friend are men of discretion, Mr Holmes?'

'I hardly understand your Grace.'

'I must put it plainly, Mr Holmes. If only you two know of the incident, there is no reason why it should go any farther. I think twelve thousand pounds is the sum that I owe you, is it not?'

But Holmes smiled, and shook his head.

'I fear, your Grace, that matters can hardly be arranged so easily. There is the death of this schoolmaster to be accounted for.'

'But James knew nothing of that. You cannot hold him responsible for that. It was the work of this brutal ruffian whom he had the misfortune to employ.'

'I must take the view, your Grace, that when a man embarks upon a crime he is morally guilty of any other crime which may spring from it.'

'Morally, Mr Holmes. No doubt you are right. But surely not in the eyes of the law. A man cannot be condemned for a murder at which he was not present, and which he loathes and abhors as much as you do. The instant that he heard of it he made a complete confession to me, so filled was he with horror and remorse. He lost not an hour in breaking entirely with the murderer. Oh, Mr Holmes, you must save him – you must save him! I tell you that you must save him!' The duke had dropped the last attempt at self-command, and was pacing the room with a convulsed face and with his clenched hands raving in the air. At last he mastered himself and sat down once more at his desk. 'I appreciate your conduct in coming here before you spoke to anyone else,' said he. 'At least we may take counsel how far we can minimize this hideous scandal.'

'Exactly,' said Holmes. 'I think, your Grace, that this can only be done by absolute and complete frankness between us. I am disposed to help your Grace to the best of my ability; but in order to do so I must understand to the last detail how the matter stands. I realize that your words applied to Mr James Wilder, and that he is not the murderer.'

'No; the murderer has escaped.'

Sherlock Holmes smiled demurely.

'Your Grace can hardly have heard of any small reputation which I possess, or you would not imagine that it is so easy to escape me. Mr Reuben Hayes was arrested at Chesterfield on my information at eleven o'clock last night. I had a telegram from the head of the local police before I left the school this morning.'

The duke leaned back in his chair and stared with amazement at my friend.

'You seem to have powers that are hardly human,' said he. 'So Reuben Hayes is taken? I am right glad to hear it, if it will not react upon the fate of James.'

'Your secretary?'

'No, sir; my son.'

It was Holmes's turn to look astonished.

'I confess that this is entirely new to me, your Grace, I must beg of you to be more explicit.'

'I will conceal nothing from you. I agree with you that complete frankness, however painful it may be to me, is the best policy in this desperate situation to which James's folly and jealousy have reduced us. When I was a young man, Mr Holmes, I loved with such a love as comes only once in a lifetime. I offered the lady marriage, but she refused it on the grounds that such a match might mar my career. Had she lived, I would certainly have never married anyone else. She died, and left this one child, whom for her sake I have cherished and cared for. I could not acknowledge the paternity to the world; but I gave him the best of educations, and since he came to manhood I have kept him near my person. He surprised my secret, and has presumed ever since upon the claim which he has upon me and upon his power of provoking a scandal, which would be abhorrent to me. His presence had something to do with the unhappy issue of my marriage. Above all, he hated my young legitimate heir from the first with a persistent hatred. You may well ask me why, under these circumstances, I still kept James under my roof. I answer that it was because I could see his mother's face in his, and that for her dear sake there was no end to my long-suffering. All her pretty ways, too – there was not one of them which he could not suggest and bring back to my memory. I *could* not send him away. But I feared so lest he should do Arthur – that is, Lord Saltire – a mischief that I dispatched him for safety to Dr Huxtable's school.

'James came into contact with this fellow Hayes because the man was a tenant of mine, and James acted as agent. The fellow was a rascal from the beginning; but in some extraordinary way James became intimate with him. He had always a taste for low company. When James determined to kidnap Lord Saltire it was of this man's service that he availed himself. You remember that I wrote to Arthur upon that last day. Well, James opened the letter and inserted a note asking Arthur to meet him in a little wood called the Ragged Shaw which is near to the school. He used the duchess's name, and in that way got the boy to come. That evening James cycled over – I am telling you what he has himself confessed to me – and he told Arthur, whom he met in the wood, that his mother longed to see him, that she was awaiting him on the moor, and that if he would come back into the wood at midnight he would find a man with a horse, who would take him to her. Poor Arthur fell into the trap. He came to the appointment and found this fellow Hayes with a led pony. Arthur mounted, and they set off together. It appears – though this James only heard yesterday – that they were pursued, that Hayes struck the pursuer with his stick, and that the man died of his injuries. Hayes brought Arthur to his public-house, the Fighting Cock, where he was confined in an upper room, under the care of Mrs Hayes, who is a kindly woman, but entirely under the control of her brutal husband.

'Well, Mr Holmes, that was the state of affairs when I first saw you two days ago. I had no more idea of the truth than you. You will ask me what was James's motive in doing such a deed. I answer that there was a great deal which was unreasoning and fanatical in the hatred which he bore my heir. In his view he himself should have been heir of all my estates, and he deeply resented those social laws which made it impossible. At the same time, he had a definite motive also. He was eager that I should break the entail, and he was of opinion that it lay in my power to do so. He intended to make a bargain with me – to restore Arthur if I would break the entail, and so make it possible for the estate to be left to him by will. He knew well that I should never willingly invoke the aid of the police against him. I say that he would have proposed such a bargain to me, but he did not actually do so, for events moved too quickly for him, and he had not time to put his plans into practice.

'What brought all his wicked scheme to wreck was your discovery of this man Heidegger's dead body. James was seized with horror at the news. It came to us yesterday as we sat together in this study. Dr Huxtable had sent a telegram. James was so overwhelmed with grief and agitation that my suspicions, which had never been entirely absent, rose instantly to a certainty, and I taxed him with the deed. He made a complete voluntary confession. Then he implored me to keep his secret for three days longer, so as to give his wretched accomplice a chance of saving his guilty life. I yielded – as I have always yielded – to his prayers, and instantly James hurried off to the Fighting Cock to warn Hayes and give him the means of flight. I could not go there by daylight without provoking comment, but as soon as night fell I hurried off to see my dear Arthur. I found him safe and well, but horrified beyond expression by the dreadful deed he had witnessed. In deference to my promise, and much against my will, I consented to leave him there for three days under the charge of Mrs Hayes, since it was evident that it was impossible to inform the police where he was without telling them also who was the murderer, and I could not see how that murderer could be punished without ruin to my unfortunate James. You asked for frankness, Mr Holmes, and I have taken you at your word, for I have now told you everything without an attempt at circumlocution or concealment. Do you in your turn be as frank with me.'

'I will,' said Holmes. 'In the first place, your Grace, I am bound to tell you that you have placed yourself in a most serious position in the eyes of the law. You have condoned a felony, and you have aided the escape of a murderer; for I cannot doubt that any money which was taken by James Wilder to aid his accomplice in his flight came from your Grace's purse.'

The duke bowed his assent.

'This is indeed a most serious matter. Even more culpable in my opinion, your Grace, is your attitude towards your younger son. You leave him in this den for three days.'

'Under solemn promises –'

'What are promises to such people as these? You have no guarantee that he will not be spirited away again. To humour your guilty elder son you have exposed your innocent younger son to imminent and unnecessary danger. It was a most unjustifiable action.'

The proud lord of Holdernesse was not accustomed to be so rated in his own ducal hall. The blood flushed into his high forehead, but his conscience held him dumb.

'I will help you, but on one condition only. It is that you ring for the footman and let me give such orders as I like.'

Without a word the duke pressed the electric button. A servant entered.

'You will be glad to hear,' said Holmes, 'that your young master is found. It is the duke's desire that the carriage shall go at once to the Fighting Cock Inn to bring Lord Saltire home.'

'Now,' said Holmes, when the rejoicing lackey had disappeared, 'having secured the future we can afford to be more lenient with the past. I am not in an official position, and there is no reason, so long as the ends of justice are served, why I should disclose all that I know. As to Hayes I say nothing. The gallows awaits him, and I would do nothing to save him from it. What he will divulge I cannot tell, but I have no doubt that your Grace could make him understand that it is to his interest to be silent. From the police point of view he will have kidnapped the boy for the purpose of ransom. If they do not themselves find it out I see no reason why I should prompt them to take a broader view. I would warn your Grace, however, that the continued presence of Mr James Wilder in your household can only lead to misfortune.'

'I understand that, Mr Holmes, and it is already settled that he shall leave me for ever and go to seek his fortune in Australia.'

'In that case, your Grace, since you have your-self stated that any unhappiness in your married life was caused by his presence, I would suggest that you make such amends as you can to the duchess, and that you try to resume those relations which have been so unhappily interrupted.'

'That also I have arranged, Mr Holmes. I wrote to the duchess this morning.'

'In that case,' said Holmes, rising, 'I think that my friend and I can congratulate ourselves upon several most happy results from our little visit to the North. There is one other small point upon which I desire some light. This fellow Hayes had shod his horses with shoes which counterfeited the tracks of cows. Was it from Mr Wilder that he learned so extraordinary a device?'

The duke stood in thought for a moment, with a look of intense surprise on his face. Then he opened a door and showed us into a large room furnished as a museum. He led the way to a glass case in a corner, and pointed to the inscription.

'These shoes,' it ran, 'were dug up in the moat of Holdernesse Hall. They are for the use of horses; but they are shaped below with a cloven foot of iron, so as to throw pursuers off the track. They are supposed to have belonged to some of the marauding Barons of Holdernesse in the Middle Ages.'

Holmes opened the case, and, moistening his finger, he passed it along the shoe. A thin film of recent mud was left upon his skin.

'Thank you,' said he, as he replaced the glass. 'It is the second most interesting object that I have seen in the North.'

'And the first?'

Holmes folded up his cheque, and placed it carefully in his notebook. 'I am a poor man,' said he, as he patted it affectionately, and thrust it into the depths of his inner pocket.

'Holmes,' said I, as I stood one morning in our bow-window looking down the street, 'here is a madman coming along. It seems rather sad that his relatives should allow him to come out alone.'

My friend rose lazily from his armchair, and stood with his hands in the pockets of his dressing-gown, looking over my shoulder. It was a bright, crisp February morning, and the snow of the day before still lay deep upon the ground, shimmering brightly in the wintry sun. Down the centre of Baker Street it had been ploughed into a brown crumbly band by the traffic, but at either side and on the heaped-up edges of the footpaths it still lay as white as when it fell. The grey pavement had been cleaned and scraped, but was still dangerously slippery, so that there were fewer passengers than usual. Indeed, from the direction of the Metropolitan station no one was coming save the single gentleman whose eccentric conduct had drawn my attention.

He was a man of about fifty, tall, portly, and imposing, with a massive, strongly marked face and a commanding figure. He was dressed in a sombre yet rich style, in black frock-coat, shining hat, neat brown gaiters, and well-cut pearl-grey trousers. Yet his actions were in absurd contrast to the dignity of his dress and features, for he was running hard, with occasional little springs, such as a weary man gives who is little accustomed to set any tax upon his legs. As he ran he jerked his hands up and down, waggled his head, and writhed his face into the most extraordinry contortions.

'What on earth can be the matter with him?' I asked. 'He is looking up at the numbers of the houses.'

'I believe that he is coming here,' said Holmes, rubbing his hands.

'Here?'

'Yes; I rather think he is coming to consult me professionally. I think that I recognize the symptoms. Ha! did I not tell you?' As he spoke, the man, puffing and blowing, rushed at our door, and pulled at our bell until the whole house resounded with the clanging.

A few moments later he was in our room, still puffing, still gesticulating, but with so fixed a look of grief and despair in his eyes that our smiles were turned in an instant to horror and pity. For a while he could not get his words out, but swayed his body and plucked at his hair like one who has been driven to the extreme limits of his reason. Then, suddenly springing to his feet, he beat his head against the wall with such force that we both rushed upon him, and tore him away to the centre of the room. Sherlock Holmes pushed him down into the easy chair, and, sitting beside him, patted his hand, and chatted with him in the easy, soothing tones which he knew so well how to employ.

'You have come to me to tell me your story, have you not?' said he. 'You are fatigued with your haste. Pray wait until you have recovered yourself, and then I shall be most happy to look into any little problem which you may submit to me.'

The man sat for a minute or more with a heaving chest, fighting against his emotion. Then he passed his handkerchief over his brow, set his lips tight, and turned his face towards us.

'No doubt you think me mad?' said he.

'I see that you have had some great trouble,' responded Holmes.

'God knows I have! – a trouble which is enough to unseat my reason, so sudden and so terrible is it. Public disgrace I might have faced, although I am a man whose character has never yet borne a stain. Private affliction also is the lot of every man; but the two coming together, and in so frightful a form, have been enough to shake my very soul. Besides, it is not I alone. The very nobles in the land may suffer, unless some way be found out of this horrible affair.'

'Pray compose yourself, sir,' said Holmes, 'and let me have a clear account of who you are, and what it is that has befallen you.'

'My name,' answered our visitor, 'is probably

familiar to your ears. I am Alexander Holder, of the banking firm of Holder & Stevenson, of Threadneedle Street.'

The name was indeed well known to us, as belonging to the senior partner in the second largest private banking concern in the City of London. What could have happened, then, to bring one of the foremost citizens of London to this most pitiable pass? We waited, all curiosity, until with another effort he braced himself to tell his story.

'I feel that time is of value,' said he, 'that is why I hastened here when the police inspector suggested that I should secure your co-operation. I came to Baker Street by the Underground, and hurried from there on foot, for the cabs go slowly through this snow. That is why I was so out of breath, for I am a man who takes very little exercise. I feel better now, and I will put the facts before you as shortly and yet as clearly as I can.

'It is, of course, well known to you, that in a successful banking business as much depends upon our being able to find remunerative investments for our funds, as upon our increasing our connection and the number of our depositors. One of our most lucrative means of laying out money is in the shape of loans, where the security is unimpeachable. We have done a good deal in this direction during the last few years, and there are many noble families to whom we have advanced large sums upon the security of their pictures, libraries, or plate.

'Yesterday morning I was seated in my office at the Bank, when a card was brought in to me by one of the clerks. I started when I saw the name, for it was that of none other than – well, perhaps even to you I had better say no more than it was a name which is a household word all over the earth – one of the highest, noblest, most exalted names in England. I was overwhelmed by the honour, and attempted, when he entered, to say so, but he plunged at once into business with the air of a man who wishes to hurry quickly through a disagreeable task.

'"Mr Holder," said he, "I have been informed that you are in the habit of advancing money."

'"The firm do so when the security is good," I answered.

'"It is absolutely essential to me," said he, "that I should have fifty thousand pounds at once. I could of course borrow so trifling a sum ten times over from my friends, but I much prefer to make it a matter of business, and to carry out that business myself. In my position you can readily understand that it is unwise to place oneself under obligations."

'"For how long, may I ask, do you want this sum?" I asked.

'"Next Monday I have a large sum due to me, and I shall then most certainly repay what you advance, with whatever interest you think it right to charge. But it is very essential to me that the money should be paid at once."

'"I should be happy to advance it without further parley from my own private purse," said I, "were it not that the strain would be rather more than it could bear. If, on the other hand, I am to do it in the name of the firm, then in justice to my partner I must insist that, even in your case, every business-like precaution should be taken."

'"I should much prefer to have it so," said he, raising up a square, black morocco case which he had laid beside his chair. "You have doubtless heard of the beryl coronet?"

'"One of the most precious public possessions of the Empire," said I.

'"Precisely." He opened the case, and there, embedded in soft, flesh-coloured velvet, lay the magnificent piece of jewellery which he had named. "There are thirty-nine enormous beryls," said he, "and the price of the gold chase is incalculable. The lowest estimate would put the worth of the coronet at double the sum which I have asked. I am prepared to leave it with you as my security."

'I took the precious case into my hands and looked in some perplexity from it to my illustrious client.

'"You doubt its value?" he asked.

'"Not at all. I only doubt –"

'"The propriety of my leaving it. You may set your mind at rest about that. I should not dream of doing so were it not absolutely certain that I should be able in four days to reclaim it. It is a pure matter of form. Is the security sufficient?"

'"Ample."

'"You understand, Mr Holder, that I am giving you a strong proof of the confidence which I have in you, founded upon all that I have heard of you. I rely upon you not only to be discreet and to refrain from all gossip upon the matter, but, above all, to preserve this coronet with every possible precaution, because I need not say that a great public scandal would be caused if any harm were to befall it. Any injury to it would be almost as serious as its complete loss, for there are no beryls in the world to match these, and it would be impossible to replace them. I leave it with you, however, with every confidence, and I shall call for it in person on Monday morning."

'Seeing that my client was anxious to leave, I said no more; but, calling for my cashier, I ordered him to pay over fifty thousand-pound notes. When I was alone once more, however, with the precious case lying upon the table in front of me, I could not but think with some misgivings of the immense responsibility which it entailed upon me. There could be no doubt that, as it was a national possession, a horrible scandal would ensue if any misfortune should occur to it. I already regretted having ever consented to take charge of it. However, it was too late to alter the matter now, so I locked it up in my private safe, and turned once more to my work.

'When evening came, I felt that it would be an imprudence to leave so precious a thing in the office behind me. Bankers' safes had been forced before now, and why should not mine be? If so, how terrible would be the position in which I should find myself! I determined, therefore, that for the next few days I would always carry the case backwards and forwards with me, so that it might never be really out of my reach. With this intention, I called a cab, and drove out to my house at Streatham, carrying the jewel with me. I did not breathe freely until I had taken it upstairs, and locked it in the bureau of my dressing-room.

'And now a word as to my household, Mr Holmes, for I wish you to thoroughly understand the situation. My groom and my page sleep out of the house, and may be set aside altogether. I have three maid-servants who have been with me a number of years, and whose absolute reliability is quite above suspicion. Another, Lucy Parr, the second waiting-maid, has only been in my service a few months. She came with excellent character, however, and has always given me satisfaction. She is a very pretty girl, and has attracted admirers who have occasionally hung about the place. That is the only drawback which we have found to her, but we believe her to be a thoroughly good girl in every way.

'So much for the servants. My family itself is so small that it will not take me long to describe it. I am a widower, and have an only son, Arthur. He has been a disappointment to me, Mr Holmes, a grievous disappointment. I have no doubt that I am myself to blame. People tell me that I have spoiled him. Very likely I have. When my dear wife died I felt that he was all I had to love. I could not bear to see the smile fade even for a moment from his face. I have never denied him a wish. Perhaps it would have been better for both of us had I been sterner, but I meant it for the best.

'It was naturally my intention that he should succeed me in my business, but he was not of a business turn. He was wild, wayward, and, to speak the truth, I could not trust him in the handling of large sums of money. When he was young he became a member of an aristocratic club, and there, having charming manners, he was soon the intimate of a number of men with long purses and expensive habits. He learned to play heavily at cards and to squander money on the turf, until he had again and again to come to me and implore me to give him an advance upon his allowance, that he might settle his debts of honour. He tried more than once to break away from the dangerous company which he was keeping, but each time the influence of his friend Sir George Burnwell was enough to draw him back again.

'And, indeed, I could not wonder that such a man as Sir George Burnwell should gain an influence over him, for he has frequently brought him to my house, and I have found myself that I could hardly resist the fascination of his manner. He is older than Arthur, a man of the world to his fingertips, one who has been everywhere, seen everything, a brilliant talker, and a man of great personal beauty. Yet when I think of him in cold blood, far away from the glamour of his presence, I am convinced from his cynical speech, and the look which I have caught in his eyes, that he is one who should be deeply distrusted. So I think, and so, too, thinks my little Mary, who has a woman's quick insight into character.

'And now there is only she to be described. She is my niece; but when my brother died five years ago and left her alone in the world I adopted her and have looked upon her ever since as my daughter. She is a sunbeam in my house – sweet, loving, beautiful, a wonderful manager and housekeeper, yet as tender and quiet and gentle as a woman could be. She is my right hand. I do not know what I could do without her. In only one matter has she ever gone against my wishes. Twice my boy has asked her to marry him, for he loves her devotedly, but each time she has refused him. I think that if anyone could have drawn him into the right path it would have been she, and that his marriage might have changed his whole life; but now, alas! it is too late – for ever too late!

'Now, Mr Holmes, you know the people who live under my roof, and I shall continue with my miserable story.

'When we were taking coffee in the drawing-room that night, after dinner, I told Arthur and Mary my experience, and of the precious treasure which we had under our roof, suppressing only the name of my client. Lucy Parr, who had brought in the coffee, had, I am sure, left the room; but I cannot swear that the door was closed. Mary and Arthur were much interested, and wished to see the famous coronet, but I thought it better not to disturb it.

'"Where have you put it?" asked Arthur.

'"In my own bureau."

'"Well, I hope to goodness the house won't be burgled during the night," said he.

'"It is locked up," I answered.

'"Oh, any old key will fit that bureau. When I was a youngster I have opened it myself with the key of the box-room cupboard."

'He often had a wild way of talking, so that I thought little of what he said. He followed me to my room, however, that night with a very grave face.

'"Look here, dad," said he, with his eyes cast down. "Can you let me have two hundred pounds?"

'"No, I cannot!" I answered sharply. "I have been far too generous with you in money matters."

'"You have been very kind," said he; "but I must have this money, or else I can never show my face inside the club again."

'"And a very good thing, too!" I cried.

'"Yes, but you would not have me leave it a dishonoured man," said he. "I could not bear the disgrace. I must raise the money in some way, and if you will not let me have it, then I must try other means."

'I was very angry, for this was the third demand during the month. "You shall not have a farthing from me," I cried, on which he bowed and left the room without another word.

'When he was gone I unlocked my bureau, made sure that my treasure was safe, and locked it again. Then I started to go round the house to see that all was secure – a duty which I usually leave to Mary, but which I thought it well to perform myself that night. As I came down the stairs I saw Mary herself at the side-window of the hall, which she closed and fastened as I approached.

'"Tell me, dad," said she, looking, I thought, a little disturbed, "did you give Lucy, the maid, leave to go out tonight?"

'"Certainly not."

'"She came in just now by the back door. I have no doubt that she has only been to the side-gate to see someone but I think that it is hardly safe, and should be stopped."

'"You must speak to her in the morning, or I will, if you prefer it. Are you sure that everything is fastened?"

'"Quite sure, dad."

'"Then, goodnight." I kissed her, and went to my bedroom, where I was soon asleep.

'I am endeavouring to tell you everything, Mr Holmes, which may have any bearing upon the case, but I beg that you will question me upon any point which I do not make clear.'

'On the contrary, your statement is singularly lucid.'

'I come to a part of my story now in which I should wish to be particularly so. I am not a very heavy sleeper, and the anxiety in my mind tended, no doubt, to make me even less so than usual. About two in the morning, then, I was awakened by some sound in the house. It had ceased ere I was wide awake, but it had left an impression behind it as though a window had gently closed somewhere. I lay listening with all my ears. Suddenly, to my horror, there was a distinct sound of footsteps moving softly in the next room. I slipped out of bed, all palpitating with fear, and peeped round the corner of my dressing-room door.

'"Arthur!" I screamed, "you villain! you thief! How dare you touch that coronet?"

'The gas was half up, as I had left it, and my unhappy boy, dressed only in his shirt and trousers, was standing beside the light, holding the coronet in his hands. He appeared to be wrenching at it, or bending it with all his strength. At my cry he dropped it from his grasp, and turned as pale as death. I snatched it up and examined it. One of the gold corners, with three of the beryls in it, was missing.

'"You blackguard!" I shouted, beside myself with rage. "You have destroyed it! You have dishonoured me for ever! Where are the jewels you have stolen?"

'"Stolen!" he cried.

'"Yes, you thief!" I roared, shaking him by the shoulder.

'"There are none missing. There cannot be any missing," said he.

'"There are three missing. And you know where they are. Must I call you a liar as well as a thief? Did I not see you trying to tear off another piece?"

'"You have called me names enough," said he; "I will not stand it any longer. I shall not say another word about this business since you have chosen to insult me. I will leave your house in the morning, and make my own way in the world."

'"You shall leave it in the hands of the police!" I cried, half mad with grief and rage. "I shall have this matter probed to the bottom."

'"You shall learn nothing from me," said he, with a passion such as I should not have thought was in his nature. "If you choose to call the police, let them find what they can."

'By this time the whole house was astir, for I had raised my voice in my anger. Mary was the first to rush into my room, and at the sight of the coronet and of Arthur's face, she read the whole story, and, with a scream, fell down senseless on the ground. I sent the housemaid for the police, and put the investigation into their hands at once. When the inspector and a constable entered the house, Arthur, who had stood sullenly with his arms folded, asked me whether it was my intention to charge him with theft. I answered that it had ceased to be a private matter, but had become a public one, since the ruined coronet was national property. I was determined that the law should have its way in everything.

'"At least," said he, "you will not have me arrested at once. It would be to your advantage as well as mine if I might leave the house for five minutes."

'"That you may get away, or perhaps that you may conceal what you have stolen," said I. And then realizing the dreadful position in which I was placed, I implored him to remember that not only my honour, but that of one who was far greater than I, was at stake; and that he threatened to raise a scandal which would convulse the nation. He might avert it all if he would but tell me what he had done with the three missing stones.

'"You may as well face the matter," said I; "you have been caught in the act, and no confession could make your guilt more heinous. If you make such reparation as is in your power, by telling us where the beryls are, all shall be forgiven and forgotten."

'"Keep your forgiveness for those who ask for it," he answered, turning away from me with a sneer. I saw that he was too hardened for any words of mine to influence him. There was but one way for it. I called in the inspector, and gave him into custody. A search was made at once, not only of his person, but of his room, and of every portion of the house where he could possibly have concealed the gems; but no trace of them could be found, nor would the wretched boy open his mouth for all our persuasions and our threats. This morning he was removed to a cell, and I, after going through all the police formalities, have hurried round to you, to implore you to use your skill in unravelling the matter. The police have openly confessed that they can at present make nothing of it. You may go to any expense which you think necessary. I have already offered a reward of a thousand pounds. My God, what shall I do! I have lost my honour, my gems, and my son in one night. Oh, what shall I do!'

He put a hand on either side of his head, and rocked himself to and fro, droning to himself like a child whose grief has got beyond words.

Sherlock Holmes sat silent for some minutes, with his brows knitted and his eyes fixed upon the fire.

'Do you receive much company?' he asked.

'None, save my partner with his family, and an occasional friend of Arthur's. Sir George Burnwell has been several times lately. No one else, I think.'

'Do you go out much in society?'

'Arthur does. Mary and I stay at home. We neither of us care for it.'

'That is unusual in a young girl.'

'She is of a quiet nature. Besides, she is not so very young. She is four-and-twenty.'

'This matter, from what you say, seems to have been a shock to her also.'

'Terrible! She is even more affected than I.'

'You have neither of you any doubt as to your son's guilt?'

'How can we have, when I saw him with my own eyes with the coronet in his hands?'

'I hardly consider that a conclusive proof. Was the remainder of the coronet at all injured?'

'Yes, it was twisted.'

'Do you not think, then, that he might have been trying to straighten it?'

'God bless you! You are doing what you can for him and for me. But it is too heavy a task. What was he doing there at all? If his purpose were innocent, why did he not say so?'

'Precisely. And if he were guilty, why did he not invent a lie? His silence appears to me to cut both ways. There are several singular points about the case. What did the police think of the noise which awoke you from your sleep?'

'They considered that it might be caused by Arthur's closing his bedroom door.'

'A likely story! As if a man bent on felony would slam the door so as to awake a household. What did they say, then, of the disappearance of these gems?'

'They are still sounding the planking and probing the furniture in the hope of finding them.'

'Have they thought of looking outside the house?'

'Yes, they have shown extraordinary energy. The whole garden has already been minutely examined.'

'Now, my dear sir,' said Holmes, 'is it not obvious to you now that this matter really strikes much deeper than either you or the police were at first inclined to think? It appeared to you to be a simple case; to me it seems exceedingly complex. Consider what is involved by your theory. You suppose that your son came down from his bed, went, at great risk, to your dressing-room, opened your bureau, took out your coronet, broke off by main force a small portion of it, went off to some other place, concealed three gems out of the thirty-nine, with such skill that nobody can find them, and then returned with the other thirty-six into the room in which he exposed himself to the greatest danger of being discovered. I ask you now, is such a theory tenable?'

'But what other is there?' cried the banker with a gesture of despair. 'If his motives were innocent, why does he not explain them?'

'It is our task to find out,' replied Holmes, 'so now, if you please, Mr Holder, we will set off for Streatham together and devote an hour to glancing a little more closely into details.'

My friend insisted upon my accompanying them in their expedition, which I was eager enough to do, for my curiosity and sympathy were deeply stirred by the story to which we had listened. I confess that the guilt of the banker's son appeared to me to be as obvious as it did to his unhappy father, but still I had such faith in Holmes's judgement that I felt that there must be some grounds for hope as long as he was dissatisfied with the accepted explanation. He hardly spoke a word the whole way out to the southern suburb, but sat with his chin upon his breast, and his hat drawn over his eyes, sunk in the deepest thought. Our client appeared to have taken fresh heart at the little glimpse of hope which had been presented to him, and he even broke into a desultory chat with me over his business affairs. A short railway journey, and a shorter walk, brought us to Fairbank, the modest residence of the great financier.

Fairbank was a good-sized square house of white stone, standing back a little from the road. A double carriage sweep, with a snow-clad lawn, stretched down in front to the two large iron gates which closed the entrance. On the right side was a small wooden thicket which led into a narrow path between two neat hedges stretching from the road to the kitchen door, and forming the tradesmen's entrance. On the left ran a lane which led to the stables, and was not itself within the grounds at all, being a public, though little used, thoroughfare. Holmes left us standing at the door, and walked slowly all round the house, across the front, down the tradesmen's path, and so round by the garden behind into the stable lane. So long was he that Mr Holder and I went into the dining-room, and waited by the fire until he should return. We were sitting there in silence when the door opened, and a young lady came In. She was rather above the middle height, slim, with dark hair and eyes, which seemed the darker against the absolute pallor of her skin. I do not think that I have ever seen such deadly paleness in a woman's face. Her lips, too, were bloodless, but her eyes were flushed with crying. As she swept silently into the room she impressed me with a greater sense of her grief than the banker had done in the morning, and it was the more striking in her as she was evidently a woman of striking character, with immense capacity for self-restraint. Disregarding my presence, she went straight to her uncle, and passed her hand over his head with a sweet womanly caress.

'You have given orders that Arthur should be liberated, have you not, dad?' she asked.

'No, no, my girl, the matter must be probed to the bottom.'

'But I am so sure that he is innocent. You know what women's instincts are. I know that he had done no harm, and that you will be sorry for having acted so harshly.'

'Why is he silent, then, if he is innocent?'

'Who knows? Perhaps because he was so angry that you should suspect him.'

'How could I help suspecting him, when I actually saw him with the coronet in his hand?'

'Oh, but he had only picked it up to look at it.

Oh, do, do take my word for it that he is innocent. Let the matter drop, and say no more. It is so dreadful to think of our dear Arthur in prison!'

'I shall never let it drop until the gems are found – never, Mary! Your affection for Arthur blinds you as to the awful consequences to me. Far from hushing the thing up, I have brought a gentleman down from London to inquire more deeply into it.'

'This gentleman?' she asked, facing round to me.

'No, his friend. He wished us to leave him alone. He is round in the stable lane now.

'The stable lane?' She raised her dark eyebrows. 'What can he hope to find there? Ah, this, I suppose, is he. I trust, sir, that you will succeed in proving, what I feel sure is the truth, that my cousin Arthur is innocent of this crime.'

'I fully share your opinion, and, I trust with you, that we may prove it,' returned Holmes, going back to the mat to knock the snow from his shoes. 'I believe I have the honour of addressing Miss Mary Holder. Might I ask you a question or two?'

'Pray do, sir, if it may help, to clear this horrible affair up.'

'You heard nothing yourself last night?'

'Nothing, until my uncle here began to speak loudly. I heard that, and I came down.'

'You shut up the windows and doors the night before. Did you fasten all the windows?'

'Yes.'

'Were they all fastened this morning?'

'Yes.'

'You have a maid who has a sweetheart? I think that you remarked to your uncle last night that she had been out to see him?'

'Yes, and she was the girl who waited in the drawing-room, and who may have heard uncle's remarks about the coronet.'

'I see. You infer that she may have gone out to tell her sweetheart, and that the two may have planned the robbery.'

'But what is the good of all these vague theories,' cried the banker impatiently, 'when I have told you that I saw Arthur with the coronet in his hands?'

'Wait a little, Mr Holder. We must come back to that. About this girl, Miss Holder. You saw her return by the kitchen door, I presume?'

'Yes; when I went to see if the door was fastened for the night I met her slipping in. I saw the man, too, in the gloom.'

'Do you know him?'

'Oh, yes; he is the greengrocer who brings our vegetables round. His name is Francis Prosper.'

'He stood,' said Holmes, 'to the left of the door that is to say, farther up the path than is necessary to reach the door?'

'Yes, he did.'

'And he is a man with a wooden leg?'

Something like fear sprang up in the young

lady's expressive black eyes. 'Why, you are like a magician,' said she. 'How do you know that?' She smiled, but there was no answering smile in Holmes's thin, eager face.

'I should be very glad now to go upstairs,' said he. 'I shall probably wish to go over the outside of the house again. Perhaps I had better take a look at the lower windows before I go up.'

He walked swiftly round from one to the other, pausing only at the large one which looked from the hall on to the stable lane. This he opened, and made a very careful examination of the sill with his powerful magnifying lens. 'Now we shall go upstairs,' said he, at last.

The banker's dressing-room was a plainly furnished little chamber with a grey carpet, a large bureau, and a long mirror. Holmes went to the bureau first, and looked hard at the lock.

'Which key was used to open it?' he asked.

'That which my son himself indicated – that of the cupboard of the lumber-room.'

'Have you it here?'

'That is it on the dressing-table.'

Sherlock Holmes took it up and opened the bureau.

'It is a noiseless lock,' said he. 'It is no wonder that it did not wake you. This case, I presume, contains the coronet. We must have a look at it.' He opened the case, and, taking out the diadem, he laid it upon the table. It was a magnificent specimen of the jeweller's art, and the thirty-six stones were the finest that I have ever seen. At one side of the coronet was a crooked cracked edge, where a corner holding three gems had been torn away.

'Now, Mr Holder,' said Holmes; 'here is the corner which corresponds to that which has been so unfortunately lost. Might I beg that you will break it off.'

The banker recoiled in horror. 'I should not dream of trying,' said he.

'Then I will.' Holmes suddenly bent his strength upon it, but without result. 'I feel it give a little,' said he; 'but, though I am exceptionally strong in the fingers, it would take me all my time to break it. An ordinary man could not do it. Now, what do you think would happen if I did break it, Mr Holder? There would be a noise like a pistol shot. Do you tell me that all this happened within a few yards of your bed, and that you heard nothing of it?'

'I do not know what to think. It is all dark to me.'

'But perhaps it may grow lighter as we go. What do you think, Miss Holder?'

'I confess that I still share my uncle's perplexity.'

'Your son had no shoes or slippers on when you saw him?'

'He had nothing on save only his trousers and shirt.'

'Thank you. We have certainly been favoured

with extraordinary luck during this inquiry, and it will be entirely our own fault if we do not succeed in clearing the matter up. With your permission, Mr Holder, I shall now continue my investigations outside.'

He went alone, at his own request, for he explained that any unnecessary footmarks might make his task more difficult. For an hour or more he was at work, returning at last with his feet heavy with snow and his features as inscrutable as ever.

'I think that I have seen now all that there is to see, Mr Holder,' said he; 'I can serve you best by returning to my rooms.'

'But the gems, Mr Holmes. Where are they?'

'I cannot tell.'

The banker wrung his hands. 'I shall never see them again!' he cried. 'And my son? You give me hopes?'

'My opinion is in no way altered.'

'Then for God's sake what was this dark business which was acted in my house last night?'

'If you can call upon me at my Baker Street rooms tomorrow morning between nine and ten I shall be happy to do what I can to make it clearer. I understand that you give me *carte blanche* to act for you, provided only that I get back the gems, and that you place no limit on the sum I may draw.'

'I would give my fortune to have them back.'

'Very good. I shall look into the matter between

this and then. Goodbye; it is just possible that I may have to come over here again before evening.'

It was obvious to me that my companion's mind was now made up about the case, although what his conclusions were was more than I could even dimly imagine. Several times during our homeward journey I endeavoured to sound him upon that point, but he always glided away to some other topic, until at last I gave it over in despair. It was not yet three when we found ourselves in our room once more. He hurried to his chamber, and was down again in a few minutes dressed as a common loafer. With his collar turned up, his shiny seedy coat, his red cravat, and his worn boots, he was a perfect sample of the class.

'I think that this should do,' said he, glancing into the glass above the fireplace. 'I only wish that you could come with me, Watson, but I fear that it won't do. I may be on the trail in this matter, or I may be following a will-o'-the-wisp, but I shall soon know which it is. I hope that I may be back in a few hours.' He cut a slice of beef from the joint upon the sideboard, sandwiched it between two rounds of bread, and, thrusting this rude meal into his pocket, he started off upon his expedition.

I had just finished my tea when he returned, evidently in excellent spirits, swinging an old elastic-sided boot in his hand. He chucked it down into a corner and helped himself to a cup of tea.

'I only looked in as I passed,' said he. 'I am going right on.'

'Where to?'

'Oh, to the other side of the West End. It may be some time before I get back. Don't wait up for me in case I should be late.'

'How are you getting on?'

'Oh, so-so. Nothing to complain of. I have been out to Streatham since I saw you last, but I did not call at the house. It is a very sweet little problem, and I would not have missed it for a good deal. However, I must not sit gossiping here, but must get these disreputable clothes off and return to my highly respectable self.'

I could see by his manner that he had stronger reasons for satisfaction than his words alone would imply. His eyes twinkled, and there was even a touch of colour upon his sallow cheeks. He hastened upstairs, and a few minutes later I heard the slam of the hall door, which told me that he was off once more upon his congenial hunt.

I waited until midnight, but there was no sign of his return, so I retired to my room. It was no uncommon thing for him to be away for days and nights on end when he was hot upon a scent, so that his lateness caused me no surprise. I do not know at what hour he came in, but when I came down to breakfast in the morning, there he was with a cup of coffee in one hand and the paper in the other, as fresh and trim as possible.

'You will excuse my beginning without you,

Watson,' said he; 'but you remember that our client has rather an early appointment this morning.'

'Why, it is after nine now,' I answered. 'I should not be surprised if that were he. I thought I heard a ring.'

It was, indeed, our friend the financier. I was shocked by the change which had come over him, for his face, which was naturally of a broad and massive mould, was now pinched and fallen in, while his hair seemed to be at least a shade whiter. He entered with a weariness and lethargy which was even more painful than his violence of the morning before, and he dropped heavily into the armchair which I pushed forward for him.

'I do not know what I have done to be so severely tried,' said he. 'Only two days ago I was a happy and prosperous man, without a care in the world. Now I am left to a lonely and dishonoured age. One sorrow comes close upon the heels of another. My niece Mary has deserted me.'

'Deserted you?'

'Yes. Her bed this morning had not been slept in, her room was empty, and a note lay for me upon the hall table. I had said to her last night, in sorrow and not in anger, that if she had married my boy all might have been well with him. Perhaps it was thoughtless of me to say so. It is to that remark that she refers in this note:

My Dearest Uncle – I feel that I have brought this

trouble upon you, and that if I had acted differently this terrible misfortune might never have occurred. I cannot, with this thought in my mind, ever again be happy under your roof, and I feel that I must leave you for ever. Do not worry about my future, for that is provided for; and, above all, do not search for me, for it will be fruitless labour, and an ill service to me. In life or in death, I am ever your loving

MARY

'What could she mean by that note, Mr Holmes? Do you think it points to suicide?'

'No, no, nothing of the kind. It is perhaps the best possible solution. I trust, Mr Holder, that you are nearing the end of your troubles.'

'Ha! You say so! You have heard something, Mr Holmes: you have learned something! Where are the gems?'

'You would not think a thousand pounds apiece an excessive sum for them?'

'I would pay ten.'

'That would be unnecessary. Three thousand will cover the matter. And there is a little reward, I fancy. Have you your cheque-book? Here is a pen. Better make it out for four thousand pounds.'

With a dazed face the banker made out the required cheque. Holmes walked over to his desk, took out a little triangular piece of gold with three gems in it, and threw it down upon the table.

With a shriek of joy our client clutched it up.

'You have it?' he gasped. 'I am saved! I am saved!'

The reaction of joy was as passionate as his grief had been, and he hugged his recovered gems to his bosom.

'There is one other thing you owe, Mr Holder,' said Sherlock Holmes, rather sternly.

'Owe!' He caught up a pen. 'Name the sum, and I will pay it.'

'No, the debt is not to me. You owe a very humble apology to that noble lad, your son, who has carried himself in this matter as I should be proud to see my own son do, should I ever chance to have one.'

'Then it was not Arthur who took them?'

'I told you yesterday, and I repeat today, that it was not.'

'You are sure of it! Then let us hurry to him at once, to let him know that the truth is known.

'He knows it already. When I had cleared it all up I had an interview with him, and finding that he would not tell me the story, I told it to him, on which he had to confess that I was right, and to add the very few details which were not yet quite clear to me. Your news of this morning, however, may open his lips.'

'For Heaven's sake tell me, then, what is this extraordinary mystery!'

'I will do so, and I will show you the steps by which I reached it. And let me say to you, first, what it is hardest for me to say and for you to hear. There has been an understanding between Sir George Burnwell and your niece, Mary. They have now fled together.'

'My Mary? Impossible!'

'It is, unfortunately, more than possible; it is certain. Neither you nor your son knew the true character of this man when you admitted him into your family circle. He is one of the most dangerous men in England – a ruined gambler, an absolutely desperate villain; a man without heart or conscience. Your niece knew nothing of such men. When he breathed his vows to her, as he had done to a hundred before her, she flattered herself that she alone had touched his heart. The devil knows best what he said, but at last she became his tool, and was in the habit of seeing him nearly every evening.'

'I cannot, and I will not, believe it!' cried the banker with an ashen face.

'I will tell you, then, what occurred in your house that night. Your niece, when you had, as she thought, gone to your room, slipped down and talked to her lover through the window which leads into the stable lane. His footmarks had pressed right through the snow, so long had he stood there. She told him of the coronet. His wicked lust for gold kindled at the news, and he bent her to his will. I have no doubt that she loved you, but there are women in whom the love of a lover extinguishes all other loves, and I think that she must have been one. She had hardly listened to his instructions when she saw you coming downstairs, on which she closed the window rapidly, and told you about one of the servants' escapade with her wooden-legged lover, which was all perfectly true.

'Your boy, Arthur, went to bed after his interview with you, but he slept badly on account of his uneasiness about his club debts. In the middle of the night he heard a soft tread pass his door, so he rose, and looking out, was surprised to see his cousin walking very stealthily along the passage, until she disappeared into your dressing-room. Petrified with astonishment the lad slipped on some clothes, and waited there in the dark to see what would come of this strange affair. Presently she emerged from the room again, and in the light of the passage lamp your son saw that she carried the precious coronet in her hands. She passed down the stairs, and he, thrilling with horror, ran along and slipped behind the curtain near your door, whence he could see what passed in the hall beneath. He saw her stealthily open the window, hand out the coronet to someone in the gloom, and then closing it once more hurry back to her room, passing quite close to where he stood hid behind the curtain.

'As long as she was on the scene he could not take any action without a horrible exposure of the woman whom he loved. But the instant she was gone he realized how crushing a misfortune this would be for you, and how all-important it was to set it right. He rushed down, just as he was, in his bare feet, opened the window, sprang out into the snow, and ran down the lane, where he could see a dark figure in the moonlight. Sir George Burnwell tried to get away, but Arthur caught him, and there was a struggle between them, your lad tugging at one side of the coronet, and his opponent at the other. In the scuffle, your son struck Sir George, and cut him over the eye. Then something suddenly snapped, and your son, finding that he had the coronet in his hands, rushed back, closed the window, ascending to your room, and had just observed that the coronet had been twisted in the struggle and was endeavouring to straighten it, when you appeared upon the scene.'

'Is it possible?' gasped the banker.

'You then roused his anger by calling him names at a moment when he felt that he had deserved your warmest thanks. He could not explain the true state of affairs without betraying the one who certainly deserved little enough consideration at his hands. He took the more chivalrous view, however, and preserved her secret.'

'And that was why she shrieked and fainted when she saw the coronet,' cried Mr Holder. 'Oh, my God! What a blind fool I have been. And his asking to be allowed to go out for five minutes! The dear fellow wanted to see if the missing piece were at the scene of the struggle. How cruelly I have misjudged him!'

'When I arrived at the house,' continued

Holmes, 'I at once went very carefully round it to observe if there were any traces in the snow which might help me. I knew that none had fallen since the evening before, and also that there had been a strong frost to preserve impressions. I passed along the tradesmen's path, but found it all trampled down and indistinguishable. Just beyond it, however, at the far side of the kitchen door, a woman had stood and talked with a man, whose round impression on one side showed that he had a wooden leg. I could even tell that they had been disturbed, for the woman had run back swiftly to the door, as was shown by the deep toe and light heelmarks, while Wooden-leg had waited a little, and then had gone away. I thought at the time that this might be the maid and her sweetheart, of whom you had already spoken to me, and inquiry showed it was so. I passed round the garden without seeing anything more than random tracks, which I took to be the police; but when I got into the stable lane a very long and complex story was written in the snow in front of me.

'There was a double line of tracks of a booted man, and a second double line which I saw with delight belonged to a man with naked feet. I was at once convinced from what you had told me that the latter was your son. The first had walked both ways, but the other had run swiftly, and, as his tread was marked in places over the depression of the boot, it was obvious that he had passed after the other. I followed them up, and found that they led to the hall window, where Boots had worn all the snow away while waiting. Then I walked to the other end, which was a hundred yards or more down the lane. I saw where Boots had faced round, where the snow was cut up, as though there had been a struggle, and, finally, where a few drops of blood had fallen, to show me that I was not mistaken. Boots had then run down the lane, and another little smudge of blood showed that it was he who had been hurt. When he came to the high-road at the other end, I found that the pavement had been cleared, so there was an end to that clue.

'On entering the house, however, I examined, as you remember, the sill and framework of the hall window with my lens, and I could at once see that someone had passed out. I could distinguish the outline of an instep where the wet foot had been placed in coming in. I was then beginning to be able to form an opinion as to what had oc-curred. A man had waited outside the window, someone had brought him the gems; the deed had been overseen by your son, he had pursued the thief, had struggled with him, they had each tugged at the coronet, their united strength caus-ing injuries which neither alone could have ef-fected. He had returned with the prize, but had left a fragment in the grasp of his opponent. So far I was clear. The question now was, who was the man, and who was it brought him the coronet?

'It is an old maxim of mine that when you have

excluded the impossible, whatever remains, however improbable, must be the truth. Now, I knew that it was not you who had brought it down, so there only remained your niece and the maids. But if it were the maids, why should your son allow himself to be accused in their place? There could be no possible reason. As he loved his cousin, however, there was an excellent explanation why he should retain her secret – the more so as the secret was a disgraceful one. When I remembered that you had seen her at that window, and how she had fainted on seeing the coronet again, my conjecture became a certainty.

'And who could it be who was her confederate? A lover evidently, for who else could outweigh the love and gratitude which she must feel to you? I knew that you went out little, and that your circle of friends was a very limited one. But among them was Sir George Burnwell. I had heard of him before as being a man of evil reputation among women. It must have been he who wore those boots, and retained the missing gems. Even though he knew that Arthur had discovered him, he might still flatter himself that he was safe, for the lad could not say a word without compromising his own family.

'Well, your own good sense will suggest what measures I took next. I went in the shape of a loafer to Sir George's house, managed to pick up an acquaintance with his valet, learned that his master had cut his head the night before, and finally, at the expense of six shillings, made all sure by buying a pair of his cast-off shoes. With those I journeyed down to Streatham, and saw that they exactly fitted the tracks.'

'I saw an ill-dressed vagabond in the lane yesterday evening,' said Mr Holder.

'Precisely. It was I. I found that I had my man, so I came home and changed my clothes. It was a delicate part which I had to play then, for I saw that a prosecution must be avoided to avert scandal, and I knew that so astute a villain would see that our hands were tied in the matter. I went and saw him. At first, of course, he denied everything. But when I gave him every particular that had occurred, he tried to bluster, and took down a life-preserver from the wall. I knew my man, however, and I clapped a pistol to his head before he could strike. Then he became a little more reasonable. I told him that we would give him a price for the stones he held – a thousand pounds apiece. That brought out the first signs of grief he had shown. "Why, dash it all!" said he, "I've let them go at six hundred for the three!" I soon managed to get the address of the receiver who had them, on promising him that there would be no prosecution. Off I set to him, and after much chaffering I got our stones at a thousand apiece. Then I looked in upon your son, told him that all was right, and eventually got to my bed about two o'clock after what I may call a really hard day's work.'

'A day which has saved England from a great public scandal,' said the banker, rising. 'Sir, I cannot find words to thank you. But you shall not find me ungrateful for what you have done. Your skill has indeed exceeded all that I have ever heard of it. And now I must fly to my dear boy to apologize to him for the wrong which I have done him. As to what you tell me of poor Mary, it goes to my heart. Not even your skill can inform me where she is now.'

'I think that we may safely say,' returned Holmes, 'that she is wherever Sir George Burnwell is. It is equally certain, too, that whatever her sins are, they will soon receive a more than sufficient punishment.'

The Engineer's Thumb

Of all the problems which have been submitted to my friend Mr Sherlock Holmes for solution during the years of our intimacy, there were only two which I was the means of introducing to his notice, that of Mr Hatherley's thumb and that of Colonel Warburton's madness. Of these the latter may have afforded a finer field for an acute and original observer, but the other was so strange in its inception and so dramatic in its details, that it may be the more worthy of being placed upon record, even if it gave my friend fewer openings for those deductive methods of reasoning by which he achieved such remarkable results. The story has, I believe, been told more than once in the newspapers, but, like all such narratives, its effect is much less striking when set forth *en bloc* in a single half-column of print than when the facts slowly evolve before your own eyes and the mystery clears gradually away as each new discovery furnishes a step which leads on to the complete truth. At the time the circumstances made a deep impression upon me, and the lapse of two years has hardly served to weaken the effect.

It was in the summer of '89, not long after my marriage, that the events occurred which I am now about to summarize. I had returned to civil practice, and had finally abandoned Holmes in his Baker Street rooms, although I continually visited him, and occasionally even persuaded him to forgo his Bohemian habits so far as to come and visit us. My practice had steadily increased, and as I happened to live at no very great distance from Paddington Station, I got a few patients from among the officials. One of these whom I had cured of a painful and lingering disease was never weary of advertising my virtues, and of endeavouring to send me on every sufferer over whom he might have any influence.

One morning, at a little before seven o'clock, I was awakened by the maid tapping at the door, to announce that two men had come from Paddington, and were waiting in the consulting room. I dressed hurriedly, for I knew by experience that railway cases were seldom trivial, and hastened downstairs. As I descended, my old ally, the guard, came out of the room, and closed the door tightly behind him.

'I've got him here,' he whispered, jerking his thumb over his shoulder; 'he's all right.'

'What is it, then?' I asked, for his manner suggested that it was some strange creature which he had caged up in my room.

'It's a new patient,' he whispered. 'I thought I'd bring him round myself; then he couldn't slip away. There he is, all safe and sound. I must go now, Doctor, I have my dooties, just the same as you.' And off he went, this trusty tout, without even giving me time to thank him.

I entered my consulting room, and found a gentleman seated by the table. He was quietly dressed in a suit of heather tweed, with a soft cloth cap, which he had laid down upon my books. Round one of his hands he had a handkerchief wrapped, which was mottled all over with blood-stains. He was young, not more than five-and-twenty, I should say, with a strong masculine face; but he was exceedingly pale, and gave me the impression of a man who was suffering from some strong agitation, which it took all his strength of mind to control.

'I am sorry to knock you up so early, Doctor,' said he. 'But I have had a very serious accident during the night. I came in by train this morning, and on inquiring at Paddington as to where I might find a doctor, a worthy fellow very kindly escorted me here. I gave the maid a card, but I see that she has left it upon the side table.'

I took it up and glanced at it. 'Mr Victor Hatherley, hydraulic engineer, 16a Victoria Street (3rd floor).' That was the name, style, and abode of my morning visitor. 'I regret that I have kept you waiting,' said I, sitting down in my library chair. 'You are fresh from a night journey, I understand, which is in itself a monotonous occupation.'

'Oh, my night could not be called monotonous,'

said he, and laughed. He laughed very heartily, with a high ringing note, leaning back in his chair, and shaking his sides. All my medical instincts rose up against that laugh.

'Stop it!' I cried. 'Pull yourself together!' And I poured some water from a carafe.

It was useless, however. He was off in one of those hysterical outbursts which come upon a strong nature when some great crisis is over and gone. Presently he came to himself once more, very weary and blushing hotly.

'I have been making a fool of myself,' he gasped.

'Not at all. Drink this!' I dashed some brandy into the water, and the colour began to come back to his bloodless cheeks.

'That's better!' said he. 'And now, Doctor, perhaps you would kindly attend to my thumb, or rather to the place where my thumb used to be.'

He unwound the handkerchief and held out his hand. It gave even my hardened nerves a shudder to look at it.

'Good heavens!' I cried, 'this is a terrible injury. It must have bled considerably.'

'Yes, it did. I fainted when it was done; and I think that I must have been senseless for a long time. When I came to, I found that it was still bleeding, so I tied one end of my handkerchief very tightly round the wrist, and braced it up with a twig.'

'Excellent! You should have been a surgeon.'

'It is a question of hydraulics, you see, and came within my own province.'

'This has been done,' said I, examining the wound, 'by a very heavy and sharp instrument.'

'A thing like a cleaver,' said he.

'An accident, I presume?'

'By no means.'

'What, a murderous attack!'

'Very murderous indeed.'

'You horrify me.'

I sponged the wound, cleaned it, dressed it; and, finally, covered it over with cotton wadding and carbolized bandages. He lay back without wincing, though he bit his lip from time to time.

'How is that?' I asked, when I had finished.

'Capital! Between your brandy and your bandage, I feel a new man. I was very weak, but I have had a good deal to go through.'

'Perhaps you had better not speak of the matter. It is evidently trying to your nerves.'

'Oh, no; not now. I shall have to tell my tale to the police; but, between ourselves, if it were not for the convincing evidence of this wound of mine, I should be surprised if they believed my statement, for it is a very extraordinary one, and I have not much in the way of proof with which to back it up. And, even if they believe me, the clues which I can give them are so vague that it is a question whether justice will be done.'

'Ha!' cried I, 'if it is anything in the nature of a problem which you desire to see solved, I should strongly recommend you to come to my friend Mr

Sherlock Holmes before you go to the official police.'

'Oh, I have heard of that fellow,' answered my visitor, 'and I should be very glad if he would take the matter up, though of course I must use the official police as well. Would you give me an introduction to him?'

'I'll do better. I'll take you round to him myself.'

'I should be immensely obliged to you.'

'We'll call a cab and go together. We shall just be in time to have a little breakfast with him. Do you feel equal to it?'

'Yes. I shall not feel easy until I have told my story.'

'Then my servant will call a cab, and I shall be with you in an instant.' I rushed upstairs, explained the matter shortly to my wife, and in five minutes was inside a hansom, driving with my new acquaintance to Baker Street.

Sherlock Holmes was, as I expected, lounging about his sitting-room in his dressing-gown, reading the agony column of *The Times*, and smoking his before-breakfast pipe, which was composed of all the plugs and dottles left from his smokes of the day before, all carefully dried and collected on the corner of the mantelpiece. He received us in his quietly genial fashion, ordered fresh rashers and eggs, and joined us in a hearty meal. When it was concluded he settled our new acquaintance upon the sofa, placed a pillow beneath his head, and laid a glass of brandy and water within his reach.

'It is easy to see that your experience has been no common one, Mr Hatherley,' said he. 'Pray lie down there and make yourself absolutely at home. Tell us what you can, but stop when you are tired, and keep up your strength with a little stimulant.'

'Thank you,' said my patient, 'but I have felt another man since the doctor bandaged me, and I think that your breakfast has completed the cure. I shall take up as little of your valuable time as possible, so I shall start at once upon my peculiar experiences.'

Holmes sat in his big armchair, with the weary, heavy-lidded expression which veiled his keen and eager nature, while I sat opposite to him, and we listened in silence to the strange story which our visitor detailed to us.

'You must know,' said he, 'that I am an orphan and a bachelor, residing alone in lodgings in London. By profession I am a hydraulic engineer, and have had considerable experience of my work during the seven years that I was apprenticed to Venner & Matheson, the well-known firm of Greenwich. Two years ago, having served my time, and having also come into a fair sum of money through my poor father's death, I determined to start in business for myself, and took professional chambers in Victoria Street.

'I suppose that everyone finds his first independent start in business a dreary experience. To me it has been exceptionally so. During two years I have had three consultations and one small job, and that is absolutely all that my profession has brought me. My gross takings amount to twenty-seven pounds ten. Every day, from nine in the morning until four in the afternoon, I waited in my little den, until at last my heart began to sink, and I came to believe that I should never have any practice at all.

'Yesterday, however, just as I was thinking of leaving the office, my clerk entered to say there was a gentleman waiting who wished to see me upon business. He brought up a card, too, with the name of "Colonel Lysander Stark" engraved upon it. Close at his heels came the colonel himself, a man rather over the middle size but of an exceeding thinness. I do not think that I have ever seen so thin a man. His whole face sharpened away into nose and chin, and the skin of his cheeks was drawn quite tense over his outstanding bones. Yet this emaciation seemed to be his natural habit, and due to no disease, for his eye was bright, his step brisk, and his bearing assured. He was plainly but neatly dressed, and his age, I should judge, would be nearer forty than thirty.

'"Mr Hatherley?" said he, with something of a German accent. "You have been recommended to me, Mr Hatherley, as being a man who is not only proficient in his profession, but is also discreet and capable of preserving a secret."

'I bowed, feeling as flattered as any young man would at such an address. "May I ask who it was who gave me so good a character?" I asked.

'"Well, perhaps it is better that I should not tell you just at this moment. I have it from the same source that you are both an orphan and a bachelor, and are residing alone in London."

'"That is quite correct," I answered, "but you will excuse me if I say that I cannot see how all this bears upon my professional qualifications. I understood that it was on a professional matter that you wished to speak to me?"

'"Undoubtedly so. But you will find that all I say is really to the point. I have a professional commission for you, but absolute secrecy is quite essential – *absolute* secrecy, you understand, and of course we may expect that more from a man who is alone than from one who lives in the bosom of his family."

'"If I promise to keep a secret," said I, "you may absolutely depend upon my doing so."

'He looked very hard at me as I spoke, and it seemed to me that I had never seen so suspicious and questioning an eye.

'"You do promise, then?" said he at last.

'"Yes, I promise."

'"Absolute and complete silence, before, during, and after? No reference to the matter at all, either in word or writing?"

'"I have already given you my word."

'"Very good." He suddenly sprang up, and

darting like lightning across the room he flung open the door. The passage outside was empty.

'"That's all right," said he, coming back. "I know that clerks are sometimes curious as to their masters' affairs. Now we can talk in safety." He drew up his chair very close to mine, and began to stare at me again with the same questioning, and thoughtful look.

'A feeling of repulsion and of something akin to fear had begun to rise within me at the strange antics of this fleshless man. Even my dread of losing a client could not restrain me from showing my impatience.

'"I beg that you will state your business, sir," said I; "my time is of value." Heaven forgive me for that last sentence, but the words came to my lips.

'"How would fifty guineas for a night's work suit you?" he asked.

'"Most admirably."

'"I say a night's work, but an hour's would be nearer the mark. I simply want your opinion about a hydraulic stamping machine which has got out of gear. If you show us what is wrong we shall soon set it right ourselves. What do you think of such a commission as that?"

'"The work appears to be light, and the pay munificent."

'"Precisely so. We shall want you to come to-night by the last train."

'"Where to?"

'"To Eyford, in Berkshire. It is a little place near the borders of Oxfordshire, and within seven miles of Reading. There is a train from Paddington which would bring you in there at about 11.15."

'"Very good."

'"I shall come down in a carriage to meet you."

'"There is a drive, then?"

'"Yes, our little place is quite out in the country. It is a good seven miles from Eyford station."

'"Then we can hardly get there before midnight. I suppose there would be no chance of a train back. I should be compelled to stop the night."

'"Yes, we could easily give you a shakedown."

'"That is very awkward. Could I not come at some more convenient hour?"

'"We have judged it best that you should come late. It is to recompense you for any inconvenience that we are paying you, a young and unknown man, a fee which would buy an opinion from the very heads of your profession. Still, of course, if you would like to draw out of the business, there is plenty of time to do so."

'I thought of the fifty guineas, and of how very useful they would be to me. "Not at all," said I; "I shall be very happy to accommodate myself to your wishes. I should like, however, to understand a little more clearly what it is that you wish me to do."

'"Quite so. It is very natural that the pledge of secrecy which we have exacted from you should have aroused your curiosity. I have no wish to commit you to anything without your having it all laid before you. I suppose that we are absolutely safe from eavesdroppers?"

'"Entirely."

'"Then the matter stands thus. You are probably aware that fuller's earth is a valuable product, and that it is only found in one or two places in England?"

'"I have heard so."

'"Some little time ago I bought a small place – a very small place – within ten miles of Reading. I was fortunate enough to discover that there was a deposit of fuller's earth in one of my fields. On examining it, however, I found that this deposit was a comparatively small one, and that it formed a link between two very much larger ones upon the right and the left – both of them, however, in the grounds of my neighbours. These good people were absolutely ignorant that their land contained that which was quite as valuable as a gold mine. Naturally, it was to my interest to buy their land before they discovered its true value; but, unfortunately, I had no capital by which I could do this. I took a few of my friends into the secret, however, and they suggested that we should quietly and secretly work our own little deposit, and that in this way we should earn the money which would enable us to buy the neighbouring fields. This we have now been doing for some time, and in order to help us in our operations we erected a hydraulic press. This press, as I have already explained, has got out of order, and we wish your advice upon the subject. We guard our secret very jealously, however, and if it once became known that we had hydraulic engineers coming to our little house, it would soon rouse inquiry, and then, if the facts came out, it would be goodbye to any chance of getting these fields and carrying out our plans. That is why I have made you promise me that you will not tell a human being that you are going to Eyford tonight. I hope that I make it all plain?"

"'I quite follow you," said I. "The only point which I could not quite understand, was what use you could make of a hydraulic press in excavating fuller's earth, which, as I understand, is dug out like gravel from a pit."

"'Ah!" said he carelessly, "we have our own process. We compress the earth into bricks, so as to remove them without revealing what they are. But that is a mere detail. I have taken you fully into my confidence now, Mr Hatherley, and I have shown you how I trust you." He rose as he spoke. "I shall expect you, then, at Eyford, at 11.15."

"'I shall certainly be there."

"'And not a word to a soul." He looked at me with a last long, questioning gaze, and then, pressing my hand in a cold, dank grasp, he hurried from the room.

'Well, when I came to think it all over in cool blood I was very much astonished, as you may both think, at this sudden commission which had been entrusted to me. On the one hand, of course, I was glad, for the fee was at least tenfold what I should have asked had I set a price upon my own services, and it was possible that this order might lead to other ones. On the other hand, the face and manner of my patron had made an unpleasant impression upon me, and I could not think that his explanation of the fuller's earth was sufficient to explain the necessity for my coming at midnight, and his extreme anxiety lest I should tell anyone of my errand. However, I threw all my fears to the winds, ate a hearty supper, drove to Paddington, and started off, having obeyed to the letter the injunction as to holding my tongue.

'At Reading I had to change not only my carriage but my station. However, I was in time for the last train to Eyford, and I reached the little dim-lit station after eleven o'clock. I was the only passenger who got out there, and there was no one upon the platform save a single sleepy porter with a lantern. As I passed out through the wicket-gate, however, I found my acquaintance of the morning waiting in the shadow upon the other side. Without a word he grasped my arm and hurried me into a carriage, the door of which was standing open. He drew up the windows on either side, tapped on the woodwork, and away we went as hard as the horse could go.'

'One horse?' interjected Holmes.

'Yes, only one.'

'Did you observe the colour?'

'Yes, I saw it by the sidelights when I was stepping into the carriage. It was a chestnut.'

'Tired-looking or fresh?'

'Oh, fresh and glossy.'

'Thank you. I am sorry to have interrupted you. Pray continue your most interesting statement.'

'Away we went then, and we drove for at least an hour. Colonel Lysander Stark had said that it was only seven miles, but I should think, from the rate that we seemed to go, and the time we took, that it must have been nearer twelve. He sat at my side in silence all the time, and I was aware, more than once when I glanced in his direction, that he was looking at me with great intensity. The country roads seemed to be not very good in that part of the world, for we lurched and jolted terribly. I tried to look out of the windows to see something of where we were, but they were made of frosted glass, and I could make out nothing save an occasional blur of a passing light. Now and then I hazarded some remark to break the monotony of the journey, but the Colonel answered only in monosyllables, and the conversation soon flagged. At last, however, the bumping of the road was exchanged for the crisp smoothness of a gravel drive and the carriage came to a stand. Colonel Lysander Stark sprang out, and, as

I followed after him, pulled me swiftly into a porch which gaped in front of us. We stepped, as it were, right out of the carriage and into the hall, so that I failed to catch the most fleeting glance of the front of the house. The instant that I had crossed the threshold the door slammed heavily behind us, and I heard faintly the rattle of the wheels as the carriage drove away.

'It was pitch dark inside the house, and the Colonel fumbled about looking for matches, and muttering under his breath. Suddenly a door opened at the other end of the passage, and a long, golden bar of light shot out in our direction. It grew broader, and a woman appeared with a lamp in her hand, which she held above her head, pushing her face forward and peering at us. I could see that she was pretty, and from the gloss with which the light shone upon her dark dress I knew that it was a rich material. She spoke a few words in a foreign tongue in a tone as though asking a question, and when my companion answered in a gruff monosyllable she gave such a start that the lamp nearly fell from her hand. Colonel Stark went up to her, whispered something in her ear, and then, pushing her back into the room from whence she had come, he walked towards me again with the lamp in his hand.

'"Perhaps you will have the kindness to wait in this room for a few minutes," said he, throwing open another door. It was a quiet little plainly furnished room, with a round table in the centre, on which several German books were scattered. Colonel Stark laid down the lamp on the top of a harmonium beside the door. "I shall not keep you waiting an instant," said he, and vanished into the darkness.

'I glanced at the books upon the table, and in spite of my ignorance of German, I could see that two of them were treatises on science, the others being volumes of poetry. Then I walked across to the window, hoping that I might catch some glimpse of the countryside, but an oak shutter, heavily barred, was folded across it. It was a wonderfully silent house. There was an old clock ticking loudly somewhere in the passage, but otherwise everything was deadly still. A vague feeling of uneasiness began to steal over me. Who were these German people, and what were they doing, living in this strange, out-of-the-way place? And where was the place? I was ten miles or so from Eyford, that was all I knew, but whether north, south, east, or west, I had no idea. For that matter, Reading, and possibly other large towns, were within that radius, so the place might not be so secluded after all. Yet it was quite certain from the absolute stillness that we were in the country. I paced up and down the room humming a tune under my breath to keep up my spirits, and feeling that I was thoroughly earning my fifty-guinea fee.

'Suddenly, without any preliminary sound in the midst of the utter stillness, the door of my room swung slowly open. The woman was standing in the aperture, the darkness of the hall behind her, the yellow light from my lamp beating upon her eager and beautiful face. I could see at a glance that she was sick with fear, and the sight sent a chill to my own heart. She held up one shaking finger to warn me to be silent, and she shot a few whispered words of broken English at me, her eyes glancing back, like those of a frightened horse, into the gloom behind her.

'"I would go," said she, trying hard, as it seemed to me, to speak calmly; "I would go. I should not stay here. There is no good for you to do."

'"But, madam," said I, "I have not yet done what I came for. I cannot possibly leave until I have seen the machine."

'"It is not worth your while to wait," she went on. "You can pass through the door; no one hinders." And then, seeing that I smiled and shook my head, she suddenly threw aside her constraint, and made a step forward, with her hands wrung together. "For the love of Heaven!" she whispered, "get away from here before it is too late!"

'But I am somewhat headstrong by nature, and the more ready to engage in an affair when there is some obstacle in the way. I thought of my fifty-guinea fee, of my wearisome journey, and of the unpleasant night which seemed to be before me. Was it all to go for nothing? Why should I slink away without having carried out my commission, and without the payment which was my due?

This woman might, for all I knew, be a mono-maniac. With a stout bearing, therefore, though her manner had shaken me more than I cared to confess, I still shook my head, and declared my intention of remaining where I was. She was about to renew her entreaties when a door slammed overhead, and the sound of several footsteps was heard upon the stairs. She listened for an instant, threw up her hands with a despairing gesture, and vanished as suddenly and noiselessly as she had come.

'The newcomers were Colonel Lysander Stark, and a short thick man with a chinchilla beard growing out of the creases of his double chin, who was introduced to me as Mr Ferguson.

'"This is my secretary and manager," said the Colonel. "By the way, I was under the impression that I left this door shut just now. I fear that you have felt the draught."

'"On the contrary," said I, "I opened the door myself, because I felt the room to be a little close."

'He shot one of his suspicious glances at me. "Perhaps we had better proceed to business, then," said he. "Mr Ferguson and I will take you up to see the machine."

'"I had better put my hat on, I suppose."

'"Oh no, it is in the house."

'"What, do you dig fuller's earth in the house?"

'"No, no. This is only where we compress it.

But never mind that! All we wish you to do is to examine the machine and to let us know what is wrong with it."

'We went upstairs together, the Colonel first with the lamp, the fat manager and I behind him. It was a labyrinth of an old house, with corridors, passages, narrow winding staircases, and little low doors, the thresholds of which were hollowed out by the generations who had crossed them. There were no carpets, and no signs of any furniture above the ground floor, while the plaster was peeling off the walls, and the damp was breaking through in green, unhealthy blotches. I tried to put on as unconcerned an air as possible, but I had not forgotten the warnings of the lady, even though I disregarded them, and I kept a keen eye upon my two companions. Ferguson appeared to be a morose and silent man, but I could see from the little that he said that he was at least a fellow-countryman.

'Colonel Lysander Stark stopped at last before a low door, which he unlocked. Within was a small square room, in which the three of us could hardly get at one time. Ferguson remained outside, and the Colonel ushered me in.

'"We are now," said he, "actually within the hydraulic press, and it would be a particularly unpleasant thing for us if anyone were to turn it on. The ceiling of this small chamber is really the end of the descending piston, and it comes down with the force of many tons upon this metal floor.

There are small lateral columns of water outside which receive the force, and which transmit and multiply it in the manner which is familiar to you. The machine goes readily enough, but there is some stiffness in the working of it and it has lost a little of its force. Perhaps you will have the goodness to look it over, and to show us how we can set it right."

'I took the lamp from him, and I examined the machine very thoroughly. It was indeed a gigantic one, and capable of exercising enormous pressure. When I passed outside, however, and pressed down the levers which controlled it, I knew at once by the whishing sound that there was a slight leakage, which allowed a regurgitation of water through one of the side-cylinders. An examination showed that one of the india-rubber bands which was round the head of a driving-rod had shrunk so as not quite to fill the socket along which it worked. This was clearly the cause of the loss of power, and I pointed it out to my companions, who followed my remarks very carefully, and asked several practical questions as to how they should proceed to set it right. When I had made it clear to them, I returned to the main chamber of the machine, and took a good look at it to satisfy my own curiosity. It was obvious at a glance that the story of the fuller's earth was the merest fabrication, for it would be absurd to suppose that so powerful an engine could be designed for so inadequate a purpose. The walls were of wood, but the floor consisted of a large iron trough, and when I came to examine it I could see a crust of metallic deposit all over it. I had stooped and was scraping at this to see exactly what it was, when I heard a muttered exclamation in German, and saw the cadaverous face of the Colonel looking down at me.

'"What are you doing there?" he asked.

'I felt angry at having been tricked by so elaborate a story as that which he had told me. "I was admiring your fuller's earth," said I; "I think that I should be better able to advise you as to your machine if I knew what the exact purpose was for which it was used."

'The instant that I uttered the words I regretted the rashness of my speech. His face set hard, and a baleful light sprang up in his grey eyes.

'"Very well," said he, "you shall know all about the machine." He took a step backward, slammed the little door, and turned the key in the lock. I rushed towards it and pulled at the handle, but it was quite secure, and did not give in the least to my kicks and shoves. "Hallo!" I yelled. "Hallo! Colonel! Let me out!"

'And then suddenly in the silence I heard a sound which sent my heart into my mouth. It was the clank of the levers, and the swish of the leaking cylinder. He had set the engine at work. The lamp still stood upon the floor where I had placed it when examining the trough. By its light I saw that the black ceiling was coming down upon me, slowly, jerkily, but, as none knew better than myself, with a force which must within a minute grind me to a shapeless pulp. I threw myself, screaming, against the door, and dragged with my nails at the lock. I implored the Colonel to let me out, but the remorseless clanking of the levers drowned my cries. The ceiling was only a foot or two above my head, and with my hand upraised I could feel its hard rough surface. Then it flashed through my mind that the pain of my death would depend very much upon the position in which I met it. If I lay on my face the weight would come upon my spine, and I shuddered to think of that dreadful snap. Easier the other way, perhaps, and yet had I the nerve to lie and look up at that deadly black shadow wavering down upon me? Already I was unable to stand erect, when my eye caught something which brought a gush of hope back to my heart.

'I have said that though floor and ceiling were of iron, the walls were of wood. As I gave a last hurried glance around, I saw a thin line of yellow light between two of the boards, which broadened and broadened as a small panel was pushed backwards. For an instant I could hardly believe that here was indeed a door which led away from death. The next I threw myself through, and lay half fainting upon the other side. The panel had closed again behind me, but the crash of the lamp, and a few moments afterwards the clang of the two slabs of metal, told me how narrow had been my escape.

'I was recalled to myself by a frantic plucking at my wrist, and I found myself lying upon the stone floor of a narrow corridor, while a woman bent over me and tugged at me with her left hand, while she held a candle in her right. It was the same good friend whose warning I had so foolishly rejected.

'"Come! Come!" she cried breathlessly. "They will be here in a moment. They will see that you are not there. Oh, do not waste the so precious time, but come!"

'This time, at least, I did not scorn her advice. I staggered to my feet, and ran with her along the corridor and down a winding stair. The latter led to another broad passage, and, just as we reached it, we heard the sound of running feet and the shouting of two voices – one answering the other – from the floor on which we were, and from the one beneath. My guide stopped, and looked about her like one who is at her wits' end. Then she threw open a door which led into a bedroom, through the window of which the moon was shining brightly.

'"It is your only chance," said she. "It is high, but it may be that you can jump it."

'As she spoke a light sprang into view at the further end of the passage, and I saw the lean figure of Colonel Lysander Stark rushing forward with a lantern in one hand, and a weapon like a butcher's cleaver in the other. I rushed across the bedroom, flung open the window, and looked out.

How quiet and sweet and wholesome the garden looked in the moonlight, and it could not be more than thirty feet down. I clambered out upon the sill, but hesitated to jump, until I should have heard what passed between my saviour and the ruffian who pursued me. If she were ill-used, then at risk I was determined to go back to her assistance. The thought had hardly flashed through my mind before he was at the door, pushing his way past her; but she threw her arms round him, and tried to hold him back.

'"Fritz! Fritz!" she cried in English, "remember your promise after the last time. You said it should not be again. He will be silent! Oh, he will be silent!"

'"You are mad, Elise!" he shouted, struggling to break away from her. "You will be the ruin of us. He has seen too much. Let me pass, I say!" He dashed her to one side, and, rushing to the window, cut at me with his heavy weapon. I had let myself go, and was hanging with my fingers in the window slot and my hands across the sill, when his blow fell. I was conscious of a dull pain, my grip loosened, and I fell into the garden below.

'I was shaken, but not hurt by the fall; so I picked myself up and rushed off among the bushes as hard as I could run, for I understood that I was far from being out of danger yet. Suddenly, however, as I ran, a deadly dizziness and sickness came over me. I glanced down at my hand, which was throbbing painfully, and then, for the first time, saw that my thumb had been cut off, and that the blood was pouring from my wound. I endeavoured to tie my handkerchief round it, but there came a sudden buzzing in my ears, and next moment I fell in a dead faint among the rose-bushes.

'How long I remained unconscious I cannot tell. It must have been a very long time, for the moon had sunk and a bright morning was breaking when I came to myself. My clothes were all sodden with dew, and my coat-sleeve was drenched with blood from my wounded thumb. The smarting of it recalled in an instant all the particulars of my night's adventure, and I sprang to my feet with the feeling that I might hardly yet be safe from my pursuers. But, to my astonishment, when I came to look round me neither house nor garden were to be seen. I had been lying in an angle of the hedge close by the highroad, and just a little lower down was a long building, which proved, upon my approaching it, to be the very station at which I had arrived upon the previous night. Were it not for the ugly wound upon my hand, all that had passed during those dreadful hours might have been an evil dream.

'Half dazed, I went into the station, and asked about the morning train. There would be one to Reading in less than an hour. The same porter was on duty, I found, as had been there when I arrived. I inquired from him whether he had ever heard of Colonel Lysander Stark. The name was strange to him. Had he observed a carriage the night before waiting for me? No, he had not. Was there a police station anywhere near? There was one about three miles off.

'It was too far for me to go, weak and ill as I was. I determined to wait until I got back to town before telling my story to the police. It was a little past six when I arrived, so I went first to have my wound dressed, and then the doctor was kind enough to bring me along here. I put the case into your hands, and shall do exactly what you advise.'

We both sat in silence for some little time after listening to this extraordinary narrative. Then Sherlock Holmes pulled down from the shelf one of the ponderous commonplace books in which he placed his cuttings.

'Here is an advertisement which will interest you,' said he. 'It appeared in all the papers about a year ago. Listen to this – "Lost on the 9th inst., Mr Jeremiah Hayling, aged 26, a hydraulic engineer. Left his lodgings at ten o'clock at night, and has not been heard of since. Was dressed in," etc. etc. Ha! That represents the last time that the Colonel needed to have his machine overhauled, I fancy.'

'Good heavens!' cried my patient. 'Then that explains what the girl said.'

'Undoubtedly. It is quite clear that the Colonel was a cool and desperate man, who was absolutely determined that nothing should stand in the way of his little game, like those out-and-out pirates who will leave no survivor from a captured ship. Well, every moment now is precious, so, if you feel equal to it, we shall go down to Scotland Yard at once as a preliminary to starting for Eyford.'

Some three hours or so afterwards we were all in the train together, bound from Reading to the little Berkshire village. There were Sherlock Holmes, the hydraulic engineer, Inspector Bradstreet of Scotland Yard, a plain-clothes man, and myself. Bradstreet had spread an ordnance map of the county out upon the seat, and was busy with his compasses drawing a circle with Eyford for its centre.

'There you are,' said he. 'That circle is drawn at a radius of ten miles from the village. The place we want must be somewhere near that line. You said ten miles, I think, sir?'

'It was an hour's good drive.'

'And you think that they brought you back all that way when you were unconscious?'

'They must have done so. I have a confused memory, too, of having been lifted and conveyed somewhere.'

'What I cannot understand,' said I, 'is why they should have spared you when they found you lying fainting in the garden. Perhaps the villain was softened by the woman's entreaties.'

'I hardly think that likely. I never saw a more inexorable face in my life.'

'Oh, we shall soon clear up all that,' said Bradstreet. 'Well, I have drawn my circle, and I only wish I knew at what point upon it the folk that we are in search of are to be found.'

'I think I could lay my finger on it,' said Holmes quietly.

'Really, now!' cried the inspector, 'you have formed your opinion! Come now, we shall see who agrees with you. I say south, for the country is more deserted there.'

'And I say east,' said my patient.

'I am for west,' remarked the plain-clothes man. 'There are several quiet little villages up there.'

'And I am for north,' said I; 'because there are no hills there, and our friend says that he did not notice the carriage go up any.'

'Come,' said the inspector, laughing; 'it's a very pretty diversity of opinion. We have boxed the compass among us. Who do you give your casting vote to?'

'You are all wrong.'

'But we can't *all* be.'

'Oh, yes, you can. This is my point,' he placed his finger on the centre of the circle. 'This is where we shall find them.'

'But the twelve-mile drive?' gasped Hatherley.

'Six out and six back. Nothing simpler. You say yourself that the horse was fresh and glossy when you got in. How could it be that, if it had gone twelve miles over heavy roads?'

'Indeed it is a likely ruse enough,' observed Bradstreet thoughtfully. 'Of course there can be no doubt as to the nature of this gang.'

'None at all,' said Holmes. 'They are coiners on a large scale, and have used the machine to form the amalgam which has taken the place of silver.'

'We have known for some time that a clever gang was at work,' said the inspector. 'They have been turning out half-crowns by the thousand. We even traced them as far as Reading, but could get no further; for they had covered their traces in a way that showed that they were very old hands. But now, thanks to this lucky chance, I think that we have got them right enough.'

But the inspector was mistaken, for those criminals were not destined to fall into the hands of justice. As we rolled into Eyford station we saw a gigantic column of smoke which streamed up from behind a small clump of trees in the neighbourhood, and hung like an immense ostrich feather over the landscape.

'A house on fire?' asked Bradstreet, as the train steamed off again on its way.

'Yes, sir,' said the stationmaster.

'When did it break out?'

'I hear that it was during the night, sir, but it has got worse, and the whole place is in a blaze.'

'Whose house is it?'

'Dr Becher's.'

'Tell me,' broke in the engineer, 'is Dr Becher a German, very thin, with a long sharp nose?'

The stationmaster laughed heartily. 'No, sir, Dr Becher is an Englishman, and there isn't a man in the parish who has a better lined waistcoat.

But he has a gentleman staying with him, a patient as I understand, who is a foreigner, and he looks as if a little good Berkshire beef would do him no harm.'

The stationmaster had not finished his speech before we were all hastening in the direction of the fire. The road topped a low hill, and there was a great widespread whitewashed building in front of us, spouting fire at every chink and window, while in the garden in front three fire-engines were vainly striving to keep the flames under.

'That's it!' cried Hatherley, in intense excitement. 'There is the gravel drive, and there are the rose-bushes where I lay. That second window is the one that I jumped from.'

'Well, at least,' said Holmes, 'you have had your revenge upon them. There can be no doubt that it was your oil lamp which, when it was crushed in the press, set fire to the wooden walls, though no doubt they were too excited in the chase after you to observe it at the time. Now keep your eyes open in this crowd for your friends of last night, though I very much fear that they are a good hundred miles off by now.'

And Holmes's fears came to be realized, for from that day to this no word has ever been heard either of the beautiful woman, the sinister German, or the morose Englishman. Early that morning a peasant had met a cart, containing several people and some very bulky boxes, driving rapidly in the direction of Reading, but there all traces of the fugitives disappeared, and even Holmes's ingenuity failed to discover the least clue to their whereabouts.

The firemen had been much perturbed at the strange arrangements which they found within, and still more so by discovering a newly-severed human thumb upon a windowsill of the second floor. About sunset, however, their efforts were at last successful, and they subdued the flames, but not before the roof had fallen in, and the whole place reduced to such absolute ruin that, save some twisted cylinders and iron piping, not a trace remained of the machinery which had cost our unfortunate acquaintance so dearly. Large masses of nickel and of tin were discovered stored in an outhouse, but no coins were to be found, which may have explained the presence of those bulky boxes which have been already referred to.

How our hydraulic engineer had been conveyed from the garden to the spot where he recovered his senses might have remained for ever a mystery were it not for the soft mould which told us a very plain tale. He had evidently been carried down by two persons, one of whom had remarkably small feet, and the other unusually large ones. On the whole, it was most probable that the silent Englishman, being less bold or less murderous than his companion, had assisted the woman to bear the unconscious man out of the way of danger.

'Well,' said our engineer ruefully, as we took our seats to return to London, 'it has been a pretty business for me! I have lost my thumb, and I have lost a fifty-guinea fee, and what have I gained!'

'Experience,' said Holmes, laughing. 'Indirectly it may be of value, you know; you have only to put it into words to gain the reputation of being excellent company for the remainder of your existence.'

The Red-Headed League

I had called upon my friend, Mr Sherlock Holmes, one day in the autumn of last year, and found him in deep conversation with a very stout, florid-faced, elderly gentleman, with fiery red hair. With an apology for my intrusion, I was about to withdraw, when Holmes pulled me abruptly into the room, and closed the door behind me.

'You could not possibly have come at a better time, my dear Watson,' he said cordially.

'I was afraid that you were engaged.'

'So I am. Very much so.'

'Then I can wait in the next room.'

'Not at all. This gentleman, Mr Wilson, has been my partner and helper in many of my most successful cases, and I have no doubt that he will be of the utmost use to me in yours also.'

The stout gentleman half rose from his chair, and gave a bob of greeting, with a quick little questioning glance from his small, fat-encircled eyes.

'Try the settee,' said Holmes, relapsing into his armchair, and putting his fingertips together, as was his custom when in judicial moods. 'I know, my dear Watson, that you share my love of all that is bizarre and outside the conventions and humdrum routine of everyday life. You have shown your relish for it by the enthusiasm which has prompted you to chronicle, and, if you will excuse my saying so, somewhat to embellish so many of my own little adventures.'

'Your cases have indeed been of the greatest interest to me,' I observed.

'You will remember that I remarked the other day, just before we went into the very simple problem presented by Miss Mary Sutherland, that for strange effects and extraordinary combinations we must go to life itself, which is always far more daring than any effort of the imagination.'

'A proposition which I took the liberty of doubting.'

'You did, Doctor, but none the less you must come round to my view, for otherwise I shall keep piling fact upon fact on you, until your reason breaks down under them and acknowledges me to be right. Now, Mr Jabez Wilson here has been good enough to call upon me this morning, and to begin a narrative which promises to be one of the most singular which I have listened to for some time. You have heard me remark that the strangest and most unique things are very often connected not with the larger but with the smaller crimes, and occasionally, indeed, where there is room for doubt whether any positive crime has been committed. As far as I have heard, it is impossible for me to say whether the present case is an instance of crime or not, but the course of events is certainly among the most singular that I have ever listened to. Perhaps, Mr Wilson, you would have the great kindness to recommence your narrative. I ask you not merely because my friend Dr Watson has not heard the opening part, but also because the peculiar nature of the story makes me anxious to have every possible detail from your lips. As a rule, when I have heard some slight indication of the course of events I am able to guide myself by the thousands of other similar cases which occur to my memory. In the present instance I am forced to admit that the facts are, to the best of my belief, unique.'

The portly client puffed out his chest with an appearance of some little pride, and pulled a dirty and wrinkled newspaper from the inside pocket of his greatcoat. As he glanced down the advertisement column, with his head thrust forward, and the paper flattened out upon his knee, I took a good look at the man, and endeavoured after the fashion of my companion to read the indications which might be presented by his dress or appearance.

I did not gain very much, however, by my inspection. Our visitor bore every mark of being an average commonplace British tradesman, obese, pompous, and slow. He wore rather baggy grey shepherds' check trousers, a not over-clean black frock-coat, unbuttoned in the front, and a drab waistcoat with a heavy brassy Albert chain, and a square pierced bit of metal dangling down as an ornament. A frayed top-hat, and a faded brown overcoat with a wrinkled velvet collar lay upon a chair beside him. Altogether, look as I would, there was nothing remarkable about the man save his blazing red head, and the expression of extreme chagrin and discontent upon his features.

Sherlock Holmes's quick eye took in my occupation and he shook his head with a smile as he noticed my questioning glances. 'Beyond the obvious facts that he has at some time done manual labour, that he takes snuff, that he is a Freemason, that he has been in China, and that he has done a considerable amount of writing lately, I can deduce nothing else.'

Mr Jabez Wilson started up in his chair, with his forefinger upon the paper, but his eyes upon my companion.

'How, in the name of good fortune, did you know that, Mr Holmes?' he asked. 'How did you know, for example, that I did manual labour? It's as true as gospel, and I began as a ship's carpenter.'

'Your hands, my dear sir. Your right hand is quite a size larger than your left. You have worked with it, and the muscles are more developed.'

'Well, the snuff, then, and the Freemasonry?'

'I won't insult your intelligence by telling you how I read that, especially as, rather against the strict rules of your order, you use an arc and compass breastpin.'

'Ah, of course, I forgot that. But the writing?'

'What else can be indicated by that right cuff so very shiny for five inches, and the left one with the smooth patch near the elbow where you rest it upon the desk.'

'Well, but China?'

'The fish which you have tattooed immediately above your right wrist could only have been done in China. I have made a small study of tattoo marks, and have even contributed to the literature of the subject. That trick of staining the fishes' scales of a delicate pink is quite peculiar to China. When, in addition, I see a Chinese coin hanging from your watch-chain, the matter becomes even more simple.'

Mr Jabez Wilson laughed heavily. 'Well, I never!' said he. 'I thought at first you had done something clever, but I see that there was nothing in it after all.'

'I begin to think, Watson,' said Holmes, 'that I make a mistake in explaining. "Omne ignotum pro magnifico," you know, and my poor little reputation, such as it is, will suffer shipwreck if I am so candid. Can you not find the advertisement, Mr Wilson?'

'Yes, I have got it now,' he answered, with his thick, red finger planted half-way down the column. 'Here it is. This is what began it all. You must read it for yourself, sir.'

I took the paper from him and read as follows:

To the Red-Headed League – On account of the bequest of the late Ezekiah Hopkins of Lebanon, Penn., USA, there is now another vacancy open which entitles a member of the League to a salary of four pounds a week for purely nominal services. All red-headed men who are sound in body and mind, and above the age of twenty-one years, are eligible. Apply in person on Monday, at eleven o'clock, to Duncan Ross, at the offices of the League, 7 Pope's Court, Fleet Street.

'What on earth does this mean?' I ejaculated, after I had twice read over the extraordinary announcement.

Holmes chuckled, and wriggled in his chair, as was his habit when in high spirits. 'It is a little off the beaten track, isn't it?' said he. 'And now, Mr Wilson, off you go at scratch, and tell us all about yourself, your household, and the effect which this advertisement had upon your fortunes. You will first make a note, Doctor, of the paper and the date.'

'It is *The Morning Chronicle*, of 27 April 1890. Just two months ago.'

'Very good. Now, Mr Wilson?'

'Well, it is just as I have been telling you, Mr Sherlock Holmes,' said Jabez Wilson, mopping his forehead, 'I have a small pawnbroker's business at Coburg Square, near the City. It's not a very large affair, and of late years it has not done more than just give me a living. I used to be able to keep two assistants, but now I only keep one;

and I would have a job to pay him, but that he is willing to come for half wages, so as to learn the business.'

'What is the name of this obliging youth?' asked Sherlock Holmes.

'His name is Vincent Spaulding, and he's not such a youth either. It's hard to say his age. I should not wish a smarter assistant, Mr Holmes; and I know very well that he could better himself, and even twice what I am able to give him. But after all, if he is satisfied, why should I put ideas in his head?'

'Why, indeed? You seem most fortunate in having an employee who comes under the full market price. It is not a common experience among employers in this age. I don't know that your assistant is not as remarkable as your advertisement.'

'Oh, he has his faults, too,' said Mr Wilson. 'Never was such a fellow for photography. Snapping away with a camera when he ought to be improving his mind, and then diving down into the cellar like a rabbit into its hole to develop his pictures. That is his main fault; but on the whole, he's a good worker. There's no vice in him.'

'He is still with you, I presume?'

'Yes, sir. He and a girl of fourteen, who does a bit of simple cooking, and keeps the place clean – that's all I have in the house, for I am a widower, and never had any family. We live very quietly, sir, the three of us; and we keep a roof over our heads, and pay our debts, if we do nothing more.

'The first thing that put us out was that advertisement. Spaulding, he came down into the office
just this day eight weeks with this very paper in
his hand, and he says:

'"I wish to the Lord, Mr Wilson, that I was a
red-headed man."

'"Why that?" I asks.

'"Why" says he, "here's another vacancy on
the League of the Red-Headed Men. It's worth
quite a little fortune to any man who gets it, and I
understand that there are more vacancies than
there are men, so that the trustees are at their
wits' end what to do with the money. If my hair
would only change colour, here's a nice little crib
all ready for me to step into."

'"Why, what is it, then!" I asked. You see, Mr
Holmes, I am a very stay-at-home man, and, as
my business came to me instead of my having to
go to it, I was often weeks on end without putting
my foot over the door-mat. In that way I didn't
know much of what was going on outside, and I
was always glad of a bit of news.

'"Have you never heard of the League of the
Red-Headed Men?" he asked, with his eyes open.

'"Never."

'"Why, I wonder at that, for you are eligible
yourself for one of the vacancies."

'"And what are they worth?" I asked.

'"Oh, merely a couple of hundred a year, but
the work is slight, and it need not interfere much
with one's other occupations."

'Well, you can easily think that that made me prick up my ears, for the business has not been over good for some years, and an extra couple of hundred would have been very handy.

'"Tell me all about it," said I.

'"Well," said he, showing me the advertisement, "you can see for yourself that the League has a vacancy, and there is the address where you should apply for particulars. As far as I can make out, the League was founded by an American millionaire, Ezekiah Hopkins, who was very peculiar in his ways. He was himself red-headed, and he had a great sympathy for all red-headed men; so, when he died, it was found that he had left his enormous fortune in the hands of trustees, with instructions to apply the interest to the providing of easy berths to men whose hair is of that colour. From all I hear it is splendid pay, and very little to do."

'"But," said I, "there would be millions of red-headed men who would apply."

'"Not so many as you might think," he answered. "You see it is really confined to Londoners, and to grown men. This American had started from London when he was young, and he wanted to do the old town a good turn. Then, again, I have heard it is no use your applying if you hair is light red, or dark red, or anything but real, bright, blazing, fiery red. Now, if you cared to apply, Mr Wilson, you would just walk in; but perhaps it would hardly be worth your while to put yourself out of the way for the sake of a few hundred pounds."

'Now, it is a fact, gentlemen, as you may see for yourselves, that my hair is of a very full and rich tint, so that it seemed to me that, if there was to be any competition in the matter, I stood as good a chance as any man that I had ever met. Vincent Spaulding seemed to know so much about it that I thought he might prove useful, so I just ordered him to put up the shutters for the day, and to come right away with me. He was very willing to have a holiday, so we shut the business up, and started off for the address that was given us in the advertisement.

'I never hope to see such a sight as that again, Mr Holmes. From north, south, east, and west every man who had a shade of red in his hair had tramped into the City to answer the advertisement. Fleet Street was choked with red-headed folk, and Pope's Court looked like a coster's orange barrow. I should not have thought there were so many in the whole country as were brought together by that single advertisement. Every shade of colour they were – straw, lemon, orange, brick, Irish setter, liver, clay; but, as Spaulding said, there were not many who had the real vivid flame-coloured tint. When I saw how many were waiting I would have given it up in despair; but Spaulding would not hear of it. How he did it I could not imagine, but he pushed and pulled and butted until he got me through the crowd, and right up to the steps which led to the office. There was a double stream upon the stair, some going up in hope, and some coming back dejected; but we wedged in as well as we could, and soon found ourselves in the office.'

'Your experience has been a most entertaining one,' remarked Holmes, as his client paused and refreshed his memory with a huge pinch of snuff. 'Pray continue your very interesting statement.'

'There was nothing in the office but a couple of wooden chairs and a deal table, behind which sat a small man, with a head that was even redder than mine. He said a few words to each candidate as he came up, and then he always managed to find some fault in them which would disqualify them. Getting a vacancy did not seem to be such a very easy matter after all. However, when our turn came, the little man was more favourable to me than to any of the others, and he closed the door as we entered, so that he might have a private word with us.

'"This is Mr Jabez Wilson," said my assistant, "and he is willing to fill a vacancy in the League."

'"And he is admirably suited for it," the other answered. "He has every requirement. I cannot recall when I have seen anything so fine." He took a step backwards, cocked his head on one side, and gazed at my hair until I felt quite bashful. Then suddenly he plunged forward, wrung my hand, and congratulated me warmly on my success.

'"It would be injustice to hesitate," said he. "You will, however, I am sure, excuse me for taking an obvious precaution." With that he seized my hair in both his hands, and tugged until I yelled with the pain. "There is water in your eyes," said he, as he released me. "I perceive that all is as it should be. But we have to be careful, for we have twice been deceived by wigs and once by paint. I could tell you tales of cobbler's wax which would disgust you with human nature." He stepped over to the window, and shouted through it at the top of his voice that the vacancy was filled. A groan of disappointment came up from below, and the folk all trooped away in different directions, until there was not a red head to be seen except my own and that of the manager.

'"My name," said he, "is Mr Duncan Ross, and I am myself one of the pensioners upon the fund left by our noble benefactor. Are you a married man, Mr Wilson? Have you a family?"

'I answered that I had not.

'His face fell immediately.

'"Dear me!" he said gravely, "that is very serious indeed! I am sorry to hear you say that. The fund was, of course, for the propagation and spread of the redheads as well as for their maintenance. It is exceedingly unfortunate that you should be a bachelor."

'My face lengthened at this, Mr Holmes, for I thought that I was not to have the vacancy after all; but after thinking it over for a few minutes, he said that it would be all right.

'"In the case of another," said he, "the objection might be fatal, but we must stretch a point in favour of a man with such a head of hair as yours. When shall you be able to enter upon your new duties?"

'"Well, it is a little awkward, for I have a business already," said I.

'"Oh, never mind about that, Mr Wilson!" said Vincent Spaulding. "I shall be able to look after that for you."

'"What would be the hours?" I asked.

'"Ten to two."

'Now a pawnbroker's business is mostly done of an evening, Mr Holmes, especially Thursday and Friday evening, which is just before pay-day; so it would suit me very well to earn a little in the mornings. Besides, I knew that my assistant was a good man, and that he would see to anything that turned up.

'"That would suit me very well," said I. "And the pay?"

'"Is four pounds a week."

'"And the work?"

'"Is purely nominal."

'"What do you call purely nominal?"

'"Well, you have to be in the office, or at least in the building, the whole time. If you leave, you forfeit your whole position for ever. The will is very clear upon that point. You don't comply with the conditions if you budge from the office during that time."

'"It's only four hours a day, and I should not think of leaving," said I.

'"No excuse will avail," said Mr Duncan Ross, "neither sickness, nor business, nor anything else. There you must stay, or you lose your billet."

'"And the work?"

'"Is to copy out the *Encyclopedia Britannica*. There is the first volume of it in that press. You must find your own ink, pens, and blotting-paper, but we provide this table and chair. Will you be ready tomorrow?"

'"Certainly," I answered.

'"Then good-bye, Mr Jabez Wilson, and let me congratulate you once more on the important position which you have been fortunate enough to gain." He bowed me out of the room, and I went home with my assistant, hardly knowing what to say or do, I was so pleased at my own good fortune.

'Well, I thought over the matter all day, and by evening I was in low spirits again; for I had quite persuaded myself that the whole affair must be some great hoax or fraud, though what its object might be I could not imagine. It seemed altogether past belief that anyone could make such a will, or that they would pay a sum for doing anything so simple as copying out the *Encyclopedia Britannica*. Vincent Spaulding did what he could to cheer me up, but by bedtime I had reasoned myself out of the whole thing. However, in the morning I determined to have a look at it anyhow, so I bought a penny bottle of ink, and with a quill pen, and seven sheets of foolscap paper, I started off for Pope's Court.

'Well, to my surprise and delight everything was as right as possible. The table was set out ready for me, and Mr Duncan Ross was there to see that I got fairly to work. He started me off upon the letter A, and then he left me; but he would drop in from time to time to see that all was right with me. At two o'clock he bade me good day, complimented me upon the amount that I had written, and locked the door of the office after me.

'This went on day after day, Mr Holmes, and on Saturday the manager came in and planked down four golden sovereigns for my week's work. It was the same next week, and the same the week after. Every morning I was there at ten, and every afternoon I left at two. By degrees Mr Duncan Ross took to coming in only once of a morning, and then, after a time, he did not come in at all. Still, of course, I never dared to leave the room for an instant, for I was not sure when he might come, and the billet was such a good one, and suited me so well, that I would not risk the loss of it.

'Eight weeks passed away like this, and I had written about Abbots, and Archery, and Armour, and Architecture, and Attica, and hoped with diligence that I might get on to the B's before very long. It cost me something in foolscap, and I had pretty nearly filled a shelf with my writings. And then suddenly the whole business came to an end.'

'To an end?'

'Yes, sir. And no later than this morning. I went to my work as usual at ten o'clock, but the door was shut and locked, with a little square of cardboard hammered on to the middle of the panel with a tack. Here it is, and you can read for yourself.'

He held up a piece of white cardboard, about the size of a sheet of note-paper. It read in this fashion:

THE RED-HEADED LEAGUE IS DISSOLVED
OCT. 9, 1890

Sherlock Holmes and I surveyed this curt announcement and the rueful face behind it, until the comical side of the affair so completely over-topped every other consideration that we both burst out into a roar of laughter.

'I cannot see that there is anything very funny,' cried our client, flushing up to the roots of his flaming head. 'If you can do nothing better than laugh at me, I can go elsewhere.'

'No, no,' cried Holmes, shoving him back into the chair from which he had half risen. 'I really wouldn't miss your case for the world. It is most refreshingly unusual. But there is, if you will excuse me saying so, something just a little funny about it. Pray what steps did you take when you found the card upon the door?'

'I was staggered, sir. I did not know what to do. Then I called at the offices round, but none of them seemed to know anything about it. Finally, I went to the landlord, who is an accountant living on the ground floor, and I asked him if he could tell me what had become of the Red-Headed League. He said that he had never heard of any such body. Then I asked him who Mr Duncan Ross was. He answered that the name was new to him.

'"Well," said I, "the gentleman at No 4."

'"What, the red-headed man?"

'"Yes."

'"Oh," said he, "his name was William Morris. He was a solicitor, and was using my room as a temporary convenience until his new premises were ready. He moved out yesterday."

'"Where could I find him?"

'"Oh, at his new offices. He did tell me the address. Yes, 17 King Edward Street, near St Paul's."

'I started off, Mr Holmes, but when I got to that address it was a manufactory of artificial knee-caps, and no one in it had ever heard of either Mr William Morris, or Mr Duncan Ross.'

'And what did you do then?' asked Holmes.

'I went home to Saxe-Coburg Square, and I took the advice of my assistant. But he could not help me in any way. He could only say that if I waited I should hear by post. But that was not quite good enough, Mr Holmes. I did not wish to lose such a place without a struggle, so, as I had heard that you were good enough to give advice to poor folk who were in need of it, I came right away to you.'

'And you did very wisely,' said Holmes. 'Your case is an exceedingly remarkable one, and I shall be happy to look into it. From what you have told me I think that it is possible that graver issues hang from it than might at first sight appear.'

'Grave enough!' said Mr Jabez Wilson. 'Why, I have lost four pounds a week.'

'As far as you are personally concerned,' remarked Holmes, 'I do not see that you have any grievance against this extraordinary league. On the contrary, you are, as I understand, richer by some thirty pounds, to say nothing of the minute knowledge which you have gained on every subject which comes under the letter A. You have lost nothing by them.'

'No, sir. But I want to find out about them, and who they are, and what their object was in playing this prank – if it was a prank – upon me. It was a pretty expensive joke for them, for it cost them two-and-thirty pounds.'

'We shall endeavour to clear up these points for you. And, first, one or two questions, Mr Wilson. This assistant of yours who first called your attention to the advertisement – how long had he been with you?'

'About a month then.'

'How did he come?'

'In answer to an advertisement.'

'Was he the only applicant?'

'No, I had a dozen.'

'Why did you pick him?'

'Because he was handy, and would come cheap.'

'At half wages, in fact.'

'Yes.'

'What is he like, this Vincent Spaulding?'

'Small, stout-built, very quick in his ways, no hair on his face, though he's not short of thirty. Has a white splash of acid upon his forehead.'

Holmes sat up in his chair in considerable excitement.

'I thought as much,' said he. 'Have you ever observed that his ears are pierced for ear-rings?'

'Yes, sir. He told me that a gipsy had done it for him when he was a lad.'

'Hum!' said Holmes, sinking back deep in thought. 'He is still with you?'

'Oh, yes, sir, I have only just left him.'

'And has your business been attended to in your absence?'

'Nothing to complain of, sir. There's never very much to do of a morning.'

'That will do, Mr Wilson. I shall be happy to give you an opinion upon the subject in the course of a day or two. Today is Saturday, and I hope that by Monday we may come to a conclusion.'

'Well, Watson,' said Holmes, when our visitor had left us, 'what do you make of it all?'

'I make nothing of it,' I answered, frankly. 'It is a most mysterious business.'

'As a rule,' said Holmes, 'the more bizarre a thing is the less mysterious it proves to be. It is your commonplace, featureless crimes which are really puzzling, just as a commonplace face is the most difficult to identify. But I must be prompt over this matter.'

'What are you going to do, then?' I asked.

'To smoke,' he answered. 'It is quite a three-pipe problem, and I beg that you won't speak to me for fifty minutes.' He curled himself up in his chair, with his thin knees drawn up to his hawk-like nose, and there he sat with his eyes closed and his black clay pipe thrusting out like the bill of some strange bird. I had come to the conclusion that he had dropped asleep, and indeed was nodding myself, when he suddenly sprang out of his chair with the gesture of a man who had made up his mind, and put his pipe down upon the mantel-piece.

'Sarasate plays at the St James's Hall this afternoon,' he remarked. 'What do you think, Watson? Could your patients spare you for a few hours?'

'I have nothing to do today. My practice is never very absorbing.'

'Then put on your hat, and come. I am going through the City first, and we can have some lunch on the way. I observe that there is a good deal of German music on the programme which is rather more to my taste than Italian or French. It is introspective, and I want to introspect. Come along!'

We travelled by the Underground as far as Aldersgate; and a short walk took us to Saxe-Coburg Square, the scene of the singular story which he had listened to in the morning. It was a pokey, little, shabby-genteel place, where four lines of dingy two-storied brick houses looked out into a small railed-in enclosure, where a lawn of weedy grass and a few clumps of faded laurel bushes made a hard fight against a smoke-laden and uncongenial atmosphere. Three gilt balls and a brown board with JABEZ WILSON in white letters upon a corner house, announced the place where our red-headed client carried on his business. Sherlock Holmes stopped in front of it with his head on one side and looked it all over, with his eyes shining brightly between puckered lids. Then he walked slowly up the street and then down again to the corner, still looking at the houses. Finally he returned to the pawnbroker's, and, having thumped vigorously upon the pavement with his stick two or three times, he went up to the door and knocked. It was instantly opened by a bright-looking, clean-shaven young fellow, who asked him to step in.

'Thank you,' said Holmes, 'I only wished to ask you how you would go from here to the Strand.'

'Third right, fourth left,' answered the assistant promptly, closing the door.

'Smart fellow, that,' observed Holmes as we walked away. 'He is, in my judgement, the fourth smartest man in London, and for daring I am not sure that he has not a claim to be third. I have known something of him before.'

'Evidently,' said I, 'Mr Wilson's assistant counts for a good deal in this mystery of the Red-Headed League. I am sure that you inquired your way merely in order that you might see him.'

'Not him.'

'What then?'

'The knees of his trousers.'

'And what did you see?'

'What I expected to see.'

'Why did you beat the pavement?'

'My dear Doctor, this is a time for observation, not for talk. We are spies in an enemy's country. We know something of Saxe-Coburg Square. Let us now explore the paths which lie behind it.'

The road in which we found ourselves as we turned round the corner from the retired Saxe-Coburg Square presented as great a contrast to it as the front of a picture does to the back. It was one of the main arteries which convey the traffic of the City to the north and west. The roadway was blocked with the immense stream of commerce flowing in a double tide inwards and outwards, while the footpaths were black with the hurrying swarm of pedestrians. It was difficult to realize as we looked at the line of fine shops and stately business premises that they really abutted on the other side upon the faded and stagnant square which we had just quitted.

'Let me see,' said Holmes, standing at the corner, and glancing along the line, 'I should like just to remember the order of the houses here. It is a hobby of mine to have an exact knowledge of London. There is Mortimer's, the tobacconist, the little newspaper shop, the Coburg branch of the City and Suburban Bank, the Vegetarian Restaurant, and McFarlane's carriage-building depot. That carries us right on to the other block. And now, Doctor, we've done our work, so it's time we had some play. A sandwich and a cup of coffee, and then off to violin land, where all is sweetness and delicacy and harmony, and there are no red-headed clients to vex us with their conundrums.'

My friend was an enthusiastic musician being himself not only a very capable performer, but a composer of no ordinary merit. All the afternoon he sat in the stalls wrapped in the most perfect happiness, gently waving his long thin fingers in time to the music, while his gently smiling face and his languid, dreamy eyes were as unlike those of Holmes the sleuth-hound, Holmes the relentless, keen-witted, ready-handed criminal agent, as it was possible to conceive. In his singular character the dual nature alternately asserted itself and his extreme exactness and astuteness represented, as I have often thought, the reaction against the poetic and contemplative mood which occasionally predominated in him. The swing of his nature took him from extreme languor to devouring energy; and, as I knew well, he was never so truly formidable as when, for days on end, he had been lounging in his arm-chair amid his improvisations and his black-letter editions. Then it was that the lust of the chase would suddenly come upon him, and that his brilliant reasoning power would rise to the level of intuition, until those who were unacquainted with his methods would look askance at him as on a man whose knowledge was not that of other mortals. When I saw him that afternoon so enwrapped in the music at St James's Hall I felt that an evil time might be coming upon those whom he had set himself to hunt down.

'You want to go home, no doubt, Doctor,' he remarked, as we emerged.

'Yes, it would be as well.'

'And I have some business to do which will take some hours. This business at Coburg Square is serious.'

'Why serious?'

'A considerable crime is in contemplation. I have every reason to believe that we shall be in time to stop it. But today being Saturday rather complicates matters. I shall want your help tonight.'

'At what time?'

'Ten will be early enough.'

'I shall be at Baker Street at ten.'

'Very well. And I say, Doctor! there may be some little danger, so kindly put your army revolver in your pocket.' He waved his hand, turned on his heel, and disappeared in an instant among the crowd.

I trust that I am not more dense than my neighbours, but I was always oppressed with a sense of my own stupidity in my dealings with Sherlock Holmes. Here I had heard what he had heard, I had seen what he had seen, and yet from his words it was evident that he saw clearly not only what had happened, but what was about to happen, while to me the whole business was still confused and grotesque. As I drove home to my house in Kensington I thought over it all, from the extraordinary story of the red-headed copier of the *Encyclopedia* down to the visit to Saxe-Coburg Square, and the ominous words with which he had parted from me. What was this nocturnal expedition, and why should I go armed? Where were we going, and what were we to do? I had the hint from Holmes that this smooth-faced pawnbroker's assistant was a formidable man – a man who might play a deep game. I tried to puzzle it out, but gave it up in despair, and set the matter aside until night should bring an explanation.

It was a quarter past nine when I started from home and made my way across the Park, and so through Oxford Street to Baker Street. Two hansoms were standing at the door, and, as I entered the passage, I heard the sound of voices from above. On entering his room, I found Holmes in animated conversation with two men, one of whom I recognized as Peter Jones, the official police agent; while the other was a long, thin, sad-faced man, with a very shiny hat and oppressively respectable frock-coat.

'Ha! our party is complete,' said Holmes, buttoning up his pea-jacket, and taking his heavy hunting-crop from the rack. 'Watson, I think you know Mr Jones, of Scotland Yard? Let me introduce you to Mr Merryweather, who is to be our companion in tonight's adventure.'

'We're hunting in couples again, Doctor, you see,' said Jones in his consequential way. 'Our friend here is a wonderful man for starting a chase. All he wants is an old dog to help him to do the running down.'

'I hope a wild goose may not prove to be the end of our chase,' observed Mr Merryweather gloomily.

'You may place considerable confidence in Mr Holmes, sir,' said the police agent loftily. 'He has his own little methods, which are, if he won't mind my saying so, just a little too theoretical and fantastic, but he has the makings of a detective in him. It is not too much to say that once or twice, as in that business of the Sholto murder and the Agra treasure, he has been more nearly correct than the official force.'

'Oh, if you say so, Mr Jones, it is all right!' said the stranger, with deference. 'Still, I confess that I miss my rubber. It is the first Saturday night for seven-and-thirty years that I have not had my rubber.'

'I think you will find,' said Sherlock Holmes, 'that you will play for a higher stake tonight than you have ever done yet, and that the play will be more exciting. For you, Mr Merryweather, the stake will be some thirty thousand pounds; and for you, Jones, it will be the man upon whom you wish to lay your hands.'

'John Clay, the murderer, thief, smasher, and forger. He's a young man, Mr Merryweather, but he is at the head of his profession and I would rather have my bracelets on him than on any criminal in London. He's a remarkable man, is young John Clay. His grandfather was a Royal Duke, and he himself has been to Eton and Oxford. His brain is as cunning as his fingers, and though we meet signs of him at every turn, we never know where to find the man himself. He'll crack a crib in Scotland one week, and be raising money to build an orphanage in Cornwall the next. I've been on his track for years, and have never set eyes on him yet.'

'I hope that I may have the pleasure of introducing you tonight. I've had one or two little turns also with Mr John Clay, and I agree with you that he is at the head of his profession. It is past ten, however, and quite time that we started. If you two will take the first hansom, Watson and I will follow in the second.'

Sherlock Holmes was not very communicative

during the long drive, and lay back in the cab humming the tunes which he had heard in the afternoon. We rattled through an endless labyrinth of gas-lit streets until we emerged into Farringdon Street.

'We are close there now,' my friend remarked. 'This fellow Merryweather is a bank director and personally interested in the matter. I thought it as well to have Jones with us also. He is not a bad fellow, though an absolute imbecile in his profession. He has one positive virtue. He is as brave as a bulldog, and as tenacious as a lobster if he gets his claws upon anyone. Here we are, and they are waiting for us.'

We had reached the same crowded thoroughfare in which we had found ourselves in the morning. Our cabs were dismissed, and, following the guidance of Mr Merryweather, we passed down a narrow passage, and through a side door, which he opened for us. Within there was a small corridor, which ended in a very massive iron gate. This also was opened, and led down a flight of winding stone steps, which terminated at another formidable gate. Mr Merryweather stopped to light a lantern, and then conducted us down a dark, earth-smelling passage, and so, after opening a third door, into a huge vault or cellar, which was piled all round with crates and massive boxes.

'You are not very vulnerable from above,' Holmes remarked, as he held up the lantern and gazed about him.

'Nor from below,' said Mr Merryweather, striking his stick upon the flags which lined the floor. 'Why, dear me, it sounds quite hollow!' he remarked, looking up in surprise.

'I must really ask you to be a little more quiet,' said Holmes severely. 'You have already imperilled the whole success of our expedition. Might I beg that you would have the goodness to sit down upon one of those boxes, and not to interfere?'

The solemn Mr Merryweather perched himself upon a crate, with a very injured expression upon his face, while Holmes fell upon his knees upon the floor, and, with the lantern and a magnifying lens, began to examine minutely the cracks between the stones. A few seconds sufficed to satisfy him for he sprang to his feet again, and put his glass in his pocket.

'We have at least an hour before us,' he remarked, 'for they can hardly take any steps until the good pawnbroker is safely in bed. Then they will not lose a minute, for the sooner they do their work the longer time they will have for their escape. We are at present, Doctor – as no doubt you have divined – in the cellar of the City branch of one of the principal London banks. Mr Merryweather is the chairman of directors, and he will explain to you that there are reasons why the more daring criminals of London should take a considerable interest in this cellar at present.'

'It is our French gold,' whispered the director. 'We have had several warnings that an attempt might be made upon it.'

'Your French gold?'

'Yes. We had occasion some months ago to strengthen our resources, and borrowed, for that purpose, thirty thousand napoleons from the Bank of France. It has become known that we have never had occasion to unpack the money, and that it is still lying in our cellar. The crate upon which I sit contains two thousand napoleons packed between layers of lead foil. Our reserve of bullion is much larger at present than is usually kept in a single branch office, and the directors have had misgivings upon the subject.'

'Which were very well justified,' observed Holmes. 'And now it is time that we arranged our little plans. I expect that within an hour matters will come to a head. In the meantime, Mr Merryweather, we must put the screen over that dark lantern.'

'And sit in the dark?'

'I am afraid so. I had brought a pack of cards in my pocket, and I thought that, as we were a *partie carrée*, you might have your rubber after all. But I see that the enemy's preparations have gone so far that we cannot risk the presence of a light. And, first of all, we must choose our positions. These are daring men, and, though we shall take them at a disadvantage they may do us some harm, unless we are careful. I shall stand behind this crate, and do you conceal yourself behind those. Then, when I flash a light upon them, close in swiftly. If they fire, Watson, have no compunction about shooting them down.'

I placed my revolver, cocked, upon the top of the wooden case behind which I crouched. Holmes shot the slide across the front of his lantern, and left us in pitch darkness – such an absolute darkness as I have never before experienced. The smell of hot metal remained to assure us that the light was still there, ready to flash out at a moment's notice. To me, with my nerves worked up to a pitch of expectancy, there was something depressing and subduing in the sudden gloom, and in the cold, dank air of the vault.

'They have but one retreat,' whispered Holmes. 'That is back through the house into Saxe-Coburg Square. I hope that you have done what I asked you, Jones?'

'I have an inspector and two officers waiting at the front door.'

'Then we have stopped all the holes. And now we must be silent and wait.'

What a time it seemed! From comparing notes afterwards it was but an hour and a quarter, yet it appeared to me that the night must have almost gone, and the dawn be breaking above us. My limbs were weary and stiff, for I feared to change my position, yet my nerves were worked up to the highest pitch of tension, and my hearing was so acute that I could not only hear the gentle breathing of my companions, but I could distinguish the deeper, heavier in-breath of the bulky Jones from the thin sighing note of the bank director. From my position I could look over the case in the direction of the floor. Suddenly my eyes caught the glint of a light.

At first it was but a lurid spark upon the stone pavement. Then it lengthened out until it became a yellow line, and then, without any warning or sound, a gash seemed to open and a hand appeared, a white, almost womanly hand, which felt about in the centre of the little area of light. For a minute or more the hand, with its writhing fingers, protruded out of the floor. Then it was withdrawn as suddenly as it appeared, and all was dark again save the single lurid spark, which marked a chink between the stones.

Its disappearance, however, was but momentary. With a rending, tearing sound, one of the broad, white stones turned over upon its side and left a square gaping hole through which streamed the light of a lantern. Over the edge there peeped a clean-cut, boyish face, which looked keenly about it, and then, with a hand on either side of the aperture, drew itself shoulder high and waist high until one knee rested upon the edge. In another instant he stood at the side of the hole, and was hauling after him a companion, lithe and small like himself, with a pale face and a shock of very red hair.

'It's all clear,' he whispered. 'Have you the chisel and the bags. Great Scott! Jump, Archie, jump, and I'll swing for it!'

Sherlock Holmes had sprung out and seized the intruder by the collar. The other dived down the hole, and I heard the sound of rending cloth as

Jones clutched at his skirts. The light flashed upon the barrel of a revolver, but Holmes's hunting-crop came down on the man's wrist, and the pistol clinked upon the stone floor.

'It's no use, John Clay,' said Holmes blandly; 'you have no chance at all.'

'So I see,' the other answered with the utmost coolness. 'I fancy that my pal is all right, though I see you have got his coat-tails.'

'There are three men waiting for him at the door,' said Holmes.

'Oh, indeed. You seem to have done the thing very completely. I must compliment you.'

'And I you,' Holmes answered. 'Your red-headed idea was very new and effective.'

'You'll see your pal again presently,' said Jones. 'He's quicker at climbing down holes than I am. Just hold out while I fix the derbies.'

'I beg that you will not touch me with your filthy hands,' remarked our prisoner, as the handcuffs clattered upon his wrists. 'You may not be aware that I have royal blood in my veins. Have the goodness also when you address me always to say "sir" and "please".'

'All right,' said Jones, with a stare and a snigger. 'Well, would you please, sir, march upstairs, where we can get a cab to carry your highness to the police station.'

'That is better,' said John Clay serenely. He made a sweeping bow to the three of us, and walked quietly off in the custody of the detective.

'Really, Mr Holmes,' said Mr Merryweather, as we followed them from the cellar, 'I do not know how the bank can thank you or repay you. There is no doubt that you have detected and defeated in the most complete manner one of the most determined attempts at bank robbery that have ever come within my experience.'

'I have had one or two little scores of my own to settle with Mr John Clay,' said Holmes. 'I have been at some small expense over this matter, which I shall expect the bank to refund, but beyond that I am amply repaid by having had an experience which is in many ways unique, and by hearing the very remarkable narrative of the Red-Headed League.

'You see, Watson,' he explained in the early hours of the morning, as we sat over a glass of whisky-and-soda in Baker Street, 'it was perfectly obvious from the first that the only possible object of this rather fantastic business of the advertisement of the League, and the copying of the *Encyclopedia*, must be to get this not over-bright pawnbroker out of the way for a number of hours every day. It was a curious way of managing it, but really it would be difficult to suggest a better. The method was no doubt suggested to Clay's ingenious mind by the colour of his accomplice's hair. The four pounds a week was a lure which must draw him, and what was it to them, who were playing for thousands? They put in the advertisement; one rogue has the temporary office, the other rogue incites the man to apply for it, and together they manage to secure his absence every morning in the week. From the time that I heard of the assistant having come for half-wages, it was obvious to me that he had some strong motive for securing the situation.'

'But how could you guess what the motive was?'

'Had there been women in the house, I should have suspected a mere vulgar intrigue. That, however, was out of the question. The man's business was a small one, and there was nothing in his house which could account for such elaborate preparations and such an expenditure as they were at. It must then be something out of the house. What could it be? I thought of the assistant's fondness for photography, and his trick of vanishing into the cellar. The cellar! There was the end of this tangled clue. Then I made inquiries as to this mysterious assistant, and found that I had to deal with one of the coolest and most daring criminals in London. He was doing something in the cellar – something which took many hours a day for months on end. What could it be, once more? I could think of nothing save that he was running a tunnel to some other building.

'So far I had got when we went to visit the scene of action. I surprised you by beating upon the pavement with my stick. I was ascertaining whether the cellar stretched out in front or behind.

It was not in front. Then I rang the bell, and, as I hoped, the assistant answered it. We have had some skirmishes, but we had never set eyes on each other before. I hardly looked at his face. His knees were what I wished to see. You must yourself have remarked how worn, wrinkled and stained they were. They spoke of those hours of burrowing. The only remaining point was what they were burrowing for. I walked round the corner, saw the City and Suburban Bank abutted on our friend's premises, and felt that I had solved my problem. When you drove home after the concert I called upon Scotland Yard, and upon the chairman of the bank directors, with the result that you have seen.'

'And how could you tell that they would make their attempt tonight?' I asked.

'Well, when they closed their League offices that was a sign that they cared no longer about Mr Jabez Wilson's presence; in other words, that they had completed their tunnel. But it was essential that they should use it soon, as it might be discovered, or the bullion might be removed. Saturday would suit them better than any other day, as it would give them two days for their escape. For all these reasons I expected them to come tonight.'

'You reasoned it out beautifully,' I exclaimed in unfeigned admiration. 'It is so long a chain, and yet every link rings true.'

'It saved me from ennui,' he answered, yawning.

'Alas, I already feel it closing in upon me! My life is spent in one long effort to escape from the commonplaces of existence. These little problems help me to do so.'

'And you are a benefactor of the race,' said I.

He shrugged his shoulders. 'Well, perhaps, after all, it is of some little use,' he remarked. '"*L'homme c'est rien – l'oeuvre c'est tout*," as Gustave Flaubert wrote to George Sand.'

Iconic classics
you can't live without . . .

9780141331829

9780141331836

9780141329741

9780141329734

9780141335377

9780141335360

9780141334417

9780141336596

6 BOOKS THAT MATTER

6 books we fell in love with – and you will too.
As chosen by the Spinebreakers crew

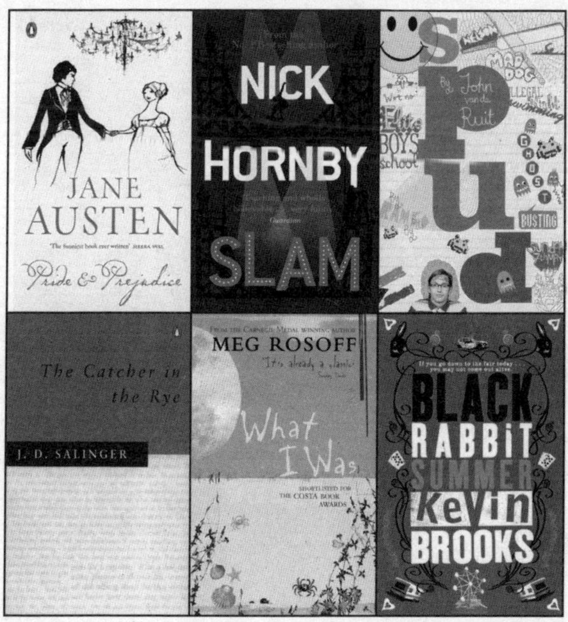

The list continues at spinebreakers.co.uk

DO YOU WANT TO JOIN THE CREW?

If you are a story-surfer, word-lover, day-dreamer,
reader/writer/artist/thinker . . . BECOME one of us

spinebreakers.co.uk

GET INSIDE YOUR FAVOURITE BOOK